# THE
# HITCHCOCK
# MURDERS

# THE HITCHCOCK MURDERS

Gavin Collinson

Cutting
Edge
Press

A Cutting Edge Crime Paperback

Published in 2014 by Cutting Edge Crime, an imprint of Cutting Edge Press

www.cuttingedgepress.co.uk

ISBN: 978-1-908122-85-8
E-PUB ISBN: 978-1-908122-86-5

# A note from the killer

Good evening.

It is a rare man whose past does not return to haunt him. My past is about to catch up with me in this very book.

If you are interested in reading you will be treated to a macabre succession of murders, mysteries and crimes of passion. I freely confess my guilt, but remember this. I did it for you. The you who read my crimes with such excited disbelief and disapproval. I did it for you. You were there by my side as I did them all in, just as I will be there peeping over your shoulder as you turn these pages at midnight.

And so this happy burden of guilt I am pleased to share with you in the story which follows immediately.

Alfie

## *Pre-titles*

When they first visited the place, his dad parked the car on top of the hill, wound down the window and asked if he knew what the building was.

'It looks like a castle where monsters live.'

'Yeah, I suppose it does.' A short burst of laughter. 'You know, you're dead right.'

And with that otherworldly instinct peculiar to small children, Jamie Diaz knew there and then that this would be a special place for both of them. So, three sleeps later, he wasn't surprised when his dad woke him in the middle of the night. 'Quick, Jamie! Get your coat on.'

He rubbed his eyes. 'Where are we going?'

'The cathedral.'

'What?'

'The castle where monsters live.'


His dad pushed open the door and Jamie was relieved to see they were at the top of the tower. No more steps. Just a vastness of darkness and stars, and floating over them both on a long, strong pole, the huge Golden Angel.

'Stand by the wall.'

Jamie didn't need to be told twice. He was glad Mum wasn't there. She'd have ordered him to stay away from it. To *be careful!* But not Dad. He was like a big brother sometimes, running up slides, using broom handles as light sabres and bringing him to the Cathedral Tower at midnight. Even fetching a toy gun along. One he'd not seen before.

Jamie could feel the wind was picking up, buffeting against his face as he rested his chin on the wall and gazed across the twinkling sprawl of Guildford. Without thinking he pulled up the hood of his parka.

'You know,' he heard his dad saying, 'how much I love you?'

'Love you, too,' he replied automatically.

'No, Jamie, listen to me. This is important. Special important.'

'Is that *my* gun?'

But another voice answered.

'No, it's not your gun, Jamie.' A pause. 'Why don't you give it to me, Thom?'

'Hello, Danny.'

The grown-ups kept chatting until a loud crack shattered the night. Like a gunshot off TV, except much, much louder. A chunk of wall about the size of Jamie's fist exploded and a fragment of stone flew into his face. As he raised his hand to touch the small, bloody cut it had made, he felt his dad wrap an arm around his waist and lean back over the wall.

'I love you, son!'

And then they were both about to fall, Jamie suddenly wishing with all his heart that Mum was there, and reaching out to the man who was pelting forward, hand outstretched, towards him.

*FIVE YEARS LATER*

# CHAPTER 1

## *Tuesday, 7 March*

Alfred Hitchcock was smiling at her. Jill Kennedy sipped her champagne, placed the flute carefully on a coaster and looked back at the paused image on the 50-inch plasma screen. She called over her shoulder. 'What film is this?'

She sat on a comfortable leather sofa in an expensively furnished room. Modern, like the home cinema system, mixed with old, like the rosewood side table with its mother-of-pearl inlay. The only elements she wasn't in love with were the cheap red rug at her feet and the bland throw he'd slung across the sofa. But in a curious way, that lapse made her host even more attractive to her. A throw-over across a Ligne Roset! Bless his bachelor's naivety! The sofa had its back to an archway which led onto to a kitchen where she could hear him tinkering with something metallic on a work surface.

'Not a film,' came his reply. 'It's a voice test. For a young Swedish actress Hitch was using for his first talkie. *Blackmail.*' He walked across the kitchen towards her.

'What's a voice test?' As soon as she asked the question she knew it sounded stupid and she hoped he didn't think she was foolish. Jill wanted to impress. She'd never been out with someone like him before. She was twenty-eight, thinking about kids and trying not to think about the gene pool options her usual boyfriends sloshed towards her. They were okay, but Jill wanted better. She had always felt she didn't belong on the estate, not out of any sense of snobbery, but through an awareness that what made her friends happy was great, but not for her. Her brother had married money, and the people she met through him – their refinement, gentle humour and understated kindness – had contrasted with the lads whose idea of courtship was a half of Strongbow on a Saturday evening. But tonight … tonight she was with what her mother would call a proper gentleman.

He walked into the room carrying a tripod and began setting it up in front of the sofa. 'Well, in 1929 a director wouldn't know how an actor would sound on film because chances were they'd only done silent movies. So they did voice tests.' He began screwing a small digital video camera into the top of the tripod. 'In this case, with Anny Ondra, after seeing the test Hitch decided her accent was too strong, so he had another actress called Joan Barry speak her lines.' He looked through the camera, now secured to the tripod. 'Uh-huh. Perfect.' And then glanced up. 'So what you actually see in *Blackmail* is Anny mouthing away as if she's talking but the words are really spoken off-set. By Joan.'

With most blokes a camera by the couch meant one thing.

'Is there anything about Alfred Hitchcock you don't know?'

Jill's host laughed and Jill felt she had redeemed herself for asking such a stupid question earlier.

'Oh, there are always new ways of appreciating Hitchcock.'

But with him she wasn't worried. He'd explained he wanted to record her reactions to a set of sequences. What he called Hitchcock moments. For his latest work on the director he was collecting 'visceral responses' and he found her innocence and honesty – what had been the word he'd used? *Enthralling.*

She was enthralling. She enjoyed being enthralling. For previous boyfriends she'd been hot or fit or fine, but to him she was enthralling.

'Okay. We're rolling. I want you to press play and just, well, react to what you experience.'

'Okay. Ready for my close-up.'

'But don't talk.'

She made a play of closing an imaginary zip across her mouth. She found the remote and started the DVD.

He walked behind the sofa and Jill could hear him in the kitchen. She wanted to watch him but didn't, opting to face forward and maintain the fiction that she was as interested in the

sound test as he clearly was. She knew how men sharing their passion for something like to feel they have opened eyes and enthused their woman with excited monologues. That was fine. She'd come across a lot weirder hobbies, and an obsession with a dead director was pretty harmless. Surely?

'Now, Miss Ondra,' Hitchcock begins. 'We are going to do a sound test. Isn't that what you wanted? Now come right over here.'

He sounds at once bullying and charming.

'I don't know what to say,' Anny replies. 'I'm so nervous.'

And Hitchcock's immediate response: 'Have you been a good girl?'

Anny starts laughing. It's a mixture of nerves and amusement. 'Oh, no!' she says, not in response to his actual question but the type of question he's sprung on her.

'No? Have you slept with men?'

More laughter. Hitchcock throws a glance towards the cameraman.

Eighty-three years later, Jill Kennedy catches that glance. She's seen it a thousand times. Lads in the pub exchanging looks when they think they're getting somewhere. Clumsy, demeaning, dreadful in her want-better eyes. Eighty-three years later, Jill Kennedy understands that look. Doesn't care if the camera records her reaction, and for the first time that evening she feels uncomfortable.

Her host quietly approaches the back of the sofa and his shadow slips over her.

Some women could do it with ease. Josa Jilani had seen them on Underground trains rattling along the District Line, applying lipstick and mascara as if they were sat at their dressing tables on a Friday night. But even gliding along a perfectly smooth stretch of the Embankment, her attempts to apply basic make-up in the back of a black cab were haphazard.

'Sorry for being a bit late for the pick-up!'

Josa looked at the cabbie in the rear-view mirror. His gaze was fixed on the road ahead. 'No problem,' she said.

'Cos it's a Tuesday, you see? Busiest night of the week for us, now! I shouldn't say it, but these murders ...' And he didn't say it. Just shook his head. 'Do you think they'll catch him?'

'Or her.'

'What?'

'The killer. Could be a woman.'

'Suppose so.' His eyes flicked towards the mirror and he looked at his passenger more closely. 'Don't like to think of that,' he added, as if the possibility admitted a more ghastly dimension to the matter.

They drove along in silence. Josa, slightly fearful that her lipstick would be looking like the cardiograph of a heart attack victim, studied her own reflection in the passenger window. She examined her *almost* features. Almost good-looking, dark hair that almost reached her shoulders, eyes that were almost pretty. But not quite. Still, the lipstick that her mother invariably said looked so great on her sister had been pasted on pretty well. Not too shabby!

Her sister, however, was undoubtedly one of those women with the knack, and when they met later that night to wish her mother *bon voyage* for her trip to India, Josa knew she would be looking perfect. Which was fine, except that her mother would draw her attention to it. 'Look how well-groomed your sister is, you see?' she would say, as if her sibling was a show pony. And her sister would privately roll her eyes and then cross them and they'd share a secret laugh as they always had done, but it still hurt. Josa felt a stab of guilt, admitting to herself that she'd have preferred to be spending the evening with her sister, just the two of them on their own. They could have had a few drinks to celebrate her promotion, but her mother still hoped her daughters would turn into good Muslim girls and both of them – for as long as Josa could remember – shared an unspoken understanding that they never consumed anything stronger than black coffee around their relatives. The old woman knew this, of course, but this tactic was just one of many that allowed the Jilanis to square their faith with their various lifestyles. Josa may have ticked 'Muslim' on the forms that her job occasionally threw her way, but she did so with the same insouciance as ticking 'Yes' when asked if she'd read the terms and conditions for the latest app she was downloading.

Still peering at her reflection in the window, Josa wiped away the Rouge Dior like a bad memory. It looked good on her sister, but … She refocused. Looked over the Thames.

She was thirty, but felt an almost childish thrill whenever she surveyed London after dark. Across the river she could see the lively South Bank and the British Film Institute, swathed in red light for another movie premiere. But on a small slick of the shimmering Thames, the light's ruby reflection reminded Josa of the cabbie's words and she shuddered involuntarily.

Ten minutes later the taxi drew to a halt and the driver swivelled around in his seat. 'The building you're after. Can't get any closer than this, I'm afraid. No access by road, but you see that?' He pointed to a passageway. 'Just walk up there. The concourse to the building's less than a minute away.' He paused, noticing the large cardboard box on the back seat. 'You can't miss it.'

'Thanks.' She paid him and struggled with the container that had occupied the seat next to her. As she tottered down the dimly lit passageway he wound down his window. 'Are you going to be okay, luv? It's Tuesday, you know!' He sounded uneasy. 'And d'you wanna hand with that?'

But she didn't even look around as she disappeared further into the shadows.

'Thanks! It's a kind offer,' Josa replied as she vanished entirely from the cabbie's sight. 'But I've got it, so no.'

'No!' screeches Anny Ondra.

Hitchcock counters with an incredulous, 'No?'

Anny is giggling now and something strikes Jill; that she and the actress from another era are physically very similar. Round face, pale skin, Cupid lips. Blond hair.

'Oh, Hitch!'

And Anny is doing exactly what Jill would do in that situation. Not knowing what to say, so laughing, hoping to flatter and divert attention from the awkwardness of the exchange.

But tonight, Jill won't have that problem. She reaches across for her glass of champagne and takes another sip. Because the man she'll be spending tonight with isn't like that. Isn't like all the fumbling boys she's wasted so many years on. He's a gentleman. He stands behind her, patiently waiting for her to put down her drink so he can murder her without breaking his champagne flute.

No, Jill is very happy.

'You make me so embarrassed!' says Anny.

'Now, come over here,' Hitchcock tells her, 'and stand still in your place, or it won't come out right, as the girl said to the soldier!'

Anny Ondra cracks up completely, Alfred Hitchcock beams to camera and Jill Kennedy starts laughing. She feels the champagne bubbles at the bridge of her nose, puts down her glass and at that moment she realises she's the happiest she's been in years.

*Thwack!*

Jill's host, the man who has made her so happy, swings the blunt object downwards, smashing her skull. A very slight pause. He's taking in the moment. Then in a quick, frenzied succession –

*Thwack! Thwack! Thwack!*

A blur of bloodied hands and it's done. Jill's dead by the fourth blow.

Hitchcock grins. 'Cut!'

# CHAPTER 2

Josa reached the building, took a lift to the thirteenth floor and crossed the deserted, open-plan office. Light sensors picked her up, illuminating where she had walked but not where she was heading. She kicked open the door to an enclosed corner office and dumped the box on an apparently empty desk, straightening her back with a celebratory, '*Thank God for that.*' She hadn't noticed the solitary sealed envelope that rested on the desk, now underneath the box.

Josa Jilani looked around her new office. She'd never worked in a room by herself before. Her team would be just outside, of course, but still *outside*.

A television stood in a corner of the room and she found a remote control in an otherwise empty drawer. Glanced at her watch. She didn't have much time to kill before she needed to leave for the restaurant but it surely wouldn't hurt to –

Josa froze as she heard lights flickering to life in the office space outside. She looked through the door and spotted a thin figure approaching. A twenty-something guy in a Top Man suit. Five ten. Bad complexion. Smelt of Lynx. A slight, light shading where he'd removed his wedding ring. 'Don't make yourself at home here.' He leant against the doorframe. 'We're getting a new DCI tomorrow.' He was being friendly. Josa guessed he was married, probably having an affair. But it was with someone outside the team, otherwise he wouldn't have bothered to remove his wedding ring, so she didn't mind too much. He offered an amiable smile. 'And you are?'

'The new DCI you're getting tomorrow.'

Detective Chief Inspector Jilani didn't need to be a mind reader to see what was running through his head. 'Oh! Sorry!' he spluttered, standing to attention. 'I've been on leave. Haven't seen you about and –'

'No problem.'

According to the last report she'd skimmed through, less than 1.5 per cent of chief inspectors in England and Wales were from what was termed an 'Asian or Asian British' background, and so Josa wasn't annoyed by his surprise. He apologised again, muttered something about having popped back after forgetting his Oyster card, and she watched him hurriedly leave. She looked across the open-plan office, pausing at an incident board about half-way across the room. At the top of it she could see a row of three photographs – a trio of portraits. Murdered women.

Photographs of victims were routinely used to ensure that they never became anonymous, and even though she'd seen a thousand similar boards, Josa always found them unnerving. Eerie.

Still, *not her case*.

Another glance at her watch. She hadn't wanted her new colleagues to see her struggling with the box, but the building was on the way to the restaurant, so swinging by had seemed a sensible move. It also allowed her to get a feel for her new office, to familiarise herself not just with the room, but *having* the room. When she next came into work she knew curious eyes would be regarding her with judgmental interest – *How's she settling in?* – and she wanted it to feel like her office from the get go. But aside from all that, the stop had been a delaying tactic because she knew her mother would be dismissive about the promotion, and for just a few minutes longer, Josa wanted to enjoy it. Her new office. She smiled. Nodded. Still, it was getting late and she'd better crack on. She shook her head at the box on her desk. She could create a mess in moments. Been here barely five minutes and already she'd –

Josa grunted as she shoved the box across the desk, guiding it over the edge and letting it crash to the floor, out of the way. She stood back. As she had moved it to one side, the box had swept the envelope along the desk; it fell unseen to the carpet and now lay concealed beneath the container.

Josa massaged the small of her back with her left hand. Took a final glance around her office. She pursed her lips and strode towards the lifts.

The envelope had been addressed, quite simply, *To Josa*.

As she passed the incident board she could feel the three murdered women watching her leave.

Alfred Hitchcock was looking at him. *Into* him. He gazed at the picture and into Hitchcock's eyes. The canvas photograph hanging on the wall directly in front of the sofa was an iconic image of the director looking towards camera as if nothing was amiss. Stark white background and, as though it was as natural as a pet poodle at his feet, an enormous raven was perched on his shoulder.

He often stared at the unframed image because, for him, it was more than a photograph. It was Alfred Joseph Hitchcock, the man himself, as if the ink stamped onto the canvas formed a portal and those printed eyes were the real eyes of Hitchcock, watching him, following his progress and altering ever so slightly to demonstrate approbation or enquiry or, best of all, but very rarely, a respect that was born of understanding.

'I know, I know … I've got to de-rig.'

He'd once spent time on a movie set and knew that at the end of a shoot, the crew would de-rig. In other words, tidy away a set or a location, leaving it in its original, pre-production state. During his inner monologues about murder, he enjoyed using the vocabulary of film-making, believing Hitchcock would appreciate his phrasing.

*Very elegant, old chap.*

But right now, Hitch looked a little disdainful.

He playfully wagged a finger at the canvas as he stepped over the corpse in his living room. 'But before I do, there's another scene that needs my attention!'

Hitchcock had never shown any desire to dawdle or delay over his art. And so nor should he. During his early period, between

1925 and 1935, Hitch directed nineteen movies, a clear instruction that for beginners, work should be regular and uninterrupted. He would follow the master's lead. One murdered tonight. She would be put on ice. Now it was time for his second work of the evening. He checked his watch. She should already be waiting for him. He pictured her in a demure cream blouse, ever so slightly see-through and therefore necessitating a white bra. Fabulous! Blood always looks better against virginal lingerie, in the same way that, like it or not, incisions look sexier across young, unmottled flesh.

He looked up. Caught Hitchcock tapping into his thoughts and laughed. He was beginning to understand the scale of what he had planned for tonight.

# CHAPTER 3

Josa Jilani looked across the street and could see her sister and mother seated in the restaurant, chatting over a menu. She stopped. Watched them. Her mother wore a long, deep green Mysore sari, all pleats and folds and finished off with the grey cardigan she always slipped over her shoulders like it was a cape. Her sister wore a gold and black sari but had it wrapped and draped to resemble a Western-style summer dress. Josa gazed at them both for about a minute, half to put off the dressing down she'd get from her mum for being late, and half because she took a masochistic fascination in seeing how smiley the old woman became around her sister.

In a second or two, Josa will steel herself to face her mother. She will begin to cross the road but never reach the other side, because her phone will ring. 'Hello?' she'll say.

'Is that DCI Jilani?'

'Speaking!' She'll put her left index finger in her ear. 'How can I help?'

'You didn't have any plans for tonight, did you?'

And although she'll guess that it probably means murder, Josa will still allow herself a smile of relief.

But for the moment, she just watches and feels outside.

He punched 999 into his phone and took a deep breath.

As the lift rose, he felt his spirits soar, unconsciously associating the physical ascent with something more spiritual.

'Emergency – which service do you require?'

'I require the police service. And please don't ask any more questions. Just listen and then pass on this message.' He spoke calmly and crisply, aware that the distortion app would disguise his voice. 'Tell the police to go to the Shard building immediately. On the fifty-eighth floor they will find a corpse. The body of a young lady who has been murdered. Her name is Elaine Hargreaves. *Elaine Hargreaves*. Good evening.'

He pressed 'end call' and felt the lift slide to a halt. He smiled.

Hearing the *ping* as the lift's doors parted, the suite's solitary occupant whirled around, offered a professional smile and moved towards him.

'Good to meet you,' she said, extending her hand.

His smile broadened. The view across the apartment, with its stunning panorama of London, proved as visually high-impact as he had anticipated. He nodded. Another great choice of location. The perfect set. But the best view was offered by the creature in front of him, the girl trying to look like a woman with her mother's court shoes and grown-up smile. She wore a light, tight cream blouse.

'I'm Elaine Hargreaves,' she said.

# CHAPTER 4

The lift slid smoothly to a halt. Its doors parted and Josa Jilani stepped into hell.

She took a single step, paused and peered around the luxury apartment, immediately aware it was bad news. The corpse was the only person in the room who didn't look anxious, and you could have cut the tension with a carving knife, pretty much like the one that lay on the Egyptian rug by the dead woman's head. A narrow line of blood ran straight along the middle of the suite; a thin red river that exposed the groove of two carpets meeting.

Josa walked further into the living room. This was the fifty-eighth floor of the Shard, the tallest building in Europe, and even the view was expensive. Shimmering lights, Tower Bridge, St Paul's and skyscrapers that vied for –

'Hold it right there, girly!' Arm raised, Detective Inspector Don Walters stepped in front of Josa, blocking her way. He was a big, balding man who smelt of old cigarettes and bad habits. 'I know you ...' He looked Josa over. 'The young *British Asian* detective. Fast-tracked to DCI because you're a Muslim. Well, this is my investig-'

'And I know you,' Josa interrupted. 'The old, white detective, slow-tracked because you're an alcoholic. I had no idea it was a crime scene.' She held his furious gaze, willing herself not to flinch. 'I'm here because Gilmour told me to be here.'

Walters looked like he was about to explode and Josa brushed past him, heading towards the murder victim. The body lay on the floor behind a sofa, meaning Josa could only see the corpse from the shoulders upwards. But it was enough to reveal it was ... *Oh, dear God, no!* The body of a young woman. Mid-twenties. Long auburn hair. Snow-white skin. Josa shuddered. Didn't want any part of this, not now. Let someone more experienced deal with it because *she just knew.*

For the past four weeks the British public had been both terrified and mesmerised by a serial killer. A predator who struck at random, left no trace evidence and became invisible around would-be witnesses. Within a month he had become the stuff of urban mythology, and #whonext? was trending, not just in his hunting ground of London, but right across the UK. In the space of three weeks he had slaughtered three young women in grimly different ways. One defenceless female victim, every Tuesday.

And today was Tuesday.

As she rounded the sofa to reach the body, Josa glanced across the apartment. Elegant but spartan furniture. All leather and chrome. Two tiny video cameras in opposite corners of the room, one with a winking red light. And aside from Walters, two other officers, both young detective constables she recognised from her new station. The nearest one to her was in his early twenties but looked younger. Medium build, light ginger hair. He stood over the victim.

'How you doing, Stevie?'

Marc Stevenson was momentarily taken aback that she'd recalled his name. 'I'm good, thanks, Detective Chief Inspector.' He didn't look good, with only slightly more colour in his cheeks than the corpse. Josa paused by a grey tray on a low coffee table. 'These her effects?'

'She's got nothing in her pockets,' Walters grunted. 'I had Stevie bag the stuff that was in her jacket – found it on the couch.'

The tray held half a dozen transparent evidence bags containing keys, a packet of tissues, a purse, USB stick, some loose change and a couple of pens. 'Odd …' Josa muttered.

Walters didn't bother to conceal his annoyance. 'What is?'

Through a doorway leading to an unlit bedroom, Josa glimpsed a fourth man. A tall, shabby-looking figure silhouetted against a window. He was hidden by the gloom but she sensed him watching her. Josa knew that her black, knee-length dress and long, elegant camel-coloured coat were wildly inappropriate for a crime scene. But she'd wanted to look her best for dinner with her mother and sister.

Tonight's meal at the restaurant was supposed to have been a farewell to her mother who was embarking on a trip to India to see 'the old family'. But earlier in the day, Josa had phoned with her news. Her promotion to Detective Chief Inspector was official. After a decade in the police service, she'd finally reached the rank she'd set out to achieve. She'd waited a moment for her mother's reply.

'Always thinking about *yourself*! Your sister tells me she has an interview with a *highly respectable* private surgery.' Her mother managed to make 'highly respectable' sound like a royal appointment. 'Doesn't that strike you as more important?'

Josa walked around the tan sofa. She saw for the first time the full horror of the corpse and tried in vain not to gasp as she took in the injuries which had killed the young woman. From the neck upwards she remained pale and perfect, almost porcelain, but her clothes had been slashed away and her body carved open, exposing the insides of her torso. This had been recent, Josa reflected. Very recent. Blood, when exposed to air, quickly changes colour to a dull brown tincture, so far from scarlet that many witnesses mistake it for dried mud. But this scene was gleaming, glowing in a sheen of electric red. This was fresh.

'She's had her heart torn out,' Stevie said.

Josa hitched up her best dress and knelt down to take a closer look. 'I know how she feels,' she murmured.

'Her name's Elaine Hargreaves,' the DC added.

Josa studied the lifeless face. 'I'm so sorry, Elaine …' she said quietly, before abruptly turning away. Elaine's arm had fallen in the direction of a low, large chair in the corner of the room and now Josa's hand swept below it.

Walters stood over her. 'I asked you what was so odd.'

'Her effects. No phone.'

'So what?' He instinctively threw a glance at the grey tray. 'She might not have had a mobile.'

'Young woman in her twenties. No mobile phone?' Her arm continued to sweep this way and that, like a windscreen wiper below the chair. 'Really?'

'It's entirely –'

'Gotcha!' Josa declared. She rolled away from the chair and her hand, wrapped in an evidence bag, was grasping a smartphone. She recognised the make and model – an old Sony Ericsson – the same type she'd used for years until recently. She turned the bag inside out, ensuring the mobile phone fell neatly into it, before clambering to her feet. 'What do you make of that, Walters?' Josa asked, nodding towards the sheet of paper that lay on top of the sofa.

The Detective Inspector regarded it for less than a second but it was enough time for Josa to drop the bagged phone into her coat pocket. She had no intention of keeping it but was curious and wanted to check out the call history before surrendering it to the black hole of forensics.

'You know bloody well what it is!' Walters replied.

Stevie moved a step closer to Josa. She knew he'd seen her conceal the handset but noted his face and body language revealed nothing. Josa squirreled the fact away. 'Do you think it's him?' the young man asked her.

Of course she knew who he meant. The butcher who'd already murdered three women. Josa looked at Elaine. Make that four.

'Of course it's not bloody him!' Walters roared, shaking his head as if the question was an idiotic one. 'Completely different MO to our chummy. Obviously, some snotty-nosed little DC leaked the news about our serial killer's calling card. Some other nutcase heard about it and left it here to make us think it was the work of –'

'It's him!' Josa cut in. 'Bloody hell, Walters!' She was annoyed by his attitude towards Stevie. 'What d'you think? The butler did it?' She nodded towards the 'calling card', a triangle scrawled on the sheet of white paper. 'That's *exactly* like the ones he's left at previous crime scenes, and all this …' she gestured to the mutilated body. 'It *feels* like his work. Don't you think? It's an escalation –'

'Rubbish!'

'– and that's what worries me. If his modus operandi is stepping up a gear, who's to say the frequency with which he's –' Josa stopped. She was staring at the broad-shouldered man in the bedroom. He was prodding his phone. 'Hey! Hey, what the hell do you think you're doing?'

Walters shrugged. 'He's with us.'

Josa marched across to the bedroom. 'If you're tweeting about any of this I'll have you banged up faster –'

'Hello!' He held up his phone, screen towards her. 'It's her Facebook page,' he said. 'Elaine's.'

Josa studied him for a moment. She'd seen hundreds of his sort at crime scenes and assumed he was one of the cleaners, contracted to restore bloodbaths to normality after forensics and photographers had finished with the area. 'You're a bit keen, aren't you?' she asked. 'It'll be hours until –'

'She was into am-dram,' he interjected.

'What?'

'Am-dram. Amateur dramatics. Had it on the brain. That's got to be a crucial factor, I think.'

Despite herself, Josa shrugged. 'That's pure speculation.'

'Oh, good speculation is never pure.' He smiled. 'And look! It *also* says on her Facebook page that right now she's rehearsing for the lead in a production of *Good Queen Bess.*'

'Right. And? So? Look, I think –'

'She was going to play Elizabeth I,' he persisted. 'Doesn't that strike you as important?'

Josa looked into his beaming blue eyes and paused.

His choice of words brought a flashback to her mother. If her father had been alive he'd have been euphoric, greeting the news of her promotion with his customary cry of *What are we waiting for? Crack open the champers, I tell you!* Of course, she'd only heard from other people that this had almost been his catchphrase. She'd been a young girl when he died, succumbing to the cancer and leaving her mother to –

'I'm sorry.' The man in front of Josa offered her an

understanding smile. *Understanding*? How the hell could he be understanding? He appeared to be in his mid-thirties. The frayed, thigh-length, navy blue overcoat wasn't doing him any favours and, combined with the open-necked blue shirt and torn jeans, it gave him a look that suggested artisan. His face was hidden by shadows but his hair was dark and fell to his shoulders.

'Sorry? For what?'

'For whatever it was.'

There was a physical openness about him that she found inexplicably attractive and she heard herself overcompensating with a waspish, 'Who exactly are you?'

'Oh, just a friend! Passing through.' A grin. Broad. Upbeat. 'You know!'

'No, as a matter of fact I don't, and I want to see some identific-'

'Jilani!'

Josa whirled round to face Walters. 'What?'

He raised his eyebrows and tilted his head towards the lift. A woman had just emerged from it. Skinny. Pencil skirt and smart jacket, too much make-up but still good looking. Long dark hair clipped back. 'I'm the concierge,' she said, and to Walters, 'Hello, again.'

Josa noted that she positioned herself so the sofa blocked her view of the corpse. 'Concierge?'

'These are private apartments but the holding company provides a concierge for the convenience of all residents.' Her French accent was unmistakable. Josa wondered if she was laying it on a bit thick and imagined the British businessmen enjoyed her Parisian twang.

'And Elaine Hargreaves was one of your residents?'

'*Non.* This apartment is one of three recently acquired by a family business looking to rent them out. The other two are immediately above this one. Miss Hargreaves was one of that company's employees, retained to ensure the rooms are kept fresh, tidy et cetera. The apartment below is currently occupied by the family who own the property.' She paused. Bit her lip. 'Strictly speaking, she should not have treated the apartment as her own but …'

Josa looked through the vast window, across the city, taking in the broad, dizzying view of London. 'But you get the keys to a pad like this and the temptation to spend time here must be enormous.' She gazed down, feeling vaguely queasy as she took in the 700-foot drop. Her eyes wandered from the window and noticed some tiny white flecks of dried paint on the carpet. 'Nice new place like this. Can't say I blame her.'

'*Oui.*'

'What's with the cameras?'

'Webcams. Installed by the overseas company to allow prospective clients to view the apartment before –'

'Are they active?'

'Sadly not. They were due to be activated tomorrow.'

'That's a bugger.' Josa clicked her tongue against the roof of her mouth. 'So we don't know how he got in.'

The concierge shrugged. 'It can only have been one of two ways. The lift or via the emergency staircase.'

'What about though a window?'

Walters laughed. 'We're not looking for Spider-Man, Jilani! Bugger me! They can give you lot promotions but not common sense! Get a grip!' he snorted.

Josa ignored him and addressed the Frenchwoman. 'Could he have used that?' She pointed downwards, through the pane of glass towards what looked like a window cleaner's platform, halted on the level below them.

The concierge didn't need to move from her spot. '*Non.* That is an EMP. An external maintenance platform. But none of the windows open so it would have been impossible for him to have gotten from the EMP into a room.'

'Do you have security cameras positioned by all entrances and exits?'

'*Oui, madame.*'

'I'll need all recent footage by morning. Is that do-able?'

'It will be done immediately.'

'Thank you,' Josa replied. 'Right!' She looked at Walters. 'Can I have a word?'

'Anything to help, DCI Jilani.'

Josa led him into the bathroom, closed the door and lowered her voice. 'The cameras!'

'Look, I know we haven't exactly covered ourselves in glory trampling over the crime scene before forensics got here, but we're both the sort who like to get stuck in and I was told they'd been delayed, so I *deemed* it –'

Josa was shaking her head. 'The cameras!' she repeated.

Walters scratched his neck. 'What about them? They're webcams. Not working yet.'

'One of them has been activated. The blinking red line indicates it's working right now. Only it's not a webcam. I've actually used one myself on a surveillance job. It's used for very short-range feeds and, judging by the chipped paint on the floor underneath where it's been fitted, it was only installed tonight.'

'What are you saying?'

'The killer installed it and is watching everything that's happening in that room, *right now*.'

'Good God!'

'It's very short range. That means he's very close. Can't be in the apartment below us, as that's occupied. So, to be more specific, he's in the apartment immediately above us.'

Walters blanched. Looked up at the ceiling as if he might magically gaze through it and into the face of the murderer. 'What are you saying?'

'The country's most dangerous serial killer is upstairs.' Josa leant forward and said quietly, 'Let's go and get him.'

# CHAPTER 5

If he'd looked more closely, he'd have seen that his black leather gloves were still freckled with the blood of Elaine Hargreaves. But the man who tore open her warm body less than an hour earlier sat approximately ten feet above its remains in a suite identical to the one below, having too good a time to care. Hunched over a small table, eyes fixed on the laptop it supported, he was enjoying the scene he'd set up and grinned at the sight of Stevie looking everywhere except towards the corpse at his feet. The other young officer was still waiting in a corner, but ... where was the old guy? Or the woman in the dress?

He drummed gloved fingers on the table. Pulled back the sleeve of his suit to reveal his watch. One minute. He'd give them a minute, then he was off. Alfred Hitchcock had always cannily insisted that his assistant directors shoot the dangerous-to-get shots, and he admired such a cautious stance. No, *admired* was the wrong word. *Empathised*. Always empathised with the great man.

He ended the recording and transferred the video file to a USB. He had captured enough for his purposes. Another time check. Thirty seconds. He slipped the USB stick into his pocket and began to stand up, but something on the screen caught his eye. Something in the room below that he found more remarkable than the corpse or the uneasy coppers. He sank down into the chair.

'I don't believe it ...'

Don Walters licked his lips. 'We've got to call it in. Wait for backup and –'

Josa was shaking her head. 'No time! We know that perps often stick around to watch what happens. This is just taking it another step further, but he's not going to wait much longer before scarpering. In fact, we can only stay in here for a minute before he gets suspicious. You take the emergency staircase. I'll take the lift. Surprise attack. Pincer movement.'

'Listen to yourself! Are you seriously suggesting we tackle him – just the two of us?'

'He's watching right now. He'll get suspicious if we leave with one of the others.'

'Christ! We don't have to do this!' Walters threw his head right back and exhaled before looking into Josa's eyes. 'Jilani, you don't have to prove anything to me.'

'To *you*?' She suppressed the urge for ironic laughter.

'All that through there,' Walters whispered, 'it's just banter. You know?'

'I know what it is.'

'You just don't get it.'

'Oh, I get it. I get it every day of my life.'

'It doesn't mean anything.'

'Every. Day. Of my life.' Josa showed her palms. No time for this. 'Okay. I'm going up there alone. You go through there. Start walking around. Give him something to watch. Fake a heart attack or something.'

'How am I supposed to do that?'

'I dunno. Imagine having to take orders from a woman.'

'I meant … Jesus, Jilani, of course I'm coming with you.'

Josa wondered if the odds had just got better or worse. She nodded. 'Then let's do it.'


The unkempt man who had so casually made such a big impression on Josa had moved out of the unlit bedroom and was handing Stevie a glass of water. He then dropped to his haunches, studying Elaine as a mechanic might visually appraise an engine that wasn't turning over.

The killer pressed the 'up' button on his laptop and the man's face filled the screen. He was pausing. Looking up. Into the camera. *Into his face.*

Elaine Hargreaves' murderer felt curiously exposed but couldn't resist a brief smile. 'Hello, again,' he said.

Walters had been right, of course. Josa stepped into the lift and pressed the button for the suite above. Her plan *was* crazy. The doors slid shut and for the first time since her arrival at the Shard, she felt alone. She knew that the DI was right about having something to prove, as well. *But not to him.* The lift started to rise. Josa took a deep breath.

She quickly affixed her Bluetooth earpiece. 'You there?'

'I'm in position by the door to chummy's suite.' Walters' voice, out of breath from climbing the stairs. 'Give me the word and I burst in like John Wayne.'

Josa rolled her eyes. 'Great,' she replied with more sarcasm than she'd intended. She tried to visualise the room the lift doors would open onto and picture her opponent. The *ping* as the lift arrived would claim his attention. He'd look her way and she'd say '*Now!*' At that moment, Detective Inspector John Wayne would crash into the room from the far corner. There'd be distraction and confusion and Josa would launch herself at the killer. Walters might not be in the best shape but it would still be two against one. Josa's head was selling this reassuring prediction but her stomach, heavy as lead, wasn't buying.

The lift started to slow down. This would work, Josa told herself. It had to. She'd only be in trouble if the killer had a gun, and clearly one hadn't been used on the victim downstairs. The lift stopped. Without realising what she'd done, Josa had edged into the corner of the lift and now she had to force her feet forward.

*Ping!*

The doors began to open. She tried to give the vital command clearly and crisply, but even as she croaked 'Now!' she knew it hadn't been loud enough for Walters to pick up.

She could hear someone nearing the lift. Swift movements that implied confidence. The doors had slid apart by about one foot and her heart lurched as she saw the killer aiming a gun directly at her.

# CHAPTER 6

'Now!' Josa screamed. She stepped back, instantly regretting the move as it boxed her in.

Walters' desperate voice via her earpiece: 'The door's locked! It's bloody locked! Pull back!'

The killer glided forward, gun arm extended.

'I can't!' Josa shrieked.

And then the muzzle of the pistol moved fractionally to the right, tracking her. In that moment, Josa took in everything. The *thump, thump, thump* of Walters' useless banging on the door across the room. The tall gunman dressed in a dark, expensive suit. The intensely bright light behind him that made it impossible to look directly into his face. She actually saw his finger pull back on the trigger.

And her last thought before the gunshot: *she should have stopped trying to prove things to herself years ago.*

Then confusion, quickly followed by understanding.

Josa had heard enough gunshots to know this one hadn't come from the pistol in front of her. The man holding it whirled around to face the direction of fire and Josa saw his trigger finger relax. She knew he'd come within a millisecond of squeezing it sufficiently to click back the striker latch spring, an action that would have discharged the bullet. She threw herself forward. If the seconds before had felt like eternity, the quick, chaotic tumble of events that followed seemed to occur all at once.

Josa saw that Walters had burst into the room. He held a revolver in his right hand and she guessed he'd used the gun to blast away the lock. But he'd shoulder-charged the door, and with the impetus carrying him forward, he offered a clear target. The man directly in front of her didn't pause a second time, opening fire on the Detective Inspector.

It was difficult to see which shots hit their mark but Walters kept moving forward. The vast window behind him took several hits, a spider's web of thick cracks appearing where bullets had been pumped through the pane. And then Walters took a shot in his torso, the impact pushing him backwards so his spine smashed into the badly damaged glass. Josa heard a sickening crack as the window began to splinter and give way, but Walters wasn't finished, pushing himself forward. Then another shot – an eruption of blood across his chest – and he spun to the floor.

All of this only took a couple of seconds. Josa was almost on her quarry when he swung his pistol in a tight arc to cover her. And then, stillness again. Josa froze, once more in a corner, this time of the room, trapped. She knew he wouldn't have many bullets left, but one would be enough. 'Put the gun down!' she requested in a tone of such reasonableness that even she was surprised. The figure in front of her paused. Josa slipped her hands into the pockets of her long, stylish coat. 'We can talk about this.'

While keeping his right hand steady, pointing the muzzle at Josa, the gunman raised his left hand –

In the pocket of her coat, Josa pressed the call back button of Elaine Hargreaves' phone.

– and the man flapped his fingers, tapping their tips against the butt of his palm. Waving like a child. *Goodbye*. Then he stopped. This was it. Josa held her breath.

And for the second time that night, a distraction saved her life. This time a tiny, nonsensical diversion as the phone in his suit pocket began to vibrate. Josa had anticipated it, and as he glanced down she raced forward. She could never reach him – he'd have pulled the trigger automatically and she was directly in the firing line. Nor could she head to the lift. Too long for the doors to close, making her a sitting duck. Instead, she moved forward towards the only exit she could reach with the moment she had bought herself, and knew that the audacity – make that *insanity* – of her plan might just stun the killer and thereby give her another precious second to escape. Well, a kind of escape.

Josa Jilani hurtled along the side of the room towards the window. Her right foot hit the top of the leather sofa and she kicked off it, the momentum of her run allowing her to spring through the air.

The gunman had recovered quickly and was loosing off another barrage of shots. But Josa was focussed on one thing. Mess this up and she knew she'd be at his mercy.

Josa dived headlong through the hail of bullets towards the window and the web of cracks the previous salvo had created. Her shoulder smashed into the glass and it gave way, half-buckling, half-splintering. Somehow her body slammed into the pane and it gave way entirely. Josa felt an ice-cold blast of air as she crashed through the window. *She was through.*

Josa plunged through the glass into nothingness, falling from the fifty-ninth floor towards the ground.

# CHAPTER 7

His latest triumph – the murder of Elaine Hargreaves – had come too late in the evening for reviews to appear in the next day's newspapers. He knew that, but he'd already pulled over, taken out his phone and gone online to see if anything had percolated through to the internet. Of course it had, and he reflected that sometimes he enjoyed living in an instant age. The Twittersphere was loving it, the laughably named 'news' sites couldn't get enough and ... Yes! When he turned on his car radio and spun through a few stations, he found several talk shows were gossiping about the murders, trying to sound saddened but obviously more excited than mournful. The fake concern of a friend asking, *have you heard* ...

Well, soon everybody would have heard. And they would hear more and more and *more* until every last person on the planet, from the barefoot Baka to the bowler-hatted banker would shudder, smile and understand.

The stretchered body was rushed across the concourse and eased into the helicopter, blades still whirling as it rested on the forecourt in front of the Shard. It was getting late but a considerable crowd had gathered to see what was happening, hopeful of glimpsing an injured body or getting their face on the news. A line of constables, including Stevie, kept them at a safe distance. The helicopter started to rise. The noise and take-off blast of air was stronger than most onlookers had anticipated and the majority instinctively pulled back.

Stevie looked over his shoulder. The crowd's retreat had left one man exposed. He was tall, with shoulder-length hair, and pummelled by the chopper's ascent, his coat was blown back from his body. He stood, apparently unconcerned by the hullabaloo around him, watching the helicopter depart. The guy from the crime scene. Stevie had assumed the stranger had been with Walters, and had never asked his name or requested ID. Come to think of it, he couldn't be certain that any of them had.

'Would you mind waiting a moment, sir?' Stevie called across to him.

A smile of acknowledgement – he'd heard him all right and didn't look flustered – and the young policeman began walking towards him. He'd made no sign of moving but now the helicopter had flown, the coppers were stepping aside and the crowd became a stream of pedestrians. Stevie reached the spot where the man had stood. Looked around the surge of late-night Londoners.

'Bugger!' This would not look good on his report. 'Bugger, bugger, bugger!'

The stranger had disappeared.

Josa Jilani had briefly drifted into consciousness moments earlier and seen the helicopter. Now her eyes fluttered open again and she guessed she was inside it. She vaguely recognised Don Walters on a stretcher next to hers, huge green bumble bees buzzing over him.

Josa had never travelled in a chopper before. Once the reinforced carbon fibre door had slid shut, it was quieter than she'd expected, but much colder. Somehow she'd assumed there would be some kind of heating and –

And then the pain kicked in. Her hands burning and head throbbing. A short period of screaming pain before mercifully, Josa lapsed back into unconsciousness.

As the helicopter banked steeply, swerving eastwards over London, she came to again but this time her eyes remained closed. *Voices.* The intense pain in her head had reduced to a dull ache and she felt lighter. The drugs were kicking in. She could hear voices, lowered to suggest clandestine intent. Two men. She knew the first. The head of her new station. Chief Superintendent Kim Gilmour.

'So what do we do now?' he was asking.

The second voice was older, more assured, and as silky as a public school tie. It held the casual arrogance that Josa associated with off-camera politicians. 'Will she live?'

'I'm reliably informed she will.'

'Thank God for small mercies.' A pause. 'Would have been a PR disaster if she'd died tonight. We maintain our course, Kim. Our dear Home Secretary is sticking to her ridiculous scheme. But like all politicians she'll drop it the moment it becomes unpopular.'

'What are you saying?'

'We must expose the rotten fruits of her plan. Make Jilani head up the hunt for this serial killer fellow. When she fails and this psychopath really starts ratcheting up the body count, well … The media will hold her accountable and by extension the Home Secretary's little flight of fancy. The scheme will be quietly shelved and we can all get back to a more agreeable status quo.'

Gilmour cleared his throat. 'I'm not entirely happy –'

'No one is ever *entirely* happy!' the second man barked. 'You just do as you're told.' His tone returned to Home Counties affability. 'There's a good chap.'

Josa was distracted as through her blurred vision she saw the green bumble bees turn and hover over her face. She blinked and they gradually became paramedics. 'How is she?' one of them asked.

'Seemed okay before. Just kept going on about her hands.'

'What wrong with them?'

'That's the funny thing. Nothing at all.'

And the two bumble bees exchanged glances.

Josa Jilani carried very few childhood fears around with her, but her dread of Jahannam, the Islamic equivalent of hell, had been carefully ingrained by her mother and remained deep in her bones. She recalled the old woman – as she'd always seemed to Josa – beckoning her with a crooked index finger. A palm on the back of her neck and whispered words. Eyes that shone with fervour as her mother conveyed what waited for those who failed to attain the paradise of Jannah. And always the same implication.

For years, Josa had problems understanding how anyone could be blasé about hell. Even non-Muslims accepted a version of Jahannam, so why didn't the prospect of it scare them to death? She gradually began to realise that for most people, 'hell' was a metaphorical notion or just a fairy tale no more real than the wolf in grandma's clothing. And even as a young child she recognised that the Christian view of hell was too woolly to be worrying. Not enough accepted wisdom about what actually happened there or the environment itself. She'd seen old cartoons where it was little more than a coalmine ruled over by an impish devil; even serious works like Dante's *Divine Comedy* portrayed hell as a romantic realm, full of dead celebrities that always had time for a chat. There was nothing too terrifying about it.

But Josa's mother made it clear that Jahannam was an actual, *physical* place. She would grasp her hand and hold it over the lighted stove. *'As real as the heat on your hand, girl!'*

She painted a detailed picture of Jahannam, right down to what those confined there were compelled to eat and drink – pus from open wounds and boiling water – and the precise nature of the tortures that waited. Most of them entailed burning. Garments of fire. Bodies being scorched with the roasted flesh replaced, only to be burnt over and over again.

Her hand forcibly lowered, closer to the flame. *'As real as that, Josaphata! Can you feel it, child? Can you?'*

Josa tried to open her eyes as the pain in her palms returned. She opened her mouth to scream but felt a needle puncture the skin of her forearm. Someone said, 'It's all right, luv,' coaxing her back into unconsciousness, a troubled sleep crowded with bad dreams and distorted memories. Elaine Hargreaves. Fire. Elizabeth I. The navy blue coat. Auburn hair …

*Why did that last image feel like the most important?*

# CHAPTER 8

He arrived home in the early hours, parking a few streets from his house and entering by the back door, just in case any nosey neighbours had mounted a net curtain vigil. As he'd feared, Alfred Hitchcock was waiting up for him.

'I know! I heard it on the car radio as I was driving back! Don't look at me like that!' He crossed his sitting room. Poured himself a large cognac. 'Both of them might still be alive. Damn and blast!' He fired a look at the photograph of Hitchcock. 'Sorry. It's just … The shoot didn't go exactly how I'd planned. I don't think they saw my face because of a strong light behind me, but …' He knocked back a mouthful of the brandy and felt emboldened by the fire in his throat. 'Even *you* must have had …' He stopped. Started to laugh. What on earth had he been thinking? This was perfect!

He raised his glass to Hitchcock and saw the crafty old devil knew exactly what he had planned. After all, it was he who had given him the idea.

He drained the rest of his cognac in a single tilt of his head. He had work to do.

# CHAPTER 9

He'd introduced himself with a slight bow. 'Doctor Taylor!' White coat, bow tie and a stethoscope, like he was playing a doctor on a sketch show. 'How do you do?' He peered over his half-moon spectacles. 'Have we met?'

'I don't think so,' Josa replied. The truth was that a couple of months ago she'd been on the London Underground and spotted a guy stepping off her carriage without taking his rucksack. And somehow she had known. The man escaped, but she just managed to make it back onto the train before the doors bumped shut and then she knelt over the rucksack. And weeks later she could still feel its coarse fabric and thick stitching on her fingertips. It contained a bomb that could have blown a hole in the Northern Line, bringing the River Thames and about half a mile of tunnelling crashing into the tube network. Unwilling to risk waiting for the bomb disposal officers, she'd disabled the explosive device and for a few uneasy days had been the media's sweetheart with even the Home Secretary, Liz Canterville, noticing the headlines and name-checking her on *Loose Women*. She found the spotlight intense and uncomfortable, boggling at the sheer absurdity of how certain tabloids tried to blame Islam for the UNDERGROUND TERROR ATTACK while admitting (paragraph five) that the long-serving officer who had thwarted the mysterious operation was Muslim. A fortnight later she took a call from Liz, who was starting a fast-track initiative ... 'I've got one of those faces,' Josa added, and Doctor Taylor nodded, apparently satisfied.

He gave her a brief examination, becoming the third of three medics who'd subjected her to a similar scrutiny since her arrival. After a couple of minutes he once again peered over the top his glasses. 'How did you do it?' He indicated he was referring to the cut on the back of her head.

'I jumped out of a building.'

Josa lay propped up by pillows in her hospital bed. She'd woken up in the drab, single-occupancy room in London's Albion Hospital and now this genial doctor – she pegged him as early forties, despite greying hair – stood on one side of her, with Gilmour tapping his toes on the other. 'What on earth did you think you were playing at?' the Chief Superintendent snapped.

'Just trying to keep the customers satisfied.'

'First floor? Second floor?' enquired the doctor.

'Fifty-ninth floor.'

'I just asked you to meet me there!' Gilmour continued. 'You were only at the scene five minutes before turning it into a horror movie! One of my officers in intensive care and you lucky to escape with your life!'

'Fifty-ninth?' The doctor whipped off his specs and stood back. 'Well in that case you're in pretty good nick, Josa.' He mispronounced her name, articulating the soft middle 's' as a 'z'.

'It's *Josa*. As in rhymes with *closer*. And fortunately, I didn't fall all the way down. I grabbed the cable holding up an external maintenance platform. Fell onto that. Kind of slithered down its cable but I was going too fast, fell the last six feet or so and …' She gestured to the cut on the back of her head.

'God knows how this is going to play with the press, Jilani!'

'Well, we've put stitches in and people won't be able to see it because it's hidden by your hair. But out of sight shouldn't mean out of mind. I'll be giving you another couple of injections, otherwise you'll have the devil's own headache, and although I'm not too worried by the cut, as you were rendered unconscious it *is* standard practice to give you a number of tests and a scan.'

'A scan?'

'A brain scan.'

Josa gave a weak smile followed by a weak joke. 'D'you think you'll find one?'

Doctor Taylor produced the polite smile of a man who'd heard the gag a thousand times.

'I doubt it,' Gilmour muttered.

The doctor looked across at him. 'You look pale. Drawn. Those eyes …' he shook his head.

'What would you recommend?'

'A little courtesy to officers who risk their lives, Chief Superintendent. Plus a trip to your GP and some healthy meals. And cut back on the … sherry?'

'Brandy.' Gilmour gave a curt nod as if he'd been fooled and resented it. 'Thank you, Doctor.'

The medical man offered Josa a paternal smile. 'I'll be back shortly to see how you're doing. The tablets I gave you should get rid of the pains.' He glanced at Gilmour. 'Well, most of them, anyway.'

'*Thank you, Doctor!*' he repeated.

Taylor gave a final cheery wave to Josa and a nod to Gilmour before leaving the room. The door clicked shut. There was silence for a moment and Gilmour nodded to himself, suddenly aware that they were alone. 'Right. Down to business!' But he hesitated, and Josa sensed he was steeling himself to deliver something seismic. He looked to one side. 'You're heading up the hunt for the serial killer.'

Josa leant forward, sharply. She must have misheard him. 'I'm sorry, what?'

'You're heading up the case, Jilani.'

She instantly felt light-headed. '*What?* You can't be –'

'You're senior investigating officer. It's your case.'

Her head injury began to throb. 'You're not serious! This case is … *is huge*! He's killed four young women already! The media interest is massive! I'm … I'm not ready for this, for an investigation so –'

'You are now a Detective Chief Inspector. This investigation befits your rank.'

Technically speaking, he was right. But less than a month earlier, Josa had been a Detective Sergeant based in Guildford, never expecting to be thrown into the spotlight when she became the poster girl for the new Home Secretary's latest initiative.

'Besides,' Gilmour pointed out, 'Don Walters is hardly in any condition to continue as SIO on these killings.'

'Sir … I really don't feel I'm ready for this. The thought of it … well, it terrifies me, if I'm being honest.'

'I understand. Jilani … Josa. Look … I can easily have you transferred to another station. Somewhere more bucolic. Far away from London. We'll simply say you weren't up to it. No shame in –'

'That's what this is all about, isn't it, *sir*?' The half-remembered conversation flitted through her aching head. 'Discredit me and you discredit the scheme.'

'That's enough!'

'It's more than enough!'

'One simple question! Four women have been murdered. I'm asking you to find the man responsible. Do you accept?' Gilmour presented the life-changing dilemma with stark simplicity. 'Can you take the case?'

Doctor Taylor walked from Josa's room with a smile on his face. It was all starting to come back to him. He'd missed it.

Two young nurses walked towards him, parted – so for a couple of paces they were either side of him – before continuing on their way. They were pretty enough to distract him and he casually glanced over his shoulder. A tug of nostalgia. He remembered when nurses' uniforms were one of the things that made hospitals bearable. He suspected many an old boy had turned away from the bright light to sneak another gander at matron's legs. These days they looked like dinner ladies with their acrylic black slacks and baggy blue smocks. Still, the nurse on the left did have a very nice –

'Steady, sir!'

Taylor had collided with a different kind of uniform. He stepped back. A police constable stood in the middle of the corridor.

'What's going on?'

'Laying on extra security tonight, sir.'

Taylor noticed a young policewoman by his side.

'Extra security? What for? Oh, God! Not another royal visit is it?' he groaned. 'Ah! No! It'll be for Miss Jilani and –'

'Not at liberty to say, sir.'

'I know the drill!' Taylor handed the constable his plastic identification card and didn't mind the lengthy scrutiny his ID received. By way of hello, he raised his eyebrows at the policewoman. She had a mole on her left cheek and he tapped his own face in the corresponding spot. 'I could get rid of that for you.'

The first PC returned his identification. 'That'll be all, sir.'

'I'm all right, thanks,' said his colleague, and before any further pleasantries could be attempted, a whole shuffling pack of student doctors arrived at the checkpoint and the two PCs began verifying their IDs.

Taylor continued on his way. *Oh, well, you can't win …*

As he turned the corner his phone rang. He glanced at its screen. Recognised the number. He ducked into a walk-in cupboard lined with cleaning supplies and shut the door. 'Hello?' He waited while the voice at the other end of the line sought urgent reassurances about the latest developments. 'Yes, yes, yes. They *have* set up security checks but I'm already in. And my ID opens all doors.' Taylor pulled a syringe from his pocket as he waited for a pause. 'But I'm glad you called. I need you to confirm you definitely want me to go ahead with this. It's all happened so fast, I wanted to be certain you're one hundred per cent resolved to –'

He pulled the phone from his ear as the answer he received was more emphatic than he'd expected. 'Okay. Okay! Murder is a big step and I'm not cheap, but if you're certain, then I'll go ahead.' Another pause. 'Don't you worry for one moment! I've told you!' He idly examined the tip of the needle. 'Everything is on point.'

## CHAPTER 10

Alfred Hitchcock's final movie, *Family Plot*, was playing on his television set. He sat in the sanctuary of his home, watching the film while occasionally passing comment to the portrait of its director. He knew that by his later movies, Hitch always got one of his assistant directors, or ADs as they were known, to direct the dangerous stuff. And that's what he had done with Taylor, effectively making the doctor his first AD.

He knew he would have been looking at the tip of the syringe when he made the 'on point' remark. The pun riled him, in the way private jokes can irritate those who are deliberately excluded. But at least it showed Taylor had confidence, and maybe that's all he needed for such an easy scene.

At about 11 p.m. Josa Jilani peeled back her bedding, swung her legs over the mattress and felt the cold floor on the soles of her feet. Tried to stand. For some reason she thought she would sway or tumble to her knees, but her limbs were working just fine. She slipped into her camel coat, wearing it like a dressing gown over the ghastly paper nightie they'd insisted she put on.

She walked slowly from her room and down the corridor.

'You shouldn't be out of bed.'

He was a young-looking doctor. Asian. The name badge on his Ben Sherman shirt read *Doctor Hameer*.

'You're looking after Don Walters.' She had heard Gilmour mention it earlier. 'He's a colleague of mine. And a friend.'

'Yes, I am,' Hameer answered, although it hadn't been a question.

'Is he going to make it?'

Josa saw he was caught off guard by such a direct question so early in the exchange. 'It's touch and go.'

Her heart fell. Subconsciously or not, Hameer had shaken his head as he'd replied. One of the nurses opened the door to Walters' room and stood back. Josa moved forward. She could see the DI, eyes closed and unmoving on his bed, and as she slowly approached him she already felt like she was visiting a corpse that was lying in state.

She pushed the door gently shut and pulled a chair to his side. Sat down. 'Hello, Don.' He looked like the centrepiece in some weird piece of art. Half a dozen straps and sensors attached to his skin. Countless tubes looping-the-loop before ending up in his mouth or his flesh. A bank of monitors blipping in the background, casting his face in a green hue.

'I came to say I'm sorry.' Josa started crying, almost immediately giving in to loud, wailing sobs as she buried her head in her hands. 'Oh, God ...'

She sniffed. Wiped her eyes on the cuffs of her coat. 'Sorry. Came to apologise for dragging you up there with me. Sometimes I don't know when to stop. But I shouldn't have involved you ... Oh, Don. You'd better get back soon. Because Gilmour asked me to take over the case.' She looked around the room. It felt cold and impersonal when something within Josa suggested the environment should be more welcoming. Beckoning him back to life, not freezing him out.

'And I said yes. Don't be cross. I had to take it and now ... Everything is on the line. Justice for the victims. The lives of the girls he intends to kill. And yeah, my career. Everything I ever wanted. So ...' Another loud sniff. 'I need your help. I can't do this on my own. Do you think ...' Her voice fell to a whisper, close to tears, again. 'Do you think you could help me?'

She gazed at his eyelids as if her plea might be enough to rouse him. Finally, Josa shook her head. 'I'm sorry. This is my mess. You just concentrate on getting better soon.'

She stood. What would Don Walters want to hear her say? She

had no idea and simply kissed the side of his head. She was half-way across the room when she realised what a fool she'd been. Whirled around.

'I promise you,' she said in a firm voice. 'I will get the bastard that did this to you.' But she couldn't stop herself from blowing him a tiny kiss. 'Night, Don.'

After she'd left, a figure stepped from the shadows in the corner of the room.

# CHAPTER 11

He had loaded the syringe with a solution of potassium chloride. Strong enough to kill, and once it was in her bloodstream, she'd react almost immediately, lurching into fatal cardiac arrest. Small doses of the compound were routinely given to patients suffering from hypokalaemia or digitalis poisoning and yet this same milky-white substance – albeit in a different concentration and dosage – was injected into condemned prisoners in the US. Death normally occurred within seven minutes, and most medical experts were agreed that it represented the most effective and reliable option when all you wanted to do was kill a man.

Or a woman.

11.15 p.m. Josa traipsed back to her room and found Gilmour had returned, eager to brief her more thoroughly on the case she'd inherited. He'd hardly begun when the door flew open.

Jack Dempsey burst into the room, looked from the patient to Gilmour and gave the latter a cheeky wink. 'Not interrupting anything, am I?'

In spite of herself, Josa laughed. 'Dempsey!'

'How are you, darling?' He'd been in England for over thirty years, most of them spent serving in the UK police, but he'd never lost his American accent. 'I heard what happened! Had to come and see you! Brought you a little something.' He stopped. Beamed at her. But Gilmour had recovered himself enough to stand in the big man's way.

'No visitors for DCI Jilani unless on police business!' And with a little more emotion, 'How the hell did you get past the constables out there? You've been out of the police service for –'

'Flashed them my old warrant card!'

'That is a clear breach of … How the hell did you even hang onto …' He shook his head and extended an open palm. 'Your police ID, please!'

Dempsey simply grasped the other man's hand and shook it as if greeting an old friend, slapping his shoulder with his left palm and deftly manoeuvring him to one side. 'Good to see you, too, buddy!' Now standing before the patient, he broadened his grin. 'Josa Jilani! A DCI for two minutes and already lying down on the job! Atta girl!' He handed her a brown paper bag. 'I come bearing gifts!'

She took a peek. 'Grapes!'

'Ah, fuck those.' He plucked out the bunch of seedless and tossed them into the bedside bin. 'That was in case the woodentops looked in …'

Josa peered into the bag and could now see a half-bottle of Glenlivet.

'Terr-der!' said the American.

Josa began laughing. She'd worked with Dempsey after he'd left the police service. His final months as a serving officer had been dogged by allegations and internal investigations. Up to his pips in trouble until he'd jumped, taking early retirement. No charges. He was even back in the nick now and again working on cold cases. Josa had been his liaison officer for a few of them and liked him, although in her view he was as bent as a right angle. He'd moved down to Cornwall and lost weight, although probably not enough. Dempsey's hair was peppered grey but he still looked good for a guy in his fifties. He had powerful shoulders, a broad, handsome face and eyes that made you disinclined to turn your back on him. 'Hey! How you doing?' he asked Josa.

'I'm fine!' She gestured to the whisky. 'And you shouldn't have!'

'Come here!' Dempsey leant across and embraced her.

Gilmour cleared his throat. 'Seeing as how you're here, former

DCI Dempsey, perhaps you could assist. Or were you here mainly for the whisky?'

'Mainly for the whisky,' he replied without missing a beat, and then laughed. 'I'm joking!' He perched on the edge of the bed. 'How can I help you guys?'

Even at the time it struck Josa as odd that Gilmour had requested his assistance; looking back, she wondered if she'd half-known, even then. Jack Dempsey and Daniel Blake were rumoured to have a father-son relationship … Had her boss been trying to get Blake's help without having to directly ask for it?

'DCI Jilani,' Gilmour continued, 'has been placed in charge of the hunt for the serial killer who last struck at the Shard building earlier this evening.'

'I heard that's what you were gonna try to pull.' Dempsey looked from Gilmour to Josa and whistled under his breath. 'Looks like someone high up is sure as hell out to get you, and whoever it is means –'

'We've already been through this,' Josa cut in gently. 'It's all right. Honestly.'

'Okay. It's your baseball game.' Dempsey shrugged. 'So what do we know about the killer?'

Gilmour paused, but after a moment took a file from his attaché case and extracted an A4-sized photograph. 'Becka Hoyle, the first victim,' he declared, placing it on the hospital table that arched over Josa's bed. Becka was smiling in the photograph, her blue eyes twinkling in sunlight. 'Do you both feel up to seeing this?' He held a second photo now, image towards his chest, shielded. 'It's a post-mortem shot.'

'Sure. How did she die?' Dempsey enquired.

'She was drowned.' Gilmour made no move to reveal the second photo. 'Haemorrhaging in the middle ears, diatoms in the bloodstream, water in the lungs and stomach … the usual indicators you'd expect, plus, marks on her wrist. Taken as a whole we're fairly confident that her killer bound her hands behind her back and held her head underwater until she was dead.'

Josa's voice was firm but respectful. 'We've both seen drown victims before, sir.'

But he remained hesitant. 'Any drowning is bad enough. But what he did afterwards …' He straightened his back. 'I'm afraid what you're about to see and what happened was …' His face held a trace of fear. 'Appalling.'

# CHAPTER 12

'There were marks around her neck,' Gilmour began.

'What?' Dempsey raised his eyebrows. 'Strangulation marks?'

'No. Too light for that. Something had been affixed to her throat. Or rather, *around* her throat.'

'Do we know what?' Josa asked.

'Here's the gruesome bit. We found foodstuff on her skin. Or, to be more precise, we discovered traces of meat-based stock granules that had been rubbed into her face. You're probably wondering why.' He handed Dempsey the photograph.

The American shook his head. 'I've seen it done before. It's to encourage rats and other vermin to feast on the dead victim. I'm guessing it did the trick in Becka's case or at least –' Dempsey stopped dead in his tracks as he looked down at the dead girl's face. 'Oh, my God …'

Josa said, 'Show me,' and Dempsey laid the photograph of Becka Hoyle on the table.

Josa had scrutinised murder victims many times before, but as she looked down at the image of this young woman she felt a triple stab of anger, sorrow and determination. She had to take a moment to visually get her bearings on the photograph. Which side of the bloody oval was the top of Becka's head and which the bottom. Most of the flesh had been gnawed away, either to muscle or bone. Her hair was scarlet and matted against her scalp, barely distinguishable from the flaps of red skin that hung from the edge of what had been her face. Her lips were completely absent and the line of teeth, stained with blood and mud, was the most obvious indicator. From there it was easier to locate the eyes, or rather the ocular sockets. Becka's pretty blue eyes had been devoured.

Without anger, without malice, without show, Josa Jilani said, 'I'd like to meet the man who did this to her.'

Doctor Taylor had almost reached Josa's room when another constable stopped him and demanded to see his ID. The security had pleased him as it indicated that Josa was inside. He'd tried the room a few minutes earlier and panicked a little when he found it empty. He shouldn't have waited for his client to confirm he wanted the job doing! He should have ... But what did it matter? This copper's presence confirmed she was back. He murmured 'No problem,' when his ID was returned, knocked on Josa's door and pushed it ajar without waiting for a reply.

'– *the man who did this to her.*'

'Not interrupting anything, am I?' he said breezily.

'As a matter of fact ...' Gilmour began.

Taylor held up a hand. 'I shall be discretion personified!' He grabbed Josa's notes. 'But I *will* need my patient on her own for a few minutes very shortly. So if you can wrap this up –'

'Now, you see here –'

'He's just doing his job!' Josa interjected.

'If she needs her meds ...' Dempsey shrugged. 'She needs her meds.'

'Very well! But just give us a moment, would you?'

'Your wish ...' – Taylor gave a mock bow and moved into the corner of the room – '... is my command.' He half-turned away.

'This is the second victim. Ebba Lovgren.' Taylor could hear every word, despite the fact that Gilmour had lowered his voice. 'There was no mutilation this time, thank God. But the same calling card was left. The scrawled triangle.' Taylor risked a darting glance. The two men were huddled around the bed, a Hogarth print of conspiracy in action. He caught a quick glimpse of a photo as the Chief Super laid it on the table. The same snap he'd seen in the papers. 'She was only eighteen. Swedish. Over here for work experience. She'd wanted to go to New York but her mother told her it was too dangerous …'

'How was she killed?' Josa whispered. She'd read press reports, of course, but wanted an insider's take.

'Stabbed. Several times. All the injuries were from one set of scissors which was found lodged between her first and second thoracic vertebrae. Ebba's corpse was discovered in a flat in Maida Vale by an estate agent who was showing it to a newly married couple.'

'Tough sell,' Jack Dempsey commented.

'Don't you believe it. Apparently the husband wanted to take a photo of the body for his blog.'

Taylor stifled a laugh, camouflaging his involuntary chuckle with a couple of coughs. He flicked Josa's notes to the last page, more for something to do than out of curiosity. Some fool had left her admittance form clipped to the board. On a whim, he slipped the single A4 sheet into his back trouser pocket.

'What about the third victim?' Josa was saying.

'Again, no mutilation.' Out of the corner of his eye, Taylor saw Gilmour pull another photograph from the file and place it beside the shot of Ebba Lovgren. 'Sarah Robinson. Early thirties. Strangled. And the item that was used to do it was found around her neck.' A heavy sigh. 'A belt. Not a leather belt or anything like that. The belt from a man's raincoat.' He placed another photograph alongside the first three. 'Elaine Hargreaves. And that completes the set.' He rested the empty envelope on the side of the bed. 'So … What do you think?'

No one responded. *What do they think?* Taylor thought. *They haven't a clue! It's hilarious!* He reasoned that the man paying him to do this job would be delighted with the good news he'd be bringing him as a surprise extra. *Might even be enough to merit a little bonus …*

The long silence was eventually broken by Dempsey. 'What have you got so far – linking the victims?'

Gilmour started talking. His tone said *we've got nothing* but he was inflating the answer with hot air. As he talked, Josa began to zone out, switching her attention to the photos in front of her.

'*Elizabeth the First* …' Her voice was quiet but edged with excitement.

Her eyes swept over the four prints. The two men were arguing about something or other. Josa didn't care. She brought each photograph closer to her face in turn. '*Yes* …' Finally she looked up. 'If you boys could turn down the testosterone for just a minute …' She gestured to the quartet of victims. 'Does anyone want to hear about the breakthrough?'

*Does anyone want to hear about the breakthrough?* Taylor looked up. *Fuck!* He had to will himself to stare at Josa's notes.

*Breakthrough* was bad. *Breakthrough* meant the client could get collared, which meant the money that he so badly needed might as well be in Fort Knox. He turned around to face the two coppers and the Yank. He had to take action right away.

Gilmour frowned. 'What?'

'The breakthrough I've just made.'

Dempsey let out a loud, celebratory *Ha!* as he clapped his hands. 'What you got, Josa?'

'The thing that connects all these women. What marked them out for death.' Josa Jilani tore her eyes away from the women whose killer she was hunting and looked at the two men stood in front of her. 'I know how he's selecting them and why he's killing them.'

Taylor cut in. 'And you can tell them all about it in about a quarter of an hour.'

'Ah, come on, doc!' Dempsey complained. 'This is important!'

'And the life of your colleague isn't?'

'Is it really that vital?' Gilmour asked. 'What you have to do now?'

'If it wasn't, do you think I'd be so insistent?'

'Do I get a say?' Josa demanded. 'Let's give the doctor the time he needs then we can finish this off and get cracking.'

Dempsey and Gilmour exchanged unhappy glances. 'All right,' said the Chief Super. 'But we'll be back in fifteen minutes.'

'Thank you, gentlemen.' Taylor beamed. His hand gripped the syringe in his jacket pocket. 'That will give me more than enough time.'

## CHAPTER 13

The hospital was a labyrinthine sprawl and it took Dempsey and Gilmour ten minutes to reach the wing housing the intensive care unit which Don Walters had just been moved to after his condition deteriorated, minutes earlier. As they walked down the long corridor that led to the ICU, Dempsey banged his fist on a window overlooking the car park. 'I don't like this. Too open. Too accessible. If laughing boy does try to reach Josa or Don, then –'

'I've drafted in all the available manpower at my disposal.'

'I still don't like it.' Dempsey took a sideways look at Gilmour, marching down the passage as if he was on a parade ground. Uniform smelling like it was fresh from the dry-cleaners. Hair immaculate. A couple of liver spots on his left hand. 'Why d'you still do it, Kim?'

'Do what, Mr Dempsey?'

'This!'

'You wouldn't understand.'

'Don't give me that.'

'A sense of duty. Old-fashioned. Many would say foolish.' Their footsteps echoed through the corridor. 'What about you?'

'I dunno. The same, I guess. Probably a misplaced sense of duty.'

'My father …' Dempsey could tell that Gilmour was uncertain whether to go on. 'My father used to say that *all* duty was misplaced.' A tight, involuntary grimace. 'Wretched man. Dreadful burden on my mother.' Another couple of paces. 'You and I never saw eye-to-eye, but let me tell you this.' He cleared his throat. 'I saw you act out of what you call a *misplaced* sense of duty many, many times and I saw you take personal risks that should have earned you

58

a medal. So, in the end … why did you do it, Jack?'

They turned a corner and hit a set of double door leading to the ICU. Dempsey stared at Gilmour. *Of all the curveballs…* He ran a hand across his face. Pushed open the doors. 'Another time,' he said.

'Some people say you joined the Protocol.'

'And you?'

'I don't think the Protocol even exists.'

Dempsey shot him a glance. 'Wise man.'

Josa's ear felt warm; her conversation with Stevie had told her very little she hadn't already known, except for the news that forensics had drawn a blank at the Shard. But the discussion had lasted longer than she'd realised. 'Sorry,' she said to Taylor. 'No more calls.' She placed her mobile phone on the bedside table. 'Pitfall of the job, I'm afraid.'

Doctor Taylor' smile was fraying at the edges. 'I understand, but as I said earlier, the quicker I can do what I came to do, the sooner we can all move on.'

'No, you're right. I agree.'

'Good.' He nodded, but clearly remained unconvinced. 'And just in case you get any more calls would you mind …'

'What? Oh, sure,' Josa nodded regretfully and switched off her phone.

Gilmour smiled across the reception desk. 'Is this the ICU?'

The nurse waited a moment before looking up. 'Yes,' she replied after what felt like half an hour. 'But visiting hours are –'

'Miss …' Gilmour tried to keep his voice calm. 'One of my men is in your ward. He was brought in earlier tonight and I was not permitted access to him. He may have vital information relating to a *very* important case and therefore we have to reach him *now*.'

'You tell her, Kim,' Dempsey murmured, *sotto voce*.

The nurse wasn't moved by Gilmour's glare. She moved a large boiled sweet from one side of her mouth to the other and then drew in air through her teeth. 'What's his name?'

'Walters,' Gilmour said. 'Detective Inspector Donald Walters.'

'Uh-huh.' The nurse took her time opening the patients' book. 'How are you spelling Walters?'

Dempsey spotted a couple of uniforms at the head of the corridor. 'This way,' he said, moving towards them.

The very first shiver of disquiet ran through Josa when she saw Taylor lock the door to her room. But she was aware that she was still slightly woozy from the drugs the previous doctors had administered. Maybe she was seeing things. The palms of her hands began to tingle. *Pull yourself together!* she thought to herself and Taylor gave her a look as if he knew exactly what she was thinking.

Dempsey addressed the constables on guard at the end of the passage. 'Evening, gentlemen. Which one of these is Don's pied-à-terre?'

'Second on the left, sir.'

'Thanks, soldier.'

Gilmour flashed his ID at one of the nurses outside Walters' room.

'I'm sorry, sir, no one's allowed in there until –'

'Now see here!' he cut in, 'I've had just about all –'

But Dempsey interrupted, 'We'll be very discreet, ma'am, and this is very important.' He gently brushed past her, opening the door as he moved forward.

Even before he had seen what was in the room, Gilmour saw Dempsey stop dead in his tracks and exclaim, 'Jesus Christ!'

Whatever was in there, it wasn't good.

Doctor Taylor stopped about a pace away from Josa, flicked the tip of the syringe and gave his best *don't worry* smile. 'You're not afraid of ...' he raised the needle.

'Is it possible to make a pun about small pricks that you've not heard before?'

'I've got three ex-wives. Does that answer your question?'

Josa smiled. She liked him. 'Do your worst,' she said, rolling up her right sleeve.

## CHAPTER 14

'Out, out, out!' Doctor Hameer began to usher them from the room. 'It's bad enough your security blitz means we cannot get some of our nurses in … and now this! You barge in –'

'All right, all right! We're sorry, doc. What the hell happened in there?'

'It's too early to say but as we were moving him into the ICU, well, it looks like Mr Walters suffered a heart attack. Those doctors in there are doing all they can. But I do not want to see you in my patient's room for another twelve hours! Minimum! Now go!' Hameer yelled. 'You hear me?'

'He makes Doctor Taylor look positively charming,' Gilmour muttered. He had already turned away and so did not see Hameer's reaction. But Dempsey paused, disturbed by the look on the medic's face.

'What is it, doc?'

Josa leant back into her pillows. Closed her eyes. Injections had always made her anxious and she didn't want him to see how tense she'd suddenly become. 'I don't know,' she said, 'I just feel nervous all of a sudden.'

'Taylor?' Hameer looked puzzled.

'Sure,' Dempsey said. 'He's the doctor looking after DCI Jilani. Doctor Taylor.'

'I've worked here over two years and I can tell you …' He shook his head. 'There's no one of that name working here, gentlemen.'

Josa heard his voice. Soft. Concerned. 'Afraid of needles, eh?'

She gave a non-committal shrug. 'Not crazy about them.'

'Don't worry.' He was so close she could feel his breath on her face. 'I'll take care of you.'

There was a second's silence, like the moment following the pin being pulled from a grenade. Dempsey and Gilmour exchanged horrified looks. They both knew what they had done and how long it would take to reach Josa. Dempsey's mobile was already in his hand. A moment passed and his face drained of colour. 'She's switched her phone off!'

'I'll be using the median cubital vein …' Taylor looked into the syringe, at the lethal solution of potassium chloride it contained, then at the still, calm face of Josa Jilani. He had already watched her swallow a couple of tablets that would reduce the feeling in her limbs. In the seven minutes she would take to die, the last thing he wanted was for her to thrash about. This way was much kinder. 'I'm so sorry,' he said, and drove the needle into the crook of her arm.

# CHAPTER 15

Like most madmen, he didn't consider himself insane. Suave, erudite, charming? Yes. One reel short of a movie? No. How could he be? Even Ebba Lovgren, in the brief time they'd known each other, had found him charismatic and irresistible. He smiled every time he thought of her elfin face. She'd had a crush on him. No doubt about it. When he'd confided in her that he wasn't good with relationships, she became a picture of incredulity. 'I can't believe that!'

'My last relationship didn't end well,' he'd replied.

'What happened?'

'I murdered her.'

Ebba had given a guilty laugh.

'No, really. I killed her.'

And something in his eyes had silenced her laughter.

He had raised the scissors and ...

When Margot Wendice stabs Captain Lesgate in *Dial M for Murder*, the scissors penetrate his body with relative ease and he slumps to the floor, dead within moments. Now, he didn't blame Hitch for shooting it like that. It looked good. But in real life he'd found that the point of a closed pair of scissors isn't sharp enough to do much damage.

In fact his initial swipes at Ebba felt more like he was bludgeoning her with the scissors, their point barely puncturing her clothes. In order to put the little minx down he'd been forced to drive the scissors into her throat, pulling hard to the left as if he was trying to rip out her windpipe. She'd clutched her gaping throat and fallen to her knees. He'd pounced on this, capturing the moment like any director worth his salt. Kicked her down, then bundled her onto her front and plunged the scissors into her spine. Even that wasn't as easy as he'd anticipated. It was like forcing a tent peg into dry, hard ground, but he'd done it. Oh yes, he'd done it.

He had proven himself.

He'd given Taylor a chance to prove himself by killing Jilani and Walters tonight, so all he could do now was wait. Wait, and imagine the moment.

The needle sank into Josa's soft flesh.

*'For Beryl Reid it was the shoes.'*

The words were enough to make Josa Jilani open her eyes, partly due to their unexpectedness, but mostly because it was not Doctor Taylor's voice. She immediately saw the medic, poised with his thumb on the syringe's plunger.

The man who'd spoken the sentence was slipping something into his pocket. A slim, metallic implement that resembled a dental sculpting tool. Of course -- a picklock -- which Josa assumed he'd wielded to unlock the door. And now, suddenly, he clapped his hands.

A loud, smart rap of his palms. 'Step back!' he barked, moving into the room, and as Taylor retreated a step, the needle of the syringe tugged from Josa's arm.

'What the hell are you doing here?' she demanded. It was the man from the Shard building. The scruffy stranger who'd expressed surprise that Elaine Hargreaves' am-dram activities had not been more illuminating.

'When it came to preparing for a role, she always started with the shoes. Said it helped her get into the character. You should have done the same.' He was talking to Taylor. 'Doctors in British hospitals very seldom wear white coats these days, and mud on the shoes is really a no-no.'

Josa glanced down. Saw what he meant. But he was talking too quickly to let anyone interrupt.

'I'm guessing you *were* a doctor. General ease around the place and its equipment. Knowledge of the median cubital vein. Your clothes are tailored and expensive, but that cheap watch is new because you had to sell your old, posh one.' A momentary pause before – 'You know what breaks my heart? I bet part of you enjoyed being back. In fact, I bet you were the model medic, right up until the point when you tried to murder your patient. Why don't you put that down, doctor, and we can find a way out of this?'

Taylor was staring at him, wide-eyed. Finally, a nod. 'Yes … Yes, I …' He made as if to put the hypodermic down on the bedside table, then took another look at the needle. 'No!' The stranger was approaching him and now Taylor thrust the syringe in his direction. Trying to avoid the point, he stepped back, arching his spine. Taylor advanced. Another hypodermic lunge.

Josa tried to move but her limbs felt impossibly heavy. Immoveable.

The cornered man was scanning the room. Nothing! Grabbed the clipboard as he retreated further. 'I'm warning you.'

'What? That's a clipboard.'

'Look, this is the bit where you run off and I comfort her. I'm not giving you a hard time for trying to kill her so why don't you just fuck off?' He pulled his arm back and skimmed the clipboard like a frisbee towards the doctor. There was a low *whoosh* as the clipboard sliced through the air, missing its target by about a metre.

'That was rubbish,' Josa sniped.

He broke off from Taylor to look at her. 'Oh, everyone's a critic! I thought I was pretty cool, coming in with the Beryl Reid line, which is true, by the –'

Taylor took one final jab with the needle. His intended victim took a further step back, catching his foot on the leg of the chair. He tumbled to the floor and Taylor moved towards him, syringe gripped in his hand like a dagger, bent on plunging it into the other man's helpless body.

# CHAPTER 16

An alarm sounded. More like a klaxon from hell – incredibly loud and painfully piercing. Taylor paused, looked around and saw Josa, her palm jammed against the *Emergency: Assistance* button.

'You've got about five seconds before the cavalry arrives,' she calmly announced. In less than three of them, he was gone. Josa saw four fingers curl around the side of her bed railing and the stranger pulled himself up until his face rose to her level, their noses only an inch apart.

'You fight like a girl,' she told him.

He moved fractionally closer. 'I don't kiss like one.'

'Is that another one of your cool lines?'

'Ah. I had time to think about the Beryl Reid one. That one needs a bit of work. I'll give you that.'

'Thanks for saving my life.'

Another move forward. 'Is that all I get?'

'I've got a bottle of Glenlivet in the drawer.'

'Not quite what I had in –'

'I know exactly what you had in –'

'Maybe ...'

Later, she put it down to lingering concussion. The way she'd tilted her head, closed her eyes. And much later, she even wondered if she'd just imagined the feel of his lips against hers. But whatever the truth, there was no clinch. Any impending kiss cut short by a frantic, '*What's going on?*'

She jerked her head towards the doorway. Stevie, out of breath and on edge. 'Gilmour told me to get here as quickly as possible because–' He saw the person by Josa's side. 'Who *are* you?'

'Pick that clipboard up!' he snapped. 'Now, soldier!'

Stevie bent down, scooped it and went to hand it to the man who –

Who was gone.

Taylor kept his head down and powered along the corridors heading towards the maternity wing. He was only forced into one route change, skipping up some stairs and through a disused ward before taking the lift back down when he'd spotted a copper doing his Checkpoint Charlie routine outside ENT.

Taylor quickly found what he was after. A small room filled with medical outfits. Blue trousers resembling trackie bottoms, cotton V-necks and paper headwear designed to keep hair in check. Fathers-to-be were directed here and changed into these clothes before joining their partners in theatre for delivery. But to the untrained eye the apparel on offer looked like scrubs. Taylor stuffed his white coat and shirt into a bin and quickly put on the blue outfit over his usual clothes. *Good!* It might buy him some extra time if they'd already circulated his description.

He reached A&E without problem and waited until an ambulance roared into the nearest bay, brushing past the copper on duty to reach it. '*Wait a minute, sir!*' but he was gone and the PC didn't notice that when a scrum of medics wheeled in the RTA victim, the man in scrubs wasn't with them.

Josa was massaging her legs, willing the feeling to return to them. Her arms had already recovered, the debilitating heaviness gradually dissipating. Next to her, Gilmour was talking on the phone to security, issuing a description of Taylor. 'I know it's difficult to check everyone but …'

Dempsey leant against the doorframe.

'Just do your best!' Gilmour concluded and hung up. 'Bloody useless! If I ran a police station the way these chaps run a hospital …'

'Josa,' Dempsey said. 'Are you all right, darling?'

In a voice so quiet that both men had to strain to hear her, she replied, 'I want to go home.'

Moments after Taylor's attack, the danger she'd faced had struck her hard.

'DCI Jilani. This is the best place for you,' Gilmour declared. 'The doctors need to keep a close watch on you.'

'They're not pumping anything else into me.'

'And here we can protect you,' he reasoned, immediately regretting his assurance.

She looked him in the eye, not needing to mock or even question his words. 'I want to go home.'

Taylor's battered BMW was parked on a gloomy side street about ten minutes from the hospital. He'd dumped the stolen clothes, quietly thanked the heavens that he was wearing a T-shirt vest and managed not to break into a run as he tracked back to his car.

He unlocked the door and sank into the passenger seat with a long sigh of relief, his muscles relaxing for the first time since he'd fled from Josa's room. He glanced in the rear-view mirror.

'Jesus Christ!' he spun around. 'You scared the shit out of me!'

'A jumpy assassin. That doesn't bode well.'

'Fucking hell!' He placed his palm over his heart. 'Don't do that!'

'How did it go?'

Taylor shook his head. 'They were both guarded. I couldn't do it.'

'You *what*?'

'I just couldn't do it. I'm sorry. It was impossible.'

'You bloody fool.'

'Think you could do better?'

'What?'

Taylor pulled out his bargaining chip. 'This has got to be worth something, I'd have thought?' The admittance form he'd pocketed earlier, containing all the patient's personal details. 'How would you like to know Josa Jilani's home address?'

# CHAPTER 17

## *Wednesday, 7 March*

'This is Josa's father. I simply wish to speak with my daughter. Is that too much to ask? I cannot believe you people.'

'Sir ...' she tried to cut in.

'I remember when nursing was a caring profession. But now? Now you tell me –'

'Sir!' the hospital receptionist shouted down the phone. She lowered her voice. 'I'm not a nurse and I'm not permitted to give out information about –'

'Even to her father? Let me speak to your superiors!'

She sighed. This was going to be a long one.

The doctors made her stay the night and, in retrospect, she conceded they had a point. She'd known victims of head traumas appear perfectly fine minutes after their injury, only to collapse with complications hours, even days later. And so a little caution was not unreasonable.

Josa slept well, waking at about 6.30 a.m. to be given more precautionary meds, after which she opened up her laptop to surf the Net and find out how much about the murders was already in the public domain. About half an hour into the research she paused for a cup of tea, and as she sipped it, she reflected how quickly she had accepted her new role and the imperative that went with it. She had less than a week until Tuesday and its expected murder. Six days to catch a killer before he took another life. That was that. She was scared – terrified – but accepted a dangerous man had to be stopped and it was now up to her to do it.

Gilmour phoned at about 9 a.m. He was handling things at the station until Josa could be there, and he promised to bring her up to speed as soon as he had a moment to breathe. Her sister phoned mid-morning. They'd already spoken once that day, at dawn when Josa had explained why she couldn't be there to wave off their mother from the train station as she began her epic journey. She'd been careful to downplay the danger she'd faced at the Shard, talking in vague terms about 'a slight injury' after giving chase. The attack she'd suffered in the hospital was totally censored. No point in worrying other people.

'So,' Josa asked. 'How did mum take it? Me not being there to wave her off?'

'She was pretty gutted but she understood.'

A ghost of a smile. 'You're a terrible liar.

For as long as Josa could remember, her sister had turned heads wherever she went. Not metaphorically, but as a physical phenomenon, like a magnet drawing the needle of a compass. She would sashay into a room and every male eye would track her progress, for one very obvious reason: Preya Jilani was beautiful. She worked moderately hard on her figure, but her face, in the words of a hundred would-be suitors, had been heaven-sent.

As a teenager, Josa had grown used to the disappointment in boys' eyes when she was introduced to lads who had already met her sister. 'And this is Josa. I told you all about her! Watch out! She's got all the brains!' And yes, the boys were kind to her, because Preya made it clear how much little sister meant to her, but they were never really interested in the studious one, unless it was to find out who Preya fancied, if Preya was seeing anyone, whether Preya preferred chocolates or roses, or would both be too much, d'you think?

Although Josa had never felt envious of her sister's eye-catching appearance, the galling thing was, they looked very similar. As a drunken uncle once put it when he thought they were out of earshot, 'Josa just missed the boat.' The remark had cut deep because she knew it was true. They both had lean faces, but whereas Preya's bone structure suggested an aristocratic geometry, Josa's was *just* too angular, her chin *just* too sharp. Both sisters were blessed with an abundance of thick, dark hair, but whereas Josa was no stranger to GHDs and an old hair band because *I can't do a thing with it*, Preya's hair was lustrous, mysteriously malleable and could be thrown into a dozen different styles, each of them striking. From the elaborate and daring to the just-got-out-of-bed look which somehow made her look even more seductive, Preya could carry off any style.

Only their eyes were identical. Preya was not vain, but they had always been the feature she disliked about her appearance. Both siblings had light brown irises but very occasionally, in certain lights, they appeared an emerald green. 'I hate them,' Preya would complain. 'Brown eyes and then bang! It's like someone photoshopped them or something.'

Josa – younger by just eighteen months – knew that most people had always murmured behind their backs. *Preya's got the looks, Josa's got the brains,* as if they were categories on a leader board. *Funny thing is, Josa doesn't seem to mind. Those two girls really do adore each other.* In truth, the 'funny thing' was, it did bother Josa. Not the fact that her sister was stunning. But the silent opinions that formed when people met them for the first time. Eyes flickering between the sisters. Their parents' male friends smiling more broadly at Preya while their wives warmed to Josa. The constant comparisons and perceptions – these bothered the hell out of Josa. But not Preya. Never Preya.

Their mother's differing attitude to her two daughters made Josa's affection for her sister all the more remarkable. Preya had always been the golden child. 'My beautiful, beautiful daughter,' her mother had called her firstborn. Josa could understand her mother's bias, but never quite forgive it.

And now she was heading home. Gilmour's chauffeured Bentley Mulsanne cruised smoothly along Tower Bridge Road and Josa, sat behind the driver, wondered how much this vanity cost her boss. She gazed through the window. This was the kind of view of the capital she enjoyed. Always had done, ever since she was a small girl and her father had brought her on day trips to London. To her right, a broad, dark, glass-fronted office block. To her left, across the river, the gleaming grandeur of 30 St Mary Axe, better known as the Gherkin. And dissecting these two symbols of modernism, the huge Victorian Gothic icon that is Tower Bridge.

As Josa sank back into the Bentley's soft, cream upholstery she could smell the leather and feel cool air blowing from the bull's-eye vents. A moment's peace before her boss burst the bubble.

'Josa,' Gilmour said, 'this is going to be uncomfortable, but I have to ask you the question.'

'Hello, miss. Yes. I believe I spoke to you earlier today. I am the father of Josa Jilani. The famous policewoman who is in your hospital. Now –'

'Before you go on, sir, could I interrupt?' She just wanted to cut this short. 'Miss Jilani is no longer with us. Left a few minutes ago. So if you do need …'

He waited until she finished prattling on, then hung up. So, she'd left a few minutes earlier. That was all he needed to know.

# CHAPTER 18

Josa nodded. 'I know.'

It was almost 6 p.m., already growing dark, and half an hour after she'd declared she'd leave the hospital with or without her doctors' approval. A consultant had expressed concern but given his consent. Gilmour had volunteered to run her home and now they sat in the back of his car, the kind of luxury coupé that cost more than her flat.

Jack Dempsey had swung by her ward as she'd been leaving and somehow insisted on riding home with her. Gilmour offered a token, bickering resistance – *I'm not running a taxi service, you know* – before a grudging acquiescence.

'You want to know,' Josa said, 'what links the killer's victims.'

Gilmour nodded. 'Back at the hospital, you said you'd worked it out. It's vital we know as soon as possible.'

Jack Dempsey sat in the front passenger seat and corkscrewed his upper body to face Josa. 'Only if you feel up to it.'

'The Chief Super is right. Best I go through it now. Do you have the photographs, sir?'

'Surely.' He handed her the file containing shots of the first four victims.

Everyone felt the Bentley decelerate. 'What's happening?' Dempsey asked. He looked ahead. 'Jesus!'

As they approached Tower Bridge, Josa peered through the windshield and saw that the blue metal gates had swung shut across it. They appeared strangely out of place, looking like the kind of railings usually found marking the perimeters of suburban parks or old-fashioned school playgrounds. Bells began to ring and warning lights flashed. 'They're raising the bridge,' she said.

'How long will that take?' Gilmour asked testily, as if he blamed her for the delay.

'No idea. Shall we crack on?'

'Please do.'

'Look at the photos, would you? The live shots.' She laid them out on the leather upholstery.

Gilmour moved closer.

Josa could see him squinting slightly and guessed he was too vain to wear spectacles. 'What am I supposed to be looking at?' he asked.

'All of them. Look!'

The first was Becka Hoyle. Long, blond hair, full lips. The epitome of glamour. Then Ebba Lovgren. Black spiky hair. Nose ring. Blue eyes and a strangely innocent face. The third photo showed Sarah Robinson, early thirties, and the oldest in the line-up. She had fair hair, turquoise eyes and a pretty smile. And finally, Elaine Hargreaves. Deep tan, auburn hair, a little obvious in her good looks.

'So what connects them?' Gilmour's impatience was making him clip his words. Traffic had come to a complete standstill and it felt as if this added to his displeasure.

'Location. All murdered in London. But that's a given, and so is gender and ethnicity …'

'Yeah, yeah …' Dempsey's voice was even as he looked over at the dead women's faces. 'Serial killers tend to hunt within one ethnic group and gender, and geographical nucleation isn't unusual.' He gave a smile. 'What else you found, Josa?'

She nodded. 'There's the big one. The one which bound all four of them. The one which meant our killer chose them. And it's right there in the photographs. The thing they all have in common and that marked them for death.'

Gilmour looked from Josa's face to the images. 'There's a physical characteristic they all share that made the killer select them?'

'Oh, yes!'

'Well? Get on with it, Jilani!'

She paused. 'They're all blonde.'

For Gilmour, it was the moment an aging relative starts talking to a person who's not there. He nodded his head slowly. 'Right. Yes. All four of them are blonde. Except the two that aren't. So they're all blonde. Except the one with black hair and the redhead. Brilliant. Are you sure that crack to your head wasn't –'

Josa was prodding her iPhone but still had time to interrupt her boss. 'Elaine was an actress, remember? She had a role that demanded red hair. Queen Elizabeth I. She's been thorough with the dye but if you look carefully you can just about make out –'

'What about Ebba?'

Dempsey snapped his fingers. 'She's Swedish!' he said. 'They're all fair-haired. Well, the majority are. She's dyed her hair, going for the emo look but I've got a feeling you're going to tell me …'

Josa held up the screen of her phone, pivoting it towards the two men. 'I Google-imaged Ebba Lovgren and what do you know?'

She registered the astonishment on Gilmour's face and looked again at the photo she'd brought up. She'd accessed an online article about Ebba's background. There she was, three years earlier, on the prow of a tiny boat, right hand raised in a comic salute and a big smile on her face.

'Well done, Jilani,' Gilmour murmured.

The fifteen-year-old Ebba had a mass of blond hair.

'I aim to please.'

'Three cherries in a row for the lady!' Dempsey's face had lit up. He turned around and drummed his hands on the passenger dash. 'Jackpot!'

'Please don't do that,' Gilmour implored. 'Finger marks, old chap. Finger marks.' He returned his attention to Josa. 'Could be a coincidence,' he reasoned.

Dempsey shook his head. 'Natural redheads are the rarest hair type. Or rather, they used to be. In the UK you're looking at about one in twenty-five being a *natural* redhead. But the incidence, if you will, of natural blondes is decreasing across Europe and hell, right across the world … Anyway, right now, pure fair hair – not dirty blondes or strawberry blondes – is about one in twenty. So the chances of choosing four natural blondes in succession are …' He paused. Looked up.

'One in 160,000,' said Josa.

'I was about to say that. One in 160,000. Yeah.' He beamed. 'That'd be one hell of a coincidence!'

'So he's going after blondes …' Gilmour's eyes moved from victim to victim. 'But not because of the way they look.'

'Yeah,' Josa murmured. She paused. Something new had just struck her. 'And you know why that's interesting?'

## CHAPTER 19

'Google, Google, Google …' he murmured, poring over the internet. 'The murderer's best friend! A-ha!' He explored the exterior of Josa's block of flats using Street View, finding the best place to wait for her and even checking for … 'No cameras!' he crowed. This was going to be easier than he'd imagined.

'*Yeah … And you know why that's interesting?*' Josa leant forward, moving to the edge of her seat. Ahead of her she could see the bridge was raised to its maximum 83-degree slant. So close to the incline, it looked weird. Like a road for magic cars that could drive upwards into the night-time sky.

'Go on,' Dempsey urged.

'It's not unusual for killers to have a type, and that type can be blondes,' she continued. 'But this is nothing to do with the way they look. Just about the fact that they're blonde.'

'Christ!' Gilmour looked like he'd aged ten years since she'd begun her explanation. 'We keep this from the press.'

'Is that wise?' Josa countered.

'DCI Jilani, I don't think you understand the catastrophic implication of what we've just discovered …' Gilmour looked ashen. 'Let me tell you why it's vital – *absolutely vital* – that this does not get out …'

'Why?'

'If the public became aware of the truth as we now know it, it would be disastrous. Disastrous! There's a real sense of panic with this one. It's playing out across social media, news updates, becoming part of urban mythology ...' Gilmour shook his head. 'This has already seeped underneath the skin of the public. Now with this revelation ... If this leaks we'll have every fair-haired woman in the country living in fear. This ... this is a nightmare!'

'It sure is,' Dempsey acknowledged, 'But lighten up. Josa just gave us your first lead on this one. That's got to be worth a moment of celebration, right?' He stuck his palm through the gap separating the front seats.

Gilmour looked aghast. 'You're not going to high-five me, are you?' He straightened his already dead-centre tie. 'Customarily, I don't do high-fives.'

'If he comes to, someone should tell Don Walters about the blonde connection,' Josa said. 'You know, let him know we've worked out what links the victims. He deserves to be kept up to date on this one. He didn't have to come with me ...'

'That's a good thought,' Gilmour agreed.

'And you know what?' Dempsey added. 'We should run a check on any other jokers who've made a habit of targeting blondes –'

Another ringing bell interrupted him.

'What is it this time?' Gilmour snapped.

'It means,' said Josa, 'they're lowering the drawbridge.'

As they approached Hammersmith Gilmour said, 'I've detailed a couple of chaps to keep an eye on you. One will remain outside your house, checking the garden, sweeping the grounds and what-have-you. The other will stand sentry outside your porch. A presence as much as anything, you understand.'

'I live in a flat, sir.'

'A flat? Really? Ah, well. They can work something out, I'm sure.'

'What time do they get here?' Dempsey asked.

'Within the next half hour. That should be all right, shouldn't it?'

Josa nodded, just desperate to get into the comfort and familiarity of her own home. 'Absolutely,' she replied.

He was there when the Bentley Mulsanne slid to a halt outside the flats, waiting in his car parked a little way along the street. Watching. *Surely this had to be her.* One of the Bentley's rear doors opened, triggering the interior light. From his position he could only see the men in front – a chauffeur and … the American. Jack Dempsey. He'd done his research, all right. That was Jack bloody Dempsey, and wherever he went, following in the shadows there was bound to be –

He shuddered. Glanced over his shoulder, taking the expression literally for a moment, and when he looked back at the Bentley, Josa Jilani had emerged. He watched her lean into the car. Final goodbyes before jogging across the street. She looked in good shape, he thought, considering everything she'd been through. He couldn't suppress a rueful smile. *Considering everything he'd put her through.*

She'd reached the broad open portico that formed the entrance to the block of flats and opened her handbag, fishing inside for her keys.

He watched, transfixed as she moved forward ever so slightly, positioning herself so that the circular overhead light shone across her and into her bag. It was as if –

*Josa looked up.*

– as if she was stepping into the spotlight.

# CHAPTER 20

She flicked the kettle on then hunted out an old notebook and placed it on a tiny writing desk that stood in the corner of her front room, intending to jot down a few observations from the previous evening.

Left hand to her temple, she began scribbling away. Short, lacklustre comments. Chin resting on her palm, she studied her words for several moments. A long sigh. This wasn't working. She was too tired. Too jaded. And – she sniffed the air, wrinkled her nose – she badly needed a shower to get rid of the hospital smell that clung to her. Then peppermint tea followed by bed.

She ripped the pages from her notebook. Four short sharp tears and the pages were in pieces. She stood, walked into the bathroom and put the ripped-up paper into the toilet basin. Closed the lid and without pausing, flushed them away. Moved to the door. Closed it.

In the hallway outside her flat, someone slipped a key into the lock of her front door. It failed to turn, just as the second and third keys proved useless. But the fourth key slid into the Yale, a perfect fit. It turned. The front door was quietly pushed open.

Even before the toilet had finished gurgling, Josa slipped off her dressing gown. It fell onto the toilet lid and she didn't bother to pick it up, stepping straight into the bath. She swished the shower curtain closed, its circular holders making a loud metallic *whoosh* as they flew across the rail. Josa exhaled. She could feel fatigue in her bones and didn't like it. She needed to be awake. Alert. She removed the wrapper from the new bar of soap and turned on the shower.

Outside the bathroom, the hand was hovering, hesitating over the handle of the door. *To go in? Not go in?* The sound of the water surging from the shower and hitting Josa's body. There was really no question.

Josa tilted her head back, letting the strong jets of water strike her lower face, throat and chest. She looked up at the shower head, raised the bar of soap to her neck, quickly building up a lather before moving down, briskly rubbing the soap across her left arm. A brief, broad smile on her face as the water hit her torso. Head right back, so that as she turned, her hair became soaked. She moved her hands back to her throbbing neck and shoulders, rubbing soap into the aches, as much for the motion of application as anything else.

Starting to relax now. This was going to be okay. She hadn't meant to get her hair wet, but what did it matter? It shouldn't take too long to dry. Josa closed her eyes. She stood in the bath letting the hot streams massage her face and body. So relaxing. Just the sound of the water and the feel of it against her skin. Somehow, *somehow*, everything was going to be fine.

She didn't notice the bathroom door open. Didn't hear its creak over the sound of the shower. Didn't see the tall figure, silhouetted in the doorway.

# CHAPTER 21

Back in the early eighties, Josa's mother, a diminutive woman called Kiran Chopra, had lived in a small town in northern India. When her parents died in a fire, her life fell apart. She moved to England to be with Jamal, her older, ambitious brother who'd made a life for himself just outside Manchester, prospering and enjoying the lifestyle that the seventies and eighties brought to the industrious and the fortunate. Kiran hated England and the English. Couldn't speak a word of the language and showed no inclination to learn.

Her brother was at first concerned. Anxious. He felt she needed male company and played matchmaker, with introductions to a string of singles. But as she treated each with a wince-inducing apathy, Jamal finally decided she secretly enjoyed spinsterhood. *You will grow old alone like a witch, I tell you!*

When he introduced her to Nasrullah Jilani, a local businessman he'd known even before arriving in the UK, he'd done so out of courtesy. He was one of four friends there for a poker night, and definitely not the type of bloke that Kiran would ever warm to. Nasrullah was gregarious, the last to leave a party. Always up for another drink, another loud joke, a great big firework of a man. Jamal had assumed that Nasrullah represented everything Kiran loathed about the British and was amazed when she threw him a coy glance. He hadn't even known she could *do* coy glances.

Nasrullah and Kiran spent hours together, simply walking, drinking tea, cooking and sharing elaborate meals. And then Jamal discovered that Nasrullah had recently lost his parents and that the two of them had somehow bonded over joint sorrow. Nasrullah – big, bold, boisterous Nasrullah – had found someone he could confide in. They were married within the year.

But within another year, the problems became obvious. Kiran both lived for Nasrullah and resented him. Her aversion to England grew more acute, and by equal degrees, her desire to return to India became more intense. *Here,* she would tell Nasrullah. *I have nothing. I am nothing!*

Nothing, until the day she gave birth to Preya and suddenly, perhaps for the very first time in her life, Kiran Jilani had something precious. It was conceivably all she had ever wanted. *Preya* was all she had ever wanted. The perfect baby who grew into the perfect child. Josa, on the other hand, had been what Kiran called 'an accident'. Josa just didn't seem able to fit in. She was a tomboy, more interested in climbing trees than learning cookery from her mother. Preya would try on a *nauvari* and become a goddess. Josa would try on the simplest sari and fall headlong down the stairs. Kiran quickly gave up on the girl she called her 'Western' daughter, but Josa didn't mind.

'Who's the most marvellous and most beautiful girl in the world?' Nasrullah had whispered to his younger daughter. 'Josa Jilani is! Daddy loves you! How much does Daddy love you?'

Josa always laughed at that one. 'To the moon and back again!' she shouted.

'That's right! Now come here! Your old man needs a hug!'

She'd never been happier than when she spent time with her dad. Walking trips, fishing weekends, playing chess in the evening and letting him win.

The cancer was at least quick. Kiran went to pieces. She seemed to see Nasrullah in Josa and couldn't bear the reminder, cold-shouldering the mourning child for many painful months. Preya was fiercely protective of her sister but felt something had died within her. The next few years were strange and difficult. Kiran, previously a lapsed Muslim, became devout and insisted her reluctant daughters follow in her footsteps.

The week after her eighteenth birthday, Preya gave Josa a present. 'Dad bought it for you, all those years ago. He stashed it away. Apparently he told Mum it was for your eighteenth birthday, just after he got the … you know.'

Cancer was always 'you know'.

'Why didn't Mum give it to me?'

'You know what she's like. But I remembered it. Dug it out of the loft'

The card read, 'One day, will you teach me to lose with such skill?' Josa tore open the wrapping paper. A chess set. Nasrullah had signed the card, 'To my darling Josa for the day you turn eighteen. Whatever you do in life, you'll always make me proud and I'll always love you … To the moon and back again! Dad. XXXXXXX'

# CHAPTER 22

Swoosh!

Josa swept the shower curtain to one side. 'Bloody hell!'

Her sister was sitting on the toilet. 'Don't hate me!' said Preya. She tried an exaggerated smile. 'I was busting. Sorry!'

'You scared the life out of me!' Josa grabbed her dressing gown from the floor and slipped into it. 'I thought you'd lost your keys.'

'Me too. Still not got used to my new keys. Still not got used to my new anything.'

Until recently Preya had been a receptionist in a private doctor's surgery, or as her mother termed it, 'a doctor'. She'd been good at her job. Enjoyed it. Enjoyed it even more when a couple of years earlier she'd started a relationship with Michael, the doctor who owned the business. They'd talked about marriage and he no longer blanched when she paused by the windows of expensive jewellers. But he'd been intractable on the subject of kids. She was desperate to be a mother and, although he was happy enough with the idea of children, he wanted to wait at least five years and build up his business. As far as Josa could tell, he was opening a string of private clinics, developing a medical franchise that could have made him seriously rich if he guided the project to its full potential. But that meant one hundred per cent focus on the expansion plan whereas Preya, although not averse to a life of some affluence, had prioritised kids over commerce. Their different stances caused minor arguments, then friction, followed by all-out hostility. When they finally parted Preya told him she loved him and if he had children with another woman within four years she'd chop his balls off. She left him, the surgery and the apartment in Portland Place they'd shared for just over eighteen months. The previous weekend she'd moved in with Josa, who had only just begun renting her place in Hammersmith.

But right now they were good for each other. Preya had too many friends to be lonely, but she felt displaced, and even the sound of her sister around the place acted like a welcome anchor. Josa felt alone and under attack, and so having her sister around offered much-needed comfort. And the little things, like the rich aromas wafting from the kitchen when Preya was rustling up dinner, made her new flat feel more like her new home.

'How was last night, Prey?'

'Brilliant. Not stayed out late with the girls, just chatting since …' She shook her head, ready to change the subject. 'Hey, I came back here for lunch and that guy called for you again.'

'What guy?' Josa asked.

'What's-his-name?' Preya stood, and in a curiously inelegant movement, waggled her hips to the left then right as she hauled her tights up. 'Like the writer.' She pulled up her Gucci jeans and rearranged her long-sleeved *kurti* so its hem fell below her waist.

Preya always managed to combine Eastern and Western styles of dress while her sister felt she'd still to grasp the rudiments of either. 'Like the writer.' Josa nodded. 'Oh, *that* guy.'

'Salinger! Professor Paul Salinger. Third time I've taken a message from him for you.' Preya sidled into the front room.

'Welcome to my world. What did he want?'

'Wanted to talk to you about your current role, believes he can be of help … You know.'

Josa paused in the hallway. 'Yeah, just another academic who's heard I'm on a *big case*.' She wrapped the phrase in speech marks using her index fingers then walked into her bedroom. 'He'll be looking to get himself published so wants to foster some kind of … Oh, I can't be bothered.'

Preya remained in the front room, curled up on the sofa. 'Tough day at work?' she called through.

'Something like that.'

'Hey! I was thinking! Now you're back with the Met, does that mean you'll be working with Simon Maxwell again?'

Josa joined her sister on the sofa. 'I dunno. Why?'

'*I dunno. Why?*' Preya laughed. 'Because you went out with him and he really liked you.'

She'd dated Simon Maxwell, a police pathologist, a couple of years earlier when they'd worked in the same division. They'd been friends at first, sharing a drink in the evening when either of them had endured a bad day. And there had been a lot of bad days. Gradually their platonic friendship became something more, but dating him had felt like a throwback to her teens when she suspected too many boys of trying to get to know Preya through her. She remembered Simon's jaw drop open by an inch when he first saw her sister. 'He really liked *you*,' Josa countered.

'Rubbish!'

'Funny how we broke up when you got serious with …' She paused, regretting the comment, but Preya didn't seem to mind.

'You broke it off, and if I remember correctly it was because you'd been seconded to London. You said you felt bad about not being able to see him, so binned him, but I always thought that was an excuse.'

'Why would I need an excuse to finish with someone?'

'I'm not saying you need an excuse. Just that you always find one.'

'I do not!'

'You do!'

Josa thought about it for a moment. She'd only had a handful of relationships, because she insisted on choosing carefully. She prided herself on that score. And with each of her serious boyfriends, it had ended amicably. Always friends and no bruises, just the way she liked it. But *Christ!* It suddenly occurred to her that she could be better at finishing relationships than sustaining them.

'Now he's working down here,' Preya said, 'and you are, too … If he tries it on, what are you going to do?'

'I buy my underwear from Sainsbury's now. I can never enter into a relationship with any man, ever again.'

Preya laughed but got the message and changed the subject.

'So ...' She mimicked the airborne speech marks. 'What's the *big case*?'

The object of the 'big case', the killer who had already slaughtered so many women, was currently sat outside the flat, listening to Radio 3. He'd watched Preya Jilani enter the building and had mulled over the added complication before deciding it shouldn't stop him. He turned off the radio, climbed from his car and began to cross the road.

'Well ...' Josa seldom discussed her job with her sister. She kidded herself it was professional discretion but knew that nine times out of ten, Preya wouldn't be interested. But this case was different. This one was juicy. And for once, Josa had no friends or allies at the station to chew over the day's findings with. She gave a brief overview of the investigation and the politics involved.

'Don't let the bastards grind you down. This is your uber-brilliant job! The one you've wanted for years! It's what you've always worked towards! Don't let them spoil it.'

'Yeah, but I always wanted it to be because of the work, my work, because of me, because of ... I dunno. I've been fast-tracked because I'm *Muslim* and it's all part of some political bollocks ...' She shrugged. 'And the reality is I've got to catch a murderer and I know he'll kill again very, very soon unless I stop him. So, no pressure, then.'

Preya didn't reply. She was thinking. Moments like this demonstrated one of her best traits. She could talk ten to the dozen but always knew when to keep her mouth shut.

Josa stood. 'I better hit the hay. And sorry. Didn't mean to bring the mood down.' She looked down on her big sister.

'You,' said Preya, as Josa reached her bedroom door. 'You didn't get this job because you're *Muslim* or *British Asian* or whatever the fuck they like to call us. You got it despite that. Never –' Josa was taken aback by the ferocity with which she delivered the word. '*Never* forget that.' Her voice softened again. 'And this guy. The guy murdering these girls. You'll get him, baby doll. It's what you do.'

Josa paused. 'Thanks, Prey.' She gave a faint smile. 'What do you think Dad would have said?'

The quizzical look on Preya's face surprised her. 'You know what I think Dad would have said.'

She spoke as if they'd already discussed it, but their father's hypothetical reaction had never been mentioned. 'Sorry,' Josa replied, uncertain what she apologising for or why.

'You must be tired.' Preya stood up and warmly embraced her sister. 'Get some sleep!'

'Yeah, you're probably right.'

'Night, Jose.'

'Sleep tight.'

Josa closed the door.

He had almost reached the block's front entrance when the liveried Vauxhall Insignia glided to a halt, right behind his car. Two constables alighted and without thinking he circled the flats. By the time he'd looped back to the road both uniforms had disappeared and no one saw him driving away into the night.

There would be other evenings.

Josa's bed had never looked so welcoming. She promised herself a full eight hours sleep and then hell-for-leather in the morning. The man she was hunting was due to kill again in five days. She slipped under her duvet and reached for the light switch.

She had no way of knowing she would not have to wait that long until the next death.

*Click.*

Darkness.

# CHAPTER 23

## *Thursday, 8 March*

*Click.*

Light.

Well, that was a good start. Most of the desk lamps in the library didn't work so –

The seat at the other side of the small table was pulled back and an old woman made herself at home. Nine times out of ten only students used this place, which meant he'd had a good chance of having some fresh-faced little temptress park opposite him. Stretching to the floor when a pen accidentally fell from the table and offering a 'Coming Soon' glimpse of teenage flesh in the process.

Never mind. At least it meant he could focus on the recent edition of the *Guardian* he'd grabbed from the archives. He swept its pages back until he reached the article about Muslim police officers being fast-tracked to ensure the service reflected something the media always called 'modern Britain'. He doubted they believed the place truly existed, certainly not how they depicted it. But if 'modern Britain' was a reality, surely he was doing something that reflected it far more accurately? And overleaf …

'Oh! Oh! Oh!' he murmured.

A whole double-page spread on the Muslim policewoman who had clearly been chosen as the face of the fast-track initiative. It had been written before she'd been placed in charge of hunting him down but the find still delighted him. He wished he could show Hitchcock the article but had to make do with reading it himself, although he spent less time on the text than he did poring over the accompanying photographs. A portrait of Josa looking almost comically young, the month she'd joined the police. She was wearing a pristine uniform and a PC's bowler hat that looked a size too large for her. She scowled as if carrying the weight of the world on her epaulettes. And years later, behind a desk at a press conference, hastily arranged by the Met's PR department after she'd foiled a plot to blow up part of the London Underground. Beneath this one he read a brief description of the would-be bomber.

'Amateur!' he murmured.

'*What did you say?*'

'Nothing!' he hissed to the old woman.

She looked up. 'What? I didn't say anything,' she told him.

He shook his head. Returned to the *Guardian*. Best of all was the inevitable photo of the dutiful copper off duty. The only shot which had her smiling. She looked to be at some sort of social function, a wedding reception perhaps, judging by the long tables of geometrical food in the background. She was raising a glass to camera and someone had her arm around her. The caption revealed it was her sister. A couple of friends were stood in front of her, leaning sideways at exaggerated angles so their heads covered her torso. He noted they were both white girls and briefly wondered whether the snap had been selected to suggest a preferred image of 'modern Britain'.

'*Make the little whore pay!*'

He stared at the old woman. 'What? What did you just say?'

She looked up from her book. 'Nothing.' A kindly smile. 'I didn't say anything.'

He momentarily held her gaze then let his eyes pinball between her face and the *Guardian* before focussing on the photograph in the newspaper again. Josa was the one sober person in the photo. In control but happy. Was that her? Did that shot capture Detective Chief Inspector Jilani?

'*That's the little trollop, all right! You know it is!*'

He could hear the old woman's voice but this time he didn't look up. She'd only deny she was haranguing him. No, he wouldn't give her the pleasure. He'd stare at the article until he'd burnt a hole into the paper.

'*The one you didn't have the stomach to get rid of! You yellow, good for nothing, worthless little boy!*'

Oh, God. Now he recognised the voice. Now he knew who the old woman sitting opposite him really was. 'I'm sorry. It wasn't that,' he said very quietly. 'I just couldn't … it would have been too dangerous to –'

'*I don't want to hear your excuses, boy! You had the wrong idea, as usual, anyway.*'

He still refused to look up, but this time it was fear preventing him from meeting her stare. And she was leaning across now. He could smell her potpourri-like perfume. See her bony finger tapping the photograph. '*Her! Kill the little bitch! And make her enjoy it!*' A croak of laughter. '*Make her ashamed to enjoy it!*'

'You want me to –'

'*Do I have to spell it out for you? This little Paki –*'

'Mother!'

'*You have to make her suffer.*' She was prodding the photograph again. '*You know what you have to do with her?*'

'I … I …' But suddenly it clicked, like the lamp coming on a few minutes earlier, and the light was strong and inescapable. Surreptitiously, he began to tear out one of the photos from the paper. Why hadn't he seen the way immediately?

'*Good …*' He saw the finger withdraw. '*You got there in the end, boy. Don't turn yellow this time!*'

'I won't!' he promised, looking up, desperate to show he was determined to go through with it, and completely in agreement that the sadism would be artistically justified.

But the old woman had gone.

# CHAPTER 24

Josa peered across the skyscrapers of files and folders that made her desk look like a mini-Manhattan. She'd read soft copies of most of them during her stay in hospital but seeing them tower before her emphasised how much documentation the case was spawning. She half-felt that her job was to add to the pile, whereas she knew her real purpose should be to make sense of the documented facts, or more practically, to co-ordinate her team so they could successfully mine and align the evidence.

She shook her head. The problem was, she didn't know her team. Had no idea who she could trust to do a good job.

At random, she opened one of the files that topped a stack. The report on the contents of the syringe that had so nearly been pumped into her body. Forensics confirmed the solution was lethal. A highly concentrated solution of –

She realised she was rubbing her arm. It had been a close thing. 'Stevie!'

He stuck his head around her door. 'Yes, guv?'

'What's all this?' She gestured at the paperwork.

'Detective Inspector Walters always demanded hard copies of everything. CS Gilmour told us to put all his files on your desk.'

'That was good of him.' She sniffed. 'You mean there's a desk under there?'

'Do you want me to move it?'

'Did we get anywhere with the phone?'

Josa felt the killer had arranged to view the apartments Elaine was looking after and that he'd made contact via the phone – the same phone that she herself had called from Elaine's handset.

'We traced the number you phoned and found that it's a pay-as-you-go. Second hand. Purchased from a market just a few hours before the suspect made contact with the victim. We pinged it and checked local CCTV but nothing.'

'When did he turn it off?'

'Just before he left –'

'The Shard,' said Josa, finishing the sentence. 'Keep on it. The minute that phone switches back on, I want to know where it is. Even if he's binned it, someone else might have …' She realised how weak it sounded. 'Offenders who've taken an unhealthy interest in blondes. Where's that getting us?'

'We've created a file of possibles. Hot, warm and tepid. We're working through it. Nothing so far.'

'Email me the list of officers following that one up.' She made a mental note to run their names past Don Walters to confirm they were the kind of coppers who'd triple check an alibi from their own grannies.

As if reading her thoughts, Stevie enquired, 'Any news on DI Walters, guv?'

'He's up and down, to be honest. What have we got on the so-called Doctor Taylor?'

'We're checking all Taylors with a medical background, just in case that's his real name, but even if it is, you have no idea how many Doctor Taylors there are out there.'

Josa lowered her voice. 'Look, I trust you, Stevie. I want you to take a personal interest in finding our Doctor Taylor. I think he's our killer, so let's circulate the screen-grabs we've got from the hospital CCTV. He knew his way around the hospital, so there's a good chance he's either worked there in some capacity or maybe spent time there. Could have been, I don't know – prolonged visits to a parent who was a patient there. So, I want as many London doctors as possible to be emailed his photo. I want everyone at the hospital to see his face. If we don't get anything by tomorrow noon we go public with his image. I want him. He is our prime suspect.'

'I'm all over it.'

'Good man.'

'And the team briefing is in five minutes, guv.'

'See you there. And Stevie!'

'Yes, guv?'

She wanted to say, *What does my new team think of me? Are they always so stand-offish at first? Which of them is nice to go for a drink or two with?* But she couldn't ask any of these things any more. 'Thanks,' she said.

'No problem.'

He half-closed the door.

She stared at the piles of paperwork. Their sheer bulk was transfixing. *Snap out of it, Josa!* She shouldn't be daunted by the scale of this thing, but it was hard not to be. She clicked her tongue against the roof of her mouth. She was the same woman who'd been a DS for almost a decade. She should use that experience, she reasoned. This was a massive case, sure, but six months ago, what would she have done?

She felt certain Taylor was the killer and suspected the victims were chosen largely at random, meaning background checks on them were of limited use. No, Taylor was the answer. She stood up.

When she'd been promoted, Josa had half-thought a new rank entailed a new wardrobe. Her work clothes were virtually a uniform. Smart blue, boot-cut jeans. A black, open-necked blouse, normally fitted. No earrings, necklace or bracelets. Chunky black boots with a Cuban heel that gave her an extra half inch, hidden below her jeans. But the step up to more formal attire had never happened, and today she was glad of it, her casual clothes giving her another link back to her DS days. It gave her another layer of confidence.

She raked her left arm across the top of her desk, sweeping the stacks of paperwork to one side. They crashed to the floor and in the open-plan office outside, everything fell quiet. Josa saw everyone pause and look towards her, wondering what the hell was going on.

She'd made up her mind.

'This man gave his name as Doctor Taylor but he also tried to kill me so I don't much trust him.' Josa pinned the screen-grab to the inquiry board at the front of the Major Investigation Team briefing room. 'He is our prime suspect. I want to know who he is. I want him found. I want a present from Tiffany's and a Christmas bonus, but most of all, I want this guy.' Her palm slammed against his photo. 'That is our number one priority.'

She turned to confront her team. About twenty faces trying to figure out their new boss. 'That is our *only* priority!'

They exchanged glances. Cups of coffee paused on the way to thirsty lips. A couple of bemused '*whoas*!' ricocheted around the room.

'For the next forty-eight hours we focus entirely on this dreamboat. Every single line of inquiry is suspended except the hunt for *him*. Has everyone at the hospital seen the photo we have of him?'

Someone piped up, 'Yes, er, DCI Jilani. No hits so far.'

'They may not have seen him for years. I want all staff asked again. This time, show them footage of him in action. Let them see how he moves, how he walks, his facial mannerisms. See if that jogs any memories. Still photos can be deceptive. Download footage onto your phones, iPods, iPads – *whatever*. No more screen-grabs. We're ushering in the era of the motion picture, ladies and gentlemen.'

Stevie threw her a grin: 'Even Cecil B. DeMille had to start somewhere!'

The guy next to him raised his eyebrows. 'Cecil B. who?'

'One of the Chief Supers at the Surrey Division,' someone suggested.

'I know we all miss Don Walters and I know many of you don't agree with my appointment, but our guy will kill again in five days if we don't stop him. That gives us something in common, right?' She struck the photo of Taylor with the side of her fist.

But before she could say another word the door at the back of the room opened and Chief Superintendent Gilmour appeared. 'DCI Jilani,' he said. 'I need to speak to you straight away. This is urgent.'

He'd set his phone to silent. He was a serial killer, sure, but he knew how to behave in a library. And so the Google news alert he'd set up the previous evening simply gave a slight vibration when a message came through. He pulled out his phone, opened the alert and clicked on the link. The item was short but big news.

He left the library within a minute because this was definitely too good to miss …

## CHAPTER 25

Despite competition from the Earls Court exhibition centres, the Empress State Building – known to its denizens as the ESB – easily dominates the skyline of West Kensington. With thirty floors and towering to a height of 385 feet, it ranks as one of Britain's twenty tallest buildings, and although a few of its office spaces are claimed by Transport for London, the overwhelming majority house members of the Metropolitan Police Service. Josa's MIT was based on the thirteenth floor and the noon press conference Gilmour had just three-lined-whipped her into attending was due to take place on the seventeenth.

In the moments leading up to it, Josa tried to gather her thoughts. She visited the ESB's prayer room, a long, light chamber which immediately helped calm her. She had the place to herself but still made a point of complying with the discreet sign that asked occupants to switch off their mobile phones. She placed her shoes by the door, knelt on a prayer mat and closed her eyes.

Josa had not visited the place to pray. All police stations and major operational buildings had prayer rooms, and Josa found them invaluable for the luxury of quiet contemplation. But today, she realised after several minutes had slipped away, she *was* praying. Asking for help. Pleading to be made better, wiser, that she could catch the man before any more innocent women were slaughtered. And she knew her prayers held a selfish motive because for Josa, failure to catch the demon meant just that: failure. Josa Jilani's palms still burnt.

She glanced at her watch. Ten minutes to noon. 'Show time,' she murmured.

A thousand flashes exploded in Josa's face the moment she entered the large, noisy room, and although Gilmour grew an inch with every snap that was taken, she recoiled in surprise and unease. She'd attended and hosted pressers – as press conferences were informally termed – many times before, discussing shifts in policing priorities or announcing new initiatives, but they'd amounted to little more than chats with friends from the local radio, TV and papers. This felt like a media event – a national event. The place was rammed with well over 150 journalists and a feeling of anticipation – of *excitement* – was palpable and scared the hell out of her.

A narrow table stood on a raised area at the front of the room. She saw her misspelt surname on a small cardboard sign and took the seat it stood in front of: *Josa Jillani*. Gilmour sprang onto the raised area, pulled out his chair and took centre stage with a welcoming smile. Josa noticed a small red cushion on his seat. To the Chief Super's left sat three pretty and hard-faced media advisers: two females with blond bobs and Blackberries, and one man in a grey suit with a PDA he consulted constantly throughout the conference.

One of the blond bobs welcomed the journos, introduced everyone at the table and then Gilmour cleared his throat and kicked things off.

The press conference would prove an extraordinary disaster.

'As you know, I'm Chief Superintendent Kim Gilmour and, for my sins, I run this place.' He didn't, of course, but no one seemed to object when he gestured airily to the building around them. 'Now. First things first. I expect you'd like me to start by telling you how I'm organising this investigation.'

Someone from the middle of the room shouted, 'No! We'd like to know if it's true DCI Jilani is now running the show!'

A murmur of agreement rippled through the audience and several questions were called out. *Is she in charge now? Why? What's happened to Don Walters? Wasn't he the original SIO on this one?*

The grey suit with the PDA looked panicked and declared, 'The Chief Superintendent will only take questions at the conclusion of his briefing!'

'That's all right,' Gilmour said, his smile not fitting quite as comfortably this time around. 'Firstly, Detective Inspector Don Walters remains in hospital. But we expect him to be out before too long – he's making splendid progress – and when he's out and about we'll get him back on the team as soon as prudence allows.'

*So Jilani is SIO on this one?*

Josa leant to her left and murmured, 'Sir, if you'd like me to …'

'Yes,' Gilmour replied, 'Jolly good.' A moment to clear his throat, and to the journalists, 'Detective Chief Inspector Jilani will supply you with some of the pertinent facts.'

Josa stood, walked to the front of the raised area and perched on the edge of the table. Without notes or hesitation she recalled details of the murdered women. With each of the four she introduced them as people – who they were and what they were like – before recounting the facts of their killing. For the first of only two occasions during the conference the journalists sat silently recording and absorbing the facts. At the close of her précis, Josa walked back to her seat where, in response to a cacophony of calls from the floor, she said only four words. 'Thank you. Any questions?'

'DCI Jilani!' A man from the middle of the room called out. 'I notice you don't wear the hijab. But would you still consider yourself to be a fundamentalist Muslim?'

'I'll tell you what I consider. I consider it interesting that if a Christian believes in a strict adherence to their sacred texts, they're called *devout*. But if a Muslim believes in a strict adherence to their sacred text, they're branded *fundamentalist*. What do you consider the reason for that is?'

A brunette on the front row raised her hand and shouted, 'Chief Superintendent Gilmour! Is it true you're hauling Daniel Blake out of retirement to help on this one?'

'Well, Miss Sherwood …'

'Call me Karen!'

A couple of wolf whistles, a few laughs and Gilmour continued, 'Well, Karen, I can categorically tell you that that particular rumour is untrue.'

'Josa!' A Brummie accent. 'Is it true you're engaged to a white bloke?'

'Why?' shouted some smart arse on the back row. 'Do you think you stand a chance with her?'

More laughter. Josa realised she was shaking her head in quiet horror. Why was no one interested in the victims? Was this whole thing unreal to them?

'DCI Jilani!' An Asian woman raised her hand.

She looked sensible enough, Josa reflected, which suggested her question would be relevant and respectful, and not one that focussed on her background. 'Yes, miss?'

'Many people in this country do not realise there are several branches of Islam. Sunni, Shia, Kharijite et cetera.' Josa's heart sank as the question was completed. 'What kind of a Muslim are you?'

'Right now,' said Josa, 'I'm a pissed-off one.'

More laughter, as if they hadn't understood she was being serious. *More laughter!* And for a moment, Josa thought she was going to be sick.

When she recalled incidents from her childhood, they often seemed to be about somebody else. It was as if the girl she was remembering was not her, or at least, the small, skinny figure was a child actor playing the role of Josa Jilani. But the little girl she remembered from one incident was her. Was palpably and emotionally her – her from years ago, her from yesterday, her at the very moment she relived the event in her head.

She is standing at the front of her classroom. To her left, a young supply teacher looks anxiously across the class of kids who have sensed her weakness. Josa had been looking forward to this moment. Telling the class about her weekend. What she did. What she learnt. Every Monday, one class member is given the privilege and now, at last, it's her turn, but this stand-in teacher can't control the children and ...

And Josa tries to tell them about Jahannam. About what will happen to those who wind up there. The place itself and its attendant physical torments and constant, recurring hell. The real place that will ...

But they just laugh. The teacher chews her nails. And they just laugh.


'Is it true Daniel Blake has turned up dead in Istanbul?'

Gilmour shook his head. 'If we could confine ourselves to questions concerning –'

But a journalist cut him off with, *'He's trying to persuade his editor to send him there for the scoop!'*

Chuckles all round.

'Ladies and gentlemen!' Gilmour began. 'I'd like to convey a message to the public ...'

Josa leant back in her chair as her boss trotted out the speech about coming forward if anyone knew anything about the crimes or ... She looked across the massed audience. Something was happening. None of them were paying heed to Gilmour any more. Something else had claimed their attention. Like the sound of crickets in a summer meadow, discreet but audible beeps denoting text messages assailed the room. The journalists were all being contacted about something. They looked up from their phones, muttered to each other. Exchanged looks with colleagues across the floor as the Chief Superintendent continued blithely on with his speech. Josa narrowed her eyes. The journalists accessed the Net on their phones and fingers blurred in a texting frenzy. The presser had become an irrelevance.

During a secondment with the Met, she'd taken part in a scheme where officers set up and oversaw football coaching for local kids. As a thank you, some of the families whose children had been involved took her along to her first Premiership match. The Gunners versus Newcastle United at the old Arsenal Stadium in Highbury. Josa recalled the London side's slick, silky skills had proven too much for the battling Magpies and the visitors had lost

2–nil. But most of all she had been struck by how tribal the experience was. As the two sets of fans made their way to and from the 'Library', for one of the rare times in her life, she had not been perceived as an Asian woman. She was simply a fan. As the match progressed, she saw that the crowd's attention was claimed one hundred per cent by the football on the pitch, until one moment late in the second half. Josa later discovered that unusually, Arsenal's nearest rivals were also playing across town and at that moment had been awarded a penalty. If they scored, they would go above Arsenal in the table. Suddenly, the match in front of them was ignored. People murmured to each other. They held their breaths and stared at their smartphones because now … now something bigger was happening elsewhere.

And looking out across the journalists, Josa sensed that same feeling as when she'd stood in the stands at Highbury, wondering what was going on. What were all their messages about?

Gilmour kept rattling away, relishing the lack of interruptions.

But now Josa was ignoring him, too busy scanning the faces of the distracted journalists, trying to catch their whispers or read the shock and excitement in their eyes.

*What the hell had just happened?*

# CHAPTER 26

He sat in front of his television, open-mouthed. What the hell was happening? He'd hurried home to catch the highlights of the press conference, but now he felt as though an old friend – the television set – was delivering bad news. Perturbed and embarrassed, he glanced up at the portrait of Hitchcock. The conference was all about Jilani. *What about his work*? For Christ's sake, what did he have to do to get some –

'You know what this is like?' He jabbed a finger at the screen. Could feel himself perspiring, like a schoolboy having to explain himself to a headmaster. 'It's like when you shot *The Lodger* and the studio didn't recognise it as a piece of a genius. Got someone in to recut it and some idiots gave him the praise for the finished movie.'

But it wasn't like that at all and they both knew it.

He looked at the director. Narrowed his eyes. What was he trying to tell him?

*Must ... try ... harder ...*

# CHAPTER 27

## *Saturday, 10 March*

Josa walked out of the ESB, crossed Lillie Road and began the short walk to West Brompton station. It was four o'clock, cold, and the streets were quiet. Heavy clouds gave the light an early evening quality and Josa turned up the collar of her coat. She paused outside the Lillie Langtry, an old fashioned pub that was a favourite with many of the ESB staff. A blackboard by the open door read, 'CLOSED. PRIVATE FUNCTION' and inside, Josa could see a cluster of police officers, all out of uniform. Men with black ties at half mast, women in jeans and smart tops. At their epicentre, Jack Dempsey was belting out 'My Way' but had changed the words as if he was singing about someone else, doing it 'His Way'. Pint pots swished with lager. Wine glasses clinked. People joined in and some wiped away tears.

Don Walters was dead.

Josa watched them. Envied them. She'd heard the news right after the press conference two days earlier. Walters' family had been informed first, at the hospital. One of his nieces had tweeted about her uncle's death, meaning most of the fourth estate had heard before the Met. A massive coronary. Very little pain. Another police officer dead before his time. The funeral was happening – Josa checked her watch – right at that moment. Close friends and family only and, to be honest, Josa was glad she didn't have to face his wife and kids. And with even more guilt she registered that her main problem with his passing was that it left her more alone as the SIO in the hunt for the serial killer. The incline of her job much steeper now, right down to having no one who could connect her to her new team, currently clustered around Jack Dempsey in the pub.

Josa sank her hands deep into the pockets of her camel-coloured coat. It cost £43 to get the bloody thing dry-cleaned after the Shard fall, but at least it kept the wind off.

More noise from the pub. They were becoming rowdier, drunker and, she imagined, more sentimental. She weighed up her options. A couple of months ago she'd have been in there with them. Large glass of Pinot and a packet of crisps. But now she was a DCI on this bloody impossible case and she had to consider that she was –

'Damned if you do and damned if you don't!' A woman's voice. Josa turned around and recognised one of the journos who'd been at the press conference. 'What do you want the headline to be? *Muslim Cop Snubs Partner's Wake*, or *Fundamentalist Muslim Cop Enjoys Boozy Knees-up?*'

That pretty much summed it up, but Josa just said, 'Karen Sherwood, isn't it?'

'This doesn't have to be a career-ender.'

'Good to know.'

Karen Sherwood shook her head. 'You still don't get it, do you? Look, the *Daily Mail* called your appointment the first step on the road to sharia law. The *Express* have already demanded your resignation after Don's death and even the broadsheets are starting to circle.' She took a step forward. 'Josa, to survive this thing you're going to need a friend in the media. Let me help you.'

Josa looked at the other woman. Mid to late thirties, slight build, long, straight brown hair. Pretty, but too many cigarettes, drinks and late nights beginning to show on her face. Well turned out. She was even wearing black. *Nice touch*, Josa thought.

'Let's work together,' the journalist concluded.

For a weary moment, Josa regretted everything that had happened over the past couple of months. She'd been a good copper for so many years. No single one thing she could point at to say, *There! That's how good I am!* Just an accumulation of doing her duty, taking the shit from her well-paid superiors, trying to help members of the public, day after day, year after year, not because of some revamped rehash of the latest government initiative, but because she cared. Then she'd made the mistake of doing something *dramatic*, and for the media, *dramatic* was good. That raising of her profile had led to Liz Canterville noticing her, and ultimately, promotion. Ironically, defusing that bloody bomb had been the most explosive thing she'd ever done.

She looked at the journalist and guessed she didn't give a damn about anything but herself and the story. 'Karen, I got your emails. I can't start giving you the inside track on this. That's not the way it's done.'

'Were the victims sexually abused before they were killed? Is it true you're trying to get Daniel Blake out of retirement to work on this? Do you think it's –'

'I just said I can't give you any exclusives.'

'You're new to all this. I wouldn't cite you. But I'd make it clear to my readers that you're doing a bloody good job. Why do you think the killer always murders on a Tuesday?'

'That's not the way I roll.'

'Don got it. It's the way he rolled.'

'Good for Don.' Josa began to walk away.

'I hadn't wanted to say this, but we *know*.'

Josa paused. 'Know what?'

'Know you've closed down every line of inquiry except the hunt for Taylor. And it's getting you absolutely nowhere.'

'It's only been two days,' Josa shot back, immediately regretting her words. Karen Sherwood smiled a little too quickly. Bugger! *She'd suspected but hadn't known for certain.*

'Two days, Josa, in a case like this where every hour is important. Where every hour brings the next murder a little closer. When are you going to admit that your strategy has been a failure?'

The chirrup of Josa's phone saved her from having to reply.

'Hello?'

'Guv! It's me!' Stevie's voice was breathless with excitement. 'You are not going to believe this!'

'She came in about Taylor! This could lead us to him, guv!' Stevie's face was animated with excitement but he turned it down a notch, adding. 'She's through there. Looks a bit … ill at ease.'

Josa peered through the slightly open door. 'I'm not surprised.' Yvonne Salter was sat at a bare table in a room normally reserved for questioning suspects. 'Get her out of there.'

The thirtieth floor of the Empress State Building is the home of Orbit, a revolving bar-cum-café that allows its seated patrons to enjoy a 360-degree sweep of London without moving from their chairs. Josa bought two hot chocolates from the central static kiosk and stepped gingerly onto the slowly moving floor. She placed one mug in front of Yvonne. 'There you go.'

'Thanks.' The smile looked easier now.

Josa guessed Yvonne was in her mid-thirties, a slightly built black woman who'd turned up at the ESB about half an hour earlier. Josa had already been informed that she was a radiographer at the hospital but by some extraordinary chance, her identification of Taylor had been unconnected to her job.

'I can't stay long,' she said. 'Got to pick the kids up.'

'Sure. And first of all, thanks for coming. You recognised the man on the footage we showed you?'

'Not at first. When I told the copper I didn't know him, I meant it. But something about him. The way he moved …'

Josa felt a twinge of disappointment that no one was around to hear her policy vindicated. 'Go on,' she said gently.

'His name's Tony Taylor. I only met him the once. He was going out with a friend of mine. They stopped by a pub one night when

I was having a few. He seemed all right. Said he was a doctor. Can't remember much more about him, to be honest.'

'Your friend.' Josa tried not to sound over-eager. 'What was her name?'

Julie Spragg jammed a cigarette in her angry mouth. 'My flat was turned over last month. It took you lot two days to turn up. But you jump one red light and suddenly –'

Josa held up her hand. 'We're not here about any driving violations, Miss Spragg.'

'And I don't like talking to you lot.' She glared at Josa.

'The police?'

A shake of the head. 'My brother was in Afghanistan fighting you lot.'

'Us lot?'

'Bloody al-Qaeda.'

'And you think that gives you the right to be stupid and rude to anyone you like?'

Julie looked from Josa to Stevie and back again. 'What's this about?'

Five minutes later they were in the small back yard of the pub where Julie worked. She was blonde. Hour-glass figure and long fake nails coloured blue. Josa fleetingly wondered how she changed the barrels with talons glued to her fingers and then guessed she was the sort of woman who wouldn't have to. Her cigarette was lit now and she inhaled quickly. 'Tony Taylor? Yeah. I knew him. About three years ago, now, it'll be.'

'How did you know him? How did you meet?'

'I was working in the Coal Hole at the time.'

'Coal Hole?'

Julie smiled at Josa's confusion. 'It's a pub. On the Strand. We got chatting. I don't normally give my number to punters, you know, but he seemed different. Said he was a doctor.'

'Are you still in touch?'

She shook her head. 'We met three times. The third time we just went out for a few drinks. That's when it became obvious. You know? It was obvious we were very different people.' She took another drag of her cigarette. 'And I think he was pissed off I wouldn't sleep with him.'

'Did he get violent?'

'No. But some blokes. They see this …' She rubbed a strand of blond hair between her thumb and index finger. 'And these.' She gestured to her chest. 'And they think I'm easy. I'm not. He thought a nice meal out on my birthday would buy him a slice. Oh, no. I'm not such a pushover.' She lingered over the word. 'But I'm worth it in the end,' she added, winking at Stevie.

Josa was not surprised to see her DC blushing and suddenly becoming very interested in his notebook.

'Do you have his address or phone number?'

'Never knew his address and I've not got his phone number. I lost it when I lost my last phone. Sorry.'

Stevie spoke for the first time. 'When's your birthday, Julie?'

## *Sunday, 11 March, 8 a.m.*

The restaurant where Julie had been wooed kept records for five years and Tony Taylor had paid for dinner using his credit card. A little checking revealed the bank account in question had been closed a couple of years earlier, but at Taylor's last known address, supplied by the bank, the landlord remembered him. 'He took to drink and drugs. Got kicked out of the doctorin' profession and hit hard times. Took quite a fall. Couldn't afford this place.' He nodded to the flats – well-kept apartments in Notting Hill. 'Moved to Mile End. No, I don't have an address as such but I helped him move some stuff, so I could probably point out the house. I remember where it was, just not the name of the street, if you get me. He'd even sold his car, poor bugger. I could take you there?'

'Go, go, go!'

Josa watched as four officers jogged across the road carrying what was known in the service as 'the big key'. Shouts, banging on the door and when she yelled the order – *Go ahead!* – the policemen began to smash it open with the Enforcer – a steel battering ram that delivers about three tonnes of kinetic energy to anything unfortunate enough to stand in its way. She knew half a dozen more men were at the back of the Eric Street ground-floor flat and that four of them would be simultaneously storming the place. She'd wanted to be with them but had been persuaded to oversee the raid from across the road. She stood by her car, then began to walk towards the terrace housing. Directive or no directive, she wanted to be in with the action.

The door crashed into the hallway, the sound of its surrender overlapping with policemen's yells as they swarmed over it.

Josa glanced to her left. *It was him.* Tony Taylor. He was on foot – had just turned on to Eric Street and seen immediately what was going on. Without fuss or apparent concern he turned around, for all the world a guy who'd forgotten the milk his wife had asked him to pick up, heading back to the shops. Within a moment he was gone. Josa was already running after him. She called to the officers in his flat, knowing her cries stood no chance against the pandemonium of the raid.

But as she sprinted around the corner, the footsteps alerted Taylor. A quick look over his shoulder and he took in the whole situation. Josa knew he'd clocked what was going on and that she was the sole pursuer: it was him versus her. He dropped his shopping bags and began to run.

Taylor sprinted across Ropery Street and into a block of three-storey flats. Josa followed his echoing footsteps as he tore up the concrete steps. He reached the top level, darted along the outside walkway, and as Josa burst out of the stairwell she saw him kick down the door at the far end.

'What's going on?'

'Hey! What the hell are you doing, man?'

Kids and older residents were emerging from the flats and shouting questions. Most of them were looking at her now, wondering what the woman in the posh coat was doing.

'Police!' Josa bellowed. 'Everyone stay in your homes, please!'

*Some hope.*

Josa held up ID as she raced along the walkway. As she neared the kicked-in door she wondered why Taylor had allowed himself to be cornered. The answer was obvious. He hadn't. No way would he have made for the flat unless it offered him some sort of advantage. Josa paused beside the shattered doorframe. Brought her police radio to her lips and gave a terse, two-line report on what was going on and where she was. Without waiting for a reply she jammed the radio back into her pocket and entered the flat.

'Tony! Tony, I just want to speak to you!' She crept slowly along the hallway. It was dimly lit, and a thick, musty smell almost made her vomit. This place hadn't been occupied for a long time. 'We can work it out.'

She heard a movement from the end room and gently pushed open the door. 'Tony?'

He was stood at the far wall, trying to force open a large sash window. Seeing Josa gave him some kind of extra strength, and with a roar he heaved it upwards then leapt out. The fall would kill him, unless …

She saw him spring from the sill, jump across a void of about three metres and grasp the drainpipe that ran down the building opposite.

'Agile little bugger,' Josa murmured.

Taylor scampered to the ground and was off. There was no way Josa could emulate his nimble exit and by the time she'd reached the stairs he'd have disappeared. She glanced down. A mound of plump black bin bags could conceivably break her fall. She could smell the old food, slops and detritus from three floors up.

Curious kids from the flats were already inching down the hallway and she knew anything she left here would be nicked in a heartbeat.

Josa looked from her newly dry-cleaned coat to the hillock of putrid rubbish below. 'You have *got* to be joking,' she muttered, and before she had time to reconsider, she hauled her upper body through the window and for the second time that week, closed her eyes and took a leap of faith.

# CHAPTER 29

He was limping. Ha! Not quite as nimble as she'd thought, and the sight of him, half-hobbling, albeit at a pace, gave her a fillip as she continued her pursuit. He was running down Cornwell Way towards the broad and busy Burdett Road, one of Mile End's main arteries. And now when he looked over his shoulder, his wide eyes revealed he knew the odds had tipped against him.

Her feet smacked the ground harder and harder. It was scarcely believable but she wasn't just gaining on him; she was nearing the goal of this whole investigation. She felt cold air whoosh over her skin; across her face and hands. *Her hands …*

He turned on to Burdett Road and Josa's heart plummeted. As quickly as the thoughts of triumph had struck her, the feeling of imminent failure replaced them. A bus was trundling past Taylor. An old Routemaster, with its open rear platform allowing passengers to hop on and off. Its speed was perfect for the fugitive. Maybe it was travelling a little fast, but Josa saw the doctor's pace accelerate towards the double-decker.

Five seconds later she hit Burdett Road. Taylor was giving it everything as the bus picked up speed. There was no way she could reach it if he found another gear and got on board but she kept on running, desperately hoping he wouldn't make it. And then just as the bus nudged in front of a lorry and entered the flow of traffic, he leapt.

Josa held her breath. *Don't make it, don't make it, don't make it …*

His left foot hit the floor of the bus. His right hand grabbed the pole that ran from the floor to the top of the stairs.

Josa's pace began to slow.

Taylor hauled himself into the bus.

Josa could already feel the stitch in her side. She shook her head. No traffic lights or impediments for a fair distance meaning he had ...

Taylor had been running hard. Must have been perspiring heavily. His grip made unsafe. Josa watched in mute horror as Taylor floundered, his palm slipping from the pole. His hand tried to grab it again but the bus's momentum denied him and she saw his fingertips uselessly scramble for the pole before his entire body lurched back. Tony Taylor crashed from the red double-decker towards the road, but he never hit the tarmac. Not alive.

The lorry behind the bus cannoned into his body, smashing it forward. The squeal of brakes and screams were deafening. Taylor's corpse landed on the road but the heavy vehicle had no chance of stopping.

By the time Josa pushed through the outer circle of pedestrians with their open mouths and pointing phone cams, Tony Taylor's frame was a mangled mass of blood and torn flesh. The inner circle of gawkers comprised men in morning suits and women in extravagant hats. They surrounded the fallen figure, looking down on him with wordless respect as if they were part of a pop-up funeral. Josa realised the bus, which had drawn to an immediate halt following the accident, was a special hire on the way to a wedding, packed with top-table guests who had streamed out to take a closer look. Josa eased through them and looked at Taylor, the man who had tried to kill her. His head a crushed red horror of jutting bone and leaking brain. Clothes and torso ripped open. She stood over him. Heart beating fast and still trying to catch her breath before shouting for everyone to get back. She looked down. Only his muddy boots were intact.

# CHAPTER 30

## *Monday, 12 March, 10.20 p.m.*

The film was finishing and Preya Jilani wiped away a tear. A nice happy ending where the girl got the guy and he got better and … She heard the rattle of the front door lock. 'Josa?'

No answer.

She swung her legs off the sofa, grabbed the remote and killed the TV. 'That you, Jose?'

'Yep. Only me.'

Something in her sister's voice made Preya walk through to the hallway. 'You okay?'

Josa was leaning against the closed front door. Preya could see from her body language she was tired but couldn't interpret the look on her face.

'What's up?'

Her sister just shook her head. Ran forward and embraced her and when Preya tried to pull back, she found herself held tighter than ever.

'I got him.' Preya could feel her warm breath against her ear. 'I did it, Prey. I did it.'

Josa put on her pyjamas and huge towelling dressing gown before joining her sister on the sofa. She found a mug of hot chocolate waiting and next to it, a tall glass cup of sweet lassi, a yogurt-based drink her mother used to give them when they were children. Josa didn't need to ask which one was hers.

'No marshmallows?' she said as she reached for the hot chocolate.

'There's cream in there but yep, no marshmallows,' Preya replied, adding with comic exaggeration, '*Someone* must have finished them off!'

Josa gave a guilty grin.

'So go on! What's happened?'

Josa gabbled a brief overview of events in Mile End. 'And then, *then* it began. Gathering information on Tony Taylor.' She shook her head. 'You wouldn't believe it when the Met swings into action. We had over 120 officers and police staff all over this guy. The facts just raining in. I felt like I was in the middle of a blizzard trying to catch snow.'

'What were you trying to find out? You know this guy tried to kill you. Isn't that enough?'

'Tony Taylor can never be tried for the four murders he did commit. But we wanted to be certain we had the right man.' Josa puffed out her cheeks and exhaled. 'Or more to the point, we had to be able to demonstrate to the media that he was the killer. And every card we turned over, Prey, was an ace. He'd had a string of blond girlfriends and the relationships have never lasted.'

Preya reached to the floor and placed her mug on a coaster. 'Sounds like every other guy in the country!' When she looked up she saw Josa wasn't smiling.

'There's a lot more than that. He was a doctor. Struck off a few years back. Never got another job. He tried writing about the profession, trying to carve out some kind of career in the media, but got nowhere. Everyone who knew him kept telling us the same thing. Same phrase, even. After he lost his job, *he just lost it.*'

Preya nodded. Kept her mouth shut.

'No one can vouch for his whereabouts at the time of the killings. We even got a psych report from some shrink he visited a year back. And in her professional opinion, he was capable of murder. He was on the edge. Something pushed him over.'

Silence. Preya felt it was her cue to talk. 'You sure he's the killer?'

Josa nodded. 'And all the people who said I couldn't do it …'

'You showed them!'

'I proved myself!' Josa clinked her mug against Preya's. 'After all these years, I proved myself.'

The call came a few minutes later – Josa was needed back at the ESB. Within the hour she was in Gilmour's office where she found him deep in conversation with Della Frank, his chief press and PR manager.

'Good of you to come in, DCI Jilani.'

'No problem. What's the news?'

'We're going for it! Press conference tomorrow – late afternoon, early evening. With all the trimmings. Before that Della is going to hold one of her little 'breakfast meetings' – a confidential briefing session with key members of the press. That is happening first thing tomorrow morning. Behind closed doors. We can't officially tell them that Tony Taylor was the killer but …'

Josa nodded. 'I understand.'

Della said, 'I'm going to reveal all the evidence you and your team have gathered and let them draw their own conclusions.' She gave a tight, professional smile. 'Or should I say foregone conclusions?'

'And more glad tidings!' Gilmour declared, brandishing a blue file. 'An eye-witness report from a passenger on the bus who confirms that Taylor wasn't killed during the pursuit. He verifies what you told us. He had made it onto the bus. Only fell off afterwards. That's crucial!'

'We'll be releasing that during the presser,' Della revealed. 'It allows us to give a story that his death, although unfortunate, was nothing *directly* to do with the police.' She smiled. 'We're going to spin a line that his death spares the public the expense of a trial.'

'Perfect!' Josa heard herself say.

The thirteenth floor was dark and deserted. Josa crossed the open office space, opened the door to her room and smiled at the mound of reports on the floor, recalling her team's reaction when she'd swept them from her desk.

She ignored the cardboard box that stood to the left of her desk – the container she'd hauled in on the evening before she'd officially been allocated her new office. It contained mugs, photographs, files and other personal ephemera she'd felt would be essential. She'd not even looked at the box since her arrival.

Josa grabbed a manila file from her in-tray and sank into her chair as she skimmed through it. The document was a complete inventory of everything found at Taylor's flat. The item that she was looking for didn't leap out at her. Where was it? She switched on her desk lamp and reread the report. Still no joy. Maybe it was unimportant. She grimaced, trying not to let it bother her, and as she glanced down, something distracted her. A triangle of white envelope jutting out from one edge of the cardboard box. It looked like an envelope. *Odd.* She leant over, reaching for it and wondering what –

'Evening, guv!' The unexpected voice gave Josa a start. She looked up. Stevie. 'Great result,' he said. 'Congratulations!'

'Thanks.' She straightened her back, the envelope instantly pushed from her thoughts. 'We've got a press conference tomorrow, announcing the *news*. Drawing a line under the whole thing.' She grinned. 'It's been quite a few days. I've not felt this relieved since the 5th of April, 2010.'

'And what happened then?'

'We got promoted back into the Premiership.' Stevie looked blank. 'I'm a Newcastle fan,' Josa added. Another smile. 'So, what are you up to?'

He lingered in the doorway. 'I'm just trying to get a head start for when it kicks off tomorrow. Massive fire at Earls Court. The team are all being put onto that.'

'I heard. I'll miss you. I'll be emailing everyone individually, but I'm glad I've caught you, Stevie. I really appreciated your support from the very beginning. You're one of the main reasons I was able to sort this out so quickly.'

Even as she spoke the words, Josa heard them and knew they sounded wrong. More than that, they *felt* wrong. She had been right to go with her initial instincts about Taylor but had she been right to follow them in such a blinkered manner? She had shown leadership at a time when she'd sensed threat from all angles, but had she betrayed her own inexperience by falling for the plaudits and back-slapping bonhomie she'd earned by apparently stopping the country's most wanted killer?

'Thanks, guv,' Stevie said.

'You get home. You can read all about the arson tomorrow morning. You need some rest.'

A nod. 'Yeah. You're right.' He started to turn away, then paused. 'We did well, yeah?'

'Yeah.' Josa nodded. Has he picked up on her doubt? There was a look in his eyes, like he had a doubt that he wanted someone, *anyone* to shake for him. She replied with a confident, 'We did very well.'

Another pause. 'Funny, though.' He nodded to the report in Josa's hand. 'We never did find it.'

'What?'

'The killer's phone. We never did find it.'

'No, no we didn't.'

'Night, guv.'

And Stevie's footsteps echoed in the darkness as he walked away, leaving Josa alone on the thirteenth floor.

# CHAPTER 31

## Tuesday, 13 March, 5 p.m.

He lay across his sofa, half-watching *Family Plot*, the other part of his brain thinking about the failed assistant director he'd manipulated into dealing with the Asian woman. He had botched the job but it really didn't matter. If Jilani or the old copper had been able to describe him, they'd have made a big song and dance about it at the press conference with urgent pleas and computer photofits. But there had been nothing. No, he was safe and remained one step ahead of them.

He conceded, however, that by now, even the dullest young woman would exercise absolute caution on a Tuesday night, but the joke was, it didn't matter. He already had today's victim ready for delivery. In the same way that Hitchcock's early films were not released in the order in which they were produced, so his victims would not be released in the order he'd created them. The sense of symmetry with Hitchcock's work pleased him, and the fact he would only face minimal risks tonight simply added to his smug satisfaction.

*Family Plot* was almost over. In the closing moments of the film, the magnificent Barbara Harris, playing Blanche, walks confidently towards the camera and – in an atypical touch for Hitchcock – she winks directly at the audience. *Shatters the fourth wall!* The final shot of his final film, a cheeky wink to the people he has thrilled and terrified for so long.

>>Pause<<

He stood up and winked back at Barbara Harris. It was time to collect her.

Even with the television silent and no music playing, he didn't hear the car pull up outside his house.

'You look good,' said Della. 'I forgot to remind you to wear black, so I'm glad you did.'

The PR woman seemed impressed with Josa's choice of attire, which pleased her. It was a new top – a variation on her standard all-black number – a luxe, black DKNY blouse with white contract collar and cuffs. 'You worried?'

'No,' said Josa. 'Not like I was the first time.'

'You ready?'

'I think so.' She smiled.

He smiled. He felt safe in his home, in the one environment in his life that he had moulded entirely to satisfy his own comfort. And so although he was a vain man in many respects, he never felt the urge to show off his 'pad'. Instead, he made certain no one ever visited him. Years ago he'd carefully ensured that the address his employers held for him was incorrect; he'd changed the name of the street minimally but significantly, given only the beginning of his postcode and, for good measure, given the house number as '60' as opposed the true designation of '16'. If the inaccuracy was found it would be dismissed as a clerical error, but he doubted that would happen. None of his friends were ever invited to meet him at home and aside from Jill Kennedy – he felt a thrill at the memory of her presence where he now stood – no one visited his house.

And so when he wandered through to his utility room he didn't bother with furtive looks over his shoulder. He simply opened the freezer, kissed Jill on the top of her head, and hauled her out of the cabinet, letting her dead weight fall to the floor.

The *rigor* had dissipated days ago, and now her frame flopped across the lino, blocking open the door, her right arm slung over her shoulder as if freeze-framed in the middle of a freak-out dance move.

He stepped over her body. Looked up, pondering how best to manhandle her. He noticed that from where he stood, he could see across the kitchen and down the short hallway, meaning his front door was visible. Not that she would be leaving via that route.

His garage was attached to the rear of his house, meaning he'd be able to move Jill from the freezer to the boot of his car without fear of being observed. He leant over and across to pick her up, grasping her right upper arm in both hands. Gave a tug. She barely moved, and without thinking he looked at her and said, 'Come on!'

Her open eyes fixed on his face. She seemed to be holding his stare. *Was she ...* His breathing became a little shallower. *Was she looking at him?*

And then, for the first time in so long that for a split second he didn't understand what the sound was, his doorbell rang.

# CHAPTER 32

He looked up, staring at the front door as if terrified it would suddenly become invisible. That slab of wood was all that stood between him and identification. He was literally face-to-face with his murder victim and the heavy wooden door had become a paper-thin barrier.

The doorbell rang again.

He froze. If he remained silent and still, whoever it was might go away. He held his breath and gradually the thud of his heart shook his chest until –

*Knock, knock, knock!*

Whoever was outside was rapping on the door now. Not a dainty, polite *anybody home?* kind of rap, but a belligerent banging. *Christ!* Who was it? The police? Couldn't be! Neighbours? Never! But who? He felt a drop of perspiration fall from his forehead. He glanced down. The droplet had landed on Jill's cheek. The tear of a dead woman. Still he tried to remain absolutely immobile, desperate to avoid the slightest sound that would give the game away.

And outside the thumping continued, harder, so that even the letterbox – in the middle of the door at waist height – rattled.

*Oh. No.*

His eyes widened, *No, no, no, no, no!*

He *had* to move. Had to move her as well. If whoever it was knelt down and pushed open the flap of the letterbox they would find more than a hall full of stylish framed photographs. They would find a picture they'd never forget.

Whoever was outside had begun talking. A male voice. Gruff. He couldn't distinguish any words. How could someone come to

124

his house and harass him like this? *Christ*!

He pulled Jill's arm. Nothing. He gave the tiniest whimper, then stopped himself. A dead weight was one thing but surely … Another pull. Nothing.

More knocking. Louder. Harder. Then a pause as if the person outside was considering.

He looked down the body of Jill Kennedy and saw that the heel of her shoe had somehow become wedged between his upright ironing board and the far wall, effectively anchoring the corpse.

Still silence outside, and then he heard the gruff, muffled voice again, but this time he caught the words: 'I'll take a look through the letterbox …'

'One last thing …' Della handed her a bottle of Olay. 'For the bags under your eyes.'

Josa took it. 'Yeah?'

'I swear by it. Saved my marriage!' Della paused. 'But hell, I still use it!'

Their laughter echoed through the rest room.

Resisting every urge to heave as hard as possible, he pulled Jill's body softly this time, almost letting out a cheer when her foot slipped out of its shoe and slid across the floor. *Almost there*!

He heard the flap of the letterbox creaking open a second before Jill's calves and feet cleared the threshold of the utility room doorway.

He'd been too late. He knew that if whoever was peering in had looked in his direction immediately they would have seen the movement. He heard another voice. 'Anything?'

The longest pause.

'Yeah …'

This time, the journalists knew exactly why they were there, and to Josa the buzz of their conversation sounded muted but excited. She and Gilmour chatted to each other as they walked to the front of the room, conducting a carefree back-and-forth exchange as if they'd not spotted the reporters. They took their places. Shared a joke. One of the blond bobs gave her usual intro but this time Gilmour gestured to Josa, indicating she should speak first. The message was unmistakeable and she appreciated it, and as she stood up, feeling like a priest in a pulpit, she felt the eyes of the world were upon her.

'Yeah … A very nice little bachelor pad. He's done all right.'

'I meant is he in?'

'Looks like we've missed him.' The flap snapped back into place. 'Come on!'

He waited, straining to hear footsteps. After a moment he tentatively poked his head around the doorway to see if –

The creak of the letterbox flap again but this time it snapped back into place immediately. The man outside had been posting something.

There were footsteps, but he remained still for several minutes, eventually peering down the hallway, taking a few quiet steps and creeping upstairs where he peeped through his bedroom curtains. They'd gone. For the first time since the doorbell had rung he let out a long, audible breath. Padded downstairs.

*But who were they? And what the hell had they wanted?*

He walked to the front door. A folded piece of white, lined A5 lay on the coir mat. He bent down. Picked it up. The paper was folded in half and across the front he could see his surname. He folded back the sheet to reveal the twelve-word message. Two lines that struck him like an icicle stabbed through his chest. 'Oh, my God …' he murmured, 'How could they …'

The press conference was going well. This, at last, was how Josa had envisaged her life during indulgent flash-forwards and now it was relief more than happiness that swept over her like an almighty yes. This is what she joined the police service for: to belong. To receive the praise and assurance she could no longer get from her –

*Don't smile!* she thought to herself.

He walked from the hallway into his living room. *He couldn't have read the note correctly.* Shoved it under a table lamp and clicked it on.

The press conference was drawing to a close and Josa knew that without explicitly stating it, the message they'd intended to convey had been received loud and clear. Tony Taylor was the killer and they'd nailed the bastard. *She'd* nailed the bastard. And strangely, the good news brushed aside any question of how and why she'd made DCI and SIO of the investigation. There was no mention of her stated faith. Later, Josa wondered why the press should play it that way, choosing not to link Islam with anything that could be considered positive.

'One last question!' someone shouted.

Josa made a show of examining her watch. 'Go on, then.'

'In your heart of hearts, do you think you've stopped the killings?'

She'd been through this one with Della. Caution first. One answer through words – a non-committal rehash of the evidence against Tony Taylor. But the other, much more direct answer, through body language, the emphatic nod of her head signalling a triumphant 'Yes!'

He looked down at the note, trying to take in the twelve block capital words that were written in dark pencil.

### WE KNOW WHAT YOU DID.

And below it:

**YOU MURDERED THOSE GIRLS. HA HA HA.**

## CHAPTER 33

## *Wednesday, 14 March, 6.40 p.m.*

From where she parked on Du Cane Road, Josa could see Queen Charlotte's Hospital and next to it, the grim, grey walls of Her Majesty's Prison, Wormwood Scrubs. She could also see, a few doors down, the home of Yvonne Salter, the woman who'd originally tipped her off about Julie Spragg's relationship with Taylor.

Josa was there to thank her for the information. With no email or phone number on file, swinging by the address she'd given had seemed the best option. She clicked the button on her keys and her car's central locking system clunked into action.

'Ten quid to make sure nothing happens to it.'

'What?'

The girl wore a blue boiler suit open at the collar. Her jet-black hair was roughly swept to one side at the front and loosely held in a 1940s-style crocheted woollen hair net at the back. Tall, skinny, she looked about twenty and so Josa pegged her as mid-teens. Pale skin, no make-up, pretty face, arsey expression.

'Your motor,' the girl replied, and Josa intuitively felt she was unused to using the expression. 'A tenner to see that –'

'I'm a copper.' Josa flashed her ID.

'Special price for you, then. Twenty quid.'

Something about the girl's eyes … And then Josa got it. 'Look,' she said, 'if anything happens to my car, I'll be back to discuss it with you when your friends are about.'

A shrugging laugh. 'Like they'd care about you giving me a hard time.'

'Oh, I wouldn't be back to give you a hard time. I'd be back to thank you for fingering the local gang members who'd done my car. I'd let everyone know you've always been a big help to the police.'

More laughter. 'Gotta love your style!'

Josa walked towards Yvonne Salter's house, sparing the girl a glance over her shoulder, but she'd already turned away and was chatting into her mobile phone. When Josa snapped her head frontward, she saw something unexpected.

Yvonne Salter was hurrying along the short path from her front door to her gate. But it was her body language that triggered Josa's suspicions. As a DS in Surrey she'd tailed a thousand subjects and could always spot the ones that suspected they were being watched. Their gait was more precise, yet artificial; like the stride of a person asked to stroll down a catwalk who suddenly couldn't look even remotely natural. And always, the head would be down but the eyes all over the shop, checking out every corner, face and pace ahead. Yvonne Salter demonstrated an extreme of that look, and without thinking twice, Josa crossed the road, bringing her phone to her ear, angling her head as if its reception was poor, while shielding her face from Yvonne.

She'd turned right out of her gate, heading eastwards towards White City. Josa followed on the opposite side of the road, making a few guesses as to the point of the pantomime. Yvonne hit Wood Lane, hung a left, hailed a taxi and leapt in. As it pulled away, Josa flagged down another and pointed to the cab that was whisking Yvonne past BBC Television Centre. 'There's no unclichéd way I can say this,' she began.

The journey lasted exactly an hour and ten minutes, taking her through West London and up the M25, along a series of minor roads and finally into a maze of country lanes. When they reached what looked like the middle of nowhere, the cab in front drew to a halt and Yvonne emerged. Josa urged her driver to hang back for a minute, then the taxi crawled cautiously forward.

Josa peered through her window, barely able to see a thing, darkness and a low-lying fog hiding everything except the narrow road and the hedgerows bordering it. With difficulty she could just about make out Yvonne pushing open a gate and disappearing from view. 'Where are we, again?'

'Dunno. Surrey.' The cabbie scrutinised the satnav. 'Nearest village is a mile or so away and I'd say Guildford is about twenty minutes by car.'

'Great.' Josa wondered why she'd been brought here. Yvonne's furtive-follow-me act had been overdone, and she'd formed a pretty good idea who the girl outside her house was. 'Wait for me here.' Josa looked in her purse and saw she was far short of the fare. A self-conscious grimace. 'When I get back you can take me back into London and I'll grab some petty cash from the station to pay you.'

'Station?'

'I'm a Detective Chief Inspector.'

He swivelled in his seat so he could get a better view of her. Squinted. Paused. Then his shoulders shook in a quick burst of laughter. 'And I'm the Queen!'

Anger replaced embarrassment and Josa held up her ID. 'Yeah? Well, you can just wait here, your majesty.'

He loved it here. Would have moved in himself if he had the money. Maybe one day. Who could say, he thought. When the owners found out what had happened here – when they saw what he was planning to create in their home – maybe they'd put the place on the market. And if they wanted a quick sale ... The notion brought a smile to his lips.

He'd driven as close as possible to the house, using narrow back roads he'd reconnoitred a thousand times without ever coming across another vehicle. Then he opened the back door, carried the corpse in, lugged it through the kitchen and into the sitting room where he'd dumped it on the floor.

It was dark outside and his car was concealed by the house itself, but he had to act quickly. He closed Jill's eyes and got to work.

She pushed open the gate and began walking along the scattering of broken slabs that passed for a path. The moonlit garden looked like an experiment in apathy, an uneven spread of knee-high grass, tangled hedges and alabaster figures obscured by wild foliage. The huge house ahead showed no sign of life. No light, no love, creeping ivy smothering its façade. As she neared the top of the path she could see there were actually four alabaster figures, each one a woman and each damaged in some way. A quartet of victims. Josa shivered. They seemed to be watching her.

She heard her cab's engine fire up. Saw it driving into the night. 'Fucker,' she murmured.

He stepped back. His modelling of Jill Kennedy was complete and he couldn't find the words to express his pleasure and pride. He took photographs and filmed the scene, finally tearing himself away. *No risks!* But he paused in the doorway, looking at his work with a parent's love. And then something occurred to him and he tiptoed back to the corpse and made one tiny alteration. Stood back again, allowing himself a moment to acknowledge the re-edit had achieved perfection.

And now that was done …

He pulled the note from his pocket.

… he had someone else to take care of.

Behind her, something creaked. Josa whirled around. A battered wooden sign that read 'Moonfleet' swung to and fro in the breeze. And beyond it –

*Of course!*

'You needn't have bothered with the theatrics,' she said. 'A text message would have done.'

'Oh, Josa!' He sat on the step leading to the front door. 'It would have been easier …' he conceded, 'but where's the fun in that?'

'The girl's your daughter. The one who gave Yvonne the message to come out of the house so I'd follow her. She's got your eyes.'

'Poor kid.'

'I know who you are.'

'I never doubted it.' It was the man she'd first met at the Shard crime scene, and later in her hospital room.

'So why did you bring me here? It had better be important.'

'It's a matter of life and death.' He stood up, his face made silver by the moonlight. 'Many lives. Many deaths, Josa. But we can stop them.' He took a pace towards her and extended his hand. 'I'm Daniel Blake.'

When she'd become a copper Josa had been astonished by the number of civilians and 'externals' she was told she'd be working with. The trainer on her induction course had rattled off the stats – the English police service employs around 80,000 civilians on either a permanent or freelance basis, and about a quarter of people working in murder investigation teams are civilians known collectively as 'police staff'. This sizeable freelance army includes expert witnesses, academics and criminologists who are customarily hired to lend their expertise on specific cases. Daniel Blake had fallen into this latter category.

Of course, Josa Jilani had heard a great deal about the man who stood before her, even caught a few stories about him from the older coppers. They rarely discussed him, as if their silence somehow protected his memory from the current crop of officers. But after a couple of pints they sometimes spoke of him, always with respect and affection, remembering bygone cases and his role in them. They called him 'the best' and his era was inevitably branded 'the good old days'. They would always end up drinking to him – frothy pint glasses colliding with a cheer. At first, the ritual irritated Josa. It had been half a decade since he'd worked with the police, and in those years he'd acquired something of a legendary status. But Josa took most anecdotes with a pinch of salt. It was her natural inclination to mistrust any legend that was perpetuated by sentiment, and she wasn't about to make an exception for the shadowy Mr Blake.

He swung open the front door and entered without saying another word. Josa followed him inside, pursuing his footsteps into darkness.

'Let there be light!' he declared.

A click and suddenly she could see again. Like a child opening her eyes after being blindfolded and whisked away to Disneyland, she literally said, '*Wow*' and after a brief silence, started to laugh. 'This is … amazing!'

But what struck Josa as remarkable was how little hard evidence there was that Blake had ever worked with the police. That he'd ever even existed. Most freelance consultants make good money from assisting the service and it's in their best interests to promote and highlight the part they have played in any successful case. They'll keep out of the media spotlight, savvy enough to let MPs and officers take the public credit. But in case notes and other official chronicles they make sure their names and deeds feature prominently.

Not so with Daniel Blake. She'd once joined a couple of senior colleagues in the pub – they'd been talking about Blake and when she'd reached the table they changed the subject. Annoyed and intrigued in equal measure, Josa had called up the case files on investigations she'd gleaned he'd worked on. In about half, he wasn't even mentioned. Not a solitary reference. This was bizarre because with most of those, she'd been told, off the record, that his involvement had led to the crucial breakthrough.

Other files were even more interesting. He'd obviously been camera-shy, and aside from a couple of blurry pictures of a clean-shaven guy who wasn't exactly a ringer for the man she'd met at the Shard, there had been almost nothing. But in several case notes the senior officer interviewed an individual apparently unconnected with the investigation or searched an ostensibly irrelevant location. More often than not these seemingly random acts proved instrumental in breaking the case. Yet time after time, when a 'brainwave' development like this had occurred she found two letters scrawled in the margin:

D.B.

Just those initials. Sometimes with an exclamation mark. In

several instances someone had attempted to hide the letters, scribbling over them or applying correcting fluid. But on countless occasions, where an uncrackable case had been cracked, D.B. was half-hidden in the margins.

She stood there, open-mouthed. It was vast, easily the size of a major hotel's lobby, but it was the old Hollywood glamour of the place that flabbergasted Josa. The floor was marble and, ahead of her, a broad central staircase dominated the room. The steps reached half-way to the first floor, then branched to the left and right. The banisters were solid oak and the staircase carpet a faded scarlet. It was threadbare down the middle where a thousand footsteps had worn away the pile, adding to the overall impression of long-lost opulence.

The furnishings were uniformly old; eccentric or eclectic depending on disposition. A dark wood hat stand and a battered teak cabinet flanked the doorway Josa had walked through and she noted a chaise longue, a green leather gentleman's chair and a mahogany highboy against the adjacent wall. But all the antiques were dwarfed by the size of the room and the massive chandelier which hung from the centre of the ceiling. Josa looked up. The paucity of light wasn't helped by the fact that its many layers of glass tearlets were caked in dust.

It reminded Josa of an abandoned film set, or at least, what she imagined a film set would have looked like for an old classic like *Gone with the Wind* or *Jezebel*. Despite the inescapable majesty and decay of it all, it still retained a strange homeliness, like someone had melded your grandmother's bungalow with the Palace of Versailles. Josa loved it.

The man in the navy blue coat sat on the bottom stair. 'Aren't you going to say it?'

'Say what?'

'Must cost you a fortune to heat.'

Josa Jilani looked at the man, studying his face.

'Where's Yvonne Salter?'

'Already left in a taxi that was waiting for her.'

'How did –'

'Yvonne's a lovely lady but she's got a big mouth on Facebook. Can you have a big mouth on Facebook? Anyway, she posted something about her meeting with you, so I contacted her and –'

'And I get the gist. *And* … I'll ask you again. Why did you bring me here?'

'Because in assuming and virtually announcing that Tony Taylor was the murderer you've made a terrible mistake. I take it the team that was hunting the killer has been disbanded and the investigation is being shelved. Do you have any idea how much time that is going to set you back?'

'Oh, oh, oh! I get it! This is the great Daniel Blake's comeback gig!'

'Does it look like I'm selling tickets?'

'A case like this that has really seized the public's attention. You just had to be a part of it and here you are, resurfacing after five years to tell the run-of-the-mill coppers like me how it's done. Well, not this lady. All my career I've had people questioning everything from my motive for having this job to my ability to do it well. Doubters and haters. But I'm still here. So if Daniel Blake wants to take a pop – fine, go ahead.'

He began to laugh. 'Jesus, Josa. I saved your life in the hospital. Doesn't that cut me any slack?'

'No. I'd like you to call me a taxi, please.'

'I don't want to be a part of the investigation. I just want you to reopen it. Now! And let the papers know you've reopened it or they will –'

'What were you doing at the Shard in the first place?' Josa cut in.

'Don Walters was an old friend. He asked for my help and I arrived a minute or so before you.'

'So, you've not helped the police for five years. You get one phone call from Don and off you go?' She sounded sceptical. 'Really?'

'Something like that.'

Josa nodded, still unconvinced, but she'd delve deeper another time. 'What about at the hospital?'

'Believe it or not I was there to see you. I felt bad about not being more help at the Shard, swung by your room but got kind of sidetracked by Doctor Death.'

'Tony Taylor?'

'Tony Taylor.'

'Our killer.'

'Not your killer.'

'Blake: news flash. He was about to pump a syringe full of potassium chloride into my veins.'

'Yeah. I'm beginning to sympathise with him.'

She shot him a look. 'What? You think it was just a radical bid to cure my headache?'

'Oh, now you want to hear what I think?'

'This is gold dust!'

'I hope you're taking notes. The real killer couldn't be certain you hadn't seen him in the Shard. So he paid Taylor to deal with the potential problem.'

She shook her head. 'I can't believe it.'

'I think you're starting to. Look, the man you're after is forensically aware, calculating and cautious. Apparently he's never been captured on CCTV. All of a sudden you think he's swanning around hospitals and his scheme to kill you involves chatting to senior policemen minutes before the deed? Oh, come on! You've not got a monopoly on making mistakes, Josa. You've got to accept you didn't call this one.'

'But if I got it wrong …' She looked up at the chandelier as if it might provide some kind of shining inspiration. 'He kills every Tuesday. We've not had any reports in.'

'I hope I'm wrong. I really do. But I suspect it's just a question of time before your phone rings and …'

'And what?'

'Just make that call. To Gilmour. Tell him you want to keep the case open and retain the men assigned to the investigation. Then contact Della Frank and get her to spin a story to the press that the case is ongoing, otherwise they will crucify you when –'

'No!'

'Josa!' He got to his feet. 'All your life you've been an outsider. I know how that feels. *Christ, I know how that feels*! But this is not the way to hit back at the people who've put you on the outside.' He stood immediately in front of her. 'I'm begging you. Make that call.'

Josa raised her hands. Blew gently on her palms. 'I asked you to call me a taxi.'

As she turned away, Blake raked his fingers through his hair. 'Okay,' he said, 'I tried my best. I can't be held responsible for what happens next.'

Josa spun around. '*I can't be held responsible*?' She stared at him. 'How lovely. To be able to say that and believe it.'

Blake could only hold her gaze for a moment. 'I'm sorry,' he said.

Josa nodded. She opened the front door and as the wind rushed into the grand old room, swirling around the two lone figures, her phone began to ring.

# CHAPTER 35

The country lanes were carpeted in a thick, low-lying fog and lined with trees. Their branches arched over the road, giving Josa the impression that they were tearing through a dark, snaking tunnel. Moonlight strobed through the canopy of foliage. She stole a glance at Blake. He was driving fast. Probably too fast for safety, but he seemed focused on the narrow lanes.

The call she'd taken in the house had been from Stevie. The killer's phone had become active again, or more precisely, had been switched on for thirty seconds earlier in the evening. It had called one number which did not pick up, and then the user switched it off. But that half minute had been enough to establish a fix. Josa's eyes glinted when she heard where the call had been made from.

'That's near here!'

Stevie was looking into the number the phone had called; he assured Josa he'd text her the details when they came in.

'Blake! No time for a taxi. Could you give me a lift? We've had a fix on the phone used by the killer.'

'Look on my works, ye mighty, and despair!'

'What?'

'How are the mighty fallen. From trusted confidante to chauffeur in five easy years.'

'Just get the keys.'

Blake insisted on driving. 'Be my guest!' Josa had told him when she'd seen his ride – a big, boxy, left-hand drive that had been guzzling petrol since the seventies. Blake mentioned it was a Cutlass and although she knew it was American, the name didn't ring any bells. Certainly, it wasn't what she'd call a vintage vehicle – not one of the classic, cool cars like a Mustang or Corvette. This baby zipped when you punched the pedal on the right but it was long, all angles, and not sleek. She noticed an ominous dent on its front, nearside bumper.

Blake took a long curve, holding at about fifty.

As his eyes were trained on the road ahead, Josa took a longer, sideways look at him.

The stories about his background were even more mysterious than his police career. The older officers remained tight-lipped on that score and Josa suspected it was because even they didn't know where he was from. In the absence of fact or even half-way reliable rumour, the tales of Daniel Blake's origins were often outlandish, bordering on the bizarre. Some said his mother was related to Anastasia, last of the Romanovs. Others claimed she had been a fortune-teller on Blackpool's Golden Mile. Some had it on very good authority that she'd been scarily high up in British intelligence, or she'd killed her husband, or he'd killed her. Depending on who you spoke to, Blake's father was a priest with a parish in the Lake District, a mercenary based in Brazil, a reformed forger now working in Langley or a madman, locked up heaven knows where because he'd learnt secrets that could topple governments and demolish royal houses. Josa believed none of these tales. There had even been a story that Daniel Blake wasn't his real name and the entire character was a fiction he had conceived and played out because –

The tyres screeched as he took a tight corner at speed.

Josa gripped the side of her seat. Looked at the driver.

'So what is it you do?' she asked.

'What is it I do? What, now, you mean?'

'No. I meant what did you do? With the police? When you used to help out. Details about you in the files were pretty scarce.'

'Good.'

'You're labelled a criminologist.'

'Nice and vague.' They hit a straight run and Blake floored the accelerator. The trees became a shadowy blur. 'You get psychological profilers, yeah? And geographic profilers. And criminal historians who can cite examples from the recent or not so recent past that give you an insight into your case. Then you have forensic psychologists, survival psychologists and social psychologists who can all throw light into the darkness. Different angles. I'm a kind of prism. I've got experience of all those disciplines, plus forensic pathology, victimology, neurolinguistic analysis, symbolic interactionism –'

'I get the picture. You're just making up words now.'

'But when I worked with the British police force my biggest attribute …'

The straight road hooked into a sharp corner. Blake dipped to twenty, took the Cutlass around it then fired her back up to fifty.

'Yes?'

'… was that I make a great pot of tea.'

'That's good to know,' Josa told him. 'For a moment I thought you were overrated.'

'It's all about the infusion.'

'I'll bear that in mind. And what have you been doing for the past five years?'

'Trying to bring up Holly Belle. My daughter. You two met.'

'She's got good hair.'

'Gets it from her mother.'

'Who is?'

'Lost.' Blake took another curve. 'Almost there,' he said.

Blake took a surreptitious glance at his passenger.

'So, do you know who's out to get you?' he asked.

'They all are. You keep your eyes on the road.'

'I'm serious.'

'So am I.'

'You gonna talk to me about how you're feeling about this whole thing?'

'Er, let me think,' Josa said. 'No.'

'I'd like to know.'

'Er, still no.'

Blake dipped his right shoulder and turned the dial that controlled the lights. Killed them. Josa shouted, 'Jesus, what are you doing?' as they hurtled through total darkness.

'You gonna talk to me?'

'All right! Just turn the bloody lights on!'

He hit the headlamps just as the road veered to the left. Decelerated slightly, negotiating the bend with ease. 'Well?'

'I've always wanted to succeed in the police service. I didn't want to reach this rank the way I have done, but if I can prove I deserve to be here on merit …' She shrugged. 'I know some of them hate me. They see me as the Muslim who elbowed aside other officers and got promoted ahead of them. But I'm just Josa Jilani. I'm just trying to do the best I can despite all this shit. Just like them. Just like everybody.'

Blake knew the answer but asked the question anyway. 'Do you think Gilmour had you assigned to this investigation?'

'God, no. Someone far higher up. Gilmour doesn't want me around. He still thinks WPCs are taking it a bit far.'

'So it's someone who wants you to fail to discredit the Home Secretary.'

'It's all political. And I'm rubbish at politics.'

'I could do some digging around. See who's gunning for you. You could confront them. Worst case scenario, they get pissed off, but hey, they're already –'

She was shaking her head.

'What? Have I said something wrong?'

'That's a bad idea. A very bad idea. And I know bad ideas. You're talking to someone who supports a club that appointed Joe Kinnear as their manager. Me and bad ideas go way back.'

'Why is it such a terrible plan?'

'I don't want to fight them,' Josa insisted, speaking more seriously, more impatiently. 'I joined the police when I was eighteen years old because I was desperate to be part of the establishment. Not to fight it.'

He slammed on the brakes and the car skidded to a halt.

'What the actual fuck! Blake! Stop driving like you're in a circus! What is it this time?'

He gestured ahead to a sign on their left.

*Shamley Green.*

'We're here,' he said.

And at that moment, something struck Josa. That in all the drama surrounding the beginning of their journey, she'd never told him the name of the village or given any indication of where the phone had been traced to. Yet he'd known and brought them here.

'Exciting, isn't it?' said Blake.

# CHAPTER 36

He shook hands with Ted Maynard like they were two old friends.

'Look who it is, Mavis!' the old man called over his shoulder.

'Well, bring him in!' There was no kindness in her instruction. 'Bring him in.'

'Aye, come in and sit yourself down.'

'Thanks.'

Ted Maynard was in his late seventies. An ex-con with eyes that looked like they were scanning for the next contraband packet of fags being passed over the table or the razor blade passed under it. He'd aged since they'd last met. Maybe it was the scruffier clothes – an old open-necked shirt, tatty cardigan and a Harris tweed jacket with holes where the elbows had worn away. But it wasn't just that. He was slouching a little and his skin appeared more sallow. Yet he remained sharp, and the grip that had shaken his hand had been firm and confident.

Ted shut the door behind him. The room's only illumination came from a crackling log fire and, despite the almost unbearable heat, Mavis Maynard sat in a rocking chair only inches from the hearth. She angled her head to regard him. A toothless smile. 'So. You came, did you?'

''Course he came, Mavis.' Ted's words were clipped. A warning to his wife that he was running the show. 'You promised you'd visit. At my leaving do. You promised.'

Ted Maynard had once been a security guard but when the era of criminal records dawned, he faced the sack, until one of his bosses 'decided' to keep him on as a caretaker. Rumours of blackmail flourished and passed into workplace folklore, but no solid facts ever emerged.

'Well, I meant to visit you earlier, but work's been insane.'

He had met Ted Maynard years ago, making the classic mistake of striking up a friendship on the first day of a new job. The caretaker seemed good value. Catch him while he was having a crafty fag and he'd tell you who was sleeping with whom and … And eventually Ted had revealed a little about his history. So when he'd needed a gun …

'Let me take your coat. There we go! Now! Can I get you a cuppa? I've not got that fancy Earl Grey stuff that you go in for, but –'

'Ted!' His voice was gentle but definite. 'We both know why I'm here.'

'We know why you've come!' croaked Mavis. She didn't look away from the fire. 'And we know what you are.'

'Mavis!' Ted rasped.

'I recognised your handwriting on the note, Ted. Block capitals, but still unmistakable.'

'Well, I thought best not to sign it. Knew there was no need. We go back such a long way …' Ted paused. 'Mavis. Why don't you go upstairs to bed? We need to talk. Go on, now.'

She shuffled across the dry wooden floor and up the stairs. Mavis Maynard had almost disappeared from view but her strident voice filled the room. 'Make sure you get a good price!'

Ted smiled at his guest. 'She's a one.'

'Yes. Quite.' He took in his surroundings. The whole downstairs of the cottage had been knocked into a single room. A living area with two battered chairs by the fire, and a kitchen space dominated by a wooden table; beyond it, a couple of old-fashioned work units, a stove and a Belfast sink. On one of the units he saw a bread knife.

They skirted the village green and Josa pointed to the house Stevie had described to her. Blake killed the engine, switched off the lights. 'Let's go,' he said.

'Wait a minute. I never told you the phone call had been made in Shamley Green, so how the hell –?'

'An educated guess. I need to see the latest victim but I've got a terrible feeling I know what's going on here.' He stepped out of the car and slammed the door.

Josa caught up with him. 'Latest victim?'

'What do you think we're going to find here?'

'You're very definite.'

'Definitely am. You might as well phone the SOCOs now.'

'SOCOs?'

Blake rolled his eyes. 'Good grief, Josa. SOCOs. Scene of the crime officers.'

She gave a short laugh. 'You mean CSIs! No one's called them SOCOs for years.' And instantly, Josa regretted her clumsiness. 'Sorry. When those TV shows – *CSI: Miami* and the rest of them – starting getting big, the SOCOs gradually became known as –'

'It's okay,' Blake interjected. They had reached the gates of the house. 'I know I'm a bit of a dinosaur. I'll need time to shake off the scales, you know?'

'Don't worry about it. Look, you stay here while I check out the house.'

'I'm coming with you.'

'I'm a big girl. I can brush my own teeth and everything.'

'Josa! Remember the Shard! The killer may be in there waiting. Why do you think he made a call? He knew it would be traced. *He wanted to draw us here.*'

'Okay. You come in with me but you stay behind me and do exactly what I say. Fair enough?'

Josa extended her hand to shake on the deal.

'Fair enough,' Blake replied.

As they shook hands, Josa's left palm moved upwards as though she was going to cup the clasp in a show of affection. Except as it neared him, her hand became a blur.

A sudden flash of silver.

*Click!*

She slapped the steel bracelet onto his right wrist.

'I'll do this alone!' *Click!* She snapped the other end of the handcuffs onto the gate. 'You wait here.'

'What? Hey! What are you doing?'

Josa brushed past him and began striding up the driveway. 'No idea!' She turned. Walked backwards for a moment. 'Exciting, isn't it?' Josa stuck out her tongue, turned, and continued her trek towards the house.

# CHAPTER 37

The two men sat at the kitchen table. 'I've got some friends in the force,' said Ted Maynard. A half-smile. 'Strange how the two sides start getting pally after retirement. Like us and the Jerries after the war.'

'Go on, Ted.'

'He told me that the fella doing all these murders on Tuesday nights … Told me that he took a few shots at a couple of coppers. And those clever buggers can tell from the bullets that the shooter he used was a Beretta. Just like the one I got you. That you said you needed for research.'

'A Beretta, eh? Well, that's a coincidence but –'

'A Beretta Cheetah. Not too many of those about. And my pal tells me that this character who's been on the news, the one who was killed on the bus … Well, he tried to inject a copper with potassium chloride. And you'll never guess who it was? Tony Taylor! Tony. My old mate from my Strangeways days. I introduced you two. Remember?'

'Yes, I believe I do.'

'You were always very interested in my friends. I thought it was because it was all a bit glamorous to you. Real-life villains and the like, but now I think you were collecting them, just in case you ever needed one to …'

Ted kept talking. About the murders. Putting the facts together and reaching what he called, 'the only reasonable conclusion. You're the serial killer.'

But the visitor was only half-listening, trying to take in the enormity of the new situation. Somebody knew he was the killer. No, two people. The chances were they'd told no one else. This was all leading to extortion, which required the blackmailers to keep what they knew secret, but still, two people with a hold over him and … He retained one advantage, however. Men like Ted Maynard thought he was weak. And sure, the old guy was still strong and could probably fight like a Doberman, but he was cleverer. His eyes rested on the bread knife. He thought of Hitchcock's *Blackmail* and the moment where …

'Ted. We're both men of the world. Both been in trouble with the law. Both know the score. We stick together.' He patted Ted's shoulder. 'Men like you and me. Remember when the bursar's cash box went missing? They thought you might have stashed it in your Cortina. What happened?'

'You gave me the wink. I moved my car before they could …' He stopped himself. 'I'm not saying it was in there, mind.'

'Of course not!'

'I want two hundred quid a month.'

'Don't we all?' He was pleased with that response. He sounded urbane, unruffled. Maybe he was calmer than he'd anticipated. Maybe he was becoming –

'That's not a lot!' Ted snapped. He gave a deep, throaty laugh that his guest didn't care for. 'You wouldn't like prison, what they'd do to you there.'

'Ted! That's no way to speak to an old chum.'

'Two hundred quid a month.'

'Do you have any olives?'

'What?'

'Olives? I'm ravenous.'

'No.'

'Bread, then?'

'There's a loaf in the box.' He gestured across the room.

'Mind if I …?'

'Help yourself. Two hundred quid's a good deal, and you know it.'

Ted Maynard, the hardened jailbird, was starting to sound worried and his guest was starting to enjoy this. The two hundred a month was not a financial problem, but he knew it would be just the start. Soon he'd be paying for Ted and Mavis' holidays in the sun and before long one of them would drink too much and spill more than their whisky. No, he had to strike now. He eyed the bread knife. Got to his feet.

Instinctively, Ted stood up too, automatically countering any advantage his guest may have been looking to achieve. The old man leant back on the kitchen table, watching him intently as he picked up a half-empty bottle of Blue Nun. 'I didn't know you were a wine drinker, Ted.'

'I know it's piss.' The first hint of a snarl. 'The wife can't taste or smell so I get her that.'

'Why does she drink wine if she can't taste it?'

'Why do you think?'

'I take your point.' He picked up the bread knife.

'Let's stop messing about. Two hundred quid. Are you going to give it to me or not?'

'Oh, yes, Ted. I'm going to give it to you.' He raised the knife and brought it down towards Ted in a swift, strong arc.

# CHAPTER 38

She looked up at the property, set well back from the village green as if it was too good for the other houses that huddled around it.

Stevie had texted her again. He had contacted the owners of the house who were half-way into a month-long tour of the Highlands. So Josa wasn't thrilled about the light blurring through the closed curtains of the bay windows. It might mean nothing, but on the other hand she preferred an empty house to look empty, whereas the lights indicated someone could be inside. Her feet scrunched along the gravel driveway.

The iron gates clanged shut behind her.

She had enough experience to avoid the front door, crossing the sloping lawn and walking directly to the side of the house. It was a large property, two floors, set in about an acre of garden. Rustic red brick work with black and white timber around the door and window frames. Josa could see a long garden extend behind the house. One rectangular lawn dissected by a stone path and beyond that, an orchard. Four rows of plum trees stretching into darkness. Back on the green there had been Blake, the weak but reassuring street lamps and signs of life from the Red Lion. Here, as she walked behind the house, she was confronted by pitch darkness and an eerie silence. She took a slim torch from her pocket and switched it on.

Josa reached the back door and her hand paused over the handle. She could walk away now. Skedaddle. Get Blake or call for backup ... She pressed her hand down, trying the door. It opened easily. Unlocked. *Christ almighty!*

Owners on holiday leaving lamps on a timer was a plausible reason for the light in the front windows, but only an idiot would leave their back door open, and people who could afford a place like this seldom fell into that category.

Josa's heart was beating like it wanted to escape her chest but she forced herself to take a step forward. *Maybe a friend of the owners had popped in to keep an eye on the place. That would explain the lights and unlocked door.* And then another step as she moved through the kitchen. She slowly tiptoed to the inner door and, as she looked down the hallway, her stomach lurched at what she saw.

Josa Jilani had reccied dozens of buildings during her days on the beat. But never alone. Never without a mate by her side, walkie-talkie in her top pocket and a telescopic truncheon on her belt. But here and now she was on her own. Or at least she fervently *hoped* she was on her own. Because Josa could see a pile of mail spilling across the carpet by the front door. Not just junk mail and takeaway menus, but square white envelopes, manila envelopes, a postcard or two. Proper correspondence. The kind that anyone looking after the house would have picked up, so whoever *had* left the door unlocked and switched on the light …

The light, the light she could see as a bright white line below the closed door of the front room, about five paces ahead to her left. Josa switched off her torch but clutched it tightly in her right hand.

*Come on, Josa!*

She forced herself to take more silent steps, inching towards the door. A floorboard creaked and she froze, straining to hear any reaction to the noise. Nothing. Two more paces, even slower as she tested the floor before committing her full weight, and now she was at the doorway. Left hand on the handle, right hand moving upwards, ready to swing with the torch if anyone sprang at her when she –

– *pushed open the door!* Stepped forward. Josa burst into the room! And immediately the horror which it held hit her. The bright light. The near emptiness. The corpse.

The body of Jill Kennedy dominated the large, white room, impossible to escape. Josa had lost count of the dead bodies she'd seen over the years, but never one like this. Never one as shocking, as gruesome – as *staged*.

Josa Jilani opened her mouth to scream but her throat constricted in terror and no sound escaped. And at that moment, she felt the hand grip her shoulder.

# CHAPTER 39

Mavis listened at the top of the stairs. Straining to piece together the goings-on downstairs. It had started promisingly enough although now ... Silence. Her hearing wasn't so good these days but she'd definitely heard him say *I'm going to give it to you* ... Then nothing. She squinted, as if narrowing her eyes would sharpen her ears. And then she heard laughing ... her husband's loud, long laughter.

Josa spun around. 'Blake! Bloody hell!'

'You forgot these,' he murmured, passing her the handcuffs. Something about their metallic glint reminded Josa of the picklock he'd used at the hospital, and she didn't need to ask how he'd worked his Houdini routine. Blake slid past her through the doorway. 'Christ ...' he said quietly.

It was a medium-sized room. No furniture, except for a two-seat sofa that was hidden by a white sheet draped across it. Cream carpets, plain beige walls, a white, Adam-style fireplace.

Jill Kennedy lay in the middle of the room, propped up against the sofa and staring blindly towards the doorway. One eye had been closed, so that for a crazy split-second, when Josa had pushed open the door, she thought she was alive and winking at her. She wore a knee-length, pleated skirt, smart blouse and a light cardigan. Simple jewellery. Sensible shoes.

About a third of her head was missing.

Her hair had been parted in a way that made the horrific injury obvious – unavoidable, like the subject of an extreme close-up. The jagged hole in her skull was the size of a rose head, rendering her brain clearly visible. Jill's exposed frontal and parietal lobes offered the only splash of colour in the blandness of the room.

There was no blood.

Josa narrowed her eyes. There was none of the mutilation that had ravaged Elaine Hargreaves' body, but there was something much more chilling about the sight of this corpse. The appalling injury was so obviously for display. Posed. Josa couldn't help thinking of a butcher's shop with all the prime cuts on show in the window to illustrate the skill of the butcher and the quality of his meat. She glanced at Blake, curious for a split-second about how he would react after so long away from this awful world.

He nodded at Josa. Looked back at Jill Kennedy. 'Let's make a start, shall we?' he said.

Josa stood back, observing. Blake circled Jill Kennedy three times, drawing steadily closer as his eyes took in her body like an electronic scanner. Now he dropped to his haunches, half-sitting, half-kneeling by her head. Josa could see him peering down her top, as if trying to look at her chest.

'A-ha!'

And then suddenly he was leaping over her, nose almost touching her throat as he moved from her neck, over her face and towards the gaping wound. His examination took Josa aback. He was fast, almost feral. Sliding over her body without ever touching it, grunting with annoyance at some apparent findings, constantly moving, eyes darting, scrutinising. Lingering on lips, fingertips, feet. Sniffing, occasionally shaking his head. Never looking up. Josa could see him consumed by the process that lasted about five minutes. Half-way through it she ferreted out her phone and called in the crime. At the end of his examination, Blake sat cross-legged by Jill's shoulders. 'I want to close her eyes,' he said. 'Stroke her hair. I know I can't.'

'So what do you think?'

'This poor, poor girl …' He shook his head. 'She thought she'd cracked it. Was finally getting somewhere. She was on a first date, of course. With a guy she thought was a real gentleman. Much better than what she was used to. That was in her mind. God, she wanted to get it spot on. And she did all the right things and she must have been happy when he took her home and offered her champagne and then ...' He paused. 'Oh, that's good. He must live in a big house. And, oh no ... He wasn't making you watch one of his films while ...' Another shake of the head.

Josa took a step forward. 'How do you know all that?'

'First date? The way she's made up. Those new clothes. She's making a big effort but doesn't want it to show. This is definitely a first-date level of effort. Now. Check out her jewellery, shoes, underwear, perfume ... She wasn't earning a bomb but spent big for this. Meant a lot to her.'

'What's with all the *thought he was a gentleman* stuff?'

'She normally went for clothes that were a lot more revealing. Judging by the tan on her chest, she customarily went for low-cut tops. But she didn't with this guy. She felt it would be inappropriate. Same way that she's actually removed the red nail varnish that she usually wore. And took off the bangles she normally had on her –'

'How can you –?'

'Tan!' said Blake, tapping his own wrist as he anticipated Josa's question.

'Champagne?'

'Judging by the slight indentation on her lipstick she was drinking out of a flute just before she died. So it could have been cava or any sparkling wine. But I'm going with champagne. And she was inside when she was killed. Look at her shoes. She's been outside recently, but dutifully wiped her feet on the way in. So, as we know she was inside when she was murdered, let's go a step further and infer the deed was done at his place, not hers. He'd have more control there and it'd be easier to clean up afterwards.'

'And you know it's a big house ... how?'

'Look at the wound. This was done from behind. From someone higher up. So, she's sat down, drinking champagne and he's behind her and ...' Blake traced the arc of the killer blow with his own right hand. '*Whack!* That just needs some space, don't you think? That swing, especially behind the chair she was sitting in.'

'It's possible,' Josa conceded.

'Yeah, it's possible,' Blake replied in a tone that said, *you know I'm right*. 'And you've spotted *that*.' He gestured to the sofa and the single item it held. A piece of A4 paper torn in two with a triangle roughly drawn on one side. 'The so-called *calling card*.'

'Then there's no doubt. It's him.' Josa blanched. 'How could I have been so ...' She swayed for a moment, just managing to grip the side of the sofa for support. She closed her eyes.

*She saw a young Asian girl, maybe six or seven, in a playground. A ring of white and black kids around her. Some pushing her, some calling her names in petty vengeance for her outburst earlier that morning when she'd blurted out they were destined for Jahannam. Others just there to see the circus. But she'd broken through the circle of children, marching purposefully away although she had no idea where she was going.*

'Josa ...'

*Always that same impulse: to run. To get out of there and to –*

'Josa!'

Her eyes snapped open to see the concerned face of Daniel Blake. 'It's okay, it's okay. Remember what I said before?' He lightly held her shoulders, smiling. 'You've not got a monopoly on making mistakes.'

She pulled away. 'You don't understand.'

'What are you afraid of?'

She looked at him. 'Going to hell.'

# CHAPTER 40

Ted Maynard looked down at the broken knife. Spoke very quietly. 'It's not like in the films, you know. A bread knife? To stab a man?' Then he laughed, shaking his head from side to side as if the whole situation amounted to the funniest thing he'd ever seen.

The knife's point had been too blunt to even penetrate the thick tweed jacket Maynard was wearing. The blade had snapped in two, reduced to a four-inch metal splinter.

'You fancy ponces really think you can step into our world, into our ...'

Ted droned on. The murder of Ebba Lovgren had taught the man that stabbing someone was more problematic than it looked. And he'd used that knowledge to craft a weapon he could now wield effectively.

'Oh, yes,' Ted was saying. 'You want to know what I think?'

'Not really.'

He thrust the jagged blade into Ted Maynard's left eye, pushed hard and felt the thin metal slice into the old man's forebrain and midbrain. There was very little resistance and he felt an odd sensation, like he was stabbing a hard, dried sponge. Gave the knife a little wiggle to make sure Maynard got the message and then stood back. He'd read somewhere that the human brain comprises over a hundred billion nerve cells but does not have pain receptors and therefore cannot feel physical sensation. The way Maynard was bawling like a scalded baby made him doubt this. This little experiment suggested quite the opposite, in fact, and he made a mental note to update the appropriate Wiki page.

'Will you be quiet? I really think this is a slight overreaction.'

Maynard's screams were like cries from hell. He'd pulled the knife from his brain and covered his useless left eye with both hands, but still the blood pumped out between his fingers.

'Help me!'

''Course I will, old chap. You sit down.' He forced him into one of the kitchen chairs. 'Don't worry. I'll be right back.'

Mavis Maynard stood at the top of the staircase, crying but too scared to move. She heard her husband's scream fade into whimpers and finally silence. Heard Ted's attacker leave the room. Where was he going? The garage? And then he returned and she felt certain he'd changed his mind and was going to do her in as well. But he simply paced around the downstairs, said goodnight to Ted and left through the back door.

Five minutes after the onslaught she crept downstairs. Her husband was sat in a kitchen chair, head lolling back to one side, his face resembling a vivid, red poppy with his gouged-out eye forming the dark button of stamens at its centre.

She put her hand to her mouth. 'Oh no! Oh no!' Moved quickly across the floor towards him. Almost slipped. Looked down, expecting to see blood but finding what she supposed was water. Mavis regained her balance, took two more steps and reached her husband. 'Ted! Ted!' Grasped his head between her two palms and straightened it. 'Can you hear me? Are you alive?'

His head moved very slightly and his jaw parted fractionally as if he was trying to speak.

'I'll call an ambulance!'

She turned but his hand grabbed her arm.

'What is it? You're going to be all right! I'm going to get a doctor straight away ...'

His jaw was rising and falling again and this time he leant forward, so Mavis moved towards him, putting her ear over his lips. 'What is it?' she said.

'Pet ...'

And Mavis' eyes filled with tears. During their months of courtship and early married life he'd always called her pet, a *nom d'amour* he'd discarded when too many years together turned affection into apathy. But now, as he hovered on the brink of death, she understood what he was trying so desperately to convey.

'Don't worry, bonny lad! I know you love me!'

Suddenly he was overcome with a fervour, shaking his parody of a head, pulling her close and trying to hiss a single word into her ear: 'Pet … Pet …' A final effort: 'Petrol!'

The feeling of blood on her flesh made Mavis recoil. She stepped back, her foot once again slipping on something. That water again, that –

*Petrol!*

But before the implication sank in the flames flew up. A line of fire from the garage where they always kept the cans of fuel, across the yard, into the room and –

'You daft bugger!' said Ted Maynard, and the cottage exploded into an all-consuming inferno.

# CHAPTER 41

'The man we're after is not the devil.'

'That's not what I mean.' Josa shook her head as if trying to clear her thoughts. 'You said before that you had a feeling you knew what was going on.'

'Yeah. And I'm happy to tell you. But d'you mind if we go through it outside? I could do with some fresh air.'

As they left the room, Josa stole another look at Jill's face, at her one-eyed countenance. She couldn't shake the feeling that it was as if the killer was winking at her by proxy.

A couple of minutes later they were standing on a strip of grass by the side of the house, overlooking the sleeping village below. Blake looked up at the sky. 'I can't stay long.'

'If you want to get back for Holly I'm sure I could call one of my female officers and ask them to –'

'It's not about Holly!' Blake snapped. 'I'm sorry,' There was genuine apology in his voice. 'I really can't stay out here much longer and I've no time to explain why. Shall we sit down?' He'd pulled a scarf from his coat pocket and now he unfurled it and spread it across the grass. 'Here. You can sit on this.'

'Thanks.'

They snuggled next each other, wordless for several seconds.

'Do you like movies, Josa?'

'Yeah. As much as the next girl. I like romcoms. Stuff you probably hate.'

'I've always been a fan. Old movies, mainly. The classics.'

'Go on.'

'After Elaine Hargreaves, when I read up on the murders, an awful thought struck me. As to why they were happening. And why they wouldn't stop for a very long time. Until …' He paused. They held each other's stare. '… *we* catch him.'

'Thank you,' she said.

'I couldn't walk away from this now. Especially now I know for certain why these murders are happening and what we need to do to stop the killer …'

And on that quiet spot beneath a lintel of stars, Daniel Blake began to explain something of the killings which would soon become known as the Hitchcock Murders. He spoke eloquently and without emphasising the shocking nature of his revelations, because he understood that both of them grasped the dire ramifications of what he knew. Dangerous, unsettling, explosive knowledge. Knowledge that had to be kept secret. And as they talked, neither of them realised that from the village green, through a powerful night-vision lens, they were being watched.

# CHAPTER 42

'It was like a Rorschach test,' said Blake. 'You ever taken one of those? Where you're shown an indistinct image. Swirls. Blocks of black. Whatever. And you have to say what it means to you.'

'I know the ones,' Josa replied.

'As I learnt about each murder I kept *almost* seeing it. But not quite. And then the blonde thing occurred to me. Who had a thing for blonde victims? And what you called his calling card. The triangle. The killer used the same thing in a movie called *The Lodger*. A triangle left at the scene of his murders. The mark of the Avenger.'

'*The Lodger*? Never heard of it.'

'It was the first thriller directed by Alfred Hitchcock. Back in 1926.'

'It's a copycat? You mean these murders are lifted from this old movie?'

'No, not just that one film. He's lifting from across all the works of Alfred Hitchcock. He started by taking elements of Hitch's early films. The first victim, Becka Hoyle, was killed the same way that Hitchcock despatched his first onscreen victim. It was a drowning in his first feature, *The Pleasure Garden*. The element of having rats feast on a victim is taken from 'Gas', a short story Hitch wrote in 1919.'

'What about Elaine Hargreaves? I don't believe we ever saw anything that horrific in an old film.'

Blake nodded his agreement. 'You're absolutely right. But *The Lodger* was roughly based on the case of Jack the Ripper. So our killer has done what Hitchcock couldn't do and shown us the reality of a Ripper victim. In this instance he'd mimicked the injuries to Mary Jane Kelly, the Ripper's fifth victim. And incidentally, that's why he's murdering every Tuesday. That's the pattern the killer in *The Lodger* stuck to.'

'Only killing on that one day of the week?'

'Yeah, exactly. One murder. Each and every Tuesday. And the blonde thing … Hitchcock had a preference for blond victims in his films. He became known for it. Some people called it a peccadillo. *The Hitchcock blonde*. One thinks of Anny Ondra, Grace Kelly, Tippi Hedren … The funny thing is, Hitch loved them all … ' Blake seemed distracted for a moment before he bared his teeth in a brief grimace. 'But our boy is starting to spread his wings. Geographically, he's experimenting. Hitchcock lived in Shamley Green for a period, just before his mega-stardom, hence the use of it as a setting. And the killer is dipping into the later films. The stabbing with the scissors. That's the way the Grace Kelly character, Margot Wendice, killed someone in *Dial M for Murder*. In a flat in Maida Vale, incidentally.'

'And the raincoat belt used to strangle someone?'

'It's the way Guy kills his wife in *Young and Innocent*. Great movie. There's this one unbelievable shot where Hitchcock tracks across an entire –'

'I'm sure it's a brilliant film but right now –'

'Right now,' Blake interrupted, 'you'd better start getting interested in Alfred Hitchcock because having an instinct for the way he worked is the only way we're going to stop this madman.' Blake leapt to his feet, 'And now …' he gazed into the sky. 'I really do have to dash.'

'What are you looking up there for?'

'Because that's why I have to dash.'

Josa took in the night-time sky. A half moon, a spread of stars, low cloud cover and a 747 in the distance. 'Are you one of those people that tells the time by aircraft flight patterns?'

Blake paused. 'Er, no. I tend to use my watch. I'll be in touch. And Josa, it's going to be okay.'

'See you.'

'Dream well.'

Josa watched him walk briskly across the lawn, through the gate and towards his car. A bank of fog was beginning to swallow him. 'Hey!' she called, but he didn't slow down. 'All those things you said in there!' She stood up. 'You gave me an analysis as if that was the way you'd worked it out, but you … *you just knew*, didn't you? How d'you do that?'

Blake stopped. Hesitated then half-turned around. 'I have an affinity for murder.'

'You must hate it.' There was complete silence. 'Thank you!'

Blake nodded, turned and walked away.

He'd not taken six steps before the fog claimed him. For a minute Josa thought she could discern his figure, but then she blinked. He was gone.

His car was stationary on the single-track road and, engine idling, window wound down, he watched the conflagration from a safe distance. The Maynards' home had been a run-down crofter's cottage in the middle of nowhere, surrounded by acres of meadows and not much more. He looked at the building's burning husk. It had been an ugly old eyesore, but in its favour, it had gone up like a tinder box.

Hitchcock had provided him with the idea, of course. He'd always felt his 1942 thriller, *Saboteur*, was an underrated work, and the shot of the hero's best friend being killed – consumed by the vast sheets of fire started by the eponymous saboteur – was a strangely beautiful piece of *mise-en-scène*. But there again, Hitch has sacrificed verisimilitude for good cinema. A blaze like that, he now saw, no one ran from, dramatically alight like a fiery daemon. *They simply screamed and fell and perished.*

The whole cottage had become lost in huge, swirling flames. A black and orange witch on the horizon.

*Probably a good thing.*

Ted had most probably got his address from correspondence he'd left lying on his desk at work sometime. Imagine looking at other people's mail … Some people! He forgave him, though. He liked to think of himself as a man who didn't bear grudges.

He wound up the car windows, popped a CD in the player and pulled away.

# CHAPTER 43

Josa sat by the side of the house, afraid to close her eyes in case she drifted off. She'd learnt about copycat killings back in a training course at Hendon. It had covered the obvious cases like Heriberto Seda, who mimicked the crimes of the Zodiac Killer, and Veronica Compton, who famously tried to murder someone in the style of the Hillside Strangler. But the course also examined instances where films and other forms of fiction influenced a murderer's modus operandi. The jury was still out as to whether violent movies and video games were directly to blame for acts of brutality, and she'd heard all the arguments, for and against.

Films like *Reservoir Dogs*, *A Clockwork Orange* and, bizarrely, *The Fisher King*, had been copycatted by unbalanced individuals, there was no denying that, the acts of aggression within them studied and replicated in real life. Josa could cite at least a dozen murders and attempted murders where the perpetrators had allegedly been influenced by *Natural Born Killers*, Oliver Stone's 1994 movie following two fictional psychopaths as they slaughter their way across the States. Indeed, shortly after the film's release, a teenager decapitated a thirteen-year-old girl and reportedly explained his actions with the casual remark, 'I wanted to be famous, like the Natural Born Killers.'

But Josa could not get her head around the idea of someone basing a series of murders on the works of Alfred Hitchcock. These were old films, lacking the ultra-violence of, say, a Tarantino or an Eli Roth flick. And these had been controlled, planned executions. The lack of forensic evidence testified to that. This was no crazy on the rampage, no loony taking a potshot at the president because of a line in *Taxi Driver*. This was someone who studied classic movies and carefully planned a bloody homage … if Blake was right.

And if he was right, it also meant another countdown to another Tuesday. Less than a week to go. She hated the fact that time had become her enemy and never wanted to see another date written in bold again.

The sound of footsteps interrupted Josa's thoughts. She peered into the fog expecting Daniel Blake to emerge at any moment. 'Couldn't stay away, eh?' she called into the darkness. There was no answer and, intuitively, without consciously recalling Blake's gait, she knew the footsteps didn't belong to him. She tried to scramble to her feet but her palms slid on the damp grass and she fell back with a heavy bump, looking up as a figure stepped from the fog.

# CHAPTER 44

'Detective Chief Inspector ...'

Josa let out an audible sigh of relief as Stevie walked into view.

'Sorry to startle you,' he said.

'You didn't. Well, maybe just a little.' She clambered to her feet and looked him over. 'I know the cutbacks are biting but ...'

'Oh!' He grinned. 'The CSI boys and the rest of the team were right behind me. Then I got a call to say they were lost in the fog and finally a text to say they're two minutes away.'

'Well, it's good to see you, Stevie.' She began striding to the back door. 'And well done for getting here so quickly.'

Josa looked at the corpse of Jill Kennedy. Surrounded by the paraphernalia of police work, it didn't look as grisly, possibly because the context of forensics removed its incongruity. She checked herself. Jill Kennedy's body had already become an *it*.

The CSIs had turned up shortly after Stevie's arrival, and just when Josa felt certain the evening could hold no more surprises for her, Simon Maxwell walked into view. She knew he was one of the force's best forensic pathologists, and ever since her new posting she'd anticipated meeting up with him again. But not here, not now. They met on the path leading up to the house, and although Josa had more important things on her mind, she still felt a pang of irritation that he was looking good, whereas if she looked half as weary as she felt ...

'Josa! Hey! Great to see you again, even though it's in these circumstances.' Her former boyfriend had been working out, and he looked tanned, radiating good health like a model in a poster for vitamin supplements.

'Simon! How are you?'

He shook his head. 'You're looking fantastic!'

That was a kind lie but it still made her smile. 'I don't think so.' They had reached each other now. Close enough for a handshake or a hug, and, uncertain of how to play it, Josa clasped his shoulder. 'Great to see you!' It was, she immediately recognised, a miscalculation that typified her occasional awkwardness. But he simply shot her hand a glance. Smiled.

'Same old Josa!' He grinned.

'Not quite.'

'I know this isn't the time, but I've missed you, you know. I've thought about you a lot and –'

'Guv!' Stevie called from the house, holding his mobile phone towards Josa. 'Chief Superintendent Gilmour is asking for an update, if that's okay.'

Josa couldn't think of anything to say to Simon Maxwell. She offered a smile then headed back to the house.

Although Josa yearned for sleep, she made a point of sticking around for an hour so no one could accuse her of sloping off early. She tried to speak to all the officers and police staff individually. *Appreciate you dropping everything … You look like you could do with a coffee … Remind me what a life is again …*

'Thanks for coming at short notice,' she said to the two constables standing sentry at the gate.

They both replied with curt nods and she recalled they were friends of Don Walters. 'Thanks for coming at short notice?' she heard one snigger to the other. 'It's not a bloody dinner party.'

It was gone 2 a.m. when she finally left, taking an unmarked Astra that Simon Maxwell thoughtfully requested for her from the station pool. Josa stumbled into the hallway of her flat about an hour later, pushing off her coat as she walked into her front room where she paused in the doorway.

Preya was asleep on the sofa. She even snored elegantly, Josa thought. Like a cat, muzzily purring. On the coffee table in front of her sister, Josa saw an empty bottle of Pinot and a pile of photographs. She gave them a glance. Preya with her ex. Some holiday shots, but mostly typical snaps. All smiles and hugs and meals out with friends. The best part of a relationship always the most photogenic.

She thought about Blake, her tired mind imagining photos where she and he grinned and laughed, had their arms around each other, kissed for the camera. *Lord! What was she thinking?* Josa felt herself blush. *Time for bed!* she realised. And this realisation sparked another imagining, making her blush even deeper.

Daniel Blake finally reached his home. Wearily closed the front door.

'Dad!'

He turned around and saw the girl with jet black hair who had confronted Josa over her car the previous evening. He smiled. 'Holly Belle.'

'You're going back, aren't you?'

'I've got to.'

She ran to him and he hugged his daughter.

'I'm glad,' she was telling him. 'It's why I love you. Just be careful. Promise me you'll be careful.'

He hugged her a little tighter, the reassuring squeeze the only answer he could give her.

Three hundred miles away, Jack Dempsey stood on the shingle beach behind his cottage in Cornwall. The stars above him looked as bright as diamonds under lights. He had just slipped his mobile phone into his pocket and was throwing stones into the roaring ocean, watching them skim across its black, choppy waters. Dempsey heard footsteps scrunch towards him but didn't look round. He knew it was his loyal friend, seventy-year-old John

Mason, checking he was okay.

'That was Danny? On the phone?'

Dempsey didn't answer. Threw another stone.

'He's going back, isn't he? Helping out with this serial killer case, and you're going to help him.'

'He was never going to walk away after what he saw in the Shard. *I knew that.* But I still …' He looked at his old comrade-in-arms. 'What would you do?'

'Throw as many stones as you want, Jack.' Mason stood at his friend's side and gazed across the ocean. 'You'll never stop it.'

And finally, with Holly Belle tucked up in bed, Daniel Blake stood in the turret room of his sprawling, falling-down house. To his left he could see Guildford, dominated by the cathedral, high on Stag Hill. To his right, the indistinct sprawl of London. Every way he turned, unfinished business.

Josa paused before closing her bedroom curtains, looking across the ruffled blanket of lights and dark shapes that was London at 3.30 a.m. She recalled how certain she'd been that Taylor was the murderer, but she'd been proved horribly wrong and the killer was still out there. She promised herself that the arrogance and her desire to be right – the twin drives that had led to her channelling everything into the belief that the doctor was their man – would never happen again. She took consolation in the fact that the corpse they'd found tonight was probably already dead when she'd been handed the investigation. She had made her one big slip and had got away with it. She would give her quarry no more chances.

The man she and Blake had sworn to hunt down recalled reading an interview with Hitchcock where the director had discussed morphic resonance – the idea of something shared without palpable contact or physical communication. Of course, he hadn't used the phrase, which had only been coined after his death. But ahead of the game, as always, he had identified the phenomenon. The man responsible for the Hitchcock murders may have been amused to know that he and Josa were at that moment sharing the same feelings: a swell of confidence and renewed optimism.

He sat in the room where he had smashed open Jill Kennedy's skull, studying the canvas of Alfred Hitchcock. The Master was being implacable tonight, not moving a muscle. That was fine. It was his right. He couldn't expect hearty encouragement all the time. After all, his magnum opus remained a work in progress.

But so far it had gone better than he could have reasonably anticipated. The tricks he'd picked up from Hitchcock, such as precise, careful planning and letting someone else direct when a scene was perilous to shoot – he thought of that idiot, Taylor – had stood him in good stead. Perhaps this murder lark was easier than people made out. Or perhaps he really was the genius he'd always suspected. Yeah, that was it! He'd had ups and downs, of course. The confrontation at the Shard, that Jilani women interfering and Blake crashing back into his life like an old actor hanging round the set of a movie he'd not been cast in. And the voices. Sometimes they helped and he found them strangely comforting, but he couldn't always like them. Sometimes they could be ... He shuddered. But with his new-found confidence he could focus on the tasks in hand. Blank them out. No more voices, then, at least for a while. *Good.* He nodded at the canvas, happy with the decision.

And he felt certain Hitch would be amazed and delighted when he grasped the full scale of his ambition. Jill Kennedy, Elaine Hargreaves and the earlier ones had been good fun and, judging by the press coverage, everyone was enjoying them. But in the same way that Hitchcock had moved from breezy crowd-pleasers to dark, psychological thrillers, he was going to up his game considerably. And then those printed hands would slowly move and applaud him! The head would bow and the eye would wink!

And to hell with just killing one specific type of victim one particular day of the week! Because now he was going to get *Rope*, going to get *Marnie*, going to get *Psycho*! He could feel his heart thumping with excitement and pride. The first few had been first-rate entertainment but now, now he was going to get serious.

# CHAPTER 45

The next morning, Josa rose early. Somehow she sensed the investigation had moved on, and despite the discovery of the corpse of Jill Kennedy, her sense of optimism from last night lingered and she felt in bizarrely high spirits.

She bobbed her head around Preya's bedroom door. She appeared to be sleeping. Josa quietly crossed the room and gently tugged the duvet over her sister's shoulders. Kissed her forehead. 'Sleep tight.' Preya gave a tiny mew and Josa left her to her dreams. She was eager to get to the ESB, but before she left her flat she had one more job to do. She still had a pile of documentation on Daniel Blake, left over from the time her curiosity had been piqued about his work with the police. She dug out a box file from one of the tea chests in the spare bedroom. It contained something she wished she'd checked out sooner. A tape.

Back in the front room, she switched on the television. Preya was a heavy sleeper at the best of times, and at this early hour Josa reckoned she could have played *Mama Mia!* at full blast without any fear of rousing her.

Josa looked at the yellowing label that ran along the spine of the VHS cassette. The words *Eyes Only: Class D* were clearly legible on a printed sticker and, next to this warning, a police case number was scrawled in biro. The numerical naming convention threw Josa for a second, then she twigged. It represented an old system, phased out years ago. But she recognised some sequences in the coded string of numbers and understood what kind of evidence the videotape held. Josa shuddered. It was, she realised, footage of an operation where someone had been killed.

She couldn't recall ever using the function before, but her

DVD recorder could also play VHS. Josa stood and walked to the machine, slipped the tape out of its box and, before putting it into her player, glanced at the label on the front of the cassette. The same handwriting as the code along the spine, but this time, just two words:

### Guildford Cathedral

Josa was intrigued, but knew that, strictly speaking, by even watching a recording of a Class D incident that was nothing to do with her, she was breaking protocol, a dangerous move in her current, vulnerable position. She clicked her tongue against the roof of her mouth three times. By the third click she was pressing the cassette into the player.

*Click.* A soft mechanical whir. Josa didn't hesitate. Pressed *play* and saw, on the TV screen, several fast-moving blurs. Grey light. The officer operating the camera is running. The movement slows and the picture sharpens. The blurs become people. Police officers in body armour. Guns. Faces lost in shadows.

Josa realised the filming had begun midway through the operation. They were in the nave near the main door of a church. Guildford Cathedral, the tape label had read. The building was vast. Wider than a football pitch, with eighty-foot arches flanking two rows of wooden pews. The stonework looked sinister in the gloom, all angles and dark detail. Josa hit the volume button, immediately regretting it because the shouts – the men trying to sound assertive but coming across as terrified – brought back too many memories of ops she'd been involved in.

'Go, go, go!'

More running, and just as the transept judders into view, the clarity deteriorates. A further series of shouts doesn't completely drown out the cameraman's heavy breathing.

'Where are they?'

'Top of the tower! Both of them and the kid.'

'Up there!' One of the blurs points to a door to the right of the altar. 'All up there!'

'Wait a minute!'

A younger voice with a Newcastle accent asks, 'What's going on?'

Clarity again. About half a dozen officers around a wooden, Norman-style door that looks like something out of a Robin Hood movie.

'Thom Diaz has shot an officer. Then he snatched his own child. He's up there now. Still armed.' Josa knew this voice, but the sound quality was poor and before she could identify the speaker the younger man was speaking again –

'Is he gonna jump? I mean, with his kid?'

'Well, he's not sightseeing up there, is he?'

'Thank God he tracked him down then.' A pause. Then the Lancashire accent added, 'I mean, thank God he figured out where Diaz was.'

'He wasn't going to tell us. *I* had him followed. And he's up there now with Diaz and the boy like he's bloody Don Quixote. He should have left this to the police.'

'If he *had* left it to us, Thom Diaz and the kid would be dead by now. Sir.'

'Now just you see here –'

A new voice interrupts. 'Sir!' It carries a deep-timbred authority and the cameraman recognises this, finding the man and zooming in on him. 'Alpha two wants to know if he should take the shot.'

Josa leant forward.

'Sir! Alpha two wants to know –'

'I heard you!'

The camera pulls back and she sees whom the officer is talking to. He's as thin as a witch and wears a pristine uniform. Neat hair, stupid moustache like he thinks he's Clarke Gable. Josa's head jerked back in surprise. It was Kim Gilmour.

'We might only get one shot, sir, but the two guys on the top of that tower are very close and the angle we've got –'

Before Gilmour can reply the Newcastle accent blurts out, 'You can't order the shot, sir, if it's that close. You might hit our man and, knowing him, he's prob'ly persuading Diaz to –'

'He's not *our* man!'

'He's the best chance we've got!'

'Take the shot!' Gilmour shouts.

'But –'

'Take the shot! Now!'

The quality of the recording worsened, so although Josa couldn't see what was happening, she got a sense of time passing before the picture and sound returned.

'One shot fired!' The man with the deep voice now has his index finger in his ear. He looks up. 'Nobody hit.'

'Bloody hell!' Gilmour closes his eyes. 'What is it with police marksmen? Are you guys trained to only hit *innocent* members of the public?' He took a deep breath. 'All right! Positions! This is war!'

Even in the gloom and pixilation, Josa could see the other man roll his eyes. Three officers aim their weapons at the wooden doorway at the bottom of the stairs. 'We go up there on my command!' Gilmour shouts. 'On three! One ... two ... *three!*'

'Bollocks!' booms an echoing voice. A voice Josa knew immediately. American. Jack Dempsey. 'Any man fires or goes up those stairs and I'll have their balls for cufflinks!'

Gilmour looks like a child whose prize balloon has just burst unexpectedly 'What are you doing here?'

Dempsey doesn't answer. He crashes into frame, gesturing towards the doorway. 'They're up there?'

Gilmour steps forward. 'Dempsey! You have no jurisdiction here or anywhere else!' He's hissing with rage. 'May I respectfully remind you, you have left the service and therefore –'

'May I respectfully remind you to fuck off!' He was standing eyeball to eyeball with Gilmour. 'Who ordered that shot to be fired?' he demanded. 'That could have cost him his life. And he's a friend of mine.'

Josa noted that none of the officers intervened to assist Gilmour. Rather they had gravitated to the big man's side. 'If anyone dies here tonight ...' Dempsey moves closer into Gilmour's face. 'Who ordered that shot?'

Josa leant forward.

The tape went blank.

She sat through a few moments of interference but when the blizzard cleared, she was returned to the door by the side of the altar where Gilmour was declaring, 'We go up there on my command!' by which Josa discerned he meant, *You go up there on my command.* 'All guns blazing!'

Josa had seen a fair few recordings of police operations but what happened next surprised even her.

# CHAPTER 46

Dempsey bulldozes forward. 'Why, you lousy little bastard!' He bends back his arm and throws a punch at Gilmour who takes a quick, stumbling step in retreat.

Josa let out a yelp of amusement and then slapped her palm over her mouth. She shouldn't really be laughing at an assault on her boss.

*Still …*

One of the other officers catches Dempsey's arm. 'Easy, JD!' There's no reprimand in the voice. Across the years, Josa can see how much Big Jack was loved by the men around him. Gilmour looks shell-shocked. *How must that feel to him?* she wondered.

There's a tense moment of silence, broken by a cry that's raw with despair. 'Where's my boy?' A series of clicks that Josa recognised as high heels on a hard surface.

'Get her back!' Gilmour yells.

She comes into shot. A pale, well-groomed woman. Slight, but striking and exquisite in a way that's normally reserved for precious objects. Josa murmured her name, 'Mara Diaz …' Even before the case she'd known about her, a prima ballerina. *The Pride of Sadler's Wells*. It had struck Josa then, and even more forcibly now, how ugly the intrusion of the 'Thom Diaz incident' must have been for a woman used to a life couched in beauty. One of the younger officers steps in her way. Mara moves back, away from him, although even this tiny movement is like a step from *Swan Lake*, Mara skipping away from dark forces. Her presence is incongruous and awful. 'Is … Jamie … dead?'

'We don't know, Mara,' Dempsey tells her. 'But it's not good.' He puts his palm to her cheek. Josa reflected that Dempsey could do things like that quite naturally. 'I'm going up there. *Alone.*' A darting glance at Gilmour. 'I'll see what I can do, darling.'

'I'm in charge here!' Gilmour snarls. 'And we do –'

'Shhhh!' Dempsey gestures for him to shut up. In the quiet – and Josa strained to hear it, too – a series of slow footsteps is audible. The sound comes from the steps behind the door. Suddenly a dozen firearms are pointing in that one direction. Mara Diaz tries to scream but her throat's too dry.

'Get her back, lads!'

A couple of officers comply with Dempsey's instruction and she's pulled away from the scene.

Gilmour is staring at the door as if he can see the footsteps through the wood and he begins to retreat. Dempsey moves forward. 'Easy lads ...' Raises a hand to push open the door. One last remark to the armed officers: 'Nobody shoot. This is a new suit.' He throws them a wink but Josa can see his face is deadly serious as he turns and puts his fingertips to the door.

'Get back, JD!' someone calls softly, but he ignores the command.

'Are you okay, son?' He's peering into the shadows. 'Guys! Jamie! Are you there?'

And from off-screen, Mara's frenzied plea: 'Is my boy alive?'

A solitary figure steps into the doorway, hidden by the shadows of the stairwell. 'I've got him,' he says. The click of rifles being cocked is in itself a warning, but the man ignores them and steps forward into the light.

It's Daniel Blake. A little younger. But the same immoveable object.

'Jamie's fine, Mara,' he says.

He's holding Jamie Diaz; the boy's legs are wrapped around him and Blake carries the child like a mother, taking the lad's weight on his hips. Jamie's head rests on his shoulder. He opens his eyes briefly, murmurs something then apparently goes back to sleep.

'Hold your fire!' Dempsey shouts.

Gingerly, as if trying not to wake the lad, Blake is handing

Jamie to his mum and now Josa sees – he's not asleep, he's terrified. Eyes tight shut and clinging tight to the man who saved him. 'He's a good boy,' Blake says softly. Jamie senses his mother is near. Relaxes his grip and allows himself to be transferred to her.

Mara is weeping, trying to kiss her son and thank his saviour at the same time. Unable to do both she buries her face in Jamie's hair.

Dempsey embraces Blake, and out of the shadows Josa saw he looked pale and gaunt. A few whispered words between the two men that Josa couldn't catch. More officers join the scene. Josa didn't recognise faces but from their paunches and pristine overcoats she figured they're high rankers.

Gilmour moves into shot. 'Now see here! I want some answers and –'

Dempsey and Blake step apart and the former snaps, 'Will you shut the fuck up?'

The high-rankers are closing in. A thousand questions are immediately fired at the tall, gaunt figure who ignores them all. Dempsey is slapping the backs of a few of the younger officers. 'You did well, lads …' Each of them grows a couple of inches with Big Jack's praise.

And the man who saved young Jamie Diaz brushes past everyone and walks from the cluster without a word. He only pauses as he passes the altar, throwing the huge cross on the limestone apse a look of fury and contempt.

Mara Diaz finally manages to speak. 'Thank you!' she calls across to him.

Blake turns, looks towards her and suddenly there's complete silence in the cathedral.

He holds up his right palm and nods.

Then he turns and walks away.

>>Rewind<< >>Pause<<

Josa froze the face of the tired, angry man, holding the moment he looked at the crucifixion.

She jumped as her phone beeped. Put her palm over her heart. 'Jesus!'

It was a text message from Stevie. They had the number the killer's phone had called from the house in Shamley Green. He gave it to Josa, but said that he had not yet tried calling it. *Something to discuss this morning?*

Josa rattled off a reply, fatigue making her put her standard three crosses – xxx – at the end of the text, as she normally only did with friends. Then she clicked on the number Stevie had sent her and her phone offered the option of calling it. She knew she should wait until later, aware that protocol demanded she make contact in the office with the tech boys there to get a fix, but she just wanted to –

Josa pressed 'call'. After a couple of seconds she could hear the ringtone. *Who had the killer been phoning?* If he or she picked up, what the hell would she say? And why on earth would the killer call this number?

The ringtone continued and Josa's mouth went dry. It was going to go to voicemail. She wouldn't have to say a thing and she could try again at the ESB under the proper –

The ringtone ended mid bar. Someone had picked up.

'*Hello?*'

Josa's mouth dropped open.

'*Hello? Who's there?*'

It was a voice she knew. She looked at the paused picture on her television set. The voice of the man she was staring at, across half a decade of legend and folklore.

'*Hello,*' said Daniel Blake for the third and final time.

Josa hung up

CHAPTER 47

As always, when Daniel Blake visited Guildford Cathedral, he was greeted by angels. The arched doors that led into the building's vestibule were about ten feet tall, each divided into four panes. Angels were engraved into the glass, meaning each figure stretched the considerable height of the doors. But these were not traditional angels. These were thin, strangely sensuous-looking creatures, more siren than seraph. Blake pushed open the centre door and walked into the cathedral. He paused by the last row of pews, looking down the nave, then marched the fifty-six paces that took him to the foot of the chancel steps.

'Daniel! Good to see you!'

Blake turned to see a young clergyman approach him. 'Father Morris!' The two men shook hands. 'How are you?'

'Fine, fine!' Jim Morris was in his late twenties, a round-faced man who wore glasses and an open, genial expression. 'Were you hoping to go …?' He gestured upwards.

Blake knew Morris was asking if he wanted to visit the top of the Cathedral Tower. For the past five years Blake had been visiting this huge, quiet place. Looking for answers. He would have been scornful of such romanticism in others, but by understanding the building he hoped to better understand what had happened here. 'No. Not today. But thanks.'

Morris regarded him for a moment. 'Let's walk,' he said, and as they drifted from the transept to the north aisle, he asked, 'What's on your mind?'

They paused. 'Nothing.' Blake looked down. Chiselled into the Italian marble flooring were the words, *This bay is the gift of Sir Edward Lewis and the Decca Record Co.*

'Do you ever question your faith?' Blake said at last.

'Ah … It's one of those days, is it?'

'I mean, you must do.'

'Daniel. I've seen you visit this place hundreds of times. I think you know every inch of it. Better than any man I know. But in all these years, I've never seen you pray. Not once.'

A long pause. Morris didn't rush him but eventually asked. 'Do you even believe? Are you an atheist? An agnostic?'

Blake paused. Looked at him. Opened his mouth to speak but someone replied.

'They don't have a word for what he is, Father.'

Blake turned and smiled when he saw Jack Dempsey striding towards them. 'Come here!' roared the American.

The two men embraced and Dempsey ruffled Blake's hair. 'How you doing? How ya been, Danny Boy? Keeping sharp?' He feigned a boxer's stance and delivered a few soft punches to Blake's torso. 'You look like hell! Even I could take you!'

'Yeah, good to see you, too!' He addressed Morris. 'This is my dad, Jack Dempsey.' And as they shook hands, 'This is Father Jim Morris.'

'Good to meet you, Father. I can see what you're thinking. This fine figure of a man is much too young to be his father. Well, he calls me Dad but it's more a term of affection, you know?'

Blake put his hand on Dempsey's shoulder. 'I owe this man a lot. I think of him like he's my own father, although if you knew my father you wouldn't think that was much of a compliment.'

'Now, Danny …' Dempsey murmured.

'You're from the States, Mr Dempsey?'

'I am, Father. And you're going to think me one of those typically brash Yanks because I've only just met you and now here I am, having to break up your conversation. Do you mind?'

Morris clearly did mind but tried to hide his chagrin. 'No, of course not.'

Dempsey threw a glance at Blake. 'It's important, Danny.'

'Yes. Yes, I know.'

Morris shook Blake's hand. 'We'll continue our conversation

sometime soon, I hope, Danny?'

'Of course.'

They exchanged farewells and Blake and Dempsey hurried from the cathedral.

The cleric stood alone. 'Pity,' he muttered to himself. 'I had hoped to raise the question of … ah, well …'

Daniel Blake and Jack Dempsey walked around the exterior of the cathedral.

'How's John?'

'He's doing good,' Dempsey replied.

They caught up on each other's news as they sauntered around the building's north elevation, all red brick and lancet windows.

At the eastern end of the cathedral, about ten steps away from the chancel wall, a wooden cross stretched over fifty feet into the sky. Made of teak timbers from the battleship HMS *Ganges*, the icon was erected in 1933, predating the foundation stone by three years and originally raised on Stag Hill to mark the site of the planned cathedral.

Blake and Dempsey paused by the Ganges Cross, aware that they now needed to address the issues which had brought them together again.

'How you doing?' The same words he'd used minutes earlier, but with a sense of gravitas.

'I've got to do this.' A pause. 'Are you with me?'

Dempsey smiled. 'In sunshine or in shadow.'

Blake grinned. 'I wasn't just saying it when I said I owe you a lot.' He hesitated. 'I don't know if you approve or not but –'

'I approve! Danny, I approve. I think you can do this thing. Period. But you know, I worry. Always I worry about you.'

'I know, I know …' Blake was avoiding the older man's eyes, choosing to gaze across to the Cathedral Gardens, a few yards east of the cross. 'I didn't want to get involved but …' He shook his head. 'And you know, she's good. This Josa Jilani. She's *going* to be brilliant but already she's something else …'

'Danny …' Dempsey's voice was low, earnest, caring. 'Are you sure ...' He put his hand on his friend's upper arm, 'Are you sure you weren't just turned on by the handcuffs?' His face broke into a grin and he gave a loud, throaty burst of laughter.

'Fucker,' said Blake, returning the smile as he realised they must have spoken on the phone earlier. 'Come on. Let's sit down and talk.'

They followed the path leading to the cathedral's 'Seeds of Hope' children's garden.

'So how are you looking to pitch and play this thing?' Dempsey asked. 'And how can I help?'

The Cathedral Gardens are made up of four separate gardens, each symbolising a season of the year and designed to help kids overcome the loss of a loved one. Blake and Dempsey drifted into the Winter Garden, also known as the Garden of Thought. It's the bleakest of the four, and Blake recalled reading it was deliberately sparse, reflecting the state of mind the bereaved child would experience immediately following their loss. But plaques around the lawns reminded the kids that unseen within the garden's seedpods, things were happening. A line on one read, 'Life goes on.'

The two men were alone in the gardens.

*Life goes on,* Blake thought. *And so does the threat to it ...*

They sat on a wooden bench. 'I think we can catch the killer through one of two ways. The first possibility is the Alfred Hitchcock connection. I'm going to follow that one up.'

'Josa's not going to like that.'

'Josa doesn't know that.'

'Natch,' Dempsey reflected. 'But you're going to stick with her?'

'Yeah. I guess for the first day we'll do the normal stuff. Tick the right boxes. Then we'll strike.'

'Daniel ...' Jack Dempsey searched the face of the man he'd known for most of his life and discovered something that made his heart miss a beat. 'You think you already know ...' He lowered his voice. 'You think you know who the killer is, don't you?'

# CHAPTER 48

Karen Sherwood studied the image of Daniel Blake. He was sitting next to Josa Jilani, outside the house where Jill Kennedy's body had been found.

'Christ, Danny. You look as bad as I feel.'

She zoomed in and shook her head at the enlarged picture of Blake on her computer screen. It was a screen-grab taken from video footage, and although in theory it should have been as distinct as a still shot, she always found grabs a little blurry even when high-res. This image was still too dark, but she could lighten it. Yeah, it would have to do.

She drained her glass of orange juice and walked through to her kitchen for a refill. She lived alone in a one-bed flat in Camberwell, south London. She didn't particularly like the place but was hardly ever there. After finally arriving home at about four in the morning, that one glass of Rioja had somehow turned into the whole bottle and a couple of chasers. What the hell? This should have been her week off, so she was allowed a drink, wasn't she? But she needed to get back into her editor's good books. She'd wasted a lot of time and effort chasing a story about a powerful criminal ring known as the Council of Dead, only to be told on the highest authority that it was just a myth old coppers told rookies to scare them. So, she needed a good story to make up for that, and now she had one. Her editor would love her for this scoop! Still, it was a hell of a hangover. A few years ago it wouldn't have been a problem, but since she'd turned thirty-four …

Whatever. She'd deserved a celebratory tipple for this one. Daniel Blake helping the police again after all these years … And not just any old police. Liz Canterville's wunderkind! Josa Jilani!

On a serial killer case! Unless the Pope decided to come out, this was going to be front-page news.

Back at her desk, armed with a carton of OJ, she took the memory card from her camera and slipped it into a reader connected to her PC. She accessed the captured content and selected the longest video. The picture was fairly static. Just Blake and Josa talking. Mostly Blake. Telling her something. But no audio. What was he telling her?

She closed the video and began converting it to a wav file. Opened MSN and contacted a friend.

>>> *You there, hon?*
<<<*Karen!!!!*
>>>*How's it going???*
<<<*What do you want?*
>>>?
<<< *Well???*
>>>*Don't be so cynical!!! Isn't a girl allowed to contact the most handsome lip-reader she knows without him thinking she needs a favour?*

Blake wasn't surprised by his old friend's intuition. His words, *You think you know who the killer is, don't you?* were delivered more as a statement than a question.

Blake asked, 'Is it that obvious?'

'No, but I'm that good. You gonna share?'

'Not before I'm more certain. I'm not trying to be mysterious, but I know me. If I start talking about it, I'll start trying to convince you, which will mean I'll get more attached to the idea, even though right now ...' A shrug. 'I'm not a hundred per cent.'

'But you're getting there?'

'We'll see.'

'There's something else,' Dempsey said, and Blake raised his eyebrows. 'If the papers hear you're back on the job, one of those tabloid jokers might dig up a story about what happened in ...' He shot a glance at the cathedral. 'I think you'd better warn Mara that she could –'

'Already done.' Blake took a deep breath. 'Called her earlier this morning.'

'She must have loved getting woken up by you on the end of a phone.'

'It wasn't a problem. She's on holiday in New Zealand. We had a video-phone conversation as she walked around Auckland Bay. She even showed me some of the sights. It made me wish ...'

'That you could be anywhere but here.'

'Something like that.'

'Okay, okay,' said Dempsey, seeing the need to pick up the pace. 'So where do I come in? You said we were going to catch this bastard one of two ways. What's the other way?'

'The other way is exactly where you come in,' Blake replied. He fell silent for a moment, as if hesitant about bringing Dempsey into the hunt. Blake looked across the garden at a bronze, life-sized sculpture of two children playing. One of the statues depicted a girl blowing dandelion seeds into the air. 'I've not shared this with Josa yet,' he revealed, 'but I don't think Becka Hoyle was our boy's first victim.'

'I'm all ears. Spill.'

'There's something so complete about her death. Like it's the work of someone who's murdered before. It's so elaborate. Think about it. If we'd seen the details of that one case in isolation we'd have assumed it was an escalation.'

'That's true,' noted Dempsey, nodding. They were both aware that often, when serial killers were hauled in, it became clear that the murders police assumed were the perpetrator's first homicides were actually preceded by assaults, and in some cases killings, that had not been linked to the murder sequence under investigation. In other words, there was a good chance that the person police thought was the first victim was in fact victim number two or three. 'Yeah. Makes sense, Danny. Any idea who the woman is? His first victim?'

Blake fired up his laptop. The screen showed five photos in a row: Becka Hoyle, Ebba Lovgren, Sarah Robinson, Elaine Hargreaves and Jill Kennedy. To the left of Becka's image was a box the same size as the portraits but empty, except for a white question mark.

'She was blonde. She was beautiful. She was young. If her body has been found it wasn't mutilated, but you know, I've a feeling it hasn't been discovered yet. I think our man knew this woman. He didn't know Becka or Jill or the others. At least he didn't know them well. Any relationship with the last five victims was created by the killer to facilitate their murder. But his relationship with the first victim was the *reason* for her murder. When he slaughtered her, he was just learning. Whether he knew it or not, that first murder was the one …'

'The one,' Dempsey chimed in, 'where if he was going to make a mistake, he'd make it.'

'Exactly.' Moving from right to left, Blake clicked on the photographs of Jill Kennedy through to Becka Hoyle. After each double-click a Word document appeared listing pages of information about the selected victim. He clicked back to the home screen and let the cursor linger over the question mark. 'Out of all of them, it's her I feel most sorry for. I know that's stupid and probably even wrong. But I do.'

'I'll find her,' Dempsey told him gently.

'Thanks.'

'And what are we going to call her?'

Blake clicked on the question mark to the left of Becka's photograph. The screen switched to a Word document, blank aside from two words:

*Victim Zero.*

Blake looked at his old friend. 'Find Victim Zero,' he told him, 'and we find the killer.'

The Palace of Westminster, better known as the Houses of Parliament, never failed to impress Josa, especially on sundrenched mornings like today when the natural light gave its Clipsham stone exterior a dazzling, honey-coloured gleam.

She'd emerged from Westminster tube station, crossed Bridge Street and headed towards the St Stephen's entrance that she remembered from a school trip, years earlier. Josa followed the clusters of people queuing around the small strip of lawn known as Cromwell Green, and as she approached the building was stopped by a small, elderly man wearing a dark three-piece suit and circular, tortoise shell glasses. He had white, wispy hair that the light breeze toyed with to lend him an air of eccentricity.

'Miss Jilani?' He came too close to her, brazenly inspecting her face as if studying an Underground map. 'Miss Josa Jilani?'

'It's DCI Jilani.'

He raised his glasses and seemed to see her for the first time. 'Ah, quite so!' A big, unexpectedly friendly smile. 'Apologies! I'm flooded with titles all day long! Memory like a sieve, and so I cling to *mister, miss* and *missus* like driftwood in a tempest. I'm so sorry.'

'It's no problem.'

'I'm Forbes. One of the minister's men.'

They shook hands.

'Which minister?'

He hooked a finger and beckoned her. 'Follow me! Follow me!'

Forbes walked with a slight stoop and Josa never caught him looking up, as if he knew his way around by some internal radar and ground recognition. He moved at a startling pace, guiding her along a walkway which followed the perimeter of the building. 'The

Members' entrance!' he called over his shoulder as they reached a doorway manned by four armed officers. Forbes waved their sub-machine guns to one side.

'I'm with him,' said Josa, following in the old man's slipstream.

He led her through a maze of progressively shabbier passageways until she realised she'd not seen anyone else for a couple of minutes. If the grand hallways and offices she'd seen on the news were intended to look good and reflect well on the country's masters, it felt like Forbes was leading her into the servants' quarters. 'Three miles of corridors, over a thousand rooms, one hundred staircases and, don't laugh, but quite a few secret doorways.' He swiped a plastic card along the side of a fire alarm trigger and a concealed door slid open. 'It looks theatrical but it's simply cheap security. It's mainly to keep out the politicians.' His eyes twinkled. 'Can't let them get anywhere near the real power.' He ushered her through and along another passage. Off-white wallpaper and worn, beige carpet. The shiny digital keypad at the far end seemed out of place. Forbes tapped in several numbers, pushed open the door it had unlocked and led Josa into an outside environment – a broad, cloistered passage that framed a neat square lawn. Above her, Josa could see an elaborate arched roof, and to her left, thin stone pillars and flying buttresses.

The tiny garden felt like an incongruous oasis. There was even a small stone fountain in the middle of it. 'Good luck,' said Forbes, disappearing into the passageway.

'Thank you!'

The door clicked shut behind him.

'Good morning!' Kim Gilmour, in full uniform as always, stood by the fountain.

'Morning, sir.'

'I've just been having a pow-wow with some of the most powerful men in Europe. And quite possibly the most ruthless. We must have a care.'

Josa stepped onto the lawn. The grass felt springy beneath her feet.

'They're not happy with the way we're running this

investigation. They fear these murders are becoming myth. The stuff of urban legend. The type of nightmare that unpicks and unravels, putting everything under threat. Do you understand me?'

'I don't need anyone to tell me how important it is to catch this man.'

He nodded. 'I'll be honest with you, I was never happy about your appointment. It's possibly quite wrong of me to say it, but I have an old-fashioned notion that people deserve promotion because of their merit. Not the colour of their skin.'

'I agree, sir. A copper's colour or creed shouldn't propel them forward. But it shouldn't hold them back, either.'

'Point taken.'

He was weary, thought Josa, unwilling or just too tired to engage.

'I read your report,' he continued. 'You brought in the elemental force that is Daniel Blake. Good God!' A weary shake of the head. 'By doing that you're openly acknowledging you need help. That we need help! And by extension you're admitting you can't cut it on your own. And if you can't cut it ...The honourable thing to do is step down.'

'You want me to resign?'

'No! I just want us to catch this ... the bastard who's carving up innocent women as if he has a right to ...' He brought his fist down onto the slate that edged the top of the fountain. 'What's all this guff about Alfred Hitchcock?'

'Hitchcock was a British director who –'

'Yes, I know who he was! That stabbing in the shower. An unfortunate victim getting gouged to death by ravens. I *have* seen some of his films.'

'Well, all the murders copy killings that have featured in the movies of Alfred Hitchcock, sir.'

'Hell's teeth, girl! Stabbings! This Kennedy woman bludgeoned to death! As modus operandi they're hardly unique in the annals of crime! If we start suggesting that every teenager who stabs someone is copying an old film ... It's absurd. No. It's more than that. It's dangerous. For our reputation, for ...' He shook his head and looked over her, around the garden. 'I told my mother I'd work here one day. I mean, when I was a little boy I told her.' He walked to the edge of the garden. Sat on a low, stone bench. 'It may surprise you to learn I come from working-class stock. Not much money in the coffers when I was a lad. When my mother brought me to London for the day, we used to walk. All day long. Along the Thames, through the great parks. The Palace of Westminster was always my favourite, though. I pointed at it, pointed at it from the South Bank and told my old mum I'd work here one day. I didn't think ...' Another lingering look across the garden. A deep breath. He returned his gaze to Josa. 'One of *his* theories, isn't it?'

'Sir?

'This Hitchcock idea. One of Blake's theories.'

'Yes, sir.'

'Thought so. It's all so Daniel Blake. Just the way he likes 'em.'

'But he's not saying that *every* stabbing is a copycat, sir, but the specific details in this sequence of murders does suggest –'

'He's charmed you, hasn't he? He always did. I saw through him, of course, but those not as perceptive as me ...'

'Like Liz Canterville?'

He narrowed his eyes. 'She can't protect you for ever.' He paused, as if regretting this last comment. He leant back slightly and continued. 'Liz is a fine woman. I respect her, despite her misguided loyalty to Blake. Even this caper of hers about accelerated promotion for ...' He waved a hand in Josa's direction. 'Even that is well-meant.'

'Can't protect me for ever. Who from?'

Karen Sherwood had showered, dressed and taken a couple of Nurofen but her headache wouldn't budge. She checked her email again. Nothing.

'Oh, come on!'

She sat at her desk. Googled *Daniel Blake,* searching for anything posted in the past twenty-four hours. Nothing. Good!

Checked her email again. At last!

She clicked open the message but was too excited to reply before she'd read the transcript he'd attached. She saved it to her desktop and opened it from there.

'Oh. My. God.' Karen began to smile as her eyes tore down the written dialogue.

'Whatever happens, let me give you a piece of advice. As a friend.' He stood up. 'Oh, don't smile, Josa, I mean this.'

She had crossed to the fountain. 'What, sir?'

'Don't get too close to Daniel Blake.'

'Why not?'

'He has his daughter, of course, and Jack Dempsey. But aside from them, have you ever stopped to consider why he is so alone?'

'No, sir.'

'This fiery messiah. Always so alone. Because he wouldn't mean to, but somehow, as sure as shadows, *somehow* he would take your breath away.'

'Isn't that what a lot of women want?'

*'He would take your breath away.'*

'You said Liz Canterville couldn't protect me. I asked who from.'

He ignored her again. 'DCI Jilani: not a word about this Hitchcock theory. To anyone. *And that is an order.* Can you imagine the media frenzy and public alarm it would cause if that got out? You've got Blake on board so I can't prevent his involvement, but you're his case officer. He messes up, as believe me, he will, and you take equal responsibility.'

'I accept that, sir.'

'We're on very dangerous ground. Both our careers are hanging by cat's whiskers and there's the small matter of having to catch this psychopath before he slaughters more women, which we know he will do very soon if we don't stop him. *If* we don't get it right.' Gilmour rubbed his eyes with the tips of his fingers. 'And right now, aside from Liz championing Daniel Blake, there's only one reason why we've not both been removed from this investigation.' He paused. 'Want to know what that is?'

There was a throbbing in Karen Sherwood's head, but this time it was pure excitement. It was all there. Blake's theories about the murders. The Hitchcock angle. The calling card. Why only blondes were being targeted and the significance of Tuesdays. 'Oh my God!'

This would be the kind of feature that would put her back on top.

'The fact,' Gilmour told Josa, 'that you've kept Blake's involvement and his ridiculous Hitchcock theory out of the press. If that leaks, we both go.'

## CHAPTER 50

Jack Dempsey paid for a standard ticket and made his way to the first class carriage, jumping on board the train moments before it departed. The announcement said they'd be in London in thirty-four minutes. That was long enough.

He took the table seat at the very top of the deserted carriage, pulled his laptop from his shoulder bag and fired it up. He sat with his back to the driver's cabin so if anybody did join him in first class they wouldn't be able to see what he was working on. As he logged on, he made a call.

'Mac! It's me! Yeah, I'm good, thanks! How you doing? That's great! Hey, buddy, I need a favour ... Of course it's legal! Are you crazy? Would I? Yeah ... Yeah ... Yeah ... They were isolated incidents!' A big laugh. 'Here's the thing. I need the details of all the missing persons you've got on your books from the last two years ... Just the females, so yeah. A walk in the park ... I don't know. How many? That many?' Dempsey gave a low whistle. Began typing away on the keyboard. 'I've got that Open Page app up and running. Can you start getting me their details across? That would be awesome!'

The train slowly pulled out of the station as Dempsey hung up and waited for his contact to establish the online connection. To his left, through a gap in the trees and the dull, grey houses, he could see Guildford Cathedral. As ever, the sight of the building took him back. The memory of that night haunted him with all the power and tenacity of an evil spirit. He had let Daniel Blake down and even now, that failure stung him. Left him sad, crippled, resentful of himself and his –

*No!*

*Must move on!*

Daniel had told him a million times that it was not his fault. How could it have been? But Dempsey knew that if he'd arrived just five minutes earlier it might have been different. Hell, who was he kidding? *Would* have been different.

A prompter appeared on his laptop screen, yanking him back to his present plight.

*Do you wish to accept image flow from source 97dqwehjg? Yes/No.*

He clicked on *Yes*.

For a moment nothing happened. He drummed his fingers on the table. And then a single photo appeared on the screen. A young woman. Messy, shoulder-length dark hair. Sallow complexion. A tiny thumbnail portrait of a missing person. He clicked on it and by doing so opened a file containing two pages of information about her. He checked hair colour. Brunette. Returned to the home screen and deleted the file.

A few seconds later another image appeared, followed almost immediately by a third. He looked at both images. Redhead and blonde. Clicked on blonde and read the details. She wasn't a natural blonde but he'd keep this file anyway. The killer may have *switched* to natural blondes but there was no guarantee that Victim Zero hadn't lightened her hair. He would have to create a folder to store all the files like this one as they came in: *possibles*.

He closed the file, returning the app to home screen. Except now he couldn't see a pixel of empty space. The entire screen was taken up by a chaos of thumbnail images, hundreds of faces, each one a missing person.

'Jesus!'

He tried to click on the file he'd just checked, but the blonde had become lost as more and more images flooded the screen. Hundreds. Thousands. An army of missing persons staring up at him, each one trying to catch his attention before she was obscured by a new recruit. He hit *escape* and tried to pause the programme, but nothing could stop them. Dempsey could only sit back and watch as the faces kept coming in a mad, incessant torrent.

# CHAPTER 51

'*Muslim Cop!*' He spoke with an exaggerated American accent. Pure Hollywood. '*She was the sexy cop whose face didn't fit! Given the break she deserved and tasked with catching a serial killer who was evil … personified. He was an aging, burnt out detective who –*'

'You're not aging!' Josa interrupted.

She was in the kitchen of her flat and Blake was sprawled across her sofa. He reverted to his normal accent although his voice rose several octaves. 'I wasn't talking about me! That's the bit about Gilmour! Jesus! I know I'm not aging! And I'm not burnt out, for that matter!' He shook his head. 'Unbelievable!'

'All right! All right!' she called through. What's the bit about you, then?'

'*He was the handsome genius sworn to –*'

'Handsome genius?' Josa cut in. 'So, it's not based on truth, then?' She walked into her front room, drying her hands on a tea towel.

'I thought you were making me a cup of tea.'

'Then you're a rubbish detective. Are you going to tell me what you've been doing today?'

'Oh, a bit of poking around here and there. By the way, I take it that was you ringing me last night and giving me the silent treatment?'

'The killer phoned your number. I had to check it.'

'He'll have watched the press conference. Seen Gilmour state that I wasn't part of the investigation. It was his way of telling us both that he knew I'm involved.'

'Yeah, I figured that out.'

'Any more leads from his phone?'

'*Nada.*'

'One: no one says '*nada*' any more. Two: so what have you been up to today?'

'One: I still do, so deal with it. And two: …' Josa sat on the seat by her small writing desk. 'Getting the team back together. They're already working hard, following up every lead we've got …'

'Except the one that will actually get us somewhere. The Hitchcock angle.'

'Gilmour doesn't want me even mentioning it at this point.'

'Oh, come on Josa, you've got –'

'Calm down, dear! Order or no order, I'll find a way to communicate the theory tomorrow. Drop hints, lead them to the conclusion without explicitly stating it.' She paused. 'You lose your temper a lot.'

He shrugged. 'I never find it. I just disguise the fact most of the time.'

She raised an eyebrow.

'Josa. I'm white. I'm English. I'm working class. Of course I'm angry.'

'What have you got to be angry about?'

'I could tell you …'

'But you'd have to kill me?'

'More likely myself.' Blake glanced at his watch. Stood up, suddenly flippant again. 'I'm offski! It's getting late. I'd better be making tracks back to the homestead.'

'You've only just got here.'

'Me, you.' He winked. 'Working the case tomorrow. Side by side.'

'I can't wait. Oh, yes. I can.' She smiled. 'Thanks.'

He stood up. 'Don't I get a kiss?'

'Are you serious?'

'Yes, I am. But I thought I'd couch it in humour in case you already had a boyfriend.'

'I need a bit of space right now.'

She secretly hoped he'd press the point but was surprised when he came back with, 'Is that code for you're gagging for it but can't be doing with walks in the park?'

'It's not code, Blake. Not everything is code.'

'Not very good with this. Social interaction. You know?'

'Right now, you and I have a serial killer to find.' She got to her feet and began pushing him out of the room. 'Let's just focus on that for the moment.'

'Is that a tentative *yes*?'

'It's a non-tentative *see you in the morning*.' She opened the door.

'And then we'll see?'

'I'll introduce you to my mother.'

She shoved him into the outside hallway and slammed the door. 'See you tomorrow morning!'

The letterbox flap was pushed open and Blake's mouth appeared behind the wire mesh. 'Look, I can see you're interested …'

*Alfred Hitchcock!* The name in her head, again and again.

She tried to close her mind and get some sleep but the name kept haunting her. *Hitchcock!* She heard a loud scream. Josa sat bolt upright. Tried to assemble her thoughts. It hadn't been Preya. Who else could be in the flat? The clock read 5.04 a.m. She was already out of bed, but paused in the doorway to the front room. Her sister had left the television on and she could see the screen, catching the tail end of a clip from an old movie.

*Hitchcock!*

Josa understood immediately and felt sick less than a second later.

' *…breaking news … serial killer … London … Hitchcock …*'

Josa froze for an instant, then moved forward, grabbed the remote control and turned the volume up. She could see a female correspondent outside New Scotland Yard. Her nick was miles across town but TV producers knew that the famous courtyard with its gently revolving sign always looked good on the telly.

'…in a remarkable turn of events it's emerged that police now think that this series of horrific killings is the work of someone who's copying murders from the films of Alfred Hitchcock. It's also emerged that all the victims were natural blondes and police believe this is not – *repeat, is not* – a coincidence. The director was known to favour blond actresses whom he often killed off in his films. It seems a deranged murderer is doing the same, but in real life.'

Josa went hot with worry. Who the hell had leaked the story?

Back in the studio a casually dressed presenter showed off his most concerned countenance. 'What I can't understand,' he said, 'is why the police didn't bother to warn us. If they knew that natural blondes are in danger, surely it's their duty to let the public know so the high-risk individuals can take proper precautions!' He tried on his baffled face. 'Do we have any sense of *why* the public weren't warned?'

Back to the reporter at New Scotland Yard, shaking her head. 'That's the mystery! There's been one murder every week for the past five weeks. Detective Chief Inspector Josa Jilani was brought in with something of a fanfare, you may remember, but she seems to be getting nowhere, and worse, she may have been behind the decision to keep the public in the dark about the threat they face. You know, people are worried, and rightly so. It turns out the police have information they could have passed to us to make us safer, but they haven't even bothered …'

Josa knew that this changed everything. She'd be even more closely scrutinised by the media, her peers and superiors. Every decision held to the light like a fifty-pound note. Pressure would increase tenfold; criticism one hundredfold. The media revealing that this serial killer case was a Hitchcock copycat was problem squared.

'… a ruthless serial killer is stalking the streets of London …' We were back to the journo outside New Scotland Yard. She was winding up her piece and Josa knew what was coming next. 'And an anxious public are demanding to know …' They switched to a photograph of Josa Jilani, giving her the full-screen treatment. 'Just what exactly are the police doing about it?'

## CHAPTER 52

Josa had been at her desk for two hours. Even before she'd arrived for work it had begun. A pack of press outside her flat, surrounding and hounding her as she started out for the tube station. Questions and accusations. She'd managed about ten paces and realised it wasn't going to work. She returned to her flat, booked a taxi and jumped into it ten minutes later. This was how it would be. Intrusion and scrutiny.

Josa ran her fingers through her hair, reread an email and hit *send*. Since six in the morning she'd been dealing with the administration of the case in light of the new revelation. Who could say what, how coppers on the investigation should react when questioned by the media. How to handle the crazies who would start to pour in, quietly confessing to the killings. And who had snitched to the fourth estate? Were any of the men on the case known to talk to the press over a whisky and wry smile?

She'd already sent emails to superiors, assuring them of what was being done, what had been achieved and discovered. Kim Gilmour had delivered the big surprise. She'd half-expected to find her marching orders waiting for her at the station, but instead he'd sent a vaguely intelligent email outlining how they would counter the avalanche of bad press.

At eight o'clock, Marc Stevenson knocked on her door.

'Come in! Stevie! How are –?'

He was holding a copy of the tabloid newspaper that had broken the story. 'Did you know about this when we had our progress meetings yesterday?'

'I'm so sorry. I'd wanted to tell you guys but I was under strict instructions not to –'

'You know,' Stevie interjected. 'No one ever said Don Walters was perfect. But at least you knew where you stood with him. At least you knew he was being straight with you … but you?' He tossed the newspaper onto Josa's desk, turned and walked away.

She had decided to give them time to chat and bitch and get their annoyance out of their systems. She certainly couldn't blame them, and a few weeks ago if she'd been a DS in their situation she'd have been muttering mutiny with the rest of them. Josa sighed. She switched on the television set in the corner of her office and began flicking through the channels. Her face was plastered all over the news programmes, usually with some earnest-looking front man demanding to know 'Why weren't the public warned?' as her portrait flashed up, suggesting the whole mess was entirely her fault. The daytime live shows were falling over themselves to cover the Hitchcock angle.

ITV1 had shanghaied some laid-back professor who was saying how Hitchcock's fascination with fear stemmed from an incident in his childhood when his father had sent him to the local police station with a note, explaining that he'd misbehaved. One of the coppers locked him in a cell and told him that this is what happened to naughty boys. Hitch had been released after a few minutes, but the trauma made a huge impact that went on to inform his later work.

Josa pressed the channel button again.

*'And in a change to our advertised film, we'll be showing Alfred Hitchcock's most famous thriller:* Psycho. *Watch out for that shower scene! Ouch!'*

ITV1+1. The Scottish presenter of a morning show was chatting to an alleged fashion expert.

At last! Surely they couldn't shoehorn Hitchcock into this item, unless –

*'Just to recap,'* the Scot was saying, *'We're not suggesting in any way that if you're blonde you should be panicking. Just that you might like to try one of these hats.'*

Straight-faced, she dutifully donned a ridiculous bonnet which the alleged fashion expert claimed was '*bang on trend and will conceal your blond hair*'.

'*Don't forget!*' the presenter concluded, '*We've been inundated with people contacting us about how they can hide their fair hair so do go to the website where there's plenty more about dyes, hats and even –*'

She flicked again.

'*– Alfred Hitchcock was a devout Catholic –*'

Again.

'*– he was more than a film director. He tapped into the very essence of fear and –*'

Again.

'*– on earth didn't the police make the link sooner –*'

Again.

'*– even got the wife into his stuff. My advice is start with the easy ones like* Torn Curtain *or* The 39 *–*'

Again.

'*– Alfred Hitchcock was a devout atheist –*'

She Googled the director's name as she surfed through the channels. As expected, the Net was in meltdown with theories and counter theories about the Hitchcock angle.

Josa realised she'd rolled through all the main channels and had strayed into sales territory. QVC and the like. Surely she'd be safe here. A man with improbably white teeth was holding up a sponge. 'Now, with these new sponges from Reduco, you can give yourself a really good body wash without having to take a shower!' He was joined by a woman with pleading eyes and too much Touche Éclat.

'That's great news, Larry,' she said. 'I'm sure none of us want to be taking showers any time soon with this crazy on the loose!' She made a stabbing motion with her hand and squeaked a few bars of Bernard Herrmann's score from *Psycho*.

'They're going fast!' Larry declared. 'Just place an order now to protect yourself and your family. Call the number on the bottom of the screen right away! It may just save your life!'

Josa pressed the channel button again and found she was back where she started with the laid-back professor. She raised the remote control to switch off the TV.

'If I was the police right now, there is one thing I'd be doing.'

Her thumb hovered over the off button.

'And what's that?'

The professor looked down the camera as if addressing Josa directly. 'Preparing the mortuary for another corpse.'

She pressed the button and the screen faded to black.

Her phone rang. 'Hello?'

'I'm guessing you're having a bad day.'

'You think? Wow. What I said about you being a rubbish detective, I take it all back. You're –'

'You've got to learn to enjoy it,' Blake interjected. 'Otherwise this job will devour you.'

'Thanks for that, Confucius.'

'I'm serious.'

'Yeah? Good for you.'

'Are you free?'

'Why wouldn't I be?'

'This is important.'

Josa glanced at her watch. 'What's the deal?'

'Buy me a coffee,' Blake said, 'and I'll catch you a killer.'

# CHAPTER 53

12:03. Josa met Blake in a Starbucks around the corner from Oxford Circus.

12:05. Josa felt the stresses of the day vanish for several marvellous moments as she sat laughing at him.

'He threw you in a cell?'

'Yes, he did. I'm delighted you find it funny. Really, that makes it bearable, you thinking –'

'Oh. Come on!' she interrupted. 'It's hilarious!'

'Well, I'm glad you think so!'

'What have you got a face on for? Gilmour let you go, didn't he?'

'Eventually!' Blake shrugged. 'He threatened to arrest me for leaking the Hitchcock angle to the press. He dug out some old non-disclosure agreement I signed back in the day and kept waving it around like he was Neville fucking Chamberlain.'

'He must really have it in for you.'

'Yeah.' He paused. 'He was delighted to see me looking like this. I didn't always look like the Piltdown Man and he seemed to think it indicated I'd fallen … That cheered him up.'

'You do look a bit rough. I mean have you ever considered a haircut? Decent shave? Wearing clothes that don't look they come from a landfill?'

Blake took a sip of espresso.

'I'm joking!' Josa said. 'Don't listen to Gilmour. He's an idiot.'

'Gilmour isn't a fool and he's not a bad man per se. I get where he's coming from. You know, at one point he said that I'd never worked on the everyday, grind-you-down stuff. The old ladies getting mugged, the burglaries on the estates, the joyriders. He called my cases *glamorous*.' Blake looked to his right, through the glass wall, across the world as it rushed by. 'He had a point.'

Josa remained tight-lipped, aware that Gilmour very possibly *did* have a point. The vast majority of police work was an exercise in mundanity, but from her research on Blake she knew that his cases tended to be dramatic and laced with the macabre. He kept his involvement out of the public eye as far as possible, but details of some of his investigations were inevitably seized on by the media. He had identified the killer in the notorious Winter's Cross incident and there was a legend floating around that he'd solved the Blackpool Ripper case. His one failure, by his standards, had also been broken by the press. A killer known as the Cuckoo had snatched babies and small children from their cots, leaving Victorian dolls in their place. Blake and DCI Dempsey, as he had been back then, were drafted in to help, but disastrously, they had –

Blake cleared his throat, returning Josa to the present. 'Gilmour might be a different man to me,' he mused, 'but at least he's always –'

'Jesus!' Josa interjected. 'I'm beginning to wish he'd kept you locked up, you morbid so and so.'

Blake grinned. 'Nah. He never intended to keep me. I didn't grass to the press, so funnily enough there's no evidence I did. It was just Gilmour showing me what he could do.'

'How *do* you think the press found out?'

'A journo called Karen Sherwood broke the story. If I was going to take a bet on it, I'd say she'd been following you for days and she was monitoring us from outside the house in Shamley Green.'

'Make sense.' Josa stirred her skinny latte. 'So what's the latest with you, then? Aside from chokey, that is.'

Blake outlined what Dempsey was up to, bringing her up to speed with his Victim Zero theory.

'Makes sense,' she admitted. 'But it'll take him a hell of a long time to wade through all those misspers.'

'He'll get there.'

'And what are we going to do in the meantime?'

From the back of his chair, Blake grabbed his navy blue coat. 'You know I said that to catch this guy you were going to have to learn all about Alfred Hitchcock?'

'Yes …'

'Well …' He slipped on the jacket. 'It's time for school.'

Capital College was just a short taxi ride from Oxford Circus, nestling in the stretch of Bloomsbury that joins Russell Square and the British Museum. Architecturally at least, it proved to be one of the grander constituents of London University. As Blake paid the cabbie, Josa cast her eyes over its buildings. They looked Victorian. Red brick and ivy. Lead-lined windows and expansive lawns in a part of London where property prices were calculated by the square inch.

'Probably make their money from overseas students,' Blake said, reading her thoughts as he joined her.

'And who's this guy we're seeing?'

'Professor Paul Salinger. We're a little early for our appointment, but hey. He teaches and lectures exclusively on Hitchcock. Supposed to be Europe's foremost authority on him and –'

'Did you just say Professor Paul Salinger?'

'I did.'

'Fuck! He's been trying to contact me for ages! I thought he was just another academic after an angle so I –'

Her phone rang and she answered it. 'How much? Bloody hell! For that kind of money you can drop it off to me.' She gave the caller brief details of her whereabouts. 'My car,' she explained to Blake. 'Expensive MOT. So, do you think Salinger made the connection and was calling to tell me?'

They crossed the road and began to stride over one of the lawns. 'You know,' Blake said. 'Hitch didn't just do thrillers. He did period melodramas, comedies, even social dramas. But from *The Lodger* onwards, his feature films all had one thing in common.'

They paused at the main entrance.

'Which is?'

'He made a cameo appearance in every one of them.' Blake held the door open. 'I'm looking forward to meeting our Professor of Hitchcock. He seems so keen to get involved. *After you.*'

A receptionist told Josa that Salinger was giving a lecture. 'He should be finished soon if you'd like to take a seat.'

'We'll join him now.' Josa flashed her warrant card and walked further into the faculty building.

Blake held up some ID and followed Josa.

'Wait a minute!' the receptionist called. 'That's a library card.'

'You've got libraries here, don't you?'

They found the lecture hall without difficulty and Josa said she'd sit in for the final few minutes.

'I'll take a look around,' Blake replied.

'Don't get into any trouble.' Josa discreetly pulled open the door and slipped in. The lecture hall was rammed. It was a large, sloping chamber with a seating capacity, Josa reckoned, of about 300 people. But this afternoon it was standing room only. Clearly, today, just as in the 1920s through to the mid-'70s, Alfred Hitchcock was packing them in.

At the front of the auditorium the lecturer noted Josa's arrival but didn't miss a beat.

He looked to be about forty years old. Dressed with a casual elegance – light grey suit and open-necked shirt. Short, smart brown hair. Just a touch of grey at the sides. He looked in good shape – tall and slender, and Josa immediately recognised him as the laid-back professor she'd seen on television earlier.

He spoke eloquently and with passion, punctuating his talk with witticisms and dramatic pauses. Salinger hopped from one fictional murder to another, but avoided the real-life killings that were dominating the headlines.

'And so we come to *Frenzy*,' he declared. 'The 1972 movie which has been described as the last Hitchcock classic. Rightly so, in my not-so-humble opinion. Although he made *Family Plot* four years later, *Frenzy* is the last Hitchcock picture, just as *The Lodger* was his first. Truffaut called *Frenzy* a young man's film. What did he mean by that? Well, he means that Hitch is experimenting, is attempting audacious shots and trickery with sound. *Frenzy* has a young man's passion and sense of adventure. It is Hitchcock's one and only R-rated film and certainly in the killings within it we see a process more brutal, more frank, more visceral than anything Hitch has attempted before. But it's done with such style, such abandon; yet at the same time, such control. He is like a skilled doctor. He finds the blood vessel with a bruising pat on your arm. Then he plunges the needle of the syringe right in! Presses down into the audience's artery with an extraordinary gusto. Here! Have it all! Without a doubt, Hitchcock is enjoying these murders.'

Josa glanced at the faces around her. They were all captivated by the man, his words and the images they conveyed.

'We're about to see a brilliant scene. It's the scene where Bob Rusk, played by Barry Foster, strangles the vile Brenda Blaney played by the divine Barbara Leigh-Hunt. It has been called a shocking scene but I prefer the phrase 'high impact'. If you've never seen it before, don't analyse it on first viewing but reflect on this. That while other directors would have been concerned with motivation, Hitchcock is concerned only with method, and that method, for the killer, becomes his motivation.'

He smiled.

'Listen to Rusk as he chokes the life out of this awful prig. *Lovely, lovely*, he intones. He enjoys the physicality of throttling these women. As we must. Because those close-ups confer a sense of prurience – voyeurism, if you like. We share in the murders. We enjoy them. At the time of the viewing experience we may not recognise that enjoyment for what it is, but later we get a ... a latent thrill from the murders Hitch serves up. The shower scene in *Psycho*. The child bludgeoning the sailor to death in *Marnie*. This strangulation in *Frenzy*. Sequences that stay with us and thrill us when we recall them. Hitchcock is not saying that you or I could be Bob Rusk or his victim. He is saying we are already them!'

Salinger nodded to the projection room at the back of the auditorium and a clip began to play.

*Bob talks to Brenda. Slowly, with a creeping sense of dread, she understands what is about to happen.*

And then a door to the right of the screen opened and Blake stepped into the room. He didn't seem bothered by the immediate attention his arrival attracted. He simply looked at the Professor, who stood at the opposite side of the screen, and nodded. Said 'Hello.' He spotted Josa and began to walk up the central aisle towards her. Only as he strode up the steps he was interrupting the projection, and so although the clip of Frenzy still played on the screen, it did so with Blake's silhouette imposed on the murder scene.

Blake winked at Josa. But something about the moment disturbed her. As he walked away from Salinger and towards her, Daniel Blake had Bob Rusk's frenzied countenance stretched across him; it flickered and became the face of Brenda Blaney as her features contorted in terror and pain, screaming in horrified awareness and only falling silent when death, and her killer, had claimed her.

# CHAPTER 54

Paul Salinger addressed Josa and Blake directly, as though oblivious to the students in the room, immediately after the short clip from *Frenzy* had finished. 'I assume you're here for me? I should be wrapping up in about five minutes. Is that all right?'

'That's fine,' Josa replied, suddenly self-conscious.

'Wonderful!' Salinger waved at someone on the front row. 'Mr Martens! Could you take my two guests to my study?'

Blake took advantage of the pause in proceedings and called down. 'What's the best bit?'

'Excuse me?'

'What's the best bit?'

'In *Frenzy*?' Salinger asked.

'Yeah. What's your favourite scene?'

'There's a sequence where the killer realises he's lost his tie pin and deduces it must be on the corpse of his latest victim. He's dumped her body in a lorry full of potatoes, and for a full ten minutes, right up close and sweaty and dirty, Hitch shows us the killer rooting through the spuds, then manhandling the corpse and scrambling for the incriminating evidence. It's so physical you want to wash your hands after watching it, and just incredibly compelling and tense. You feel for the killer. Hate him, hate his actions but can't turn away. We're left having to acknowledge that with over fifty films behind him and aged seventy-two, Hitchcock could still deliver a scene that is new and disturbing and wonderful.'

Blake turned to Josa and muttered. 'He did it.'

Todd Martens looked to be about twenty. Tall, well built, with shoulders you could chop bread on, but there was something inverted about him. It was like he was embarrassed there was so much of him, as if he'd prefer to have taken up less space.

He'd found Josa and Blake at the back of the lecture hall.

'I'll take you to the Professor's study.' Softly spoken. A little awkward.

'Thanks,' said Josa. 'Lead on.'

As they crossed a courtyard, he said. 'My name's Todd Martens. Everyone calls me Marty.'

'Nice to meet you,' Josa replied.

'Do you think the laughing professor has ever murdered anyone?' Blake asked, and Josa landed a discreet thump on his upper arm.

'Something you should know about Professor Salinger.' Marty stopped, looked at Josa and at Blake. 'He's a genius. A real genius. No other word for him. He's taught me so much. About Hitchcock. Not just his films. But his television work. He directed seventeen episodes of *Alfred Hitchcock Presents*, you know. The professor says they're terribly underrated. But much more than that, he's taught me about Hitchcock *the man* and about what we, as men, can expect from life. You'll find everyone around here loves the Professor.' He began walking again.

'Charles Schmid!' Blake rejoined. 'So charismatic they called him the Pied Piper because girls would just follow him ... He ended up killing three of them.'

'This is about those five murdered girls, isn't it?' Marty said.

Josa's tone was neutral. 'I'm afraid I can't say.' They entered one of the university buildings.

'You're police.' It was a statement, not a question. 'What about you?' Marty eyed Blake. 'What are you?'

'I'm an eccentric millionaire who uses special powers to fight crime.'

'Special powers?' Marty wasn't quite sure if he was being kidded.

'I fell off a ladder on my eighteenth birthday and now I can see around corners. The cops hate me. The underworld fears me. I always get my man but never get the girl.'

Blake smiled and looked at the kid. Josa saw he was weighing him up. Martens looked stung.

'You're Daniel Blake.'

No reply.

'The whole Hitchcock thing. It was you that sussed it out.'

Blake said nothing and Martens turned to Josa. 'Is he always like this?'

'Why d'you think he never gets the girl?'

Martens gave an unexpected smile and slight laugh. The sulky teen suddenly became a young man. 'I can see why you'd want to work with her,' he said to Blake.

They'd reached the last door in the corridor and Marty pushed it open. 'After you,' he said, indicating that they should enter. 'The Hitchcock Room!'

'Thanks,' Josa said.

The room couldn't make up its mind whether it was a study or a lounge, and was, in effect, two chambers knocked into one. At one end was a square room about twelve foot by ten. It held book shelves and wooden drawers. A mahogany desk was across the adjoining chamber, where Josa and Blake now stood. To the right of the door a long, battered sofa was draped in various exotic shawls. Above it and dotted around the room were framed pictures taken from Hitchcock movies. The famous, iconic shots were notable by their absence – Janet Leigh in the shower, the Bates Motel, Tippi and the birds and the Saul Bass posters were all missing. These were all screen-grabs, presumably taken by Salinger and blown up, lending them a grainy quality. A close-up of a blonde screaming, Kim Novak caught mid-sashay, Doris Day weeping in a ridiculous hat, an unknown man being attacked by ravens, Simon Stewart gazing at his hands and Robert Donat examining one half of a pair of cufflinks. The wall space free of pictures had been claimed by more book shelves. There was a long Ottoman chest in front of the sofa which Blake guessed served as a desk for students during tutorials. Two armchairs, a scattering of directors' chairs and a large flat-screen TV had also been crammed into the room.

Josa picked up a small alabaster bust. Hitchcock in his early days. Blake sidled up to her and nodded downwards.

'Nice bust.'

She rolled her eyes. 'You are such a child.'

Despite the clutter, one image claimed the attention of everyone who entered his study. The large, unframed canvas on the wall behind his desk. A striking publicity shot of Hitchcock. Stark white background. The director was wearing his trademark black suit and tie and, as though it was as natural as a pet poodle at his feet, an enormous raven was perched on his shoulder.

'That's his favourite picture of Hitchcock,' Marty said, noticing Josa's eye had been caught by the image. 'Do well in an assignment and he awards you a copy.'

'DVDs!' Blake snapped.

Marty turned to him. 'Excuse me?'

Blake indicated to the book shelves. 'Books, books, books. No DVDs. The movies themselves.'

'Ah …' Marty opened the Ottoman, revealing a treasure chest brimming with DVD cases.

Blake dived in. 'Oh good … very good, very, very good … rubbish … Josa, take a look. You want to complete your Hitchcock education? This is the place to start. I'm guessing there's everything he ever directed in here, yeah? Aside from *The Mountain Eagle*, obviously?'

'Why not that one?' Josa asked.

'His second movie,' Blake replied. 'And the only one that's missing. No prints are known to have survived.'

'In the early days of cinema, prints were often destroyed to save on storage costs, taxes and sometimes for the silver from the nitrate used in the actual film itself.' Marty grinned. 'But if anyone had a copy of *The Mountain Eagle* it would be Professor Salinger!'

Blake was sifting through the DVDs and, without looking up, asked, 'Which one do you watch the most, Marty? For pleasure at the end of a long day?'

'It's a difficult question. I'm asked it a lot. With all due respect,

Mr Blake, it's very limiting to commit to one favourite Hitchcock movie. His career spanned the silent era, black and white films, colour –'

'I didn't ask what your favourite movie was or what you considered his best. I asked which you watched the most.'

'*Psycho*,' Marty said.

'Blake!'

He turned to her. She was holding up a printed manuscript, about 400 pages of A4 paper, and on the coversheet, in large print: 'The Hitchcock Murders, by Professor Paul Salinger'.

'Let's skip to the last page and find out who did it,' Blake suggested.

'Put that down!' Marty blurted out. 'It's not yours!'

'On the contrary!' It was the Professor's voice. He stood in the doorway, a light smile on his lips. 'The Hitchcock Murders belong to the world.'

# CHAPTER 55

'I'm Professor Paul Salinger.' He took and shook Josa's hand.

'What a pleasure to meet you at last. You must have thought I was stalking you.'

'Excuse me?'

'My attempts to get in touch. I felt I might be of help and –'

'And we're very grateful,' Josa said. 'Thanks for seeing us. I'm Detective Chief

Inspector Jilani …'

He smiled. 'You have remarkable eyes.'

Blake popped to his feet like a jack-in-the-box. 'Hello, again.'

Salinger's smile faltered. 'Again?' The handshake was tentative.

'I'm Daniel Blake.'

The Professor's grip tightened. 'Ha! Well, of course you are! I didn't recognise you with all the …' He gestured to his stubble. 'And the rather down-at-heel clothes. Very feral. Very you. Is it for a role?'

'Isn't everything?' He turned to Josa. 'I helped out on a course here, two or three years ago. Criminal psychology. Holly Belle's idea. I gave a few guest lectures, and one sunny day I saw Professor Salinger was giving a lecture on Hitchcock and he ended up inviting me into one of his seminars …'

'They're still wiping away the blood!' Salinger laughed. 'So! Detective Chief Inspector Jilani! I take it you're here about Alfred Hitchcock?' He took a seat. 'Tell me. Are you a fan?'

'I'm not really into old movies. I had a friend who was a bit of a film buff. He showed me one or two but …'

'Then I suggest you begin with this …' Salinger rose from his chair and ferreted in the Ottoman for a moment. '*North by*

*Northwest!*' he declared plucking out a DVD. The cover showed Cary Grant tearing through a corn field pursued by a biplane. '1959. It's a good starting point.' Salinger returned to his chair. 'The year before, in 1958, he made *Vertigo*. An extraordinary, haunting, harrowing film. Of course, it's now viewed – quite rightly – as one of Hitch's finest achievements but back then it flopped at the box office and critics thought he was losing his touch. And so he came back with that.' He nodded to the DVD in Josa's hand. 'Cary Grant, Eva Marie Saint, James Mason. A huge, fun, romcom romp of a movie but I suggest it as a starting point as it still contains many of the motifs we associate with Hitchcock. The man accused of a crime he didn't commit on the run from both the bad guys and the police. A beautiful, icy blonde who joins him on his journey. A MacGuffin, a chase, plenty of wit and glamour, but also the delight of seeing a suave, sophisticated urbanite – in this case Roger Thornhill – brought down to earth. Quite literally. Getting dust on his tailored suit and blood under his manicured fingernails. It's a magnificent film.'

'Well, thank you,' Josa said.

'You know, DCI Jilani catches killers for a living.' Blake was still rummaging in the chest and didn't bother to look up. 'She looks at corpses on slabs, peers at the fatal wounds and then she writes reports and talks to their parents. Tells them that their kids won't be coming home because they've been stabbed in the kidneys for jipping down crack with talcum powder. Or maybe for no reason at all.' He held a DVD aloft. 'Ah, here it is.' Finally he faced Salinger. 'I think she could just about stomach one of his harder-hitting films.'

'And which would you suggest?'

Blake tossed him the DVD he'd unearthed. '*Blackmail.*'

'Ah …' The Professor glanced at the sleeve. 'Hitch's first talkie.' He shot an apologetic smile at Josa. 'Hitchcock began directing in the era of silent movies. In 1929 he made *Blackmail* but created two versions. One was a silent movie, the other a talkie. It's often called Britain's first talkie, but that's nonsense, of course. It's one of the first, but not the very first. Anyway,' His gaze returned to Blake.

'I'm surprised you consider *Blackmail* to be hard-hitting.'

'Well, the thing about *Blackmail* is people always bang on about it being his first talkie, and the chase scenes at the end with the British Museum, blah, blah, blah. Or the scene where Hitch draws our attention to the spoken word – knife. And that's all well and good. But what really makes it remarkable is the scene where our heroine kills her attacker. And the moments leading up to it. It's an attempted rape. It's 1929 and Hitch is showing us, quite openly, an attempted rape. And it's so modern and believable. A couple messing about, flirting, and slowly the joking gets less funny as she sees he wants to go all the way and she's trapped and it's awful.'

'And she kills him?' asked Josa.

'Oh, yes.' Salinger nodded. 'Stabs him with a bread knife. Hitch gives the character no choice. We don't see the actual killing, only the aftermath. Her total horror. And the scarring effect it has on her. It's compelling stuff.'

'So!' Blake leapt to his feet. 'A squishy romcom or a brutal, modern classic from 1929. Which will it be?'

'I can watch them both,' said Josa.

Salinger handed her *Blackmail*. 'Very diplomatic.' He looked at Blake who was circling his study, examining the posters and prints on his walls. 'And now, at the risk of sounding over-inquisitive … Mr Blake, your message said you and DCI Jilani wanted to meet me about police business and it was something to do with what the papers are calling the Hitchcock Murders? I presumed you wanted to pick my brains?'

'Yeah, yeah, yeah. I wanted to meet you again. Foremost authority on Hitchcock and all that.'

'You're too kind.'

'Not really. Took me a bit of time to track you down. You see, I assumed you'd have moved on by now so was looking for you elsewhere. Didn't you always say you'd like to teach at one of the Oxford colleges? So there I was, trying to find out where you'd gone. Google your surname and you get endless pages about J.D. Salinger. That must rankle.'

'Not unduly.'

'I like that one.' Blake studied a screenshot of an elderly lady with a strip of material across her eyes, playing blind man's buff. Then he looked at Salinger. 'I think the killer has a relationship with Hitchcock. Or rather, he thinks he does. So there's three things, really. One: he may have studied on your course. Two: I'd like you to talk to Josa about Alfred Hitchcock so she can understand the object of the killer's obsession.'

'And three?'

'I'll cover three later.'

'How enigmatic you are, Mr Blake!'

'Why, thank you.'

Josa said, 'Mr Blake is helping us with the investigation.'

Salinger nodded. 'Sure! Mr Blake. I hope you don't mind me saying –'

'Oh, say away, old chap. Say away!'

'You look a little dishevelled to be working with the police.'

'Well, how dishevelled is too dishevelled?'

Josa shot him a what-the-hell-are-you-doing look and intervened with, 'Professor Salinger, I wonder, would it be possible to obtain a list of all the students who have taken your course over the years?'

'Yes. Yes, of course. And for that I shall summon my personal assistant.' He picked up the phone on his desk, dialled and a moment later said, 'Cordelia, darling! I hate to interrupt but could you pop along to the Hitchcock Room? Could you? Thanks ever so much. See you in two.'

'Thanks, Professor,' said Josa.

'Here they are!' Blake was taking a number of slim paperbacks from the shelves. 'Your books. By Professor Paul Salinger. Here's one on Hitchcock. One on Hitchcock and look, one on, ah, Hitchcock.'

'I am an authority on the works of Sir Alfred Hitchcock. I don't see –'

'Specialist. Obsessive. What would you say the difference is, Marty?'

Todd Martens had been standing silently in the corner of the room, watching but not waiting. As the focus now moved onto him, he looked appalled to have been noticed. 'Specialist, obsessive … The two aren't mutually exclusive.'

'Obviously!' said Blake.

'Marty, Mr Blake is trying to brand me an obsessive and, in a rather ham-fisted way, suggest I could be responsible for the Hitchcock murders.'

'Can't have done your sales much harm.' Blake threw the three books onto the sofa.

'In commercial terms the murders are a godsend.'

'A godsend,' Blake repeated.

'But not for my previous books. I have a new volume out shortly that specifically examines the ways in which Hitchcock dealt with the physicality of killing.'

'What are the chances of that, eh? We get a series of murders à la Hitchcock and you're releasing a book on his modus operandi.'

'I see your implication.'

'Oh, it wasn't meant as an implication, Professor. That would imply a lack of directness.'

'And I confess,' Salinger said, 'that earlier this morning my publishers contacted me and suggested we changed the title of the tome from *Hitchcock: The Machinery of Dispatch* to quite simply *The Hitchcock Murders.*'

'Did they? Well, well, well. And you reluctantly agreed?'

'No, Mr Blake. I applauded the idea. I seized it. I've written books about Hitchcock all my life, taught his works and spoken about him all over the world. And the academic intelligentsia listened, of course, but outside those rarefied circles – nothing. But now, after a lifetime of work … Now, here is a chance to speak and be heard. By the world. To finally, *finally* be listened to. Acknowledged. But I know what you're thinking …' Salinger squared up to Blake. 'You're thinking I murdered those poor girls for the glory of Alfred Hitchcock.'

'Not at all.'

The door opened.

'I think you murdered for the spurious glory of Paul Salinger, failed author, failed academic and wannabe celebrity.' Blake's voice remained calm and confident. 'I think you murdered those girls for your own twisted sense of self.'

# CHAPTER 56

Miss Cordelia Smith was in her mid-forties but people usually assumed she was twenty years older. She took pride in that misconception. It implied seniority and experience which in turn suggested reliability, and Cordelia Smith wanted Professor Salinger to know she was reliable. She wanted the world to see that he was guarded by an old hand who didn't care about outward appearances or other such trivia. She cared about doing her job. She cared about him, protecting him, and she carried that duty of care like a tribal elder might carry a staff.

Cordelia Smith was five foot three of puritanical primness, from the soles of her comfortable shoes to the tips of her grey-shot hair. She was lean and fit, radiating the kind of rude health that hints at country walks and wholesome food. Had she ever smiled, she might have looked like the kind of grandma that TV movies bestow on angelic children, but she seldom smiled unless she was correcting an error or talking to Professor Salinger. Instead, her face was invariably set in an expression of mistrust and displeasure, as hard and warm as a butcher's slab.

Capital College swarmed with wily professors as tough and insensitive as beaten leather, but they all feared Miss Smith. No one really knew where she came from. Her accent held a hint of Scottish, but aside from her brogue, she gave nothing away, never talking about her past or her family. At a Christmas party one of the newer lecturers had attempted chit-chat about background and hobbies and had even called her by her first name. The look he received would have petrified Medusa and swiftly passed into university legend. She was simply Miss Smith, *Salinger's guard dog* or *the old harpy*. She knew all this and more and didn't care; even drew pleasure from the muttered asides and averted gazes. As long as they knew where they stood, she knew where she stood.

And although her past was a mystery, one thing about her present remained clear – her fierce loyalty to Paul Salinger. It was rumoured that she would do anything for the Professor, and as she opened the door to his study, she found him under attack.

Josa couldn't believe how far Blake was pushing it.

*'I think you murdered those girls for your own twisted sense of self.'*

Cordelia Smith stood in the doorway, and when she spoke, she immediately reminded Josa of a head teacher appearing in a classroom overrun with unruly children. 'And what,' she demanded to know, 'is going on here?'

'Hello,' said Blake. 'You must be Cordelia. Nice to meet you. I'm just accusing your boss of being a serial killer.'

'Professor. Who is this person?'

'This is Detective Chief Inspector Josa Jilani and this is Daniel Blake. He's not with the police. But apparently he's helping them, which I do find slightly baffling.'

Josa said, 'I must apologise for Mr Blake's outburst, Professor. I can assure you –'

Salinger raised a hand and smiled. 'Not at all, DCI Jilani. I encourage my students to be bold with their theories and honest about 'em. Mr Blake thinks I'm the killer because I have an interest in Hitchcock. I'm sorry to tell you that the identity parade of suspects will stretch from here to Elstree if an interest in the world's greatest director is enough to mark you down as a *wrong 'un.*'

'I'm afraid I'm going to have to ask you to leave.' Cordelia was addressing Blake directly. 'Right away.'

'Oh, that's all right, Cordelia. I like him.' Salinger flashed another Hollywood smile and placed his hand on Blake's shoulder. 'I think we're going to get along, don't you?'

'Sure. And when this is over, just let me know when visiting hours are and we'll keep in touch.'

'You honestly believe I murdered those women? I mean, you're serious?'

'Yeah. What d'you think, Cordelia?'

'I think this is a disgrace and I think you –' she shot a glance at Josa, 'are skating on very thin ice, young lady.'

'Don't bring her into it,' snapped Blake. 'I'm a spokesperson for no one but myself.'

'Can we all calm down?' Salinger implored. He pinched the bridge of his nose between his index finger and thumb. 'Look, this is madness. DCI Jilani – the first of these unfortunate girls. Do we know *when* she was murdered?'

'Yes, sir. That information is in the public domain.' She gave the exact date, adding, 'Five weeks ago last Tuesday. We estimate the time of death as being between 19.00 and 21.00 hours that evening.'

Salinger nodded. 'Cordelia. Does history record my movements for the period in question? Do I have an *alibi*?' He pronounced the word as if it was an exotic notion.

'Did you say between 7 and 9 p.m.?' Cordelia asked.

Josa nodded.

'Well, in that case you'll have to find someone else to harass. On that date, in the evening, Professor Salinger was kindly giving an extra tutorial session on the issue of sexual repression in *Shadow of a Doubt*. A number of students had, I believe, delivered essays on that film and none had mentioned the topic. The Professor was with six students all evening, showing clips of the film, discussing Teresa Wright and the way she –'

'Yeah. We get the motion picture,' Blake interjected. 'Could we have the names of the students so that can be verified?'

If looks could kill, Cordelia would have struck Blake dead with the stare she shot him. 'How dare you!' she seethed, 'You had better –'

'Cordelia,' said Salinger. 'We can clear this up right now. Marty! You attended our little ad hoc tutorial, did you not?'

The student nodded. 'I was there. It ran from about 7 till 9. Yeah. In the lecture theatre. It was really useful. A few of us were there.'

'You owe the Professor an apology!' Cordelia raged.

'Why?' Blake replied. 'I'm not interested in that week's Tuesday night. It's the Thursday night that interests me. Two evening later.'

For the first time, the expression on Cordelia's face changed from aggression to surprise.

'What?'

'The Thursday evening. That's the pertinent one, and before you ask, no, I'm not prepared to tell you why at this stage. But I'm betting Paul hasn't got an *alibi* for that evening.'

'Oh, this is preposterous!' Cordelia bulldozed past Blake and took a scarlet diary from the desk. 'I'll be making a formal complaint about this, and don't think …' She broke off, her lips creasing into an unfamiliar smile. 'Here we are. On the evening of that particular Thursday, Professor Salinger attended a dinner dance in aid of the Meredith Theatre. Gave an after-dinner speech which went down very well. I myself attended the meal but left shortly after Professor Salinger's address. The Professor stayed all night. Of course, if you need witnesses, I'm afraid you've only got two or three hundred to choose from.' She snapped the diary shut as if the matter was literally closed. 'And now, if there's nothing else, would you both leave?'

'Blake,' said Josa. 'Wait outside.'

'Why? What have I done? I haven't done anything!'

'Your behaviour is a disgrace,' hissed Cordelia. 'Your words appalling and your manners non-existent. If you don't leave this room immediately I'm going to call security.'

Blake held her stare, and for a moment his flippancy was burnt away by its intensity. 'Miss Smith, you're angry and I can understand that. Believe me, it's nothing compared to my fury. You clearly think your job is to protect Paul Salinger. That's fine. But mine is to serve the dead and the threatened. You know, your alacrity, the way you go about your job … Well, it's admirable, but unthinking. *I don't have that luxury.* Now, what does that make me? You think about that.' He took a step back, and without any hint of irony said, 'Thank you for your time, Miss Smith, Mr Martens. Good to see you again, Professor.' A brief nod at Josa and he was gone.

# CHAPTER 57

In the Professor's study, the sound of Cordelia Smith bashing away on the computer keyboard just about broke the awkward silence. Josa looked around the room, desperately searching for something to talk about. Marty had dashed off to another lecture and Cordelia had agreed to collate the annual roll calls of students who had taken the Professor's course, thereby creating a master list of Hitchcock alumni. As she worked away at the document, Salinger perched on the edge of his desk.

'You seem a trifle ill at ease, Detective Chief Inspector.'

'No, I'm fine. Mr Blake was a bit –'

'Oh, forget it. Compared to some of my students he was positively placid. Listen. Do I have to keep calling you Detective Chief Inspector? Is Josa permitted, or would I get the bracelets slapped on me for such impertinence?'

She smiled. 'Josa's fine.'

Josa noted the sound of typing paused momentarily.

'Good!' said the Professor. 'So how did you get into what you do? What Mr Blake said ... dead bodies and all that. Made me wonder. Why does someone actively pursue that career? What made you join up?'

*Sometimes*, thought Josa, *I haven't a bloody clue*. 'Oh, you know ...' She shrugged. 'It was just one of those things. There *is* the side that Mr Blake touched on, sure. But the service is full of good people, and by and large they're kind of doing it for the right reasons.'

'They?'

'What?'

'You said *they're* kind of doing it for the right reasons. Not *we*.

As if you're still not part of it all. Would that be –'

'You know,' Josa interjected, 'you and Blake might have more in common than you think.'

The Professor grinned. 'Is that a good thing?'

'He's all right, you know?'

'Then I'll take it as a good thing, Josa.'

The typing was slowing down again.

'So what did Hitchcock think of us?' Josa asked. 'How do coppers come across in his movies? Are we all bent or stupid or do we ever catch the bad guys?'

'Well, you get off to a bad start. The first copper in his films was in *The Lodger*. He was called Joe and was pretty dense. Stupid, jealous, vain, ineffective. But there's not really a typical 'Hitchcock policeman' in his works. The Scotland Yard man in *Dial M for Murder* is quick, clever and surprisingly compassionate. And don't forget that one of his most human characters – 'Scotty' Ferguson from *Vertigo* – is an ex-police officer. He's a man of honour and integrity and intelligence. Certainly, he is when the movie begins, at any rate.'

Josa raised one of the DVDs she was holding. 'What about in your choice?'

'Ah, well, in *North by Northwest* the police don't fare too well. There's one uniformed officer in it called Emile who's quite likeable, though.'

'I put it to you, Professor Salinger, that you're covering up for your friend, Mr Hitchcock, and that he generally didn't portray us in a very good light.'

'Well, it's odd. It's not that Hitch actively disliked the police, but he famously had a run-in with them once.'

'I know.'

'You do?'

'I saw you this morning on television. You spoke about his incarceration and the effect it had on him. And his movies.'

'So you were watching! But you withheld that evidence! I shall have to watch my step!' He shot her a smile. 'How did I come across?'

'Like someone who knew his stuff.'

Salinger wrinkled his nose. 'I was barely given enough time to scratch the surface. I wanted to talk about his relationship with terror! His relationship with the audience! His relationship with God! Did you know that Hitch was once driving with a friend through Switzerland, suddenly saw something and said, *That's the most terrifying sight I have ever seen*? Do you know what it was?'

'A car crash?'

'No! It was a priest talking to a little boy. The priest's hand was on his shoulder. Hitch leant out of the car and bellowed, *Run, little boy! Run for your life!* A brief, delighted laugh. 'He's the epitome of fascinating!'

'You've got quite a passion for the guy.'

'Guilty!'

'And what made you get into teaching him?'

For the first time during the exchange, Salinger broke eye contact, looking to the ground. 'A little like Hitch in the cell, I suppose.'

But he wasn't addressing Josa; she realised he was talking to himself and she moved towards him, quietly pushing further. 'What do you mean?'

'Just, well, it's nothing. I d-d-don't mean anything.'

'Go on, Paul.'

Lost for a moment. Caught in distant headlights. 'Only that ...' He was murmuring, still not prepared to look at her. 'Only that I –'

Josa put her hand on Salinger's arm. 'Tell me,' she gently implored, 'Tell me what it is!'

Blake sat on the floor in the corridor outside Salinger's room, his back leaning against the wall directly opposite the study door. He allowed himself a brief smile. His clowning had been a touch too pantomimic, he conceded that, but the loose-cannon act had yielded one very interesting piece of information. He wondered if Cordelia Smith would look back on the encounter and realise the slip his cajoling had forced her to make.

But there was something else ...

He looked down the corridor. Took in the scent of the place, the sound of young people dashing and gabbling and trying *so hard*. It was difficult not to be tugged back to his own youth and days spent in education. So many debilitating memories to be suppressed. So much of *then* that continued to threaten his *now*. He recalled Dempsey, his father and the crimes. The pain across his left shoulder and the sudden, snowy cold and … He closed his eyes, suddenly wanting to be anywhere but here.

*But there was something else …*

His eyes opened. Salinger had let something slip. Blake tried to rewind his comments. Not the obvious, showy statements about the world listening. That bombast had been calculated to imply guilt, like a member of the chorus twiddling his moustache to suggest a greater significance than his role merited. But somewhere amongst the Professor's throwaway comments he'd said something of golden importance, and Blake tried to sift it out, panning the watery words for the grain of truth.

He was still rusty. And rusty was fine for trainspotters or butterfly collectors. He slapped the floor with his open palm and the smack echoed down the corridor. But for Daniel Blake it could mean life or death.

'It's … when I was young man …'

Yes …' Josa said.

'I … I –'

'There we go!' Cordelia interrupted. She stuck her fist between Josa and Salinger. It was clutching a thin sheaf of papers. 'The master list. All the students who have taken the Professor's course. I'm not sure what good it will do you, but there you go.'

'Thank you, Miss Smith.' Josa stepped back, aware that the moment had passed. She cleared her throat. 'Well, we'll start with the obvious stuff. See if any of the names ring a bell, if any kind of record shows up for any of them. In fact, could you email me a copy of this?'

'Well, *of course!*' The reply was delivered with irritation, as if this was an obvious course of action.

'Thank you. You're …'

Salinger had taken several gulps from a glass of water and now turned to rejoin the conversation. 'Efficient and brilliant!' he interjected, finding his smile again. 'My Alma!'

Josa didn't understand the allusion, but judging from the two-foot grin on Cordelia's face, the reference meant a lot.

'Well, thanks again. Both of you.'

'Our pleasure,' Salinger replied. 'You know, Josa, with all these murders you must have a pretty dim view of Hitchcock. I'd welcome the challenge of changing your mind. And if your cross-checking fails to throw up any clues, well, I'll be more than happy to sit down with you over a bottle of decent wine and chew over a few of the names.'

'I'd appreciate that.'

As they shook hands, Josa registered that Salinger's grip lasted a fraction longer than was necessary.

'See you again,' he said.

# CHAPTER 58

Blake was walking around the grounds of Capital College, scrutinising Salinger's office from the outside. He stopped occasionally, working out the exact layout of the building and, specifically, what could be monitored from where. Salinger's room was on a corner. One side faced a quadrangle and a bank of watching windows, but the other side overlooked nothing but a strip of gravel and a tall, red brick wall. Blake smiled to himself and set off across the lawn. He glanced inside Salinger's study. Stopped.

The Professor was shaking hands with Josa but maintaining his grasp for a moment longer than he should. Was Josa enjoying the –

She had turned away.

Blake wiped the palm of his hand across his face like a flannel and continued along the perimeter of the college. He'd not been able to see her reaction to Salinger's advance, but with a modicum of surprise, he felt a sharp jab of jealousy.

Jack Dempsey felt like a man burrowing a tunnel through thick, damp earth using nothing but his fingernails. He'd spent the past several hours clawing away at the directory of missing girls but had barely made any progress. There were too many cases, and the selection criteria he was working from were proving way too broad. He'd already paid a visit to some old friends at a London station and gleaned valuable information about some of the girls. Many had been known to the police for dabbling in drugs. Some had a history of mental illness. A surprising number had been faced by crippling debts. Every such example was tragic, but suggested that their disappearance had been triggered by factors other than the serial killer they sought. And so they could be struck from the list. The difficulty was obvious: there was no computer programme to simply delete such cases from the master file. Each of the thousands of missing people had to be individually sifted. Given care and consideration and time he didn't have. Their last revenge on a world that had given up on them.

Blake and Josa walked through the university corridors in silence, but as they crossed the car park, she unleashed her pent-up anger. 'That's it, Blake. Where the hell do you get off? This is my investigation and my whole career you're messing with. This isn't just some little game for your amusement.'

'I know that!'

'Accusing him like that. The things you said. That Smith woman is going to report this whole thing and that will give Gilmour exactly the excuse he needs to hang me out to dry.' She shook her head. 'You're off the case. That was unacceptable. Just bang out of order, one hundred per cent unacceptable and I ain't covering your ass.'

'You *ain't covering my ass?*' He was gently poking fun but misjudged her mood. Badly.

Josa turned and pushed him hard with the tips of her fingers. She was shouting now: 'Don't mock me! Do you understand? Don't mock me!'

Blake had staggered back a little but Josa was unrelenting, shoving him again in the chest, harder this time.

'It's all right for you! You can just go back to your nice expensive house and make your way any way you want. All you lot! You'll be okay. But I don't have that! Do you know how hard it is for me? All that bullshit about you knowing what it's like to be an outsider! Well, you have no idea!'

For a long moment she looked as if she would vent more fury in his direction, but Blake saw the rage had exploded leaving nothing but upset. She struck him again on the shoulder, but the blow lacked force. Josa Jilani turned away and walked back to her car.

Blake ran his hand across his face. 'Josa! Josa, I'm sorry.'

'No, you're not.' She was rooting in her handbag for the car keys, impatient and annoyed that they weren't to hand. 'You're sorry I've called you on it, but you just don't get it.'

'You have no idea how much I get it.'

She gave a short, *don't-give-me-that* laugh and Blake continued: 'I had to play it that way, but I'm sorry because I should have warned you. I wanted to push them and pull them in different directions. See what cracks they were covering with their feet.'

She whipped the keys from her bag, unlocked the car and swung open the driver's door. 'Yeah. Right. You stick to that bullshit.'

'I think Paul Salinger murdered those girls.'

'Why? Because he teaches Hitchcock? Do you have any idea how many people teach courses in the history of murder? Or psychosis? Or criminology? Should we lock them up as well?'

*Well, with half of them*, Blake thought, *that wouldn't be a bad idea*, but he opted for a safer: 'Marcus Aurelius. What is each thing in itself? Forget the blizzard of facts, Josa. This guy has just written a book called *The Hitchcock Murders*. It's like a fucking guide book to the killings. He's a pompous academic who's not been connected to reality since he was bullied at sixth form. Academia all his life. A few books no one's read and a load of lectures that are completely ephemeral when – and here's the important bit – when he worships *that which is recorded*. Come on! At least accept the fact he's a suspect.'

'I accept the fact you don't like him and that's clouding your judgment.'

'Okay. I don't like him. But here's what I got out of that meeting. It's not just me that thinks he could be the killer.'

'What are you talking about?'

'The woman that probably knows him best in the world thinks it might be him.'

'Cordelia Smith?'

'Uh-huh.'

'What are you on about?'

His hands were resting on the roof of the car and he leant over it by a couple of inches. 'When I asked her what the Professor had been doing on the night of the murders she knew immediately. In every detail. Times, size of class, location. Right there.'

'She's his PA. That's her job!'

'No! Because when I asked her what he'd been up to a couple of nights later she had to look it up in her diary. This woman has clearly not got the best memory in the world. A big, fancy dinner dance that she was at! And she couldn't remember it off the top of her head! Yet she remembered the tiny little ad hoc tutorial. Why? Because it's occurred to her that he could be the killer and she's already checked his movements on the night in question. That's how she could reel off the facts. *Because she'd already checked them.*'

Several seconds of silence.

'You might have a point.'

'The woman that knows him best thinks he could be the killer. What does that tell us?'

'Yeah, all right, I get it. But you're still off the case.'

'What?' Blake looked horrified.

'Ah!' Josa jabbed a finger in his direction. 'You don't like it when someone does it back to you, do you?' She nodded to the car. 'Come on. Get in. But I'm still mad at you.' And don't think –' Her phone's ringtone interrupted. 'Hello?' A pause. 'Oh, hi … Well, nothing, but I'll be working late if that's …' A smile. 'Yeah. That would be nice. Just text me the where and when. Cool. Great.' A glance down at herself and another smile. 'See you tonight, then.' She slipped her phone back in her pocket.

'Who was that?' Blake demanded.

'My sister.'

'You are such a bad liar. Who was it?'

'Never you mind.'

'It was Salinger!'

'Okay, okay!' Josa replied, 'Yes, it was.'

She climbed into the car and Blake joined her. 'It's a date,' he said. 'You looked at your clothes before you'd even hung up because you're already wondering what you're going to wear.'

Josa pinched his cheek between her thumb and index finger and put on the exaggerated tones of a mother addressing a young child. 'You should be a detective!'

'I thought you said you needed space.'

'I thought you said you'd shut up.'

'Doesn't sound like the sort of thing I'd say. Look, Josa, seriously. Do you have any idea how dangerous this guy is?'

'I've told you before,' Josa said as she turned the engine over. 'I can look after myself.'

'Was that before or after he almost killed you at the Shard and later in the hospital?'

'After, I think,' Josa replied. She revved the engine. 'So that makes it okay, doesn't it?'

# CHAPTER 59

That evening, the murdered girl waited for him. Jack Dempsey knew he was becoming drowsy and that he should stop. He'd begun to skim-read the reports, dragging cases into the 'no interest' folder a little too quickly. A little too gratefully.

He couldn't know that she was patiently standing in the queue, several names down the list he continued to search through. She'd have stood on tiptoes if she'd been able to. Waved, smiled, called his name and put an arm around him as –

– he pinched the bridge of his nose. Suddenly Dempsey felt exhausted. If he pressed on now there was a chance he'd overlook something. Put a missing person in the 'no interest' folder when she should have been dragged into 'follow up'. But to admit defeat, even to fatigue, was not in the big American's make up.

He opened another file and his tired vision swam a little as he began to read. Leaning closer to the screen his back ached. 'Jeez,' murmured Dempsey.

But he didn't stop, and a little further down the screen, Lucy Jaeger waited.

'Well, you know, they got in touch with me this morning. They want me to present a screening here. Of *Blackmail*, funnily enough.' Salinger smiled at Josa. 'The movie your Mr Blake was so keen for you to see.' They stood in the British Museum's Great Court. 'Part of the film's chase sequence was filmed here, so it kind of makes sense. I said I'd be delighted. I mean, why not?' He

239

paused. 'I thought we could take a look around, together?'

The Professor had just emerged from a meeting with the museum's events board and, devoid of visitors and illuminated by minimal lighting, Josa felt the building held all the allure of a mausoleum. But she nodded yes. After all, she told herself, she was only spending time with Salinger to find out more about Hitchcock.

In a small, darkened room, he watched. The grey-haired guard had given him carte blanche after he'd shown her his fake Scotland Yard identification, and she'd left early, explaining that her colleague's shift began in about an hour. Her words were met with a distracted grunt. Now he sat alone in front of a bank of monitors, each connected to the cameras that peppered the museum. He was able to control the stream of video and easily follow the two figures as they floated through the museum like ghosts. Their hands never quite touching, although their shoulders brushed against each other when they found an exhibit of joint interest. And it was surprising how often he became fascinated by the relics she paused by.

They were harder to discern in the snaking series of rooms that housed the mummies and other icons of Ancient Egypt. The lighting was dimmer here. But he could see his hands rise and rest upon her shoulders.

Daniel Blake's eyes narrowed and he leant closer into the screen.

Salinger moved forward, then turned Josa's body so he stood behind her, lightly pressed against her frame as they both faced an ornate, upright coffin that housed a mummified pharaoh. Its fine gold casing, picked out by laser-bright beams of light, was radiant in the surrounding darkness.

'Magnificent,' Salinger breathed. 'Those originally viewing it wouldn't have seen it in this context, of course. It would have been more worshipful. The pharaoh may well have been on a plinth, meaning that in death he was elevated both physically and metaphorically, from mere mortals. Which means they'd have seen this from a slightly different ... here ...'

His left hand remained on her shoulder, but his right arm circled her. His fingers found her face. He cupped her cheek then moved his hand down so it was over her throat. Josa froze. Then gently, smoothly, he nudged her chin up.

'This is what they experienced,' he told her, holding the position for a split second.

Paul Salinger stood behind Josa in a stance that suggested both lovemaking and murder.

And in that split second he threw a glance over his shoulder, looked directly into the security camera, and winked.

# CHAPTER 60

If Dempsey had been driving he'd have pulled over long ago. His tiredness was growing heavier, his head dipping as he fell into a momentary microsleep. About half an hour earlier he found he'd started reading certain sentences twice, thrice, four times. But when he checked back on a file, worried he'd missed something, he found whole paragraphs that his weary eyes has passed over without registering.

And still Lucy Jaeger waited. The murdered woman, listed as missing, whose file Jack Dempsey had almost reached … He shook his head. He'd sort one more. Place in the 'follow up' folder to be examined later, or 'no interest', to be deleted at the end of the day. Then he'd go downstairs and mix himself a strong scotch and soda. That was one of the perks of staying with Blake at Moonfleet – always a good supply of excellent spirits. He'd have a nightcap and a quick chat to Holly before turning in for the night.

*Just one more.*

He clicked Lucy Jaeger's file. He wasn't struck by her beauty. He'd seen hundreds like her in the records. But the actual photograph included in her file was unusual. It showed Lucy clearly, but she had her arm around someone who had been blacked out. There was an irony in the fact that the photo showed the missing girl besides someone who had been removed. The dark silhouette indicated the 'removed' person was female, about Lucy's height. Dempsey found it odd, and for a second or two reflected that either Lucy Jaeger disliked having her photo taken, hence the need to use a doctored one, or that she always had it taken with people around her.

He shook his head again, trying to clear his thoughts. Whatever the reason for the chosen photograph, it wasn't enough to link her disappearance with the ongoing investigation.

Dempsey closed her file. He'd not even read it – a dreadful lapse brought on by extreme fatigue. He'd discounted her on one level, and his mind, keen to shut down, had resolved that this was enough.

He clicked on her file, already looking forward to switching off with a decent single malt. Dempsey dragged Lucy Jaeger over to 'no interest'.

# CHAPTER 61

Jack Dempsey's phone rang. 'Yeah?'

'It's me!'

'Danny Boy!'

'Call it a day on your missing persons trawl. I've just seen enough to convince me my prime suspect is as guilty as hell. So! I've got some new criteria for you to work with tomorrow. Should make it much easier.'

'That's what I like to hear!'

He took his finger off the mouse and Lucy Jaeger's file fell into the safety of his regular desktop. Undeleted.

It was only 11 p.m. but Josa felt early-morning tired as she unlocked her flat's front door. She'd said goodnight to Salinger downstairs and although she recognised she was a poor judge of these situations, she fancied she'd detected disappointment in his voice when he'd not been invited up for a mythical coffee.

She'd pushed open her front door, caught off guard by the sight of –

'Blake!'

He sat on the arm of her sofa, leafing through a magazine.

'Hello!'

'What are you doing here?'

'Your sister let me in.'

'Oh, you needn't have come!'

He tossed the magazine to one side. 'That's the thanks I get for giving up my evening for you, is it?'

'Don't be daft. I'm very grateful to you. Fancy a drink?'

A couple of hours before meeting Salinger she'd given Blake's theory – that he was the killer – some thought, and although she couldn't buy it completely, she was prepared to admit that spending time with him alone might not be one of her better ideas. Once she knew they'd be looking around the British Museum she'd begged Blake to follow their progress on the security cameras.

*Just blow him out!* Blake had pleaded with her. *Tell him you've just washed your car and can't do a thing with it. Anything!*

But Josa had been firm. She would learn about Hitchcock and maybe a little more about one of her suspects. With ill-grace and only after a great deal of persuasion, Blake grudgingly accepted his watching brief.

'Actually,' he said, 'I'll have a large Grand Marnier if there's one going.'

'Really? Grand Marnier? How likely is that?'

'Top left cupboard in the kitchen!' Preya called through from her bedroom. 'Help yourself!'

Josa grinned. 'You kept that quiet!' she shouted back.

They wandered through to the kitchen and Josa poured them both a liqueur. 'Well, he didn't try to beat me over the head with a guide book.' She handed Blake his drink. 'In fact he was quite charming.'

'He knew I was watching.'

'How could he know that?'

'Because he wanted me to be watching, so in his head, I was there. Cheers.'

'Cheers.'

'I've met guys like this before, Josa. He wants to be seen. To be … I don't know … feted! He's loving this!' He sipped his Grand Marnier. 'Salinger wouldn't be the first killer to murder for attention.'

'Yeah, I know that. It's just right now, I can't square those murders with that man. And hey, he's got an alibi for Becka Hoyle's killing. He was teaching when she was drowned.'

'Here's the thing. The post-mortem report on Becka said she

was a right old mess when she was brought in.'

'So?'

'And because she'd been dead for some time before she was found, time of death was established by analysis of body fluid as opposed to internal temp or analysis of the nature of her injuries … because Becka's injuries were post-mortem. Now, that's important.'

Josa nodded. 'Yeah. So? Where you going with this?'

'He takes her. Smashes the back of her head, leaving her unconscious and tied up in his study.'

'Like you do.'

'Hear me out. Then he gives his little lesson in the lecture theatre. At one point he shows a clip from *Shadow of a Doubt* that lasts six minutes. In that time he exits the theatre, returns to his study and puts Becka's head, well, her face, in a bowl of water. Drowns her. Then whips back to the lecture theatre and continues with the lesson after the clip finishes. He could have done it without being seen. I checked and it's possible for him to –'

'How many of these have you had?' Josa interrupted, holding up her glass. 'That's quite a theory.'

'Oh, come on, Josa!'

'Drowns her in a bowl of water in his study? That just sounds unbelievable.'

'Exactly!' Blake exclaimed.

'Point taken. Look. I'm too tired to think straight right now.'

'Lend me a tenner.'

'I'm not that tired!'

They laughed, the sound of Blake's phone cutting into it. 'Hello? Cool.' He ended the call. 'My taxi. Downstairs.'

'You're welcome to stay for a bit. Finish your drink.'

'Thanks. I want to get back. I've not really seen Holly today.'

'She seems like quite a girl.'

'She's amazing! You'll have to meet her. Properly I mean. I know I'm biased, but she's funny and smart and just really good company.'

'What's the deal with her mum? If you don't mind me asking.'

Blake drained his glass in one final gulp. 'Don't mind you asking. Look, I know it looks like I'm trying to cloak my past in some sort of secrecy, but it's not like that. It's just … I try not to think about it …' He looked her in the eye. 'My past is in here …' He tapped his temple. 'And it's kind of like Pandora's box. You know?'

'Not really,' Josa replied truthfully.

'Okay. Bad analogy. It's just that −' He broke off, spotting something over Josa's shoulder.

'What is it?' she asked.

Blake went through to the front room. Nodded to the windows. 'Rain on its way. I've got to go. It was nice seeing you here. Wish I could have stayed longer.'

'You can!' Preya again, calling through from her bedroom.

'Don't worry! I'm leaving the booze!'

A bashful kiss on the cheek, and, reading his body language as he pulled back, Josa felt a sense of awkwardness about him regarding his down-at-heel appearance. A nod. A smile. He was gone.

Preya appeared in the doorway of her bedroom wearing a big, thick dressing gown. 'So. You were out with a guy who's under suspicion of murder?'

'Yeah, but on the plus side I'm fairly certain he isn't married.'

'I hope you had your mace handy.'

Josa smiled and shook her head. Preya's cautionary list of stipulations was a running joke but she meant every last one of them. *Never interview a suspect alone; always wear a bullet-proof vest if there's even a hint of it kicking off; watch the women because they're often the worst; keep your mace in your pocket and not in your handbag* … More rules and regulations than the Home Office, but Josa appreciated her sister's unwavering concern.

Preya nodded towards the front door. 'He seems nice.'

'Did he try it on with you?'

'No! He sang *your* praises, talked about *you*, smiled when he spoke about *you*, and oh, yeah, asked questions about *you*.'

Josa shook her head but couldn't quite manage to keep the grin from her face. 'God! I forgot to ask! How did it go today? For you!'

In her early twenties, Preya had been a successful model and Josa had never understood why she'd walked away from the fashion industry but, to her former agent's delight, she was now back on the books and earlier today had completed her first big shoot in several years. Preya rolled her eyes. 'I'd forgotten how boring, vacuous it is, how badly you get treated and ...' She shook her head. 'Not exactly what I went to university for.'

'Talking of which ... You studied Cultural Mythology and all that.'

'Yep.'

Josa looked down through the window of the flat's front room. 'What's Pandora's box?' She could just about make out Blake getting into his taxi. He must have moved fast to reach it so soon. The wind tugged at his jacket and hair. He always looked such a mess, Josa reflected, as if the act of maintaining a half-way respectable appearance was beyond him. And if he couldn't even manage that ... But somehow he had given her leads, ideas, and more importantly, a degree of self-belief. She couldn't work him out. Not yet.

'Pandora's box? It's a Greek myth.'

Josa nodded. Watched Blake's taxi pull away and saw the first drops of rain hit the window.

'It was a box that contained all the evils of the world,' Preya told her. 'And opening it would unleash every last one of them.'

# CHAPTER 62

This felt like a council of war. The air was heavy with tension and cigar smoke. The circular walnut table they sat around was so polished that Josa could see her face in its patina. To her left, she heard Dempsey puffing on his thick Romeo y Julieta and across from her she could see a man he'd introduced minutes earlier, John Mason, studiously reading case notes. They sat in one of Moonfleet's larger study rooms on the ground floor. Books lined one wall. Another held shelves stacked with magazines, DVDs, VHS cassettes and audio tapes.

'What exactly are we here for?' Josa realised she was whispering.

'Danny thinks it's time to take it up a gear,' Dempsey replied. 'Time to get serious.'

'That'll be a first.' She looked at her watch. 'Where is he? He was supposed –'

The door opened and Josa craned her neck to see who was entering the room.

He walked into the study and that act alone was like staking a claim to it, although his manner was relaxed to the point of nonchalance. He took long strides in a quick, easy gait. Right hand in the trouser pocket of a three-button, light grey suit that was cut to show off his tall, lean frame. Blue necktie and shirt. A healthy tan, short dark hair, longer than a brush cut and although slightly outdated with a side parting and not a lock out of place, he looked well groomed as opposed to over-groomed.

Clean shaven and good looking, the man looked to be in his mid-thirties, and although she was transfixed by the handsome stranger, the trained police officer in Josa also took in the reaction of the two other people in the room; or rather, their non-response. Seeing him like this was as natural as daylight. But she'd seen this figure before; couldn't quite believe it was –

'Blake!'

He nodded. 'Morning all.'

Josa wanted to say something about his appearance but realised such frivolity would seem out of place. His transformation struck her as a physical declaration that he was well and truly back and that he was deadly serious about the hunt they had embarked on together.

Sure enough, he was immediately down to business. 'Before we get underway I'd like to thank John Mason for coming over to help us out. John's an old friend of mine and Dad's, but I think this is the first time you guys have met?'

Josa nodded. Paused. 'Dad's?'

Dempsey gave a *what you gonna do?* shrug and said, 'He sometimes calls me

Dad.'

'Well,' Blake continued, 'if I was given the option of having the entire Metropolitan Police Service at my disposal or his help for a single day, I'd tell the Met to stand down.'

'Thank you, Daniel,' Mason said. He spoke with a northern accent and Josa guessed he was from Lancashire. 'I just hope I can help you put this bastard away.'

Dempsey squeezed the other man's forearm in a gesture of *good to have you on board.* Mason looked to be in his early seventies, and although his movements were a little stiff, he carried an unmistakable air of authority. Gaunt, almost to the point of suggesting ill-health, but with lively, dark brown eyes. He retained what Josa's mother always called *a fine head of hair for an older gentleman.* He wore a two-button black suit and plain tie. Back ramrod straight. John Mason had ex-copper written all over him like a tattoo.

'This man,' Dempsey declared, 'taught me everything I know!'

'Don't try blaming it on me, son!' Mason replied.

'We're glad you could join us, sir,' Blake reiterated. 'Okay then.

Before we move onto the main point of business, Josa, have you got anywhere yet with the post-mortem report on Jill Kennedy?'

'Erm …' She was trying not to stare at the 'new' Daniel Blake. Within a short period of time, she would realise he had changed very little. Blake's gestures and characteristics remained the same. He still ran his palm over his face when he considered something. When he smiled, he always gave the broadest grin and, just as before, when he had an idea he was fond of, it fell out of him in an excited gabble.

But now, here in his Moonfleet lair, he looked more serious than she had ever known him to be, and had an almost spellbinding air. She shook her head. 'Post-mortem report. Yes. We're no further along. I mean, the report's all in and I've emailed you copies but they've still not concluded what it was that actually struck her over the head.'

Dempsey turned to her. 'What d'you mean?'

'There were traces of …' She paused. ' …*something* found in her cranial injury. The lab boys are having problems identifying what it is.'

'Who's leading on this?' Blake enquired.

'Simon Maxwell.'

'Want me to lean on him?' Dempsey asked.

'No.'

'I'll lean on him.'

'Jack, he isn't holding out on me, he's just having a hard time pinning this one down.'

'Jesus!'

'It happens!' Blake said, aiming his comment at Dempsey. 'Good. Keep me informed, would you, Josa?'

'Sure.'

'Thanks. Okay.' Blake nodded and everyone sensed they'd arrived at the main event. During the exchange with Dempsey he'd removed his suit jacket, rolled up his shirt sleeves, undone the top button of his shirt and tugged his necktie loose and low. Now he half-sat, half-stood against a desk. Behind him, the double doors to the patio were closed and covered by curtains. Thin bars of light framed them but otherwise the room was gloomy.

'I think you all know by now that I believe that the man we're hunting is Professor Paul Salinger.' Blake paused to make sure everyone was nodding. 'A lecturer. Forty-two years old. Eternal bachelor. No kids or significant other. The man has achieved fuck all in his life. A few academic books that sold about five copies each, but he wants the big time. And that's what worries me a little.'

'What do you mean?' Josa asked.

'I mean, in a way, he may want to get caught and the attendant fame. I don't think that's why he started down this scarlet street, but now? Well, he may crave that notoriety. That celebrity status.'

'I agree with Daniel,' Mason said. 'That's what makes this bugger scary. He may have already accepted that's he going to be apprehended at some stage. So he wants to make sure he's remembered as a success and, to him, that means more murders.'

'Can I play the devil's advocate here?' Josa leant forward. 'Are we absolutely convinced he's the perp? I mean, what evidence do we really have?'

'I just know,' Blake replied.

'That's good enough for me!' Dempsey announced.

'Agreed,' Mason seconded.

'Great … but guys! We're gonna need more!'

'And we'll get more,' Blake said. 'I'm gambling he's killed before. I don't think Becka Hoyle was his first victim. I believe he's murdered before and I'd bet the house his first victim was someone he knew well. A young woman he had a relationship with.'

'Whoa, whoa, whoa!' Josa raised her palms. 'There you go again. We can't conduct an investigation that's led by gut feeling.'

'Why not?' Dempsey grinned.

'I get indigestion,' Josa deadpanned.

'It's not just gut feeling,' Blake replied. 'It's common for the early victims of serial killers to get overlooked as investigators don't connect them as the work of one man. MOs tend to evolve in a sequence of murders, meaning the first few attacks are often recognised as part of a bigger picture *only* when the killer is apprehended. Donald Gaskins admitted to over a hundred murders. Peter Sutcliffe, the Yorkshire Ripper; Andrei Chikatilo, the Butcher of Rostov; Harold Shipman, the monster with over 200 murders positively ascribed to him ... these are serial killers from across the world with one thing in common.'

'Go on, then,' Josa said.

'Like dozens of others, each of them had been arrested for one set of murders and subsequently found to have earlier victims. What I'm saying is that it's common for us to pick up the scent of a serial killer when he's already notched up a few victims. And when we look at the elaborate nature of what we originally assumed were the first few killings in this case, it leads me to suspect there was at least one murder before them. One murder where he was learning. One murder that sparked it all off. And, guess what! We're going to identify his first victim. And that's how we're going to catch him. My good friend will now elaborate ...'

Blake nodded to Dempsey and then took a seat at the table.

'Thanks, Danny Boy. Now in front of you you'll find some case notes I collated for you guys. There's a profile of Salinger that the big man put together for us ...'

'My pleasure,' Mason said.

'... Danny's case notes and then a whole bunch of names. Each name is a girl who's gone missing during the past two years. It's taken me a fair few hours to whittle the list down, and I'm not there yet, not by a long shot. But now that Danny is convinced Salinger is our man, we can speed the process up and start paring these names down a lot further.'

'What do you intend to do?' Josa asked.

Blake answered. 'I think Salinger will have enjoyed his first murder. The sense of immutable achievement it gave him. So I believe the missing girl disappeared between twelve and six weeks ago. The Professor never leaves the capital so she'll have been based in London. She'll have been bright but not too bright. He wanted to be her educator. He wanted her to look up to him. So, she'll have been aged between nineteen and twenty-four. It goes without saying she was blonde, although not necessarily a natural blonde.'

Dempsey took the baton. 'So, with all those criteria I think we can really drill down into these names. We want to get to the point where we've only got a handful of names and then we can focus on them properly, get a link between one of them and Salinger.'

Josa flicked through the pages of names. 'It's still going to take you some time.'

'There's three of us and we're fast workers,' Mason replied.

'We're going to focus on this list of names,' Blake told Josa. 'You're going to go back to the station to manage your team and the investigation. But could you privately share our thoughts with the more clued-up officers in your team? I'd like them to have a heads-up, so if they come across any hint of a connection between one of the murdered girls and Salinger ...'

Josa was nodding. 'I'll have to go slow. Cordelia Smith has already complained to a few influential high-ups and Gilmour is scared of her. Well, scared of the guys she's complained to. If Cordelia gets wind that I'm targeting her boss ... But I can do it. Don't worry about that.'

'Good!' Blake stood and put his palms on the table. 'I don't think I need to remind anyone that today is Friday. If we don't stop him, he will kill again in less than four days' time.'

'I want to help!' Josa saw Holly Blake standing in the doorway. She was wearing a blue boiler suit, and her dark hair was once again up, kept in place by grips and a red handkerchief. She looked like a youthful Rosie the Riveter.

'Absolutely not!' Blake replied. 'How long have you been listening?'

She crossed the room. 'We've got four days till this freak kills again. Dad! You've got to let me help! Tell him, Uncle Jack, Uncle John.'

Mason stood and walked to the desk. Poured a glass of water. 'This is between you two.'

'Uncle Jack!'

Dempsey took a puff on his Cuban cigar. 'Like the man said ...'

'Josa!'

She looked at the young girl, so indignant, so angry, so blind to the possibility that her opinion could be anything other than a hundred per cent accurate.

'I say she could help.'

'No!' Blake replied curtly.

'Why not?' Josa asked.

'Because I don't want her involved. Because I know what it can do to you.'

Holly looked like she was on the point of exploding but checked herself, turned and stormed from the room.

'Christ. There goes Hurricane Holly Belle,' Blake muttered.

Mason took a sip of his water. 'Remind you of anyone we used to know, JD?' he asked, and Dempsey replied with quiet laughter.

Josa drove through the dark country lanes, thinking about Holly. The teenager reminded her of herself. Was the bond genuine? And if so, she wondered, what formed it? Empathy? Vanity?

She took a corner. Probably neither. Don't look so hard. She just liked her and recognised some of the artifice she relied on to create that knuckle-dusting confidence of hers. Oh, the horrors of youth. Josa glanced into her rear-view mirror.

*The young Asian girl, again. Still marching purposefully away from the kids, although they're out of sight by now. Striding with a look of resolve in her eyes, despite having no idea where she was going except out. As she passes beneath the metal arch over the school gates, it casts a shadow over her: a broad, black cross on her back.*

Josa snapped her eyes forward. No kid should ever be without a mum to rely on. Without taking her attention from the road, she reached for her phone.

Midnight. Daniel Blake closed the file he was working through. 'I'll be back in ten,' he said to Mason and Dempsey, who were both engrossed in their own dossiers.

Holly's light was still on and he gently knocked on her door. 'Yeah?'

He pushed it open. 'Hi. Can I come in?'

''Course you can.'

Her television was on mute, a black and white movie flickering across its screen while Rimsky-Korsakov's *Scheherazade* played on her hi-fi. A laptop flickered on a wiki page, her phone screen was bright and she had an open paperback in her hand.

'You got enough on the go?'

'No, but the radio's on the blink.' She smiled and lowered the music.

Blake sat on the edge of her bed. 'Thanks for not giving me a hard time today. About the decision. You know, the decision I came to this morning. You normally would have done and I'm grateful …'

She shrugged. 'I can see where you're coming from. I just think you're wrong, that's all.' She looked down. 'And it is hurtful. You don't have faith in me.'

'Oh, Holly Belle, darling, I've got so much faith in you, you wouldn't believe it. But this is something you don't want to get involved with because once you do …'

'I've seen you help so many people, Dad. And I'm not just saying it, but it's one of the reasons I love you. I want to be like my old man and help people, and in this case I want to help stop a serial killer. I think I can handle reading a few missing persons' files if that's what at stake.'

'I know. But it's not just about reading the files. It's the whole thing you'll be getting into. I know you!'

She said nothing.

'Okay,' he said. 'I'm turning in soon. Try to get some sleep yourself.'

Still she remained silent, her eyes pleading with him. He reached the doorway. Paused. 'Okay! You can give us a hand tomorrow.' He held up his palms, quick to stop the torrent of joy his daughter was straining to hold back. 'You will go through the files. You will discard those missing persons whose cases do not meet certain, easily applicable, criteria. You're helping us to whittle the names down! That's all. I mean it! After that's done, that's it. I don't want you involved in field work and you're not a part of the next stage of the investig–'

But she was already on her feet, hugging him. 'Brilliant! Thanks, Dad!' She stepped back. 'You won't regret this.'

'I already do.'

'I won't let you down,' she told him.

'I know that … Come here!' He returned her embrace. 'I love you. You know that?'

'I know.' She sprang onto her bed. 'Well, I better get some sleep. Early start.'

'Your turn to make breakfast.'

'Dad.'

'Yeah?'

'Your sudden change of heart. I mean, I'm grateful and all that. But was it anything to do with anyone else? I mean did Josa call and whisper in your ear or anything?'

'Maybe ...' Blake gave a half-smile. 'Now get some sleep. I've a feeling tomorrow is going to be ...' He paused. 'Did she call you as well? Advise you to play that conversation like ...'

But she was smiling too broadly for him to continue.

'Why do I feel like I'm suddenly outnumbered?' he said, and gently closed her door.

# CHAPTER 64

Blake looked over the landing balustrade and chandelier, across the ground floor of his home and the space where Josa Jilani had first listened to his pleas. Was she any better off for his involvement? Could he be some kind of ... *curse* was too strong a word. He glanced over his shoulder at Holly's closed door. The doubts had hit him even before he'd left her room.

*Was he doing the right thing allowing her to help?*

Sifting through the files was not, in itself, a cause for concern. But it was the precedent, the fact that this represented some kind of inaugural act – the first time she had actively and deliberately helped in one of his cases ... Blake reflected that at the time, it's sometimes difficult to spot a beginning. The camouflage of everyday life conceals its truth, passing it off as an ending or a brief divergence. Nothing more. But later, and perhaps to other people, a beginning is easy to identify. He gripped the balustrade. Remembered his earliest days, and the pain made him close his eyes. The cold. His shoulder throbbing where he'd been clutched so hard ... The falling snow. And Dempsey – Jack Dempsey, the big, strange American – miraculously arriving in time to save him when he should have been on his way back to the States. Christ, even at that point it had almost cost him his life and yet –

Blake pushed away from the balustrade. Headed upstairs. Moonlight shone through the windows of the turret room, filtering into the narrow passageway that housed the steps leading up to it. Plunged in thought, he climbed the stairs more slowly than usual.

Daniel Blake recognised that his life was much like any other, containing periods where it seemed the world was his. No dream was too extravagant, no aim too ambitious. When he could juggle planets and back-heel stars. But the other times still haunted him. The times he had lost. The crushing failures that had been down to circumstance, bad luck, his own stupidity, vanity or misjudgement. The cellar. The horrors … He had endured the loss of friends, confidence, and the shattering of his soul.

He stood in his turret room. Feelings were easy. Decisions were hard. He had let Holly in. To keep her close where he could protect her … She would work that out, over time, but he had still given his blessing for the kind of life that had almost beaten him. With all his strength and resilience and reasons to go on, he had been broken and brought to the knife-edge of –

He looked towards the floodlit cathedral and, as always, he remembered.

## CHAPTER 65

### *Five years earlier: Where the monsters live*

'Is that *my* gun?' the child asked.

'No, it's not your gun, Jamie.' A pause. He looked at the lad's father. 'Why don't you give it to me, Thom?'

'Hello, Danny.'

'Better not let Mara know you're planning to take your own life,' Blake told him. 'She'd kill you.'

Thom Diaz tried to smile. 'She probably would. And she'd guess you'd be here, trying to stop me like Don Quixote.'

'Just put the gun down, eh? Let Jamie go and –'

'How long have we known each other?'

'Too long. I don't know. I can't really focus with that banana …' Blake nodded to the police standard-issue Glock 17 in the other man's hand, 'pointing at me.'

The pair stood about fifteen feet apart, on top of the Cathedral Tower, alone except for the Golden Angel and Thom Diaz's son, Jamie. Dressed in pyjamas and a parka, the boy's chin rested on top of the wall, and when he occasionally looked up to take in the stars his teeth chattered from the cold. His father's hand gently held his left shoulder but he seemed oblivious to the grown-ups' conversation.

'I'd try not to kill you,' said Thom.

'Well, what are friends for?'

'But I'd put a bullet in your belly. A long stay in hospital. Peritonitis, knowing the hospitals around here. Bullet might shatter your spine on exit.'

Blake gave that slow nod that people give when processing bad news. 'Not really the answer I was looking for but –'

'You can't help this time. I've got to …' Thom shot a glance over his shoulder. Into the dark fall. 'And I've got to take Jamie. I love him too much to leave him.' It was a 160-foot drop.

In his peripheral vision Blake could see Jamie Diaz craning his neck to stare at the stars. The boy's teeth started chattering again. But Blake maintained eye contact with Thom, aware he was just one movement away from throwing himself and the child over the tower. The sky brooded in the background. There was a storm coming.

'About twenty-five years.'

'What?'

'We met when I was not much older than Jamie,' Blake said, 'which means, yeah, we've known each other for about twenty-five years ... '

'I'm one of the few people who knew the real you. Your real name. How all this got started. About the murders. I knew you before you became you. Never told a soul. Doesn't that count for anything, Danny?'

'I didn't tell anyone I was coming after you.'

'You promise?'

'I promise.'

'How did you even know? That it wasn't the pusher? How did you know I shot Robbo?'

'You closed his eyes. The pusher wouldn't have ... you're a good man in a bad situation.' Blake didn't add that it hadn't even been a case he'd been contracted to work on. But Detective Sergeant Roberts had enjoyed certain 'connections'. And more to the point, the police had been at a loss. That was why they'd phoned Blake. That was why they always phoned Blake. 'I knew you'd run but guessed you'd tell Mara you were leaving. When I got to your place I saw you pulling out of your drive. Followed you ...' He stopped. Suddenly uncertain because –

The muscles around Thom's eyes tightened.

He'd touched a nerve. '*What?*' Blake said, 'What are you not telling me?'

A tiny pause. 'What am I not telling you? We both know how this plays, so don't ... I'm a police officer who's embezzled thousands. Someone found out and I killed an off-duty *copper*!'

'Who was high as a kite when he came at you. But there's something else!' He didn't say it, but *something worse*. 'What are you not telling me?'

'What?' Diaz shook his head in feigned disbelief. '*Christ!* For this to get any worse I'd have to –'

'Shoot your best friend on top of a cathedral. Thom, listen to me.'

'Can you save me?'

Jamie spoke for the second time since Blake's arrival. 'I'm very cold, Daddy. Can we go home?'

'*Can you save me?*'

Blake paused. Taking stock. The top of the Cathedral Tower was dominated by the Golden Angel – an imposing, gilded, winged female on a twenty-foot pole which rose from the centre of the square. It spun when the wind blew but now came to rest so her eyes gazed down on the men below.

'Yes,' Blake replied, 'you're going to do a stretch but I can get you out the other side.'

Thom's eyes held so much hope. 'You know what, Jamie? Yeah, I think it's about time we got back home. I'll tuck you up nice and warm in bed. *How does that sound?*'

Jamie missed it but the last question was flicked Blake's way and he replied with a tiny nod.

'I don't want to go to bed, Daddy.'

Thom gave a short laugh. 'I bet Holly doesn't give you such a hard time.' And then to Jamie, 'Well, we can stay up. Just this once. Watch one of your favourite films together. How's that?'

'Yippeddy-ay!'

Thom nodded at Blake and mouthed the words, '*Thank you*.'

'Let's start the walk back to your old life, fella,' Blake told his friend. 'You know, spending time with Jamie. Getting a babysitter now and again and taking Mara out for a meal …'

Thom started to lower the Glock. 'Sounds like heaven.'

A gunshot. For a moment Blake thought Thom had accidentally pulled the trigger but he saw a spray of mortar ping from the wall and heard shouts from below. There was blood on Jamie's face. At precisely the same moment, both men realised what had happened. Thom looked directly at Blake.

'You lied!'

Blake held up his palms. 'No!'

'Oh, God … you can't help me.'

And Blake knew with a terrible certainty what was about to happen.

Thom kissed the top of his son's head. The movement was quick and slick, and while he stooped, his left arm tightened across the boy's torso. 'I love you, son.'

Blake – already moving forward. 'Thom!'

In one dreadful, elegant movement, Thom took a half-step back. The top half of his body fell backwards over the wall. His left arm, curled around Jamie's waist, carrying the boy so as his body fell from the tower, his son was with him.

*Blake is virtually in flight, but too far away, reaching out for the tiny, terrified figure of Jamie Diaz.*

# CHAPTER 66

It was a sunny Saturday morning and Detective Chief Inspector Josa Jilani crossed the station car park, heading towards her blue Ford Fiesta. A man leant against her vehicle, his face hidden by an explosive bouquet of flowers. She could see tulips and gypsy grass but not the features of the person who held them.

'Hello!' she said to the flowers.

The bouquet lowered and Paul Salinger smiled at her. 'Good morning, Josa! I was passing and I thought … No, that's not quite true. I wanted to thank you for a lovely evening.' He handed her the flowers. 'Thank you for a lovely evening!' He smiled again.

'They're gorgeous!' She looked flustered. 'Thank you!'

'I'm glad you like them. I also wondered if you're free tomorrow evening?'

'What did you have in mind?'

'Well, as you know, I have a book called *The Hitchcock Murders* being published very shortly. Well …' He gave the kind of pause that signalled he was about to talk highly of himself and felt slightly improper for doing so. 'Apparently a national newspaper is rather interested in it. In fact, they're serialising it next week and want to give …' Another pause. 'A huge launch party at the British Film Institute. Free bar. Plenty of celebrity guests. The only downside is that you have to listen to me give a speech. What do you say?'

'Well …'

'We'd love to come!' Blake's voice. 'Wouldn't we, Josa?' He had appeared at her shoulder. All smiles and bonhomie. 'Sounds like Josa's investigation has really given your career a fillip. I hope she'll be getting ten per cent.'

'I'll think of some way to repay her,' Salinger replied. 'But Mr

Blake! How different you look! What on earth could have triggered this transformation?'

'Some of the police high-ups think I'm a bit of a loose cannon. Hard to believe, I know. By looking like this I go some way to allaying their concerns.'

'Of course, of course!' his tone made it clear that he didn't believe a syllable of it. He shot a glance at Josa and gave a mischievous smile. 'And that was the only reason, was it? You weren't out to impress anybody or –'

'Lovely flowers,' Blake interrupted. 'Did you know Hitchcock wanted a scene in the rather wonderful *Foreign Correspondent* where a man was murdered in a field of tulips? He wanted to catch the moment when the victim's blood was spattered across the petals. Thought it would look good. What do you think? Appeal much?'

'Thanks for that,' Josa said, sticking the bouquet in the boot of her car.

'In the end,' Salinger replied, 'He abandoned the idea as he knew the scene required colour and *Foreign Correspondent* was black and white.' He looked at Blake. 'I'm surprised you enjoy that film.'

'Why?'

'Oh, no reason. So! Josa! Will you come tomorrow evening? It would mean a lot to me to have you there.'

'Oh, come on!' she replied playfully, 'With all those celebrity guests and shaking hands with important people, you wouldn't have time for me!'

'Ah! We're taking over all of the BFI for the party but there's a special little green room where only VIPs such as yourself will be allowed to go. We can meet there. Aside from Hitchcock, the other great love of my life is cookery, and each and every item of food in that room will have been prepared by me. I'm trying to show off and demonstrate what a good catch I am … You've got to at least give me points for trying …'

'Well, I do like a nice vol-au-vent … All right! I'll be there!'

'I'm invited, too, I hope!' Blake said. He paused and his voice became a little harder. 'There's something I'd love to chat to you about. Tony Taylor. And how he's linked to you.'

'Oh, Mr Blake, you're such a tease. And *of course* you're invited. In fact ...' And now the Professor's voice was stripped of its flippancy. 'I'm preparing a *very* special surprise for you!'

'And what's that?'

Paul Salinger smiled but said nothing.

# CHAPTER 67

Paul Salinger gave Blake a knowing smile. And then a second. And a third ... Every few paces a banner featuring the Professor's image interrupted their stroll to the British Film Institute. They showed a besuited Professor Salinger, poker-faced, sitting at an angle, neck craned over his shoulder and thus looking directly into the camera. A huge rook was perched on his right shoulder and, below this image, a friendly red font carried the words:

**Paul Salinger: The Hitchcock Murders**

The Professor looked striking and youthful, his skin flawless and hair immaculate.

Blake sniffed. 'He's been airbrushed.'

The BFI Southbank is located, as its name suggests, on London's Southbank, with much of the complex nestling beneath the concrete monstrosity that is Waterloo Bridge. Its facade is far from imposing. The rear aspect is grey and ugly and overpowered by a car park that looms beside it. From the front, or rather the elevation that overlooks the Thames, it appears to be little more than a bar and restaurant, with normally only a few posters and banners suggesting the building houses a cinema. But on that night, Salinger's publishers had ensured the BFI had gone all out on high-impact, Hollywood dressing.

Blake had parked his Cutlass nearby, and now he and Josa walked along the Southbank. To their right, the unsleeping Thames looked magnificent. Party boats and tugs ploughed through its channels. Lights from the Embankment shone like stars across its dark waters and, northwards, Westminster Bridge formed an ancient and impressive foreground to the majestic Palace of Westminster.

As they walked beneath a street lamp, Josa was able to properly see Blake's attire. She'd expected his dinner suit would be an elegant, simple affair. Black, single breasted with no frills, a plain dinner shirt and slim bow tie. Not this.

'Jesus!' she said at last and started laughing.

'*What?*'

His dinner suit was midnight blue with a black detail along the seams and edges of the lapels. His cream shirt had cover-button frills and his dark bow tie was a long, limp affair, calling to mind saloon-bar habitués in classic westerns.

'You look like a gambler on, I don't know, a Mississippi steamboat!'

Blake's face lit up. 'Thanks! For a moment I thought you didn't like it.' He beamed. 'Not bad, eh? Heard it was a black-tie event and thought I'd get this bad boy out of retirement.' He flicked imaginary dust from one of the sleeves.

'Where did you get it?'

'Dunno. Some charity shop. Marie Curie, probably, on the High Street. Years ago.'

'What about me?' As soon as she asked the question, Josa was immersed in a did-I-just-say-that moment. She hadn't meant to draw attention to how she looked and had deliberately worn a broad, black and white scarf to conceal her sister's prized John Galliano that she'd borrowed for the night. Or rather, to conceal its racy plunging neckline. The dress was black, sleek and daring, and completely at odds with the tatty scarf she wore over it.

'You look beautiful.'

He didn't sound flippant but Josa felt stung. 'You haven't even glanced at what I'm wearing.'

'I don't give a fuck what you're wearing. You always look beautiful. But, you know what, I think you should look dazzling as well tonight, Josa. Come here.'

He stopped, put his hands on her bare shoulders. She felt that unique thrill that only the touch of flesh can generate. 'Now.' He untied the scarf. She held her breath as he pulled it away, shocked and perversely proud that she hadn't tried to stop him. Josa felt naked, and with a whip-like movement Blake tossed the scarf into the Thames. Josa wanted to take a step back but found herself moving forward, into him, instead.

His hands returned to her shoulders. 'You're amazing,' he told her, his face inching closer to hers.

A loud bang, like a gunshot, made them both jump, and Josa put her palm over her heart. 'What the hell?' Her eyes followed the direction of the sound and she saw the red sparks of a firework falling across the Thames, immediately followed by another rocket.

'Fireworks,' said Blake.

They had stepped apart. 'Yeah,' said Josa. 'Fireworks.' An awkward pause. 'Right! Good!' she announced, suddenly like a games teacher addressing a gym full of apathetic school children. 'Well, I'll just dig out the invites from my handbag and we're ready to go.'

They took a couple more paces then paused by the entrance. It had been extravagantly decked out for the occasion and a thick, gold cordon looped around an outside carpeted area. Security guards stood at regular points around it, facing outwards. A sizeable gaggle of members of the public crowded around, looking in, shrieking when a star was spotted and pointing camera phones into the building. The guards allowed a few professional photographers to lurk at the end of the red square nearest the Thames, chatting to each other, digital SLRs at the ready.

Josa caught sight of a celebrity guest approaching the BFI, or rather, she saw the entourage of a celebrity guest approach the entrance. Whoever it was, she was surrounded by about half a dozen well-dressed flunkies who parted when they reached the red carpet. The crowd at last saw her, squealed and cheered. The photographers called to her and *snap, snap, snap! Lovely! Beautiful! One over the shoulder, please!*

The clamour died down as she entered the foyer and disappeared further into the building. The fuss reassured Josa. If anyone did recognise her from her work, they were unlikely to react. This was a night for celebrity-spotting, not pointing out police officers who happened to be toiling away on high-profile cases.

Another expensively dressed group approached and the crowd noise began to swell again but the photographers weren't fooled. As the new arrivals strolled across the carpet the watching public were able to see they were not famous. 'Nobodies,' shrugged one of the photographers, and the camera lenses drooped.

Josa knew that the launch of Salinger's book had turned into a distasteful stunt. The whole circus was capitalising on the real-life 'Hitchcock murders' and what would have been a standard literary launch without the crimes had mutated into something grand and grotesque.

And yet Josa still felt enormously energised by it. Her heart was still pounding from her close encounter with Blake and this glamour simply added to her excitement.

She'd never attended such a star-studded event. She'd heard about them from Preya, who had flirted with them all of her life, especially during her modelling days. But even her sister had never gone into detail about them, dismissing them as though unwilling to appear part of that world. But now, here she was. Red carpets, glamorous guests, paparazzi … Blake had already registered his disapproval of the whole thing and Josa agreed because she *knew* it was invidious. But it *felt* thrilling and she sensed an electricity in the air.

Minutes earlier Blake had been clearly – and annoyingly – unmoved by it all. As they walked beside the Thames he'd reeled off the names of local pubs and seemed inclined to delay their visit to the BFI for a quick drink in one or more of them. 'Just over the bridge there's a lovely little bar called Gordon's. You don't think it would hurt if we popped in for a swift –'

'No! Remember what we're here for,' Josa had told him. But now, as she handed over one of the invites, he took it with wordless compliance, as if he was ready.

They sauntered across the red carpet. The photographers took a couple of snaps and Josa presented their invitations to a statuesque blonde on the door who briefly checked the names on the cards against the list on her iPad. Then she smiled.

'Detective Chief Inspector Josa Jilani, Mr Daniel Blake …' She looked up from the invites. 'Welcome to *The Hitchcock Murders*.'

# CHAPTER 68

Blake buttonholed one of the attendants. 'Are you using the large green room on the first floor tonight?'

'Yes, sir.'

'And I'm guessing that's where we'd find Salinger?'

'Yes, sir.'

'Thanks.'

Blake led Josa into the building and past the doors of NFT1. They zipped down a short flight of steps, walked through a broad corridor and quickly ascended an open flight of stairs that ran along the wall of the vast foyer. This cavernous room is generally given over to the box office, queues and displays, but tonight it housed the main throng of the party. Josa glanced over it as they walked towards a large set of double doors, again guarded by a gold cordon and a standard-issue blonde holding a clipboard.

'Hi,' said Blake.

'Good evening, sir.'

'I think Professor Dillinger is expecting us.'

'Professor *Salinger*.'

'That's the monkey.'

'And you are?'

'Daniel Blake. Hello!'

She glanced down at her board. 'Ah, Mr Blake. Yes, Professor Salinger is expecting you.' She leant towards him. A flash of cleavage and a smile. 'You're one of the very few guests who has the okay to enter the green room.'

'Kind of Dillinger to arrange that.'

'Salinger.'

'Oh, yeah.'

She consulted the document clamped to her clipboard. 'You're down for a ten minute slot in …' A glance at her diamond-studded watch. 'Just under half an hour.'

'You mean I've not got, like, an *access all areas*?'

'I'm afraid not, sir. The nature of tonight's event means there are a lot of people Professor Salinger is obliged to meet and greet and so we need to enforce a rota, I'm afraid. There are drinks, canapés and entertainment in the main lounge for while you're waiting.'

'Unbelievable. He said he liked me. Didn't he, Josa? He said he liked me and then –'

'Are you Josa Jilani?' the blonde asked.

'Yeah. Why?'

'Ah, Professor Salinger gave special instructions that you were to be allowed in at any time.'

'Oh, well, that's nice of him.'

'You go in,' said Blake, stepping back.

'No. I'm not going to go in without you.'

'I'll be fine. I'll mix and mingle. That's what people do at parties, isn't it? Mix, mingle, witty repartee. I've seen it all on TV.'

'I'll come back with you, later.'

The woman on the door said, 'Professor Salinger anticipated this dilemma and asked me to tell you' – she was addressing Josa directly – 'that he has some lamb vol-au-vents he made especially for you and a bottle of Krug to accompany them!'

Despite everything, Josa's face broke into a broad grin. 'Well, I *am* starving …' The attendant was smiling too, and seeing this, the two women started to laugh.

'Oh, well, you fuck off in there, then!' Blake snapped and strode away.

'Blake!' Josa's high heels meant he'd taken a good half-dozen paces by the time she stopped him. 'What the hell d'you think you're doing? I don't appreciate you swearing at me like that and I'm not prepared to put up with it. Who the hell do you think you are?'

Blake took two angry lungfuls of air and moved closer to

whisper in her ear. 'The attendant will tell Salinger I'm acting like a love-sick schoolboy,' he revealed, in a surprisingly calm tone. 'He'll be delighted his stupid little plan is working. By acting like this I can make him underestimate me and give him more false confidence.'

He drew himself up to his full height.

Josa shook her head. '*Stupid little plan*? Don't pretend that was all an act.'

Blake gave an expansive shrug. 'The art that conceals art. I'd be willing to bet the house that Salinger forked out for this shindig tonight. Forget what he says about publishers or whoever paying for it. He sees this as his coronation. Look around you. He'll be feeling unbeatable. That makes him vulnerable.'

'Don't make it personal between you two.'

'But that's exactly what is. What it always is for me. Just like it's always personal for you. Every job a chance to square up to your mother and nestle up to you father. It's why we both flutter so close to the candlelight of insanity.'

'Candlelight of insanity? Yeah. Speak for yourself, and really ...' She wrinkled her nose. 'Don't go there.'

'I meant it as a compliment. Honestly. If more people were like you – took a stance every time they needed to, rather than just accept the *small* injustices, then the world would be a better place.' He frowned, as if unhappy with his wording. 'That ended in cliché but you get my drift.'

'Blake! Just ... just stay focussed. Don't let the theatricality of this whole thing get the better of you. We're here as part of an ongoing investigation. It's not you versus him and we're not here because it's some glamorous – oh my God!' she broke off, staring over the balcony and into the foyer. 'That's Robert Pattinson!'

'Who?'

'Do you ever watch films with any *living* people in them?'

Blake's phone rang. He glanced at the screen. *Jack Dempsey*. 'You go and say hi to the Professor. I'll catch you later.'

'Cool.' She turned away and Blake called after her. 'And be careful!'

'Yeah, yeah.'

Blake answered his phone. 'Hey.'

'Danny Boy. Which do you want first? The surprising news or the scary news?'

Blake walked down the stairs, looking over the party that was in full swing throughout the huge entrance area. He pressed his phone hard to his ear to counter the buzz of drinkers getting merry on free booze. 'Let's save the scares till last, shall we?'

'Well, the surprising news is that the lab boys have finished their analysis of the injuries that killed Jill Kennedy.'

'About bloody time!' He reached the bottom step and began to move through the mass of people. 'I thought that was finished ages ago?'

'Microscopic fibres found in the head wound. Remember? They had the devil's own job identifying what they were from.'

Blake nodded. 'Yeah, of course. I said the lab would identify them as metal. Our killer is recreating murders from Hitchcock movies. So, I'm thinking *Murder!* and *Marnie*. In both films we get victims who are cracked over the head with a poker. They don't get up in the morning.'

'Well, that's the scary news.'

A party-goer interrupted Blake. 'Hey! Look-ee here!' A hand on his shoulder. Friendly. Inappropriate. 'I'm a big fan of yours. Great to see you back! Can I have your autograph? Can you sign it *To Alex*?'

'Sure,' Blake muttered. He had never been burdened with a public profile and guessed the party-goer had him confused with an actor or one of the celebs that had hit the South Bank that night. Guessing it was quicker to simply sign something and move on, he scrawled a couple of hieroglyphs on an invite and hurried away.

'*Thanks! I'd love to buy you a drink if …*' But Blake had already disappeared, becoming lost in the crowd.

'Sorry,' he said to Dempsey. 'Go on.'

'Well, Simon Maxwell tells me that, yeah, there *are* trace elements in the head wound … but they're not metal.'

'What?' Blake narrowed his eyes. 'It's got to be metal. These murders are following a pattern. We've got to be right about this.'

Dempsey remained silent.

'Christ,' murmured Blake.

Both men knew that if Blake was wrong about the Hitchcock connection they were back to square one, clueless and adrift. 'When can we see the report?'

'I can't give you an exact time.'

'Oh, come on! This is important!'

'Look!' Dempsey replied, 'Maxwell is doing me a favour even telling me any of this. He's supposed to be delivering the report to Gilmour tomorrow morning. Gilmour asked to see it first. But from what I can gather, Maxwell has the hots for Josa so he's trying to do her a favour by giving us an early heads-up …'

'Okay, okay. I'm sorry. Look, thanks for this.' He paused. Quite aside from the investigative implications of this revelation, Kim Gilmour would inevitably seize on Blake's error and claim it was proof that he was out of his depth, too long out of the game to be trusted. He could picture the scene perfectly.

*Nothing personal, Daniel, but you did rather cock this one up. I think it best for all concerned if you simply – poof – disappear and leave it to the experts. You tried your best but …*

Blake tried to clear his thoughts. 'If it wasn't metal, did Maxwell say what they did find in the injury? Wood? Varnish, maybe? Consistent with some kind of cosh or baseball bat?'

'Nope. You see, we were on the phone. He was about to tell me but then his boss came in so he couldn't go into specifics. But …'

'But what?'

'He did say it wasn't metal or leather, then I asked the same question you did, and no … It's not wood, or varnish or anything like that.' There was a pause. The kind of pause Blake didn't like. *'He said that we wouldn't believe what it was.'*

'Will you phone me the moment Maxwell gets back to you?' As

he spoke, Blake recognised a face in the Benugo Bar, the large, swish space that dominates the north-east side of the BFI. Blake had to consciously stop himself from doing a double take as he clocked the laughing woman in the far corner of the room. 'Well, well, well …'

'What is it?' Dempsey asked.

'Nothing. Just seen an old friend I think I'd better have a word with.'

'Okay. Well, I'll call you if I get anything else.'

'You're a star.'

'Yeah. Twinkle, twinkle.'

As Blake crossed the bar room, weaving in and out of couture gowns and pristine tuxedos, dodging trays of canapés and tanned waiters proffering bottles of house champagne, his thoughts were a million miles away from the glamour and glitz of the launch. Two questions were bothering him. If Jill Kennedy wasn't attacked with something made from metal or wood, what the hell had killed her? And more pressingly, just what was the familiar figure in the corner of the bar doing here?

# CHAPTER 70

'Hello, again, Karen.'

Karen Sherwood had been a journalist too many years to allow much to startle her. So the look of surprise in her eyes was only fleeting. Yet Blake had caught it. Heard her laugh pause for a second and registered the impression of her trying to catch her breath.

'It's been a long time,' he added.

His reflection gave her a moment. Enough time for her to reboot her composure. 'Danny!' She embraced him. Held him a heartbeat too long, but when she stood back his smile was genuine. 'This is Julie …' She introduced him to a blonde with long blue nails. 'Would you excuse us for just a moment?' Karen said to her. 'I owe this man a drink.'

'You were quick at the bar,' Blake observed. He was sitting under a poster of Cary Grant playing Roger Thornhill in *North By Northwest*.

'I got you a Gibson.' She handed him the cocktail and sat down. 'Cheers.'

'Cheers.' They clinked glasses. 'Why are you following this one, Karen?'

'Oh. We're right down to business, are we?' She sipped her champagne. 'It's a good story.'

'You've been hounding Josa from the start.'

'It's a good story.' She ignored Blake's shake of the head. 'Oh, come on! A Muslim, British Asian woman gets fast-tracked and then forced to head up one of the highest-profile murder investigations we've seen for decades? Besides …' She flashed him a smile. 'It had you all over it. I knew you'd come to the aid of the defenceless young woman. She's exactly your type.'

'You don't know my type.'

'Blake: hello. Defenceless young woman. That *is* your type.'

'You shouldn't have followed her. You shouldn't have spied on us. And you shouldn't have broken the news about the Hitchcock connection.'

'You know, you're a lot less fun these days.'

'Would it help if I poured the Gibson over your head?'

'No, but it might if you poured it down your throat.'

'Just stay away from Jack.'

'Dempsey? Why? Is he Josa's guardian angel or something?'

'He's not as forgiving as I am.'

'What? Do Dempsey and Jilani have history?'

'Off the record?'

'Off the record.'

'More than she realises.'

'Who do you think the killer is?'

'Dunno. What were *you* doing on the night of Tuesday, 6 March?'

'If you want to talk about the past there are other things I'd rather cover.'

Blake's phone chirruped and he saw it was Dempsey. He stood up, hit the *silent* button. 'I've got to go,' he said. 'But just … please. This case isn't like the usual murder investigations you cover. Watch yourself. You've got my number if you need me. And good luck, Karen.'

'And that's it, is it? The great Daniel Blake prowls in, tells me off like I'm some young kid, warns me off with a growl and then pads away. Jesus, Danny!'

'Just be careful.' Blake glanced into the crowd. 'There'll be other wolves with sharper teeth. You watch yourself.'

For a moment Karen's eyes blazed and Blake wondered if she was about to toss her wine over him. 'You're priceless!' She started to laugh. 'You just don't get it!' she added, between guffaws that grew louder.

'Get what? What's so funny?'

'I've got an interview with the BBC tomorrow. A sit-down one. Prime time. I've got a new agent off the back of this. I've got champagne and a book deal. And what have you got? *Fuck all.* I've seen that look on your face before, Danny, and you know what's always followed it?'

'Tell me.'

'Death.' She challenged him with the word.

Blake reached down, grabbed his cocktail glass and swallowed the Gibson in one.

'You've got a killer you can't catch. No clues, no idea, and you know what? You better keep your *good luck.* Because you're gonna need it just to stay alive. The type of guy this psycho is ...' Karen Sherwood spoke with a chilling certainty. 'He's gonna come after you next.'

# CHAPTER 71

Josa felt uneasy. The statuesque blonde who guarded the green room had given her a conspiratorial smile as she nodded her through. Women like that never gave such secret looks to Josa, and the unspoken exchange unnerved her. Directly ahead, she could see two coat rails, angled so the gap between them formed an entrance to the main body of the room. A wooden sign that read *Jamaica Inn* hung from the ceiling. Josa's knowledge of Hitchcock movies was still sketchy, but from her conversation with Salinger back in the British Museum, she remembered *Jamaica Inn* was something to do with a band of wreckers in nineteenth-century Cornwall. She guessed the green room had been decked out as a tribute to the wreckers' favourite drinking hole – the eponymous inn.

The bar was a rough, wooden, semi-circular affair and the walls had been given a sullied, white plaster effect with period windows painted on at irregular intervals. A fifty-inch plasma screen sat on the floor to Josa's right. It played a long loop of a roaring log fire, and, further along, she saw a tight snug – small, but offering just enough space for two people to hunch over a tiny central table. The only light in the room came from a number of candles wedged in empty wine bottles.

Josa reckoned there were twenty people in the room, including Salinger, who stood chatting by the bar. He broke off his conversation and waved at Josa, beckoning her over. She smiled and stepped forward but –

Cordelia Smith appeared. As if from nowhere, she materialised in the opening between the two coat rails. Josa guessed she wasn't there to take her jacket.

'Miss Jilani.'

'Detective Chief Inspector Jilani,' Josa corrected her, but Cordelia shook her head.

'You're here tonight as a guest of Professor Salinger. Don't forget that.'

'Don't threaten me.'

'This is his moment. Professor Salinger has worked all his life to advance understanding and appreciation of Alfred Hitchcock. He's a brilliant man. People are about to recognise that and you're not going to wreck tonight. This is his moment.'

The venom of Cordelia's tone and the force of the words hit Josa hard. Her heart quickened but her face remained impassive. 'You're right. I'm here as Professor Salinger's guest. And you're here as his assistant. Right?'

'Yes.'

'Good. Then get me a drink. And after that, stay out of my face, girl. And don't tell me who to fuck with. You don't impress me. You certainly don't scare me. When I've got to deal with ten of you in the morning, that's a good day. D'you get me?'

Cordelia held her stare for a moment before turning away and scuttling into the semi-gloom of Jamaica Inn. Josa watched her go and let out a long breath. She looked across at Salinger. He'd observed the whole thing and now, vol-au-vent in one hand, champagne flute in the other, he raised his glass towards her. She couldn't decide if he was astonished or impressed. Probably a bit of both, and the vol-au-vents looked good.

# CHAPTER 72

Blake walked from the Benugo Bar, across the broad foyer, down a short flight of steps and through the double doors that led to the concourse running alongside the BFI. The double doors slid shut, sealing in the sounds of laughter and celebration. Blake hit Dempsey's mobile number and, as he waited for a reply, he could smell the pungent aroma of fine cigars. A few paces away from the side entrance, three conspicuously good-looking women in sleek gowns stood in a triangle, passing around a Havana. Blake vaguely recognised the trio as actresses from a teen soap. A few paps had spotted them and were happily snapping away. Blake walked quickly along the side of the building, past the posters that advertised a hastily planned season of Hitchcock's thrillers: *The Lady Vanishes, The Man Who Knew Too Much, Saboteur, The Lodger* – Blake ducked into a sheltered doorway. It was a work's entrance, dark, and most importantly, out of earshot of the guests and their watchers.

Dempsey picked up. 'Danny!'

'Sorry I couldn't talk a minute ago. What have you got?'

'Well, Jill Kennedy was certainly killed by several blows to the head.'

'Yeah? But what were those blows made with?'

'Flesh.'

'*What?*'

'You didn't mishear me, Danny. Flesh.'

'Human flesh? I mean, what are we talking about here? She was beaten to death with someone's bare hands? I mean come on, that's not –'

'Not human flesh. *Animal* flesh.'

The briefest of pauses. 'Go on.'

'Trace elements, buried deeply into the victim's skull, and peripheral injuries indicate she suffered blows from – and this has been double-checked – a hunk of meat. More specifically, sheep flesh.'

'What?'

Blake stepped from the doorway. He needed a better signal. He must be mishearing. He couldn't have said –

'Sheep flesh,' Dempsey repeated.

'But that's ... that's just bizarre. I mean, why? It blows everything out of the water. All our theories ...' He checked himself, wiping the palm of his left hand across his face. 'All *my* theories.' Blake suddenly felt very ill.

'You there, Danny?'

'I'm here. Christ, I've messed up.'

Blake could hear Dempsey trying to think of something to say. 'We don't know that.'

Blake stared across the row of posters advertising movies he'd felt so certain contained the answers. *The Lady Vanishes, The Man Who Knew Too Much* ...

'I just can't believe it,' he mumbled. 'She was killed by, what, a piece of sheep? That's crazy.'

... *Saboteur, Alfred Hitchcock Presents, The Lodger* ...

Blake paused. *Sounds wrong.* Something stirred.

... *Alfred Hitchcock Presents.*

'Killed by a blow from a piece of lamb ... A leg of lamb?'

Dempsey was saying, 'I can't hear you ... you're breaking up ...' but Blake wasn't listening.

*Alfred Hitchcock Presents.* Hitch's TV show.

A poster of Salinger on one of the lampposts and Blake recalled Marty's words.

*He directed seventeen episodes of* Alfred Hitchcock Presents, *you know. The Professor says they're terribly underrated.* Blake racked his memory. Wasn't there an episode directed by Hitchcock called ...

He felt dizzy.

*Lamb to the Slaughter.*

He recalled the episode, based on a short story by Roald Dahl who had later reused the plot for an episode of his British series, *Tales of the Unexpected* ... But Hitchcock had directed the original version in 1958. *Lamb to the Slaughter.* The story of a woman who kills her husband in their own home by striking him over the head with a piece of frozen lamb. And the coppers arrive, looking for the murder weapon and end up eating it as the wife had cooked it and served it ...

*Lamb vol-au-vents.*

In his peripheral vision, the flashlights of the paps' cameras exploded one after another. Blake put his hand to his face, shielding his eyes and trying to steady himself as his sense of dizziness spiralled.

*... he made especially for you ...*

'Oh, my God ...'

Blake sprinted along the side of the building.

An attendant on the double doors smiled. 'Could I see your –'

Blake pushed past her and up the stairs. The foyer was an ocean of dinner suits, dresses and diamonds. He plunged in, freefalling through wave after wave of gaudy celebration. Through the frocks and magnums and new hairdos and *Do you mind, old chap?*

Blake fought and stumbled his way through the melee, galloped up the main staircase and raced to the green room's entrance.

'I'm afraid Professor Salinger is not quite ready for you, Mr Blake.'

'I certainly hope not.'

He jostled the attendant roughly to one side and threw open the door. Immediately ahead of him he could see Salinger sandwiched between Kim Gilmour and Josa. A blond waitress stood to one side one them, clutching a silver tray which held a single vol-au-vent. He was in time!

Gilmour was reaching for it as Blake burst in. The Chief Superintendent looked appalled at the crashing arrival. His hand paused mid-air and he spluttered, 'What the devil?'

Salinger's hand swooped. 'Last one!' He held the last vol-au-vent just below Josa's lips, moving it towards her mouth.

Blake leapt forward. 'No!'

Although surprised, Josa had instinctively allowed Salinger to place the meat in her mouth and now he turned to Blake. 'I'm afraid if you're here for the lamb, Josa has just devoured the last piece.'

Gilmour looked at Salinger, evidently relieved their host was not outraged by Blake's entrance. 'Paul made them himself!' he declared. 'They were delicious!'

Blake and Salinger locked eyes.

'All gone now, though,' said the Professor. 'What a pity you didn't get here sooner.'

# CHAPTER 73

'You're a clever bugger, I'll give you that.'

Salinger acknowledged Blake's compliment by tilting his flute of champagne. 'And you're a persistent one. I'll give *you* that.'

The two opponents clinked glasses.

They were alone in the green room, sat opposite one another in the snug, lit by a solitary candle that burnt on the table between them. Minutes earlier, Cordelia Smith had announced it was almost time for the Professor's presentation in NFT1, and guests had dutifully filed out of the hospitality areas towards the main auditorium. Only Salinger and Blake lingered in the quiet of Jamaica Inn where they faced each other, with just the sound of the video fire breaking the silent pauses.

'But I'm curious,' Blake said. 'Where do you go from here? I mean, where can you go?'

'Has it ever occurred to you that you could have the wrong man? That I'm not the person you should be hunting?'

'Well, yes, it's occurred to me that you might not be the killer.'

'But not *really*. I mean, in your heart of hearts you think it's me.'

'Yes. I know you murdered those girls and I'm gonna get you.'

'You're *going to get me*?' Salinger shook his head. 'Mr Blake, even your language is so, so –'

'Oh, I could wrap it up in all the conventional phraseology. I'm going to expose you, build a case against you, have you arrested and convince the CPS to prosecute. But what it all boils down to, Professor, is I'm gonna get you.'

'You are remarkable. Really. I've never met anyone like you.'

'We found the link between you and Tony Taylor, by the way.

He did time in Strangeways where he shared a cell with a guy called Ted Maynard.'

'Dear old Ted? Really? He used to be a caretaker at the university, and, before you ask, yes, I knew him. In the same way I know hundreds of support staff who –'

'He burnt to death. With his wife. You know it and I know it. Now, they'd got up to some very nasty little tricks in their time and the world won't mourn them. And we both know that Ted Maynard is not a strong enough link between you and Taylor. Not strong enough to build a case around, anyway. But I just wanted you to know how close behind you we are. One slip, Professor, and you stumble into the noose.'

Salinger leant forward and lowered his voice. 'Do you want to know a secret?'

Blake moved closer.

'I'm glad about all this. Delighted by the attention and the boost this will give my book and my career and, well, me. Delighted. *But.* I did not kill those girls. Couldn't have done. Because the truth, the big bad truth is that Hitch and me do have one thing in common.' He paused. 'We're both cowards.'

Salinger straightened his back. Sipped his wine.

'I'm not proud of that,' he added. 'But it's not an arrestable offence, is it?'

'Why don't you have any beer here?' Blake suddenly sounded flippant. 'This is supposed to be a hospitality room and you have wine and spirits but no beer.'

'I despise beer.'

'Fair enough. You know …' Blake was instantly focussed again, intense. 'I can't decide whether you want me to believe it's you or not. I think part of you is enjoying all this. But maybe I've come along a bit too soon. You've got other things to do before it's over, haven't you?' Nothing. 'You know what I really can't figure out?'

'Pretty much most of it?'

'I can't figure out – why now? You've had no book rejected, no milestone birthday, no parents die recently or anything like that. I checked. So, why suddenly start doing all this at this moment? Why does Professor Nobody suddenly want this? Why now? What triggered it?'

Salinger sank back into his chair. The upper half of his face became hidden by jagged shadows, but by the set of his mouth, Blake knew he'd touched a nerve. This was not the nonchalant, preening professor of a moment ago. 'Let me tell you something, Mr Blake. I am better than you. The blood on your hands will not wash away so easily and that's what fuels your insanity. And it's everywhere. The blood. All over your past, all over your face and in your eyes, and that's why you, *you* can't see it anymore.'

'What do you mean?'

'I know about you. Oh, yes. That's why I've issued no formal complaint against you. I know you can't help it. Rather a fall from grace, I gather?'

'Fall from grace?'

'You cost a man his life. I hear he was a friend. If that word has any meaning for you.'

Blake looked at the tabletop and Salinger continued. 'That must weigh on your mind.' He sounded reasonable. 'You were perceived as number one before that. *Numero uno*. By others and by yourself. And then your ineptitude and your arrogance cost a man his life ... And suddenly you realise that you're not number one. You've been lucky all along, and a loss of luck has exposed you for what you are. A murderer.'

Blake's voice was fragile. 'What happened five years ago –'

'Oh, I'm aware a few people know about that and the *issues* it caused you. But I know much more about you than that.' He leant into the light. 'I know the old secrets.'

Blake hesitated. 'You're bluffing.'

Salinger scrutinised him, his eyes blazing with curiosity about the effect his words would have on his subject. 'I know who you are.'

'You can't.'

'You call yourself Daniel Blake and try *so hard* to be Daniel Blake, but I know who you were before you created that identity and its whole fiction. I know about how you met Dempsey, how he saved you, and yes, what you two did and how you became you.' A slight shake of the head. 'Oh, the bloodshed and the lies.'

Blake looked down into the flame of the burning candle. 'The old secrets ...' he murmured before returning the Professor's stare. 'I don't believe you. You don't know it all. If you knew my real name you'd have used it by now. Taunted me with it.'

Salinger smiled. 'Would I, Mr ...' His smile broadened and he gave a cheery shrug of surrender.

'You know a lot. Much more than you should,' Blake admitted. 'But you don't know it all.'

Salinger drained his champagne. 'And in that respect we are alike.'

'And you didn't answer my question.'

'Didn't I?'

'Where do you go from here? Where can you go?'

Salinger considered his response. 'Well, my next little secret,' he said after a pause, 'is quite simply –'

The door to the green room opened. 'Paul, everyone's waiting and –' Cordelia Smith fussed into view, stopping dead in her tracks as she spotted Blake.

'Show time!' Salinger declared. 'Thank you for the prompt, Cordelia. Let's go!' He stood, winked at Blake and walked across to his PA, pausing at the door. 'Come on, Mr Blake. I really don't want you to miss this.'

Blake saw Cordelia stride away in the direction of NFT1. The Professor lowered his voice. 'I promised you a surprise ... Do you still feel up to it?' He gestured towards NFT1.

'Sure, sure, sure. As long as I can take my drink in with me.'

'Good. I really wouldn't want you to miss this.'

'What have you got lined up for me?'

'Tut, tut, tut,' Salinger replied. 'As Hitch used to say, the terror is in the anticipation of the bang, not in the bang itself ...'

Josa found herself sitting towards the back of the auditorium, one space along from an empty aisle seat that she assumed had been reserved for Blake. However, as the lights dimmed, Todd Martens slipped into it.

'Detective Chief Inspector Jilani! Nice to see you again.'

'Hello, Marty. How are you?'

'Nervous,' he murmured. 'I don't think people realise what an important night this is. How much it means!'

'To Paul?'

'To the world!'

'Oh.'

'This is Professor Salinger claiming his rightful place!' He looked over his shoulder. 'I'm worried to death those fools in the projection room will play the wrong clip or ...' He shook his head. 'I'm going up there to keep an eye on things.'

'I'm sure they know what they're doing!'

'Nobody ever *really* knows what they're doing,' Marty replied, and he was gone. As he flitted towards the exit the lights were killed and for several seconds an expectant hush claimed the room. And then the music began to play, quietly at first but building to a rousing crescendo.

Charles Gounod's *Funeral March of a Marionette*.

Better known as Hitchcock's theme tune, or more precisely, the theme tune to *Alfred Hitchcock Presents*, to Josa's ear it sounded jaunty but strangely macabre. Salinger entered through a door towards the front, right-hand side of the auditorium, and a spotlight picked him out. The applause began – loud and generous, even drowning out the music. He acknowledged a few friends as he made his way to the stage, shaking hands with one or two and saluting several more who sat a few rows from the front. He bounded up the steps and reached the lectern just as the music reached its final note. 'Thank you!' he said.

Blake suddenly appeared in the seat Marty had vacated. 'This should be interesting,' he predicted.

Paul Salinger spoke well but Josa caught him repeating several of the jokes he'd made in the British Museum. Nothing wrong with that, except … Except that when he'd cracked the one-liners a couple of nights ago, he'd delivered them as though they were off the cuff. Spontaneous. And here tonight, as he gave his talk, he tried the same ruse, pausing in between details and making droll asides as though the humour of a given incident had only just occurred to him. It could be called showmanship, or good comic timing. But for Josa it was a form of mendacity and she folded the fact away for future reference.

'And now,' Salinger declared. 'I need a glamorous assistant!' There was a ripple of laughter. 'Could I call to the stage Mr Daniel Blake? Mr Daniel Blake!'

She could never explain why, but her hand shot out and she pressed her palm onto his thigh. 'Don't go!' she urged.

He was already standing up. Smiling, confident. 'I'll be fine!'

As he strode towards the stage, Josa saw him flounder for a split second. Pause. Look around. Frightened? On the huge screen a scene from *Psycho* had been playing out and, although it continued, there was nothing overtly off-putting about the clip. An exterior of the Bates Motel. The sound of rain. And Josa suddenly recalled Blake in Shamley Green, looking at the clouds and virtually racing away from her. And his fear in her flat that he'd get caught in the drizzle. And now, thrown by the sound of …

*He was terrified of rain!*

And as she looked into the face of Paul Salinger, she sensed – with an absolute certainty – that he knew it, too. In that instant, Josa understood what was about to happen.

# CHAPTER 75

*The sound of rain and Blake is virtually in flight, but too far away, reaching out for the tiny, terrified figure of Jamie Diaz.*

He shook his head slightly and saw Salinger's smiling face.

'Welcome to the stage!'

The inescapable noise of rainfall. The disc of light from the projector.

*It takes Blake six months to reach the waist-high wall. At least, that's how long it feels. His stomach hits the edge of the parapet and his torso snaps over it, his right arm lunging downwards, and, before he can even see what he's reaching for, his fingers feel something and he grasps something solid.*

*He looks down. 'It's okay,' he says to Jamie Diaz. 'I've got you.'*

'Are you okay?' Salinger asked.

'It's okay,' Blake mumbled.

A concerned pause. 'How does it feel to be up here?'

'I've got ...'

'Yes?'

'Nothing ...'

Salinger looked at Blake's hand, tightly packed into a fist, allowing his gaze to be an obvious one, contrived to draw the audience's attention to the sign of his discomfort.

Blake could sense everyone had seen it but could also feel his hand trying desperately to keep a grip on –

*Jamie!*

*He holds Jamie's forearm, or more precisely, the sleeve around it, tight in his fist. But the coat the boy is wearing is made from a smooth, shiny material and, even as Blake reassures him, he feels the arm slipping through his fingers. Something heavy – something much too heavy to hold – is pulling Jamie from his grip.*

*Clinging on to his son's leg, Thom Diaz stares up at Blake. 'Let us go! For God's sake, let us go!'*

'I can't let him die, Thom!'

'I love him too much to let him go!'

On stage, Blake closed his eyes.

*The child screams, 'Daddy!' and Blake feels Thom desperately tugging at his son, insanely trying to defeat his grip. Blake feels the sleeve slip a couple more inches through his fingers. His heart lurches.*

*'I can't hold you both! Let go, Thom!' For a second their eyes lock, and for the briefest of moments there's a weird kind of peace between the two old friends. 'Do it for your son!'*

*'I love him too much.'*

*A final tug and the sleeve slips completely from Blake's grasp.*

'And this is a murder scene,' Salinger announced, 'from Hitchcock's second American movie, *Foreign Correspondent*.'

Somewhere, in another world he vaguely recognised as the present, Blake opened his eyes and became aware of more light and more dark simultaneously. He shielded his eyes. The house lights had fallen and another clip was being played. His back was to the screen but he couldn't escape the sound of the movie: hard, heavy rainfall.

*Jamie cries out, 'Daddy!' An awful, terrified shriek.*

Blake looked to his left. Salinger blocking his exit. To his right, the huge expanse of screen and the deluge it depicted. He shrank away from the black and white rain. Looked forward, at the hundreds of horrified faces that looked captivated by his anguish. He was trapped. Couldn't do anything but –

*– grabs Jamie's hand. A last-ditch attempt to keep the boy from plummeting. This is a firmer grip, but Thom's weight means sustaining it will be impossible. Blake has got seconds – if that. Can't hold them both … Can't let the boy die … He looks at the two figures whose lives are in his hands. Their mass is inexorable, and he's lying on top of the low wall now, only his left arm and leg hanging on the tower side for some sort of balance.*

'God ...'

*He feels cold water on his cheek. A dab of rain. Hears a low rumble of thunder. More rain, finding his fingers and the flesh that holds Jamie Diaz and Thom ...*

*Lightning flashes over the cathedral. A trident of furious electricity, ripping the sky apart. Damp from the rain, Jamie's hand begins – oh, Christ – begins to slip through Blake's.*

'Let us die!' Thom screeches.

Blake teetered on the edge of the stage, the awful force of projected rainfall pushing him closer and closer to the drop ...

'No!' he screamed, as his own life and two others seemed lost, and in the audience, Josa heard him cry out and began to run to the front of the auditorium.

*Blake's left hand is groping ... He touches cold, rain-flecked metal ... His fingers tighten around something on the copper floor of the Cathedral Tower. His head snaps to one side to see what it is. Thom's gun. The rain is now a downpour. This is all he can see. The Glock, shining in the moonlight.*

Blake's cry, then and now, did not sound human. A howl that made the audience scream.

'Get the lights up!' someone yelled.

For a moment there was pandemonium, more screams and Josa still running to reach him before –

– it was too late!

As the cry was torn from his throat the onscreen clip reached its climax – a loud, single gunshot, and as though the bullet had seared from the celluloid and into his body, Blake's whole frame bowed. He spun and crashed headlong from the stage.

# CHAPTER 76

The world had decayed around Deighton Street. It was now a back street off a back street, ignored by all except the weekend learner drivers who practiced three-point turns and emergency stops beneath its shattered street lights. Fifty years ago the houses that lined it were owned by the well-to-do. Broken up into flats during the eighties, they were now abandoned, derelict. During the housing boom in the early noughties, an Irish construction company had bought most of the properties but had gone bust shortly after, leaving lawyers to argue about the empty houses.

Deighton Street had become a cul-de-sac and Holy Trinity Church stood at the sealed-off end of the road. Deconsecrated years earlier, from the outside at least, it had fared better than most buildings in the area. Its stained glass windows had been protected by thick sheets of transparent Perspex, spared the ignominy of wooden planks as the latter rotted away while the plastic was durable and deemed less of an eye sore.

The main door to Holy Trinity was also protected by a sheet of Perspex. Unlike the layers over the windows, this transparent slab was affixed to hinges allowing access to the church door which in turn opened inwardly to permit admission to the nave. Occasionally the police found squatters in the husk of Holy Trinity, but by and large, it stood forgotten and ignored. Until tonight.

Blake's unconscious face was bloody from the fall. Josa was by his side. 'Can you hear me?' she was saying.

'Someone call an ambulance!' Salinger shouted, kneeling

besides her. 'This poor man has collapsed! Had a fit! It was too much for him.'

'That's the last thing he'd want!' Josa countered. 'Blake! Blake, wake up!'

'I'm sorry, Josa,' Salinger replied. 'We've got to ship the poor man out.'

A cluster of people who half-believed the excitement was part of the show, circled Blake's still body.

'Oh, God,' Josa murmured.

'Daniel Blake is one of my men, Professor Salinger.' Kim Gilmour spoke with an authority that caught Josa off guard. The throng of people parted for the Chief Super. 'And *I* look after my men.' He strode through the crowd and put a reassuring hand on Josa's shoulder. 'He'll be all right. But you know what he's like. If he woke up in hospital he'd be …'

For a brief moment Josa loved Gilmour for not saying the word that should have finished the sentence. *Ashamed.*

'Come on, old chap!' Gilmour dropped to his haunches, took Blake in his arms and stood up. 'No need for an ambulance. Knowing this bugger …' And he winked at Josa. 'He's just faking it so we'll force brandy down his throat.'

Gilmour walked away with Blake's lifeless body and Josa could see the disappointment in Salinger's eyes.

'You can get on with your show now,' she told him. 'Although I think anything's an anti-climax after Daniel Blake.'

She caught up with Gilmour in the green room. He was standing over the unconscious Blake who was laid out across a sofa. Her boss looked tired from the effort of carrying the other man, his face grey and glistening with perspiration. And in the split second between Josa's arrival and his realisation that she was there, he looked so much older than she'd ever seen him. 'Could you tell?' he asked.

'Tell what?'

'That I almost gave myself a hernia carrying him.' He grinned, and the grin turned to laughter. 'How embarrassing would that have been if I'd collapsed as I walked up the aisle?'

'Thank you,' Josa said.

'I gave him a quick once over. Bang to the head but he'll be fine.' Josa knew she looked unconvinced. 'I've known Blake a lot longer than you,' he told her, gently. 'I know he's made from strong stuff.'

'I know …' She hesitated. 'Sir …'

'Yes?'

'I thought you hated Blake?'

'We're different creatures, Daniel Blake and I. But he once risked … he once did me an immense favour, and besides, I meant what I said back there. I know you think I'm just a politicking old man, and maybe … maybe that's what I've become, but there's one thing I will always give my all for. My men.'

'And women?'

He looked lost for a moment. 'Maybe I have got too old for this. I'm from another age. I'm so sorry, Josa. I should have –' His phone rang. 'Would you excuse me?'

'Sure.'

'Hello. This is Chief Superintendent …'

Josa began to wipe away the blood from Blake's face and Gilmour continued with the most important phone call he would ever receive.

# CHAPTER 77

The taxi dropped Gilmour outside Holy Trinity. It swung around in a 180-degree arc, zooming off down Deighton Street while the Chief Super was still standing in the middle of the road, casting his eyes over the churchyard and beyond it, the church itself. He was a man with many faults but Kim Gilmour was blessed with the wisdom of caution and knew that an abandoned building in a near-derelict street offered enough threat to make him think about walking away.

But as the taxi had taken him from the BFI to this place, one thought had consumed him. If his 'contact', as he had already dubbed the voice on his phone, was correct and knew who the Hitchcock killer was, then the prize on offer was enormous. Incalculable. The praise, respect and gratitude from press, public and politicians from across the whole bloody world! He envisaged Liz Canterville's filmed embrace, the quiet applause of the men who dwelt in the Palace of Westminster and, getting more fanciful as the cab arrived on Deighton Street, he imagined himself – pristine uniform and light smile, conducting the press conference to reveal his part in the murderer's downfall. He envisaged the front pages of tomorrow and the first line of his obituary: Sir Kim Gilmour: The Man Who Caught the Hitchcock Killer.

He looked to his left and right as if expecting support officers to somehow appear by his shoulders. But he was alone, and only the thoughts of glory made him approach the church. He couldn't see any signs of life, but on balance, wasn't sure if this represented a positive or not. Gilmour had been told to wait inside and wondered, even now, if it was too late to call for backup. The voice had been specific, demanding he came alone. Nothing strange about that – informants usually preferred to deal with just one police officer but still, maybe he could –

Gilmour walked into the Perspex that covered the door. The gloom had rendered it invisible and, despite all his trepidation and anticipation, for a few moments his overriding emotion was embarrassment. He adjusted his peaked cap. Pulled back his shoulders. Tugged the Perspex door ajar and entered the church.

'Hello? Anybody here?'

He thought he heard a muffled reply. Took a couple of steps forward and said again, 'Hello!' Another indistinct noise. 'Who's there?'

This time he realised there had been no direct response. What he had heard, and what he could hear now, was just a series of scratches and the sound of a bird. Maybe two birds. He looked up to the vaulted roof, assuming they'd flown in through a broken window and become trapped in the nave.

*Caw! Caw! Caw!*

Gilmour took another couple of steps forward. Behind him, the door swung shut. Locked.

Josa and Blake sat on a bench a little way along from the BFI, in front of County Hall. Blake looked around as he wrapped himself in a blanket, recognising the spot from the opening minutes of *Frenzy* – the scene in which a gaggle of Londoners see a corpse floating in the river below.

'How do you feel?' Josa asked. She wore a black dinner jacket over her Galliano, borrowed from one of the institute's security attendants, and she pulled its lapels close together for warmth.

Blake looked pale. He'd undone his tie and top button and was gulping in the night air, still coming to. 'I'm fine.'

They sat in silence until she said, 'I think it's time you told me.'

He nodded. 'Yes. I suppose so …'

If anyone had taken a photograph of the moment it could have wound up on the front of a greetings card. The type teenagers used to send to each other while gripped in the first flush of an affair. Blake and Josa sat below a string of twinkling lights. She had her left arm wrapped around him, and he was further enveloped in his blanket. But his right hand had found a way out and grasped the fingers of her free hand. She looked like an attentive lover taking care of her down-but-not-out man. And in a way she was, staring into his eyes as he recounted his tale. He couldn't meet her eyes, focussing instead on the light-strewn river in front of them.

He told her about the events of five years earlier on top of Guildford Cathedral Tower. About how he'd almost saved Jamie when the rain came. Josa noticed that even saying the word *rain* made him flinch, and she hugged him tighter. He told her about the rain dragging Jamie from his grip and …

'It's okay,' she whispered. 'It's over.'

'No,' Blake's voice was barely audible. 'It isn't and it can never be over. You see …' And he looked at her for the first time while delivering his account. 'I murdered him.'

Gilmour would have remained by the door but his curiosity was tugged by something directly in front of the steps leading to the altar. Upright and shaped like a coffin. A sign too small to read fixed onto its door. He took a few paces forward.

The church was in near darkness but he could see the pews had been torn out, leaving a near-empty space where congregations had once sat and prayed. The old pulpit remained and, about half-way down the nave, to his left, he could make out a row of medium-sized boxes on a long wooden platform. As he neared them he spotted they weren't so much boxes as coops. He squinted. *What the hell?*

A long line of wooden boxes with wire mesh grills on their front, allowing their contents to be seen. Or they would have, if there had been any light in the place. Gilmour was only a few feet away from them now and heard the scratching grow louder, saw the occupants move. He guessed the coops contained dogs. Medium-sized, black dogs. He reached the nearest box. Leant towards the grill.

'Hello, boy!'

*Caw!*

Gilmour came face to face with a huge raven. Sleek, dense, purple-black feathers, a sharp, vicious beak and eyes that looked pure evil. White irises, black pupils. And the thing was huge! Easily over a half metre high, and heavy! It hopped forward. Enormous! Its hooked beak tore at the mesh!

*Caw!*

Gilmour leapt back. 'Christ!' He fell and ended up on his back. The rook watched him. Tilted its head. Gilmour breathed a sigh of relief that the wire had held firm. He strained to see what kind of clasp kept the doors to the coops fastened. He narrowed his eyes. *Odd* ... Small and metallic, the locking mechanisms seemed unduly sophisticated, compared to the simple boxes they were affixed to. Still, as long as they kept those monstrous things at bay ...

He climbed to his feet. Walked faster, striding towards the steps that led to the altar. He tried to avoid looking at the birds but felt their collective gaze following him. What the hell were they doing here? He glanced to his left. There seemed to be different species. He shuddered.

Although Gilmour didn't know it, he was right in his guess that the boxes held a variety of birds from the *corvidae* genus, sometimes known as the crow family. He had peered into the face of a forest raven, one of the largest types of corvid, but further along he was watched by a variety of crows, rooks and ravens. He passed the final coop and felt a little better.

Gilmour could now see that the upright container by the steps was indeed a coffin. It looked flimsy, as if the weight of a corpse would test it to breaking point. The sign on its lid read 'Justice'.

*Caw! Caw! Caw!*

The ghastly birds were shrieking and pecking at the grills. He stared at them for a moment, shuddered again, turned back to coffin and pulled it open.

# CHAPTER 79

'I became everything I swore I'd never become, Josa. I murdered him.'

'Blake. Tell me what happened.'

'I could see his face. I knew he'd never let go and that ... Jamie would have fallen from my grip because of the rain and ... And the only thing I could see was his gun. A Glock 17. It was the only thing I could see. And I picked it up. Pointed it down. Oh, God, at my friend, and I ... Pulled the trigger. Watched his face explode ... so much blood ... His head ... My friend ...' He was weeping now. 'And he still screamed! *He still screamed*! And that sound! That whole sound! It's still in me! And I saw him die, Josa. I murdered him!'

She was hugging him tight again as he rocked back and forth. 'Oh God,' he was repeating. 'That's why I had to walk away ...'

'You didn't murder him, Blake. He tried to kill himself and his son. You managed to save his son by ...'

'It's hard to say, isn't it? By killing him ... It's terrifying ...'

'But it's over.'

'It can never be over!'

'That moment has passed! You saved Jamie Diaz! There's no need, no need for the fear anymore!'

'That's not what terrifies me about the murder ...'

'Then ...' Josa's eyes widened, suddenly so afraid of the answer. 'What is it?'

Blake looked at her again. 'I enjoyed it.'

Something tumbled towards him. No. Some *things*. He couldn't see what they were – containers of some sort, possibly, that had been balanced to fall forward when the door was opened and –

Gilmour stumbled back but it was too late and –

'Christ almighty!'

From the neck down he'd been covered in a thick, greenish-brown gloopy fluid. He tried to wipe it from his uniform but it stuck fast to his hands and clothes. Something about its consistency reminded Gilmour of frog spawn. It was thicker, but seemed to comprise of living matter, or at least something that had once been living. And here again, Gilmour was correct. The fluid was a professionally mixed amalgam of carrion, insects and water.

He repeated his oath. His contact's call was beginning to look like a prank and already his hopes of public adulation – the photocalls and back slaps – were receding. He could have felt foolish or frightened or bewildered, but as he wiped the gloop from his hands onto his trousers he just felt sad. It was not to be.

Kim Gilmour decided not to hang around. If he left now, he reasoned, he could maybe even catch the tail end of the Hitchcock Murders event. Put this whole ghastly experience behind him with the help of a large brandy. Check up on Blake, although he mustn't let him see his concern. He walked quickly down the nave but this time the birds were going crazy! A cacophony of caws and their beaks challenging the mesh grills with a manic sense of purpose. Gilmour's heart was beating fast, and as he reached the final box he looked over his shoulder and saw something that chilled his blood. The door to the coop nearest the altar was open.

Gilmour knew that the bird it housed could simply hop out at any moment. He considered his options. The first was to make a run for the door. But if the raven flew free it could swoop. He'd already worked out that whatever the substance was he'd been covered in, the vile birds wanted to rip their beaks into it. Or he could jog down the nave and slam the door shut. But if it hopped free before he reached the box …

Gilmour was already dashing down the aisle, determined to lock the wretched thing in its container. As he neared the box he saw a thick beak protrude … He quickened his pace. The head of the bird craned around the door. *Caw! Caw!*

Gilmour dived forward, slamming the door shut and trapping the bird within. He breathed a sigh of relief. *Caw!* The bloody thing stabbed at his hand with its beak through the wire and Gilmour felt the flesh of his palm gouged open. Within a moment his jacket was off and he'd wrapped it around his hand, ensuring it served as both a bandage and protection from the raven that continued to stab, stab, stab! Still, at least he'd made it!

He took a close look at the lock on the coop. It was strange, but the side of the fastening wasn't metal. He glanced along the row of boxes. All the locks had a shiny, plastic quality that he'd seen before. *But where?*

He noticed the flimsy coffin was leaning against a chair. Maybe he could kick it to one side and –

The coffin crashed to the floor allowing Gilmour to stretch and just about reach the chair. He dragged it a little closer and then picked it up. Considered for a second, then managed to lean it against the end coop in such a way as to ensure it kept the door firmly shut.

A remote control sensor! That was what the side of the locks brought to mind – the panel on his satellite box that received commands from his remote control. Gilmour frowned. Puzzled. Why would anyone fit locks that were operated by remote control?

He checked the chair against the door. It was holding firm. Gently, gingerly, he released his grip. The raven jumped forward, beak battering the door, but the chair held firm.

Gilmour allowed himself a brief smile. 'Victory!'

He turned to walk down the nave, to leave this dreadful place but –

'Christ, no!'

Every last door in the long, long line between Gilmour and the exit had swung open.

'You enjoyed it?'

'He always said I would, and everything I swore I'd never become I –'

'Almost became!' Josa interrupted, firmly. 'I don't think you're that man.'

Blake nodded.

'I want you to tell me something,' she said.

'Go on.'

*'Who are you?'*

Josa could see he was weighing up how much to reveal. So many factors to add to his calculations ... so many people from Jack Dempsey and Thom Diaz to the men like –

He suddenly snapped out of his reverie. Josa followed his eyeline and saw a uniformed constable on his beat. 'Where's Gilmour?' Blake asked.

'What?'

'Where's Gilmour?'

'After he got you to the green room he took a call from one of his contacts. Said it was pretty huge and he had to leave straight away.'

Blake was pushing off the blanket. 'Gilmour took a call from a contact? He doesn't have contacts! This is Kim Gilmour we're talking about! The closest he gets to contacts are Jerry and Tarquin down the golf club. Where did he say he was going?'

'He didn't.'

'What?' Blake's phone was already in his hand and he hit a saved number.

'He wouldn't say! Just got reception to call him a taxi and took off in it.'

'Josa, this evening was the official launch of *The Hitchcock Murders*.' He grunted and pocketed the phone. 'No answer! Gilmour gets a call in the middle of the night telling him to go somewhere alone ...' He was on his feet, swaying slightly. He ran his palm across his face. 'And you didn't think that was in any way dangerous?'

'I didn't mention *alone*.'

'It's always alone.' He swayed again, as if trying to regain his balance aboard a pitching yacht.

'Sit down before you fall down.'

'I'm fine,' he replied, clutching the back of the bench for support. 'Did he give any indication of where he was going?'

'No! Look, I'm sure he'll be fine!' Josa wasn't fooling anybody, least of all herself.

'You stay here! If he comes back, call me immediately!' Blake took several shaky steps along the Southbank.

'What are you going to do?'

'Find him!'

'And then what?'

'Save his life!'

Gilmour took a stumbling stride backwards in blind panic. His foot hit the bottom of the steps that led to the altar and he lost his balance, crashing to the floor. He looked up. The crows, rooks and ravens flocked above him, their shrieks almost deafening in the confined space and, once again, he was struck by the sheer size of the birds. Many had wingspans well over a metre-and-a-half wide and their beaks were like ebony daggers. His eyes widened as suddenly the disparate flock became a single dark cloud, as if some magnetising presence had brought them together.

He reached out to the pulpit and hauled himself up.

The noise alone from the creatures was terrifying but now he saw –

They swooped! A black ribbon of ravens unfurling from the cloud and plunging towards him. He automatically covered his face and head with his forearms but the mass of birds clawed and gored their way through his feeble defence. Gilmour yelled out in pain and seething disgust as the creatures attacked with a ravenous intensity.

Screaming, he tried to run, stumbling over the coffin. But as he started to fall his arms flailed and, even in the confusion, somewhere in his mind he registered that several crows had backed off for a moment. Gilmour began fighting back. Grasping the birds, hurling them to one side. He clutched at a raven that was gouging at his throat and could feel its skull shatter in his fingers as he seized it and flung it to one side.

But their attack was relentless. He tore several birds away from his frame but there were too many to fight. He could feel gashes all over his body, the knife-sharp beaks persistent in their onslaught.

Whatever he was covered in was driving the birds insane. Gilmour tore off his shirt and flung it to one side. Several birds zeroed in on the garment and the gunge that stained it. Within seconds the shirt was white rags, but it had given him just a moment to break free from the flock and now he was running.

Ignoring the pain from his legs that bled so profusely. Ignoring the more persistent birds that clawed at his back as he fled from them. Ignoring the mass of deep, bloody cuts that had transformed his face into a mask of agony. *Because he could see the main door was open.* He could make out a street lamp in the distance and sense some sort of salvation beyond this unholy church. Gilmour focussed on that light and sprinted down the aisle, batting away swooping attacks, summoning his last reserves of energy …

He was going to do it! As he pelted faster and faster the birds were unable to get a purchase on their prey and he felt momentarily free of the creatures. Faster, faster!

A huge crow dived onto his chest and he felt his skin ripped open but he didn't care. He was almost there. Escape! He glanced over his shoulder at the dark swarm flock that was so nearly upon him. But just another couple of steps and he'd be –

Gilmour smashed into the thick Perspex sheet that blocked the doorway. Tried to pull it open. Locked! He hammered his fists against the thick plastic because only feet away from the entrance he could see a figure, approaching the church at a jog.

'Help me!' He pounded the Perspex again but the birds were on him now, pushing him, pinning him to the plastic. Goring, gouging. His vision swam with blood. He beat his fists against the barrier. The figure had almost reached him! Thank God! Help! At last!

Gilmour pressed the front of his body hard against the Perspex, knowing his one chance of survival was in the hands of the figure who stepped from the shadows, face suddenly visible …

Gilmour gasped: 'You?'

The figure raised a hand, resting an open palm on the transparent plastic. Without knowing why, Gilmour put his palm over it and, as much as they could be, they were joined for a moment. And then the birds ended even this solace. Stabbing at his calves until he reeled from the doorway, his body felled. The figure watched from the sanctuary of outside. The palm withdrew and gave a tiny wave as Kim Gilmour's body became lost in the dark, murderous blizzard.

# CHAPTER 82

Blake had run towards his car and after a second unsuccessful attempt to contact Gilmour, made another call. 'You ordered a cab for a Chief Superintendent Kim Gilmour earlier this evening!'

On the other end of the line, the BFI receptionist answered cautiously, 'Yes, I did. Was there a problem?'

'I need you to call the cab firm you use and find out where he was dropped off. Can you do that for me *now*? Good! Do it straight away and call me right back on this number …'

Blake reached his car and threw open the door.

'Come on …come on … Hang on, Gilmour! Just hang on!'

Even before he'd swung into the driver's seat, the receptionist phoned back and Blake grabbed his satnav to punch in the postcode. 'Thanks!'

Within ten minutes of leaving the Southbank his Cutlass was tearing towards Deighton Street. 'I can still do this … come on!'

He took a corner wildly, smashing the side of his car into the corner of a red double-decker bus. 'Oi!' shouted the driver, but Blake had already screeched away, tearing through south London at the speed of insanity. He saw Deighton Street and, without having time to break, spun the steering wheel so the car skidded across the road. He felt a sudden jarring as the back of the Cutlass slammed into a postbox. He rammed her into first gear and tore down the cul-de-sac, spinning to a halt outside the church. He put his hand to his temples, his vision and thoughts still blurry from his earlier head injury, but without pause he was throwing open his door, climbing out and seeing –

He was alive! He was in time!

Blake took in the scene of horror, visible through the open

wooden door. Kim Gilmour's body in the epicentre of a maelstrom of attacking birds. And a figure watching through the Perspex barrier, seemingly indifferent to the man's fate. But that was okay. He was okay. He could save this thing.

He slammed his car door shut. Took a step forward. And that's when it hit him. Daniel Blake let out a cry of anguish as the rain began to fall.

Dempsey answered his phone. 'Josa, how are you, darling?'

Holly saw him tense. 'Is this about Dad?' she whispered.

He held up a hand. 'Give me one second, darling.' And then to Josa. 'No, he's not called me. I don't know where he's gone. But he sometimes doesn't answer his phone if –'

'Is this about Dad?' Holly asked, louder.

'No! No, it's not about your dad!' Dempsey forced himself to pause. 'Don't worry, princess. Everything's okay.'

She backed away, ashamed that her own father was all she cared about. She looked at the documents and files that covered the table. She was a part of this and had to start acting like it.

He sat in the driver's seat of his car, legs up and concertinaed so he could embrace his own thighs and calves, as if he was trying to make himself as small as possible. The deluge had hit quickly and drummed a loud tattoo on the top of the Cutlass. Blake moved his hands, opened his palms, jamming them over his ears.

'Make it stop, make it stop, make it stop …'

He looked to his right. The figure watching Gilmour's plight from the outside was still observing the onslaught with interest. The rain was easing. He tried to open his door but couldn't bring himself to touch the handle. He guessed he had a couple of minutes, if that, if he was to save Gilmour.

'*Make it stop!*'

The receptionist was on the point of leaving, zipping up her handbag as if closing her working day.

'Excuse me!'

She groaned to herself. The last one of the day always took the longest. 'How can I help?'

Blake sprinted across the road, trying desperately to focus on Gilmour. *Every raindrop dragging him back.* As he tore across the churchyard the rain fell harder, and for a moment he couldn't breathe. He closed his eyes and found himself looking down at the face of Thom Diaz. *There's a gun in his old friend's hand. A Glock. Thom shakes his head and pulls the trigger, yet Blake somehow –* screamed! The whole earth whooshed towards him, smashing into his body. Blake rolled across the grass, dragging himself to a tree. A thick canopy of leaves and tangled branches sheltered him from the storm. But Gilmour didn't have much time. So he had to get back on his feet, through this bloody rain and reach the door so he could …

He grabbed a low-lying branch and, with a growl of effort, began to pull himself up. He leant against the tree trunk, gulping down air like a drowning man.

He saw the figure at the doorway step back and wave at Gilmour. Blake pressed his back harder against the tree. Droplets of water were finding their way through the foliage and the whole universe lost its focus, cart-wheeling and collapsing. He tried to focus. Was he falling again? No. Something was heading towards him. Or someone. More blood in his eyes, stinging like hell and –

It was the figure from the doorway. Something being pulled from the person's pocket and pointed towards him. Blake saw, at the very last moment, it was a gun. A Glock. But a real one this time, and his natural instinct – causing him to move back and to one side – probably saved his life. And the noise it made as it was fired was the only thing that could have snapped Blake out of his mental turmoil.

He moved forward, flinging something towards his attacker. It was a piece of branch, substantial enough to ensure the gun was knocked to the ground. Blake saw his chance. Ran forward, shoulder-barging into the figure who had no time to dodge the move. But the figure rolled with the blow and, although they both hit the sodden grass together, Blake's opponent was up in a second, scrambling for the Glock. Blake clambered to his feet. Tried to get a fix on his attacker, but there was too much blood in his eyes … And the rain! The other figure was just a pale blur but now Blake was exposed and in the open. Defenceless.

His opponent had the gun. As if in slow motion, the figure moved backwards, leaping back in a controlled, graceful movement … so slowly, as if allowing Blake to enjoy his final moments. The gun rose and Blake saw the trigger squeezed back.

# CHAPTER 83

This would be his last moment of life unless ... the figure landed, spun round and sprinted. The trigger had not been pulled all the way back, and suddenly Blake was alone.

What had made the figure decide to –?

'Blake! Blake, are you okay?'

It was Josa. He realised her presence had done enough to discourage whoever had just tried to kill him. 'Get after him!' Blake urged, pointing to the blur that nimbly raced across the churchyard.

Josa looked from the fleet figure back to Blake. 'You are joking, aren't you? Where's Gilmour?'

'Come on!'

Blake led her to the church doorway. Through the Perspex they could see Gilmour's prone body on the floor, or rather glimpses of red amongst a seething frenzy of beaks and sleek feathers.

Josa felt sick. 'Jesus!'

Blake removed one of his shoes. He took a pen from his pocket and placed the nib end over the thick hinges on the upper left of the door. He covered the pen with his shoe and pulled it down in a sudden surge of strength. The hinge pin was pushed through its groove and fell, along with the pen, to the ground. Blake repeated the same manoeuvre on the lower hinge, ripped open the door and ran into the church.

He tore away at the birds, flinging them to one side. 'Get away! Get away!'

But he could see they had fed enough and put up little resistance to his counter-attack. As Josa squeezed through the gap between the Perspex and the door frame she saw the birds fly from their prey, although what they left behind was almost unrecognisable. She managed to give the plastic slab a final shove, and with a loud, creaking screech, it fell to the floor. A flutter of wings, and most of the birds soared into the night air.

'Kim! Kim, it's okay!' Blake was saying. 'We're here now! You okay?'

Josa was coldly aware of what needed to be done. 'It's going to be all right, sir!' She looked at her phone. *Damn it!* 'No signal!' she shouted to Blake. 'I need to call an ambulance! Stay with him! You're going to be okay, sir!'

Mindful that the birds could return at any moment, Blake took Gilmour in his arms and walked quickly to the front of the church, placing him gently on the altar. 'You're going to be okay, buddy.'

Gilmour made a movement for the first time since their arrival. 'Blake?'

Through the open doorway he could see that Josa had sprinted to the bottom of the churchyard, obviously trying to get a signal on her phone. Blake and Gilmour were alone.

'Yeah! It's me! And Josa's here! Calling an ambulance right now, so you hang on!'

'Not this time. It's …' His body convulsed in pain and Blake took in the extent of his injuries. His entire body had been gouged apart, his skin oily with blood that had seeped from his wounds and now dripped from the altar. Blake had removed his dinner jacket, using the bulk of the material to staunch the blood flow from Gilmour's throat injuries.

'You're going to be okay, you old bastard! Just for once in your life can you do something for me and bloody hang on?'

Gilmour tried a smile and then he asked something so trivial that Blake thought he'd misheard. 'Can I call you Danny?'

'What?'

'Like Dempsey does … I was always jealous of you and Dempsey. Your friendship …'

'What? Yeah! Course you can, Kim. Just hang in there, mate, and you can call me what you like. I thought you always did anyway. Eh? Eh?'

'Danny … this is important … it's about the case …'

'Save it, Kim. I know who's behind the Hitchcock Murders and I'll fucking crucify –'

But Gilmour was struggling to interrupt him. A painful shake of his head and a murmured, 'No!'

'What? What is it?'

'You'll solve this one. No doubt … but the one you could never solve … I swore I would never tell you, but …'

'What are you talking about?'

Gilmour's lip moved but no sound came out.

'Stay with me, Kim!'

And as if the physical act of speaking the words was an immense and painful process, Gilmour gasped, 'Catherine! I know the secret of Catherine!'

'What are you talking about?'

Gilmour's eyes closed.

Blake shook him. 'No! What d'you mean? You've got to tell me!'

'The man …' His words were little more than breath.

'The man,' Blake said. 'Yes? What man? Tell me! Tell me! *Tell me!*' he screamed.

Josa appeared in the doorway. She looked down the blood-stained church and saw the dying figure of Kim Gilmour on the altar with Blake standing over him, like a priest hearing a deathbed confession. He was gripping the other man's hand, urgently pressing his ear to his bloody lips.

Blake could feel Gilmour's hand become limp, literally sensing the life force drain from his body. 'Help me just this last one time, Kim. I'm begging you. What about the man?'

And Kim Gilmour's last words left his lips like a prayer. So quiet, that had Blake not been inches from his mouth they would have fallen unheard. But he caught the last two syllables that Gilmour ever uttered, hearing: 'Green … book …'

'Good, good,' said Blake. 'Green book? What green book? What's important about it? Come on, Kim! Tell me! Tell me!'

Seconds passed.

'He's gone,' Josa said gently. She had reached his side. Over Blake's ragged breathing she murmured again, 'He's gone. You did everything you –'

'No!'

Blake tried mouth-to-mouth, insisting he could bring him back, while Josa simply watched, uncertain of what would be kindest. Slowly she stepped back. She lost track of how long had passed before he stood back as well, exhausted, dripping in blood and with nothing left but his anger and his voice.

'Tell me!' Blake shouted at the dead man. 'Tell me!'

Back in her flat, Josa stood at her bedroom window, looking out across the city. In its darkness she saw Blake and his assailant outside the church. She had witnessed the near-fatal attack and replayed the scene a dozen times in her head. Always the same repetition, with something there that she couldn't quite hold on to … She saw the unknown figure moving backwards, leaping backwards … As if jumping out of her grasp, even now. But somehow …

'I know who he is …' Josa hissed. 'Just can't think …'

2.55 a.m. Almost home. Blake pulled into a lay-by and made the call. She picked up after four rings.

'I didn't wake you, did I? I take it you're still on holiday in New Zealand?' he asked.

'It's the middle of the afternoon, here,' Mara Diaz replied. 'I'm having a bath. Getting ready for a hot date tonight. In a very swish restaurant overlooking Auckland Bay. The one I pointed out on our last call.'

Blake looked at his phone screen. For some reason, Mara always preferred video calls. She lay submerged in a huge white bath, fancy little hotel bottles of shampoo and shower lotion arcing around the ledge behind her head. He saw her raise her eyebrows.

'You could at least pretend to be jealous.'

Even Blake could see she was flirting with him as she lowered her phone a fraction to afford him a better view of her naked shoulders and cleavage. Although her chest was hidden by swathes of bubble bath foam, he felt himself redden.

'Oh, all right!' Mara laughed. 'It was with an eighty-year-old expat, so you needn't worry! Bumped into him this morning. A retired police officer from the Home Counties. What are the chances, eh?'

Blake wasn't surprised. Mara had always been drawn to coppers. He'd heard she remained good friends with many of the officers who'd served alongside her husband, and knew for a fact that a couple had tried it on with her. He knew that because she'd told him, and she'd been careful to add that her refusal was nothing to do with Thom, but they'd just not been right for her …

Mara Diaz was a good-looking woman, still physically fit and careful with her appearance. After he saved her child, she'd befriended him, but he had loathed the memories her face brought back. At birthdays and Christmas she would show up with extravagant gifts and invariably promise she didn't want to talk about the past, but always, as she left his house she would make him recount one more time what had happened on the Cathedral Tower. And she'd thank him, kiss him even, after reforming the incident in his mind.

Ironically, she believed that he and Gilmour had been close friends. She praised them both equally for the operation that had led to Jamie being saved, and from this delusion sprang the close platonic friendship she had forged with the Chief Superintendent in recent years.

'Mara, it's about Kim …'

He related the facts. After a few quiet moments, Mara said, 'You can't walk away now.'

'Why do you say that?'

'Because it was guilt that made you walk away from everything five years ago.'

That was only partly the truth, but she was instinctively right about his current state of indecision.

'Danny,' she continued. 'It's too late to turn back now. If you don't finish this thing, you're lost.'

'Maybe I'm already lost.'

'Stop feeling sorry for yourself! You have to see it through to the end. It may kill you, but you have to see it through. Can't you see that? That's the way it's always been.'

The call finished moments later. Blake looked at own eyes in the rear-view mirror. She was right. As bloody usual she was dead right. He gunned the engine, shook his head, then swung the Cutlass across the road and began the long drive back to London.

Killers also get home, take off their shoes, make a cup of tea, slip into bed and unfold their dreams.

And tonight his homecoming was a raucous affair. He threw open his front door and heard deafening applause. Once the door was shut he waved modestly to the crowds lining his hallway. And even an hour later, lying in bed with the duvet pulled over his head, the exhilaration still made him shake. It had been another night of triumph. Complete victory … Except that –

The Asian girl and bloody Blake had spoilt it a little …

He turned over. Annoyed. Irritated that they should have flicked a fly into the ointment of his success.

But surely some degree of imperfection was a good thing? It meant his masterpiece would represent progress. An elevation. A revelation. And that's what the next one would be … The annoyance began to ebb away, replaced with impatience for his next great work. The one they'd all remember. And this time, Blake and Jilani would be an integral part of it. Immortalised by death in his defining moment.

He threw back the duvet. The curtains parting! His adoring audience all over his ceiling.

'Not long now,' he called to them. 'Not long now!'

7.55 a.m. Blake sat in Josa's office. The morning meeting would be starting early. Through the glass panelling he could see the MIT begin to assemble as usual, friends chatting, coffee gulped down. A few careful eyes noted Josa's demeanour and her reluctance to greet any of them. Blake couldn't hear anything through the glass but sensed the chatter was falling away.

When Josa began speaking to her team, he watched for their reactions. Some wept. Others looked around as if it searching for Gilmour to disprove the news they were hearing. A few younger men looked intense. Peering. Nodding. They politely raised their hands when their boss finished speaking, ignoring the shock of those around them. And Josa …

Josa could have been breaking any bad news. Budget cuts, mass redundancy, the brutal murder of a colleague. In the six days Blake had known her, she'd hardened.

She looked across to him, and for an awful, illogical moment he wondered if she could read his mind.

After the meeting she joined him. 'How did it go?' he asked.

'How do you think?'

A knock on her door.

'Yes?'

'Sorry to disturb you, guv.' Stevie stuck his head into the office. 'A chap has just come in. Said he did it.'

'Christ,' said Josa. 'It's started already. Good. Get his details. Have the word loony stamped on his forehead and send him home.' She sat down with an old person's sigh.

'Well, normally I would, but …'

'Yes?'

'We've not released any information to the press and I checked the Net. No details up there yet. But he knows every last detail about the church, the containers that held the birds, the birds themselves and even the fluid deposited on Chief Superintendent Gilmour that attracted the attack. Either he's psychic, or he's telling the truth. I think if you just –'

But Blake interrupted with a firm, 'Josa!'

She followed his eyeline. Walking across the office wearing the funeral ensemble of black suit and tie, she saw Paul Salinger.

Adrian Garner wore a black leather jacket over a Star Wars T-shirt. At first he would only repeat, *I'm to blame, I'm to blame*. But after three cups of tea and Josa's gentle assurance, he started to open up.

Josa had left Blake and Salinger in the office together.

'How's the head?' Salinger asked.

'Thinking,' Blake replied.

'You should be kind and courteous to me today.'

'And why's that? You just murdered a friend of mine.'

'In death he becomes your friend, does he?'

'Last night you said you knew who I was. If you were telling the truth you'd be praying right now. Praying that when I get the proof to nail you, the police reach you before I do.'

'You're amazing.'

'I know.'

'But this morning, Mr Blake, I came to give you a warning.'

'Oh, aye? And what's that about then?'

'I popped in to let you know when the next murder will occur. And where.'

'I work in the film and television industry,' Adrian Garner

explained. 'I run Canimal Ltd. We supply animals for movies, soaps … dogs mostly. But we do horses, snakes – anything really …'

'Birds?' Josa asked, and Garner nodded.

'Tomorrow night,' Salinger announced.

'You always kill on a Tuesday. That's not news.'

'Tomorrow night in Leytonstone.'

'Why's that?'

Salinger smiled. 'All the fun of the fair!'

'I've got a client. Well, my biggest client really. You've probably heard of him, Sir Lawrence Brande-Marks. Producer, director. He gives me the really big orders. The state of film and TV in this country, I tell you, if it hadn't been for Sir Lawrence, I'd have gone out of business ages –'

'Why don't you share what you came here to tell us?' Josa said quietly.

'Over the past few years I've had a lot of last-minute orders from Sir Lawrence. I mean crazy orders. But if he wants something setting up, I'll set it up. You know? And when I got this order the other day, I didn't think. It was only this morning when I arrived on Deighton Street and saw what had happened. It was only then I noticed it.'

'Noticed what?'

'The email wasn't from the normal address. I mean the email was formatted in the same way as his. Same auto signature, same style, but the address was Lawrence.Brande.Marks@Brande.Marks.co.uk. That's wrong, you see? It should have been dot com, but you don't notice, do you? You don't check! I mean, you don't think it's important, do you?'

The scent of Salinger's cologne lingered in the office. Blake brought his fist down onto the table. 'Someone emails this Adrian

Garner character and gets him to implement the practicalities of the whole murder. That's fine. I get that,' he told Josa. 'But with all the techno-wizardry at our fingertips are you really telling me we can't trace who sent it?'

She shook her head. 'I can't say for certain but the tech boys have just confirmed that their best guess is that the fake account will have been set up either in an internet café or on a pay-as-you-go smartphone. This is not an avenue of inquiry, it's a cul-de-sac. Obviously I'll detail someone to follow it up but ...'

'I understand,' Blake muttered. 'I said he was a clever bugger.'

'Talking of which, what did Paul Salinger come to warn us about?'

Blake gave a tight smile. 'You are not going to believe this ...'

He sat on the sofa where she had given him the news. He could see her now, too ashamed to look him in the eye as she ended their relationship. He'd been as understanding as ever – *not desperate* – when he'd suggested – *not begged* – that they simply took a little break instead. She'd begun shaking her head even before he'd finished the sentence. Well, that was just bloody rude. But he'd heard her out. Listened to what she had to say. 'I don't think we can be friends,' she faltered. 'It wouldn't be fair on me, so this has to be the end.' Finally she'd looked at him. 'I don't want to see you ever again. You have to *move on*. Can you promise me that this will be a final goodbye?'

'Yes,' he'd replied. 'I think I can.'

Moonfleet. 2 p.m. Holly watched proceedings with a predator's intensity. She wore jeans, a dark hoodie and, over it, a thigh-length vintage police jacket. From beneath her hood, which was pulled so far over her head that it almost obscured her eyes, she studied him, sensing he was about to say something important. He'd just walked into the study room and Holly leant against the wall by the doorway. Josa, Dempsey and Mason sat around the table.

'Right!' Blake said. 'We have one objective this evening. We are not here to bring him down, get evidence or even try to finish this tonight …'

That had been just a few short months ago. Since then, he'd taken her advice. Moved on. Moved on in so many ways. Becka Hoyle, Ebba Lovgren, Sarah Robinson, Elaine Hargreaves and … He paused. Looked at the sofa. Jill Kennedy, on this very spot! He could still feel the aftershock in his hand. The physicality of murder. He put his palms together, looked down and breathed deeply. Then he nodded, moved to the kitchen, drew the carving knife from its block and carried it across his living room …

'We are there to prevent him killing again. That is all. This is a Tuesday, and there is a fair tonight in Leytonstone, the area of east London where Alfred Hitchcock was born and raised. That's too good an opportunity for him to resist. He will go there. He will try to murder someone. It is up to us to stop him. I do not give a damn about secrecy or even subtlety. I want him to know we're all over him. I want him to know that tonight is too risky. That he is being watched every moment. And that however much he wants to kill tonight, he has to realise, he has to stop. And stop *now*.'

It was almost over, but he couldn't stop now. Sometimes he wanted to, and in those moments he reasoned that whatever happened in the future, at some point everybody in the world would know what he had done; that the sound of his name would be enough to provoke a response from anyone that heard it. Surely that was enough? But the canvas image of Alfred Hitchcock looked down on him and he could tell that the great man was trying to remind him –

*Think of me!*

Hitchcock had been kicked by critics throughout his career. Never once picked up an Academy Award. The moronic distributors who shelved *The Lodger* because it was too 'arty'. The idiots who couldn't understand *Vertigo* and tried to disguise their ignorance by sniping at the man who created it. The fools who tut-tutted at *Psycho* and bleated that it was vile and vulgar and beneath the Master of Suspense … But every time he had been critically spat at, he simply proved his detractors wrong by creating ever more beautiful works. Masterpiece after masterpiece. A string of murders to eloquently disprove the ham-fisted hacks who jeered and derided him.

He looked at the portrait of Hitchcock that hung on his living room wall. The old master and the sleek, black bird. That single image defined so much because it represented so much. An unparalleled body of work that took in over fifty movies and yet … And yet he knew that what film historians called the lesser films were only venerated because of the truly great movies. Conclusion? To ensure that all your works achieved longevity and acclaim, it was vital to create at least one masterpiece.

'Don't worry, I'll do it,' he said, and realised he was talking to Hitch.

It was almost over, but he couldn't stop now.

Blake paused, ran his palm over his face. 'Josa has assigned some of her best men to tail him. Now that's good, but we can't rely on them. We can only rely on ourselves.'

He wrapped the carving knife in a chamois leather and then, standing in his bathroom, pressed it into the small of his back so the hilt and blade ran parallel to his spine. He could feel the contours of the handle digging into his flesh, but he could endure the discomfort during the early part of the evening, knowing it wouldn't be long before he found a nice dark place to detach his knife.

He checked the look of his naked torso in the full-length bathroom mirror and, still holding the knife to his back with his left hand, began to wrap masking tape around his stomach and the makeshift scabbard. He enjoyed the sound that the tape made as it unwound and he liked the feel of it sticking to his skin. Even the bulk of the knife wedged into his spine thrilled him. He put on his shirt. Looked at himself in the mirror. Just as Hitchcock looked like an overweight accountant, so his appearance was deceptive. He smiled his sunniest smile.

Josa walked from the table, put her arm around Holly, and as they left the room together, Blake heard the older woman say, 'Don't worry, I'll look after him …' John Mason nodded good luck and followed them. Dempsey stood, moved towards Blake. 'What is it, Danny Boy? Tell me. What is it, son?'

He sat on the sofa to double-check the knife was secure when he leant back onto something relatively hard. It was. Good. By his side he saw the page he'd ripped from the old edition of the *Guardian*. The one with the article he'd read a hundred times. There it was. The piece with a portrait of Josa looking almost comically young and, beneath it, the wedding reception photo. Josa – sober – raising a glass to camera. Her sister – according to the caption – looking tipsy, and a couple of white friends stood in front of her. *Modern Britain*.

But some things were timeless, or at least, abiding. Like pathways. Instructions. *Hitchcock had never shown any desire to dawdle or delay over his art. And so nor should he*. The show didn't simply have to go on. It had to go on and on … He looked at the photograph. *And on …*

'I don't know if we can stop him,' Blake stammered. 'Something tells me tonight … tonight is going to be …'

The killer studied the photograph, examining the face of the starlet he intended to make his next leading lady.

'… terrible.'

Blake was driving Josa to the fair with Dempsey and Mason following behind. 'Remind me again,' Blake said, 'why we can't just pull Salinger in.'

'A little thing called a total lack of hard evidence,' Josa replied. 'We've questioned him and he's cooperated. And right now the mechanics of this operation are in limbo as my new boss settles in. I still can't believe Liz Canterville.'

'This traffic,' said Blake, gesturing to the gridlock surrounding them, 'is really starting to get on my nerves. What can't you believe about Liz?'

'Resigning as Home Secretary! Returning to the police! Taking over from Kim. It's a poisoned chalice. I'm amazed she can't see that.'

'Don't you worry about Liz Canterville. She has her own agenda. Christ! Leytonstone High Road is completely jammed!' Blake shook his head. 'They're going because they think there might be a murder. Some of the tabloids speculated this could be our boy's next playground. You know that? Ghoulish bastards.'

An officer that Josa had detailed to keep an eye on the professor's place had just informed her that Salinger was on his way and she guessed they'd have about an hour to recce the fair before he arrived. Blake swung his big American car to the right and began to tear through the back streets of Leytonstone village.

'You know at the church?' Josa looked across at Blake. 'You know you said you didn't recognise the man that attacked you?'

'I said that,' Blake conceded. 'But to be honest, my mind was in a blender at the time. Why?'

'Nothing. Just ... I keep thinking I recognised him.'

'Did you see his face?'

'No. No, it wasn't that. It was more the way he –'

A car shot out of a side street forcing Blake to slam on the brakes. 'Are you okay?'

Josa rubbed her shoulder. 'I'm fine. You?'

'Yeah. Go on.'

'It's nothing. Well, it's something. Just can't seem to … Hey, you missed the turning.' She pointed to a fairground sign they were passing.

'Oh, ignore that. The fair is actually on the Wanstead Flats,' Blake explained. 'We can walk it from here.'

Blake hung a left, looped around Wanstead and parked within sight of Snaresbrook station. As he locked the car, Blake could see Josa trying to grasp that slither of recognition, but he knew – they both did – that the moment had been lost.


They heard the carnival first. The screams of people already on the Magic Swings, Ghost Train and other rides. The distant laughter and dodgem cries. As they neared the Flats they became part of a stream of people heading towards the noise. That stream thickened into a fast-flowing river. Directly ahead of them, Blake could see a family of four. A pretty blonde, a man with a ridiculous quiff and their two kids: a cherubic toddler and a fair-haired lad of about three and a half. Both children were impatiently tugging the grown-ups in their wake. It seemed nobody could wait for tonight to get under way. And over the hedges and dull suburban walls rose the colourful spiralling slides, the huge hoardings of the bigger rides and the gaudy façade of the House of Fun.

*'Faster, Daddy, faster!'*

And the screams grew louder.

The Wanstead Flats is a vast area of scrubland just east of Leytonstone. It lies in a trough, and so as Blake and Josa approached it they could only see the tops of the larger attractions. But judging from the sounds, clamour and distance spanned by the rides, this was a major carnival. They jogged up the bank that led to the Flats and paused as they reached the top, taking in the twilight sight beneath them. The neon lights, the explosion of garish excitement.

'All the fun of the fair,' said Blake.

'What do people like about these places?' Josa asked as they made their way down the incline towards the carnival.

'What's your idea of a good time?'

'Crate of ale and a *Carry On* movie.'

'I'm serious!'

'Why?'

'Because I think we should go on a date.'

She stopped. 'Blake. I like you but … Did Holly force you to ask me?'

'No!'

'Did she?'

'Yes. But I was going to anyway. When all this was over. But she said I should apply my own rules. Never wait for a good time because –'

'I get it. It's just right now I need a bit of space after everything that's happened. *Is* happening.'

Blake shrugged. 'There's no such thing as *perfect* timing, you know.'

'How do I know you're not just like most of the others? All those boys who don't think I'm pretty or really want to go out with me, but just want to see what it's like to shag an Asian girl.'

'Oh, Josa. You don't believe that about me for one second, and you really don't get it, do you? You have to stop defining beauty in terms of your sister.'

'And how would you define beauty?'

'I wouldn't.' Their eyes locked. 'But I know I'm looking at it.'

The momentary silence between them was broken by a shout from someone at the bottom of the incline. 'DCI Jilani, isn't it?'

The man who'd called to them turned out to be a detective inspector and the head of the local police team patrolling the fair. Numbers were exchanged and, as a courtesy, Josa told them that some of her men would be around keeping tabs on people of particular interest.

The burly DI bristled at this news. 'Highly irregular,' he said. 'And I'd prefer to have had more notice of –'

'Highly irregular?' Blake interrupted. 'Did you just say *highly irregular*? One: coppers don't say that outside 1940s B-movies, and even then, there's really only Dennis Hoey that can get away with it. Two: let's get a bit of perspective. Six people have been murdered by the Hitchcock Killer. Tonight, we think he's going to try to murder again. That's highly fucking irregular, I'd say. Not some petty lapse of paperwork. She's told you about her men. She didn't need to. Now move on. And stop saying things like *highly irregular*. Because it *really* makes you look like a cock.'

Josa felt like a WWF referee trying to keep two wrestlers apart as she finally managed to drag Blake from the confrontation.

'How was I?' he asked when they were finally out of the DI's earshot.

'Oh, perfect, as ever. Yeah, in terms of inter-departmental cooperation, *it makes you look like a cock* was a real gem. What the hell were you thinking?'

'Just covering your back! DI Dim-wit was going to ask you for details of all your men, where they were and who they'd be trailing. Best not broadcast that information. And by the end of the conversation he was so pissed off at me he'd totally forgotten about what you'd done. You can buy me some candyfloss as a thank you.'

'*What They Don't Teach You at Hendon*, by Daniel Blake.'

'Do you fancy a go?'

'What?'

Blake nodded towards one of the amusements. A long narrow strip of grass with a plastic pail at one end and a football at the other. '*Kick the ball in the bucket and win a prize!*' the roustabout shouted.

Josa shook her head. 'I like football,' she said to Blake. 'But watching. Not playing.'

'Oh, yeah. You support Newcastle, don't you? Your family from up there?'

'Nah. First match I ever saw was Arsenal versus Newcastle. The Gunners were all over them but the boys never gave in. I kind of liked that. And the fans and the whole passion they have for …'

'For lost causes?'

Josa laughed. 'Maybe.' They continued walking. 'My dad was a big football fan. Offered to take me to a match once but I said I wasn't interested. I don't know if I've made this up in my own head, but I think I saw disappointment in his eyes.' A pause. 'I wish I could turn the clock back and say *yeah*! Let's take in a match!' She shrugged. 'But as it is, at least I can feel a bit of what he felt when –'

'You don't have to look for signs or try to turn the clock back, Josa. I can tell you now. He'd have been proud of you. And more than that – you've done him proud. Really.'

She gave a quiet but sincere, 'Thanks, Blake.' Then louder, 'What was your dad like?'

'Well …' Blake's face darkened then lit up. 'Take a look at this!'

They'd reached a large, open tent with a makeshift stage at the far end. On it they could make out a man of about sixty dressed in an ill-fitting dinner suit. A board by his side proclaimed he was Mr Memory, and Blake shouted to him, 'What is the secret of the 39 Steps?' The Hitchcock fans in the audience laughed nervously. Blake grinned like a mischievous child.

The next open tent held a similar stage, but this time a conjuror was claiming the audience's attention. Again, Josa and Blake paused in the entrance. The magician wore dark slacks and a black, long sleeved T-shirt. He held a silver coin in his left hand and, with his right hand, he tugged up his left sleeve. He then transferred the coin to his right hand and tugged up his right sleeve so that now both his wrists and forearms were exposed. He extended his right fist and opened it.

The coin was gone.

'Oh, that was very good, wasn't it? I love a bit of …' Josa caught sight of Blake's patient smile. 'Go on then, Houdini. How was it done?'

They drifted towards the heart of the fair. The mechanical

tunes played by the carousels, the shouts, screams and roustabout yells becoming a background hum. The aroma of hot dogs mingled with the smell of paraffin and oil-powered engines. Blake paused, taking it all in.

'It's called the French Drop,' he said. 'Look.' He placed a fifty pence coin in his left hand and repeated the manoeuvre they'd seen on stage.

'So how's it done?' Josa asked.

Blake set the trick up again, but this time as his right hand went to take the coin, he said, 'Watch! I actually drop the coin into the palm of my left hand and so when my right hand embraces the space where it should be, the audience assumes the coin is in my right fist. And when I pull my right hand away the coin can't be seen in my left because I've effectively palmed it. But! The most important part of the trick is in my eyes and body language. I have to follow my right hand, watching it as I talk about the coin. That's the misdirection. I'm making the audience look here –' he held his clenched right hand – 'when actually what we should be watching is here.' With a flourish he slipped the coin from his left palm to the fingers of his left hand. 'That's what he's going to try to do tonight. I can feel it. And there's something I've forgotten or overlooked or it's staring me in the face. He's going to try and misdirect us, Josa …' The sound of guns popping in a shooting gallery filled the air. 'I just don't know how.'

Dempsey and Mason arrived about twenty minutes later. 'How was Holly Belle?' Blake asked.

'About not being allowed to come and help out tonight?' Dempsey shrugged. 'Oh, she was fine. Took it real well.'

'How was Holly Belle?' Blake repeated.

'On the Richter scale she was right up there with the Frisco shake of oh-six,' Dempsey conceded.

'She just wants to help,' Josa cut in.

Blake nodded. 'I know. But I told her that this place was off bounds tonight and that's final. I should never have brought her into this in the first place, so –'

'So, what time d'you think she'll get here?' Mason pondered.

Blake looked at Josa but she simply pursed her lips and nodded.

'Jesus,' he murmured.

Josa put an arm around him. 'For a genius, you can be such an idiot at times.'

'Can I interrupt, guv?' It was Stevie, out of breath as he jogged up to her.

''Course you can. This is John Mason, Jack Dempsey, Daniel Blake …'

At the last name, the young DC's eyes widened. 'You're Daniel Blake? I mean *the* Daniel Blake?'

'Er, nice to meet you – '

'Stevie!' the lad said. 'My dad was a copper! He worked with you! You called him the Machine?' His inflection rose at the end of the sentence; a moment of doubt as he questioned whether Blake would remember his father.

'Your dad is the Machine? Ha ha! Really good to meet to you.'

'The way he speaks about you ... I mean, wow!'

'We'll have to get together some time for a few drinks. I'll let the Machine tell his stories and jump in when he's letting sentiment get the better of him.'

'I'd like that!'

Josa gave him a gentle nudge. 'Stevie ...'

'Oh, sorry, guv. Just had word. Salinger's parked up and is approaching the fair on foot. Looks like his ingress will be the main entrance. ETA six minutes. Well, probably five minutes now.'

'Thanks. You go and rejoin the team. And remember – I do not want to lose eyeball with Salinger for one moment tonight.'

'Yes, guv.'

'Actually, I'll walk with you.'

Josa had wanted to thank the team for coming out and to reinforce the importance of tonight's surveillance work. But as she walked alone with Stevie, with Blake and the others following a few paces behind, she took the opportunity to spin back to the Shard. 'Do you remember when we first met?' she asked. 'The body of Elaine Hargreaves had just been discovered. You were there with Don Walters.'

'Yeah, I remember.' A smile. 'How could I forget?'

'When I pocketed Elaine's phone, you didn't say a word.'

'What? Oh! Yeah. I mean, no. I kept *schtum*.'

'Why was that?'

'Dunno.' Stevie shrugged. 'But Walters ... he *had* known you were coming. He pretended not to, but Gilmour had phoned and given him the heads-up. He gave me a little rant about Muslim officers having a direct line to the Chief Con. Said it wasn't fair.'

Josa had heard the complaint many times before. As a member of the Association of Muslim Officers, if she identified a problem related to her background that she felt merited the Chief Constable's immediate attention, she could get through to him and discuss the issue. For normal, everyday procedures this wasn't the case, but that direct access peeved a lot of officers who felt it showed undue bias to certain groups within the service.

'I don't think he was racist,' Stevie continued. 'He was just an old man who knew the powers-that-be were on to his drinking, and he thought you were there to replace him. And the funny thing was, he did seem genuinely worried about you being given an investigation you weren't ready for. So he called Jack Dempsey.'

Josa stopped dead in her tracks. 'And said what?'

Stevie shrugged. 'Dunno. He said you might need a bit of help. That he was going to call Dempsey but he made the call in a separate room. I thought Dempsey was going to turn up and offer to give you a hand.'

'*But instead,*' Josa thought, '*Daniel Blake is the resurrection after five years away from police work.*' She surreptitiously looked over at the two men in question. *Why had Jack Dempsey taken such an interest in her that he was prepared to haul Blake out of his self-imposed exile? Maybe it was because they'd got on so well when she'd been his case officer, or maybe there was something more. Something that –*

Stevie interrupted her ruminations. 'But then he came back into the room and started being arsey again. He was obviously worried and was taking it out on me. Then you came and ... I thought you seemed okay.'

'So not mentioning the phone ...' They started walking again. 'It wasn't a procedural decision?'

'Not really.'

'It was just personal?'

They had almost reached the other officers.

'In the end,' said Stevie, 'isn't everything?'

Blake and Dempsey watched Josa chatting with her team. 'She's good with people, isn't she?'

'She sure is, Danny Boy.'

'I wish I had that knack. It's so natural with her. Look! She's so open. Like she's got nothing to hide. No madness or cruelty or anything, so she can just be herself.'

'You think too much.'

'Well ...' A mischievous glint in his eye. 'I don't get that from you.' The two men exchanged grins and Blake continued. 'But seriously, it's one of the reasons she's so good at her job. The fact she's so good with people. It isn't a flashy thing or a political thing and I bet her bosses don't even comment on it, but it means she can be a really great copper when it comes to –'

'You asked her out yet?'

'Jesus!'

'Simple question. I don't know why you always get so defensive about –'

'Can we move on, please?'

'So it was a *no*, then. That sucks, but listen, son. You don't want to let it get you down.'

'It wasn't, until you brought it up again. Thanks for that.' He smiled. 'Hey, maybe I need a bit of your magic.'

'I doubt that.'

Blake threw a glance past Josa, looking over the fairground, and his tone became more serious. 'Did you check out this place earlier?'

'Yeah. Couple of hours ago when they were setting up.' He rubbed the back of his neck. 'Even visited the fortune-teller.'

'What did she say?'

'First of all she scared the hell out of me, then said I had nothing to worry about. Crazy old witch. You know, son, talking of the future, I've a feeling you two will be good together. It may take a bit of time, but you'll get there.'

Blake slapped his arm. 'Thanks.'

Josa had persuaded Blake that, initially at least, they needed to observe Salinger covertly. If he saw he was being watched he could issue a complaint to her superiors who would simply order Josa and her people to pull out completely, so an element of discretion was essential. Blake conceded the point but made it clear that if it came to a choice of keeping the Professor in sight and being spotted, or losing him in order to remain in the shadows, he'd come down in favour of being noticed.

Stevie disappeared, and Josa, Blake, Dempsey and Mason waited a few feet away from the main entrance, mingling with a crowd watching the Magic Swings swirl high through the air. Salinger appeared as Stevie had predicted. He wore jeans, an open-necked shirt and a tweed jacket. He was alone.

'There's our man,' Josa said.

They watched the Professor pause outside the entrance and, as he scanned the sideshows ahead of him, Josa wondered if he'd spot them even before setting foot in the fair. But his gaze passed over the throng and now he moved forward, airily entering the carnival. 'And so it begins!' whispered Blake.

# CHAPTER 89

Josa found the first half-hour surprisingly easy. She wore an earpiece, and one of her police team, which comprised six officers, fed back reports every few minutes. Where Salinger was, where he lingered, which direction he was heading in. But in truth, the updates were unnecessary. Blake and Josa were maintaining visual contact with their quarry with ease. The only difficult bit was maintaining a discreet distance. Dempsey and Mason were following at a different angle and, after about thirty minutes, Josa wondered if their approach wasn't bordering on overkill.

She'd expected the crowds and confusion of the fair to pose a problem, but Salinger was on his own and wandering about the place with an observer's air. He seemed to enjoy Mr Memory and the neighbouring magician, took a few pot shots on the firing range and even had his palm read by an aged mystic sat beneath a canvas arch. But even here, he remained exposed and clearly visible.

The stress was draining from Mason's face. He'd initially appeared concerned. 'Is this all the backup we've got?' he'd asked Josa.

'Believe me, in today's financial climate within the service, we were lucky to get this.' She gave a what-you-gonna-do shrug. 'To be honest, I also think it's to do with the fact we've already had one complaint about our so-called harassment of the Professor. Flooding him didn't seem a good idea to the powers-that-be.'

It was only after Salinger had crossed the old crone's palm with silver that Josa detected a very slight upping of the ante. Nothing much at first. A slight spring in the Professor's step. He was striding, as opposed to ambling, edging his way into crowds and weaving through throngs without breaking his pace. He visited a portacabin that housed the men's toilets and, as planned, one of Josa's men followed. It had been Stevie, flustered not to find Salinger at the urinals. 'He's not here! He's not here!' Josa heard him say urgently. 'No ... it's okay. He was in a cubicle ...'

As he emerged, Salinger caught the policeman's eye for a fraction of a second. Stevie blushed but reported nothing. Despite the young copper's assurances, Josa could hear Blake breathe a sigh of relief when Salinger emerged and recommenced his walkabout.

But the Professor's pace did not slacken. If anything, his strides grew longer and now, Josa observed, he began pausing occasionally and turning around, only to march back in the direction he'd just come from. Dealing with this idiosyncrasy was not too taxing, but it meant the observers had to start thinking more about their positioning. If Salinger entered a crowd, Josa and Blake made certain they could see him, but tried to keep to the edge of any hoardings, ensuring bodies were always between themselves and their quarry, so if he happened to turn unexpectedly, they were cloaked by passers-by.

After about an hour, when Salinger strayed into certain areas, only one of the three groups – Josa/Blake, Dempsey/Mason or the MIT officers – maintained eyeball. Every now and again Salinger momentarily disappeared – for five or six seconds at most – before his distinctive Harris tweed jacket caught their eye or he stopped, as if allowing them to catch up.

'He's testing us, Josa. And testing himself,' Blake hissed.

'You think he's seen us?'

'He saw us way back. He was expecting us and looking for us. He was uncertain about MIT backup, hence the toilet stop. And when he got his palm read he was planning his next move. From this point on we're going to have to be extra vigilant.'

'Well in that case ...' Blake and Josa turned around to see her standing in front of them, smiling. 'It's a good job I came!' said Holly.

Salinger had quickened his pace again, with Dempsey and Mason obliged to accelerate to keep tabs on him. The big American glanced surreptitiously to his left. John Mason hadn't complained once, but his breath was becoming laboured. Dempsey looked back and wasn't surprised to see Holly had joined Josa and Blake. The father and daughter were arguing, which he didn't give a damn about, but they were losing ground on Salinger, and with Mason tiring, he wondered how much longer he could maintain visual contact with him.

'What the hell are you doing here?'

'I came to help you!'

'Well, now I'm going to have to keep an eye on you as well as him! How is that helping, young lady?'

'You said he wanted to kill again tonight!'

'Yes!'

'I couldn't allow that to happen!'

'I don't believe this!' Blake ran the palm of his hand over his face. 'You're at risk here! You know that? My daughter? Here! He'll love that and you've put –'

'Look!' Josa interrupted, 'Let's talk about this later. For the moment let's just try to keep up with Salinger. He's working up a head of steam again. I can't see him and can only *just* make out Dempsey, so let's get a move on, eh? Holly! You just stay with me and you'll be –'

As Josa spoke the words of encouragement she went to put her arm around Holly. Her sleeve inadvertently caught the top of the teenager's hoodie, pulling the hood down so that –

Blake was rendered momentarily speechless.

Holly's hair fell to its full length. But the long, raven-black locks he was used to had gone. His daughter had lightened her hair. Dramatically. He tried to speak, 'Wh-wh-what?'

Holly Belle Blake now had long blond hair, tumbling over her dark jacket.

Before Blake could begin to articulate any kind of coherent response, Dempsey was by his side. He'd jogged to reach them and was panting. 'It's Salinger ...' He took another gasp of breath. 'We've lost contact!'

# CHAPTER 90

Dempsey had barely finished his sentence before Josa was speaking into her comms device. 'Stevie! Do you have a visual on him?'

'No, guv.'

'What?'

'But that's only because he's just gone onto a ride. The Ghost Train.'

'And you let him?'

'I didn't know what to do! How could I have stopped him?'

'Understood. Okay, I guess so. Where are you now?'

'Waiting for him. At the end of the ride.'

'Stay put. We'll be there in two.'

Mason was furious at his inability to keep up and elected to remain by one of the smaller exits. If Salinger tried to shake off his pursuers, leaving by this route was a possibility, so at least he could help by covertly keeping an eye on it. And so when Josa met up with Stevie by the Ghost Train, her party comprised herself, Blake, Dempsey and Holly. They waited a few feet away from the ride's disembarkation area.

'Do you want to explain that?' Blake nodded towards his daughter's hair.

'I wanted to draw him out.'

Blake gestured to Holly. Looked at Dempsey. 'Can you … *can you believe this is happening?*'

'It's called a Judas Goat ploy,' the teenager said, 'It's when –'

'Yes!' Blake snapped, struggling to keep his voice calm. 'I know what a bloody Judas Goat is, Holly Belle. I've used the ploy. Used it a million times. I've *been* the Judas Goat –'

'I know! That's where I got the idea. Listening to stories people have told me about you. All those stories, and I just wanted to be like you and this was one way that –'

'Don't you get it?' Blake shouted. 'Please, don't! All those stories … I never wanted you to hear them because you're the one thing I couldn't lose. If I lost you I just –'

'Excuse me!' It was Stevie, addressing the rest of the group. 'He should be out in a minute.'

'How do you know this?' Dempsey asked.

'I remember that old couple,' he replied. 'Salinger is on the next carriage. On his own.'

They watched the end of the cloaked tunnel for what felt like an eternity. 'Come on, come on!' Josa murmured. At last a carriage began to poke its way through the canvas that covered the tracks and tunnel. She could see a sloping, laughing skull painted on the front of the carriage … then the carriage itself.

'Oh my God …' she whispered.

The carriage was empty.

# CHAPTER 91

'Come with me!' Holly urged, and began to jog through the crowds. 'I got here earlier. Asked myself what I'd do if I came to a place like this and wanted to give people the slip. Getting on a ride seemed obvious!' She was half-talking, half-shouting over her shoulder as she hurtled through the throng of revellers.

'There must be a load of service exits he could have snuck out of!' Dempsey replied, struggling to keep up.

'There are! But I went on the ride to check it out. The easiest thing is just to get out a few feet into the first tunnel where there's still a platform by your cart. That way you could just walk out of the ride and –'

She careered into an older man, almost knocking him off his feet.

'Well,' said Salinger. 'You must be Holly Blake. How nice to meet you.' He smiled. 'I hope we're going to be great friends.'

Moments earlier, the killer had closed his eyes. Temporarily alone in the darkness. He removed his jacket and shirt and then unwound the tape from his upper body, catching the chamois leather package as it fell from his back. Some of the fair's bright light shone through the top of the canvas to his left, bathing his face and naked torso in a deep red hue. He laid the bundle on top of a piece of machinery casing and pulled back the leather to reveal the knife.

The red light glinted off the steel blade.

He permitted himself a moment to enjoy the scene. A minor victory. Like Hitchcock putting Selznick in a position where he had to pump more money into *Rebecca*. Or when he'd contrived to make all those reviewers watch *Psycho* with the public, so the snooty, scathing critics had been forced to witness the public's overwhelming endorsement of the movie, even as they wrote the first disparaging lines of their reviews … Minor, but enjoyable.

He quickly put his shirt back on, wrapped the knife in the chamois and placed it in a plastic bag. He bundled this through a gap in the back of the ride's hoardings. Finally, he wiped his face and hands with a paper tissue. Put his jacket back on and prepared to face the fair once more. Just another guy at the carnival, having a great time.

'That was a cheap trick, Paul!' Josa looked daggers at the Professor.

'Well, can you blame me? I wanted to smoke you out!'

'I don't give a damn if you have seen us,' Blake told him. 'You know what I think. What I know! And I'd like you to just go home now.'

Salinger ignored him. 'You're on very dangerous ground, Josa. I don't want to have to make a complaint but –'

'Who comes to a Mardi gras on his own, anyway?' Dempsey blurted out. 'What are you doing here by yourself?'

Salinger studied him for a moment. 'And who are you?'

'Well, I was the guy who asked you what you're doing coming to a fair on your own but now I'm the guy who's noting that you're asking me something to give yourself time to think of an answer. I'll save you the brain power. Don't bother, you murdering bastard!'

Salinger threw up his arms and addressed Josa directly. 'The joke is starting to wear thin,' he said. 'Do you want to search me? Is that it? Check whether I'm carrying a bludgeon or a dagger or a big gun? As a matter of fact I was supposed to be meeting friends here earlier. They were delayed. As I waited for them I took in the fair. Is that illegal now?'

'Depends on intent,' Blake replied.

'Josa, I'm meeting friends shortly and, much as I enjoy your company … What am I supposed to tell them?'

'Tell them you've got a police escort,' Dempsey suggested.

'Tell them the truth!' Blake told him, and Salinger again threw up his hands.

'Josa! For God's sake, can't you stop this madness? I can't move without having one of your men at my elbow, and this is bordering on police harassment. I'm begging you, please –'

'Paul! Come with me a moment.' She took his elbow, guiding him away from the main group. 'Blake believes you are the killer.'

'And you? What do you believe? You're the one in charge of this investigation, aren't you?'

'Yes. Yes, I am. And no, I don't share his certainty.'

'His certainty? Well …' He gave a light smile and a sarcastic, 'Thank you, *very* much!'

'Look. We're just trying to do our job. It was you who put us on to this fair, remember?'

'Well, yes, I remember. Beginning to wish I hadn't, now.'

'Why don't you call it a day? Just go home and leave us to drag this place looking for the real killer.'

'Josa, there is one question this whole ugly incident throws up …' With a conjuror's deftness he had taken her hand and now held her fingers in his. 'What about us?'

She was saved by media intrusion.

'How are we all?' The bright, breezy voice of Karen Sherwood.

Josa turned to see the journalist approach Blake, Dempsey and Holly. And right behind her, John Mason, whom she guessed had followed her. He opened his mouth but Karen Sherwood spoke first. 'It's the old team!' she declared. 'Back together again! It's like a Christmas special! Hey, I've got some great snaps of you guys. How about a few lines to go with 'em?'

'Walk away now, Karen,' Blake advised her. 'Or if you're smart, run away.'

She replied with a pantomimic shrug. 'Now why would I want to do that?'

'Because,' said Dempsey, 'he will always go easy on you. I won't.' Mason gestured discreetly suggesting he hold back.

'I was just doing my job,' Karen countered.

'That's bullshit!' Dempsey shouted. 'Do you have any idea how much your story escalated this situation? Made it so much harder? Any idea, lady? You've got Kim Gilmour's blood on your hands! I hope you can live with that!'

This time Blake had to hold him back but Karen wasn't afraid of the American, moving forward to within inches of his face. 'Don't give me the sanctimonious bullshit, Dempsey. You're with your friends and it's all J.D.! The big, happy, say-it-like-is Jack Dempsey! But I remember how it was! You were a bent copper, Dempsey, and I don't know how that plays where you're from but over here it means you lose the right to shoot your mouth off about how other people choose to do their job.'

'Whatever my boy did,' Mason said, his hand across Dempsey's shoulder, 'he never endangered the lives of others. None of us here are perfect. Maybe the world we operate in rubs off on us. Maybe that's an excuse, I don't know. But there are lines, Miss Sherwood. Your actions put innocent folk in a more vulnerable position. For what it's worth, I don't think you acted out of malice, but I'm asking you now to move away from this one. I will personally contact you in the morning and we can see how to move forward.'

'And Holly Blake with blond hair,' said Karen. 'The plot thickens.'

Blake let go of Dempsey, turning to the journalist. 'You leave my daughter –'

But, free of his grip, Dempsey wasn't wasting any time and, enraged by the comment about Holly, he brushed past Blake. Josa could see what was about to happen and moved quickly towards them. 'Jack! Don't!'

Karen Sherwood took a stumbling step backwards. 'You wouldn't strike a lady, would you?'

Dempsey unleashed a powerful haymaker right, connecting with the journalist's jaw and sending her sprawling to the ground. She rolled onto her back, looked up at him and wiped the blood from her mouth.

'Dead right,' Dempsey replied. 'I'd never strike a lady.'

'Christ!' Josa said, kneeling down by Karen's side. 'Are you all right?'

But Karen Sherwood was looking, not at Josa or Dempsey, but

at Blake. 'You know I would never do anything to harm Holly ... You know that! You *do* know that?'

'I guess so ...' He held out a hand to help her up.

'Where's Salinger?' It was the first time Josa had heard panic in Mason's voice.

'Christ almighty!' Dempsey seethed.

Professor Paul Salinger had vanished.

And this time, Josa realised with a sickening certainty, he was not confined to the area around a single ride. She looked wildly around. *He could be anywhere.*

# CHAPTER 92

'We've got to split up!' Holly's voice was insistent.

Her father's, equally assertive. 'No! You are not leaving my side!'

But she was already pulling away from the group. 'He can't have got far. If we split up now we've got a chance of catching sight of him. If we don't, we don't. I've got my phone. We can keep in touch. Now go!' And she was away, darting in and out of the revellers, disappearing into the crowd. Blake tracked a blond blur for several seconds before his daughter was lost in the carnival.

They had followed Holly's lead and gone their separate ways, not because the teenager had suggested it, but because they had known it was the right course of action, even before she'd opened her mouth. The right course of action except for one thing, Blake thought bitterly. *Her.*

They began trawling through the fair, trying to remain vigilant despite the desperation that drove them. After about twenty minutes, Josa realised their search was growing harder. The natural light was non-existent, even the moon was masked by cloud.

And the people they had to push through to press on with their search were becoming more intractable. The effects of alcohol could be detected. Some of the shouts were louder, the cries of pleasure riper with drunken abandon. As Josa pushed past people now, even offering polite 'excuse me's, she was often shoved back. She could smell beer and see eyes that were looking for a fight. Too busy to linger, she inwardly shrugged. Pressed ahead. She had no time for this. No time!

Blake jogged up to Mason, who'd returned to his sentry point by one of the side exits. 'Any sign?' the two men asked simultaneously. 'No! Not seen Salinger or Holly Belle ...' Blake said. He raked his fingers through his hair. 'I can't believe she's ...'

'Don't be too hard on her, Daniel,' the older man said. 'She's exactly like you were when ... well, I don't have to finish that sentence.'

'I should never have allowed her into any of this.'

'You couldn't have stopped her. None of us could!'

'Maybe. But you know, I've got a weird feeling Josa could have if she'd wanted –' The chirrup of his phone interrupted. 'Holly Belle! Thank God! Why weren't you answering your phone? Where are you?'

*'Listen, Dad. My phone's almost out of juice. I think I can see him. I'm almost on him. Don't worry!'*

'No! Do not approach him! D'you hear me? Where are you?'

*'I'm –'*

John Mason saw the horror spread across his friend's face. 'She's going after him,' Blake murmured.

'Then get after her! Where is she?'

'Phone out of power and it just ...' His voice was hoarse, 'went dead. She's on her own!'


Blake closed his eyes. 'Got to think ...'

Mason had seen this before and remained silent. Blake began recalling the conversation with his daughter. Just the gist at first. The general idea of who'd said what and when. It had been a brief call, which helped, so the words came fairly easily, followed by their construction. The pacing of them, the stress placed on certain syllables. The insistence in her voice when she'd said 'listen', the use of 'Dad' as a marker, taking control. 'Don't worry' said as a genuine plea of reassurance.

And as all that fitted together like shards of a broken tile joining to form a mosaic, so the recollection of the conversation became precisely that: a recall of the moments. Right down to his breathing pattern, what he had seen – Mason's inquisitive eyes, for instance

– but not noticed during the exchange. The quality of light – slightly green from the lamps overhanging the exit arch, and even the air temperature. He went further, almost sliding through the digital stream that had linked him with Holly. Her voice had dropped an infinitesimal amount when she uttered the word 'almost' and he could see her phone moving away from her mouth as she'd spoken because ... because her eyes were following *him*. Their quarry. Blake could almost physically see her face turning to track Salinger. And as she followed him –

– there had been a bell!

He'd not noticed it at the time, but almost at the end of their snatched conversation he'd heard a bell ping as if it had been struck.

Blake's eyes snapped open.

'What is it?' Mason asked.

'D'you remember those old test-your-strength machines? You know, you get given a long hammer, swing it and bash something that shoots up a strength-o-meter and if you hit it hard enough the pointer pings to the top and strikes a bell.'

'Yeah. It's all in the wrist.'

'Yeah, never mind that. Have you seen one here?'

'Yes!'

'Where?'

'The east corner,' he said. 'I think ... yes, I'm certain! For God's sake, go! Before it's too late!'

As he sprinted through the fair, Blake phoned Josa. 'Tell all your team to focus on the east corner! Do you get that? The east corner!'

'Will do!'

Dempsey, Blake and Josa met up by the test-your-strength machine and Blake quickly explained the phone call with Holly.

'Christ!' Dempsey said. 'Well, at least we know roughly where she is and everyone's focused around here.'

''Where she *was*,' Blake corrected him. 'The call was about ten minutes ago and still no sightings.'

'She knows what she's doing,' Josa said. 'Don't worry.'

'Don't worry? Can you seriously tell me not to worry?'

Josa knew Blake's question was rhetorical but replied, 'Yes! There's something about this that –'

Stevie interrupted their conversation, bounding up to their group with urgent news. 'It's Detective Constable Grey!' he announced. 'She thinks she just spotted them. Can't be sure, as she's just replaced Barnes so she's only seen photos of Salinger and had a description of your daughter. But an older guy in a tweed jacket, open-necked shirt, distinguished looking … with a teenage girl. Long blond hair …' His voice was trailing off.

'What the hell's wrong?' Blake demanded. 'What is it?'

'Well, she reports they were together.'

'What?'

Stevie nodded, clearly regretting his role of messenger. 'Chatting. And then …'

'Then what?' Josa snapped.

'They got on the ride together. Disappeared from sight.'

Blake was right beside Stevie now. 'What ride?'

'The Tunnel of Love.'

Police officers had streamed into the end of the Tunnel of Love closest to the entrance while Josa, Blake and Dempsey jogged towards the exit. As they approached it, Josa spotted a young black woman standing by the ride's disembarkation point. 'That's DC Grey,' she panted.

They were still moving along the side of the Tunnel of Love but could see a car emerging from the tunnel itself, nosing aside plastic ivy as it neared the end of the ride. DC Grey raised her hand, pointing to the car which Josa could only see side-on. 'That's them!' the young officer shouted.

From her angle, slightly to one side of the car in question, Josa could make out a man in a brown tweed jacket and a much younger blond girl. He was trying – it appeared – to smother her somehow. Get close to her. He was smiling, laughing almost, out of his chair and trying to use his body weight to press down on her.

Josa sensed Blake quicken his pace and wondered if he'd reach them in time.

He had conceived this murder almost a week ago. Not a great deal of time in the grand scheme of things, but enough to plan with precision and flair. A fairground in Leytonstone had been the perfect setting, and in one of his more fanciful moments he even wondered if Hitchcock had had a word with the 'man upstairs' and persuaded him to make everything conspire to be absolutely, almost supernaturally *right*.

As the moment of death grew close he smiled, recalling how it all began. In the university library, reading the archived edition of the *Guardian*. The old woman's advice, and being struck by that last photograph – of Josa with her sister and two friends. He'd wondered, did that shot capture Detective Chief Inspector Jilani? The jumped-up, pumped up, *hauled*-up little nobody they had assigned to capture him. In that second he knew he'd found his next leading lady.

When he conducted his internalised interviews, he always referred to that realisation as his *Today Show* moment. In the same way that Hitchcock had first seen Tippi Hedren starring in a diet drink advertisement during the commercial break of a *Today Show*, and had instantly known she would be his next star, so he had immediately known when he saw the photograph. He would cause her pain. But he would make her famous.

The carriage slowed. Blake reached it first and hauled the man in the tweed jacket away from the blonde. *Not trying to smother her. Trying to kiss her.* The girl giggled. Said something about him being her boyfriend. Blake didn't even wait until she'd finished the sentence before he turned away. Josa could see that the two passengers were complete strangers, the girl in her late teens and the man much older than Salinger. 'It's not them!' Blake confirmed as he reached her. 'So if Holly's not there, where is she?'

Josa turned 360 degrees on the spot, searching the crowds and queues and –

She turned back to the open tent. Mr Memory. And next to it, the magician, still going through the same disappearing coin routine.

'Not them, then?' Grey had joined them.

'No,' Blake replied testily. 'How old does that guy look to you? It's clearly not Salinger! Get on to your colleagues and tell them to double their efforts.'

'Will do!' She disappeared, glad to be out of Blake's firing line.

'I think Holly's all right,' Josa said.

'You know this, how?' Dempsey asked. There was no sarcasm or antagonism in his voice. This felt like genuine interest.

'I don't know ...' Josa peered back into the conjuror's tent. 'It's just ...'

'Dad!'

Blake was almost knocked off his feet as Holly bowled into him, all hugs and explanations. 'Saw a guy ... tweed jacket ... got into the Tunnel of Love ... thought it was ... but it wasn't ... so sorry ...'

'It's okay, it's okay. Just, thank God you're safe. Never, ever do anything like again! Do you prom–'

'Detective Chief Inspector Jilani?' Josa turned, recognising the interrupting voice. It was the brawny DI who headed up the local police's presence at the fair.

'Hello.' She sounded wary and was anticipating trouble, but was surprised by the grin on the man's face.

'Just thought I'd let you know. The fair's winding down. Our lads are calling it a day. Nothing reported. I think our presence did the trick. No murders this Tuesday!' He paused and shot a wink at his colleagues. 'Any time you fancy city officers want help from some real police catching this Hitchcock Killer, you just let us know.'

'I wish I shared your optimism, Detective Inspector,' Blake said.

'Oh, come on! The crowds are thinning, the rides closing. Everything becoming nice and visible. If he was going to try anything he'd have gone for it earlier on. What d'you say, DCI Jilani?'

'I say,' Josa replied, glancing at her watch, 'That the worst is yet to come. And at any moment now.'

He'd done his research. Knew that the top floor wasn't occupied and contained no security cameras. And so he stepped into its hallway without fear of being spotted. Sauntered to the far end by the window and took his time preparing. Knife on one side of the window ledge. And then he opened the bag and took out the dress.

'He murders every Tuesday …' Blake insisted.

He was talking to Josa, Dempsey and Holly. None of them moved as the fair-goers filed past them, finally heading for home. The music was dying, the whir of engines fading, and lights right across the carnival were being switched off. Josa could see that the magician was taking a final bow.

'Blake. D'you remember what you told me, before? About misdirection.'

'Yeah. I said he'd try to misdirect us tonight. Draw our attention to one thing when we should be focussing on something else. And a fairground was perfect for him because it's so noisy, so chaotic, so much going –'

'You're not getting it!'

'What d'you mean?'

'Suppose this … suppose this fair is the misdirection?'

He smoothed down the pleats of the skirt. Straightened his back. Reached inside his bag and removed the wig. He held it like a crown, placing it on his head and adjusting it slightly as if the moment merited august solemnity. Because, for him, it did. This was the one people always remembered. And when history came to record *his* Hitchcock Murders, when people spoke of it in pubs and on panel shows, this would be the act that would revile and excite them the most. This was it. His hands moved away from the wig. His crowning moment.

'Blake …' Josa was talking faster now. 'Suppose Salinger is behind all this.'

'There's no suppose about it.'

'Well, he must know that on a Tuesday we'll be all over him.'

'Agreed.'

'So what does he do? He makes us look one way. Tells us about the fair. Even turns up here. *Tells us where he'll be and turns up.* Nice and obliging. But …' Josa closed her eyes.

*In the end, isn't everything?*

'Oh, God …' She was starting to feel sick.

He opened the door to the stairwell and listened for any sound, but everyone always took the lift, even when moving between single floors. After a moment, satisfied that no one was around, he began to descend the steps leading to Josa's apartment. And as he neared his victim, he slipped something into his pocket, something he had just enjoyed looking over again. His next victim's face on the scrap of torn paper. On the newspaper photograph.

'Gilmour is dead,' Josa said. If he wants to attack, to hurt the next person in the chain of command for the case, what does he do?'

Holly gave a confused shrug. 'Kill you!'

But Blake was beginning to understand, and his voice dropped to a horrified whisper. 'No, not Josa …'

The photograph of Josa Jilani. And her sister, Preya.

# CHAPTER 95

Preya and Josa seldom fought, but tonight they'd had one of their infrequent rows. A stupid little spat about washing up and keeping the flat tidy. Josa had admitted she didn't do her share, but insisted that as she'd been working all hours following her promotion, her sister should have stepped up to the plate and handled domestic duties. Tired and irritated, Preya counter-claimed that she was busier than ever trying to secure employment, and that Josa was lucky with her job for life, whereas she had to –

And so the thing had blown up. Two sisters. Exhausted. Stressed. In retrospect, they both recognised they'd handled the disagreement clumsily, but they assumed it was no big deal. They'd be friends again in the morning. Apologies and gentle self-recrimination all around.

But Preya Jilani had always worried about any contretemps with her little sister. She'd looked after her all through school and, it seemed to her, well into her adult life. The disparity in their physical beauty had always pained Preya. She had never once mentioned it, but she saw that Josa lived in a much more bruising world; it was a world her looks protected her from, and to see her sister caught there resolved Preya to let Josa know that whatever happened, she had her. Had her safe. Had her close. Had her for ever.

And so even the tiniest argument upset her, because the thought of Josa doubting her love for even a single second was agony. It was the reason she decided to write a note. When Josa got in, she'd see it, read it and even before turning in for the night, she'd be aware that whatever the following day brought, big sis Preya was in her corner, just like she'd always been. Just like she always would be.

Preya sat at the writing desk in the front room. Left hand to her temple, she began scribbling away. Short, lacklustre comments. Chin now resting on her palm, she studied them for several moments. A long sigh. This wasn't working. She was too tired. She needed some coffee and to –

She ripped the pages out of her notebook. She'd wanted to speak openly and honestly to her sister, sure, but her words were sounding too measured, too serious. Why couldn't she just write something simple and funny instead of this long, rambling prose that read like *The Waltons*?

Four short, sharp tears and the torn-out pages were in pieces. She looked around for the bin, deciding to try again after she'd freshened up. It was too late to take a walk, so she'd put the kettle on. Make a coffee. Take a shower.

In the hallway outside her flat, he slipped a pick and tension wrench into the lock. The two steel tools resembled medical instruments and he handled them with the deftness of a surgeon. It took less than thirty seconds to spring the pins and tumblers and, very gently, he pushed open the door.

Preya slipped off her dressing gown. It fell onto the toilet lid and she didn't bother to pick it up, stepping straight into the bath. She swished the shower curtain closed, its circular holders making a loud metallic *whoosh* as they flew across the rail.

He could barely believe his luck. She was in the shower. He had to control his breathing because he felt exhilarated to the point of dizziness about the imminent murder. In the past, a small percentage of his thoughts had been given over to technique and security, but here and now he knew that nothing could go wrong.

Preya tilted her head back, letting the strong jets of water strike her lower face, throat and chest. She looked up at the shower head, raised the bar of soap to her neck, quickly building up lather before moving down, briskly rubbing the soap across her left arm.

A brief, broad smile on her face as the water hit her torso. Head right back, so that as she turned, her hair became soaked. She moved her hands back to her throbbing neck and shoulders –

The bathroom door opened and the killer was silhouetted in the threshold. He wore an old woman's dress and a grey wig. His right hand grasped a long, sturdy carving knife, and as he moved forward he raised it to the level of his chin, the tip of its lethal blade pointing towards the shower curtain and Preya Jilani.

# CHAPTER 96

'Not Josa ...' Blake repeated. 'Her sister!'

Josa was already on her mobile. A moment later her horrified eyes looked up. 'She's not picking up.'

He had to force himself not to run. To take slow, measured paces. He tried not to become too excited by Preya's naked body, visible through the transparent curtain. She wasn't facing him. Hadn't heard him. And even through the plastic he could see she was slender and toned. He had never seen an Asian woman naked before and in that moment he somehow felt nobody had and that he was the first person ever to see – no, to behold – this vision.

His left hand swept back the shower curtain.

Preya turned. Screamed.

His knife was raised but for a couple of seconds he just stared. Only Hitchcock had ever seen the view he now enjoyed. The beautiful woman, naked, with a knife raised before her. The millions of people who had watched the killing with fear and delight in the cinema or on television screens had enjoyed glimpses and guilty imaginings, but he was experiencing the ultimate murder exactly as it should be savoured. Even the actor portraying Norman would have played the scene to a camera. No, only he and Hitchcock had shared this vision. This knowledge gave him the impetus to go on, and he drove the knife hard into Preya's body.

She tried to parry the blade with her hand, but it was odd. He could see that even now she believed he wouldn't do it. He perceived that much in her eyes, and, correspondingly, her feeble defence remained mindful of the knife, fearful of getting her hands cut! He would have grasped the sharp steel and fought off any attacker but this woman was used to the protection her beauty gave her, and even when faced with a knife slicing towards her, she still instinctively believed nothing could hurt her.

He withdrew the blade. Held it aloft.

She screamed, 'No!'

At last, beginning to understand!

He slashed at her again but this time she caught his wrist! Tried to wrestle! The whore! But, *yes!* Her right foot slipped a little and as she tried to regain her balance he wrenched his hand back, then plunged the knife forward, more firmly this time, so although she made contact with his arm, the blade sunk into her flesh for a second time, again just under her left shoulder.

She was trying to fight back, arms flailing as she lunged for the weapon and he noticed with a shock of fury that she made no attempt to cover her nakedness. Both her hands grasped the base of the blade and her stance meant she stood squarely in front of him.

*I know your game, lady!* he thought. He guessed she was positioning herself to seduce him with what cheap directors called a full-frontal. Had she no shame? Or sense? He was above that! She was beautiful, yes, but was that enough to warrant her tempting him? And he was tempted, even now, and yet ... *No!* Did she think he was turned on by her? That he wanted her? That wasn't it at all! *No, no, no!* How come he was killing her, but she retained the upper hand?

Livid, he delivered five stabs in swift succession. Each time, ramming home the knife good and proper, forgetting to look at her face, intent solely on plunging it into her. She must know by now it was over.

But now the little trollop – *oh, no* – the little bitch was turning her back on him! No! That was his whole life, right there. Past and present colliding in that single, symbolic act.

And he screamed, ruining the scene even further in his own eyes. The added anger at this realisation drove him forward again and he stabbed her in the back. Felt the blade splinter bone, and, as he pulled back the knife, it remained lodged in Preya's spine so her body was drawn back with it. She tumbled out of the bath, knocking her murderer to the floor.

*No! Not like this!* He had wanted to finish her off properly, or rather leave as she was dying, completing the ultimate re-enactment.

But he felt her lifeless, curiously heavy mass pinning him to the bathroom floor, and he knew with an absolute certainty that Preya Jilani was already dead.

Her blood covered his dress. He used his palms to push her off and quickly tried to heave her back into the shower. He grasped her wrists but they were damp and slid through his fingers. So he leant over her, embraced her corpse and straightened his back to haul her from the floor.

At least when she was found it would look as if the re-enactment had gone to plan and that he'd successfully –

Over her shoulder, he saw the floor space where her body had been. Let out a sob as he registered the huge red slick of blood and water. Her body fell through his arms as he let out another sob. They would piece together what happened. No problem. Realise he had bungled the scene that should have been his *pièce de résistance*. He heaved her up again but his heart wasn't in it, and just like before, she slipped through his fingers, thudding to the floor.

No good. They'd be able to tell. He caught sight of himself in the mirror. '*Messed it up again, eh, boy?*'

Josa's phone fell from her hand. Without saying another word to Blake, Holly or Dempsey, she began to run.

# CHAPTER 97

Josa sprinted from the carnival. She ran, tearing under the exit arch, her shoes blurring over the scrubland, never having run this fast since she'd been –

*– a young girl. All she sees as she runs is her own pair of shoes. The scuffed black leather and silver buckles blurring as she races from the school. She'd waited until the playground was out of sight before she'd begun to walk a little faster, finally breaking into a sprint with no thought of where she was heading, propelled only by a desire to leave the other children far behind.*

*Gradually her pace slackens. She looks up. No idea where she is. A back alley somewhere. Broken, uneven ground. A vast, mud-coloured puddle, so wide that she has to press her back to the wall so she can side-step past it. The alley widens to accommodate turning space for a row of three garages. The ground is more even here, but more dangerous, as she sees a group of older boys watching her. As she nears them she tries to run again, but her foot catches on something and her ankle twists. She's sent flying towards the ground and then something happens that always happens.*

*In a minute or two the boys will be trying to make her laugh and giving her sweets. But before that, as the ground seems to fly towards her she lets out a cry and –*

*Preya catches her.*

*Doesn't ask what she's doing or where she's going. Just holds her sister in a tight, everything-is-all-right embrace and says three words that Josa, from that day onwards, believes should only be said if you mean them properly. Mean them for ever.*

*Preya strokes her sister's hair, holds her tight and whispers, 'I've got you.'*

Josa sat on her bathroom floor. She held the body of her dead sister tight to her own body. Preya was wearing her thick, striped dressing gown. Somewhere in Josa's head she'd known that the CSIs would come and take their photographs and she didn't want them to see her beautiful sister naked. And so she'd struggled to put Preya's lifeless arms into the sleeves, turn her over and …

And now that was done she just sat with the weight of her sister against her chest and in her arms. The shower still ran, gradually steaming up the room. Josa put her lips and nose against the top of Preya's head, feeling the damp hair against her skin. She could smell the shampoo and see the back of her neck. The tiny tattoo at the very top of Preya's spine she'd got done on her eighteenth birthday. Even before the ink had fully seeped into her skin she'd shown it to Josa and they'd both sworn that they'd keep it a secret from their mother. She'd not seen it for years. A tiny broken heart.

In time the water ran cold and the steam faded.

Blake was the first to arrive, slowly pushing open the bathroom door and standing in the hallway, taking in the whole scene. Josa wasn't weeping. She looked up, calm. 'When he writes the post-mortem report, would you ask Simon to omit the presence of the tattoo? Mum might read it and … It's a secret.' And then she turned from Blake, once again burying her face in sister's hair.

# CHAPTER 98

Blake rang the doorbell. Stood back and glanced at his watch. 3.02 a.m. He had sent a text – *You home yet?* – and received the equally terse reply: *Just back*. But he knew he should have phoned ahead to spare her the dread that she must now be feeling. No one gets good news at three in the morning, and Blake could imagine the horrors running through her –

A rattle of locks interrupted his thoughts.

The door swung open a couple of inches. She was peering over the safety latch and saying 'Yes?' even before she had time to focus.

'Hello,' Blake replied, stepping forward a little so she could see him. He saw her catch her breath. 'I should have phoned ahead. I'm so sorry.'

'No. No, don't be. You never need to …' She paused. 'Wait a second.' She closed the door and Blake heard a metallic clink as the safety chain was unfastened. He looked over his shoulder. Above the rooftops of the houses opposite, the sky was dark purple. No stars. A pale, crescent moon. The next moment the door was thrown wide open. 'Come in,' said Mara Diaz.

Simon Maxwell stood in the middle of Josa's living room. He could still taste the strong, bitter coffee he'd gulped down on the way over but the caffeine hadn't fully kicked in yet. Josa emerged from her bedroom and he threw a smile in her direction.

'They didn't tell me you were the SIO on this one! In fact they've told me nothing about it at all. Typical, eh?' He grinned. Saw the lack of response and lowered his voice. 'Is everything okay,

Josa? I hope Jack Dempsey told you I tried to help you guys out with the Jill Kennedy post-mortem reports?' Still nothing. 'Look, I'll leave if –'

She stepped away. His brow furrowed and he opened his mouth to speak, but as Josa had walked to one side he could see a shelf in the corner of the room and a framed photograph on top of it. The two Jilani girls, their beaming faces squashed together on a bright summer's day.

He glanced into the bathroom. Back at the photograph. *This was her new place!* She'd forbidden him to visit until she had it looking how she wanted it, but he recalled her sister was flat-sharing with her, which meant … He closed his eyes. 'Oh, my God …'

Mara had lived here almost five years, but in Blake's mind it was still her 'new home'. He had visited her old place a thousand times. Happier days when he'd called on Thom for cards nights, or when they'd been out for an evening on the town, inevitably arriving back the worse for wear, alcohol anesthetising them against the frost in Mara's reception. '*And where did you rats get to tonight?*' But she'd always relent with a smile. In fact, Blake had suspected she was always delighted to join them for a nightcap. He recalled that Thom's arm around her waist and his winning smile always seemed to do the trick when it came to –

Blake froze. He had just stepped into the hallway and, even before he'd taken anything else in, he was struck by a large studio portrait of Thom and Mara Diaz. It was a terrible photograph. Both of them looked awkward, cajoled into an unnatural stance with Mara seated and Thom standing by her side, one hand resting on her shoulder. Both wore too much make-up and unconvincing smiles. But it was the unnatural quality of the photograph that unnerved Blake. His old friend not quite himself, as if the figure in the photograph was trying to be Thom Diaz. Even in death, trying to get back. To defeat the state that Blake had inflicted upon him.

'It's a poor picture, I know,' said Mara, reading his thoughts.

'But it's one of the few I have of us together.'

Blake tore his eyes from the face of Thom Diaz and looked at his widow. She was in her late thirties. Long dark hair, sultry eyes, pretty face. A former dancer who still had a toned, trim body, and the dressing gown she wore was only loosely tied, meaning Blake had to make an effort to focus on her eyes.

'You answered the door very quickly,' he said. 'I'm hoping you weren't asleep and I don't have to apologise for –'

'I only got back here an hour ago. My body is still on New Zealand time so, no, I was wide awake. As a matter of fact, I was about to come down to start unpacking.'

Blake saw three large suitcases by the front door.

'And you never have to apologise for coming around. God knows, I've been trying to persuade you for years. Come here, Danny.'

She embraced him and he could feel the contours of her body beneath the thin silk of her dressing gown. Mara held him close for several seconds and he returned the hug, rubbing her back. She slowly pulled away and, for a moment, Blake thought she was going to kiss him. In that split second of uncertainty, he wondered how he would respond, but she simply smiled. 'So what is it?' she asked. 'Run out of sugar?'

'Mara, it's Thom.' Blake ran his fingers through his hair. 'I need to speak to you about Thom.'

'So what do we do?' Holly Blake asked. 'I want to phone Josa now. Let her know we're here for her.'

Dempsey shook his head. 'Send her a text if you want, but give her a few hours before you phone, darlin'. Believe me, she'll just need a bit of space, then she'll appreciate your call.'

Holly, Dempsey and John Mason were gathered around the circular table in Blake's study room. The men looked tired and ashen-faced. Both of them sat behind large tumblers of whisky while Holly sipped a mug of chocolate. 'What do *we* do now?' she persisted.

'We've done all we can do,' Mason replied.

Against the far wall they had pinned A4 photographs of six young women. Mason pointed at them. 'When we agreed to help we promised to whittle down the thousands of missing persons to just six people so your father could investigate them and find out which one is Victim Zero. When we got back tonight, your uncle Jack and I finally finished that undertaking. Now it's up to your father to discern which girl is the link with Salinger.'

'And from there,' Dempsey added, 'to find the evidence that links him to her, and from *there*, to put Salinger away.'

'But after everything that's happened,' Holly said, 'do you think he'll go on killing?'

'After everything that's happened?' Dempsey finished his whisky in a single gulp. 'Do you think he'll ever stop?'

It was not the reaction Blake had anticipated. Mara Diaz was laughing, covering her face with her hands, shoulders rising and falling. 'You think Thom is still alive?' she said at last, dropping her hands.

Blake could see tears in her eyes.

'I don't know …' he replied. 'It's just with everything that's happened it feels as if …'

'Danny! You shot him. His body fell 160 feet. You saw the post-mortem report. You think he has a ghost?'

'I just don't know,' Blake told her honestly.

'How many times have you replayed that night in your head? But every time you play it, it ends the same because you can't go back. Danny, you saved Jamie. You couldn't save Thom. Without you, I'd be without the single most important thing in my life. My son. My God, d'you think I haven't replayed those final weeks in my head? Wondered what I did wrong? Wondering what I could have changed that would have stopped him from going up there and …' She shook her head. 'Want to hear something funny? When you told me about Kim Gilmore's death I was due to catch a plane to South Island the very next morning. They say it's one of the most beautiful places on earth. But instead, I came straight back here because I thought you might need me. But I didn't think it would be to answer that question.'

Blake suddenly felt very tired. He closed his eyes. 'I'm sorry.'

'Don't be.'

He felt her lips on his. His eyes sprang open and he stepped back, surprised.

'Thom is dead,' Mara told Blake.

He looked at her and knew there was a guilt he had never considered.

'Thom is *dead*!' she repeated, narrowing her eyes, as if looking into Blake's mind. 'And no amount of guilt can change that.'

Liz Canterville's breezy 'Good morning!' into the phone disguised the fact that the call had woken her. She leant on her elbow and glanced at the time. A frown crossed her face. She took the news of

Preya's murder quietly, asked what kind of state Josa and Blake were in, and then made assurances she'd handle the situation. Moments after the conversation ended she took her mobile phone from her bedside table. Her call was answered immediately. 'Get me the Prime Minister,' she said.

When Blake stepped through his front door, John Mason was there to greet him. 'How are you, Daniel?'

'You've really got it down to six people?'

'If Victim Zero exists, she's waiting for you, through there. We've done all we can. We've probed and investigated and collected all the facts, but we can't narrow it down any more. She could be any one of those half-dozen girls.'

Dempsey appeared at the top of the stairs and, as he joined them, said, 'You're going to have to read all the files we've put together and investigate each individual girl. That could take weeks. Even months.'

Blake strode beneath the huge chandelier and walked quickly to the room that had become their centre of operations. Across one wall he saw where Dempsey had pinned the six photographs, one for every possible Victim Zero. Blake marched towards the images, scanning them as he approached the line-up.

'He's right,' Mason conceded. 'Narrowing it down from here could take –'

'It's her!' Blake snatched a photograph from the wall.

'What?' Dempsey stammered.

'No doubt about it,' Blake said. 'This is the woman that started it all. This is the woman Salinger thought he loved and the woman he murdered. Let me introduce you to Victim Zero.' He glanced at the name pencilled across the back of the photograph. *He just knew.* 'Lucy Jaeger.'

# CHAPTER 100

## *The day after Preya's murder: Josa*

Josa opened her door and looked into the pale, round face of the family liaison officer, the woman with the job of telling her that everything would be all right. All sympathy, pamphlets and common sense passed off as wisdom and psychological insight.

She'd have been sent automatically, dispatched by an email that gave the name and address of her new *client* (as they were bizarrely termed) and in about 200 words, an overview of their relevant 'issue'. The bland face tried a tentative smile.

That morning, Josa had tried without success to reach her mother and had already spoken to a few friends. She'd had a good social circle before her promotion – a small group of close friends as opposed to an address book full of acquaintances – a close-knit gang that went back more years than seemed plausible. They'd even started to say, *D'you remember, fifteen years ago* … which although mathematically correct, always felt exaggerated. But since her move from Surrey to London she'd not caught up with any of them, too busy with the new flat at first, and then work. Some of her friends even prefaced their call of condolence with, *Sorry I've not been in touch, Jose* … In the end she'd started screening the calls, not because she didn't want to talk, but as a kindness to the people she loved. Josa could easily imagine the relief on their faces when her voicemail kicked in. And besides, there was nothing they could say that would offer any hope or comfort.

She knew the way it worked, and at this point she let process take over. If she went into work, colleagues would conceal their surprise at her presence until a senior officer would wander over and gently suggest that in her current state …

Josa knew she needed to make statements, sign forms and

engage with the machinery of police work, not as a copper, but as a – the thought occurred to her – a client. Yet for the first time she understood the blank look in the eyes of the bereaved she'd interviewed over the years. So often she'd felt the urge to slap them and bawl, *We want to catch the person responsible for this!* unable to fathom the look of apathy – hostility even – that her words engendered. Now she got it. The fury was not directed at her, it was levelled at the situation, because of the unshakeable, unquestionable, unalterable knowledge that it didn't matter. None of it. Nothing anyone could say or pray or do could bring back the dead or help in any meaningful way, and so the pretence was absurd, grotesque.

Josa wanted to focus on doing the right thing for Preya. The tenets of Islam demanded the burial should take place as soon as possible. This meant dealing with the police, calling in a few favours, letting friends and family know what had happened and what was being planned. After that, she'd think about falling apart. But she wouldn't afford herself the luxury of reflection until everything was right for Preya.

The Family Liaison Officer inclined her head and pursed her lips in a move that said, *I know how difficult this must be for you and, believe me, I understand, luvvie.*

But Josa simply closed the door before either of them had a chance to say anything.

# CHAPTER 101

## *The day after Preya's murder: Blake*

Lucy's mother, Jeanette Jaeger, lived in a once-grand house on the edge of the Hanwell flight of locks – the stretch of waterway that raises the Grand Union Canal by just over fifty feet. Although ensconced in London, West 7, the area has a rural feel to it, with meadows bordering one section of the canal and woodlands surrounding the lower locks. On the day Blake first called to see Jeanette, a fallen oak had restricted road access and he left his Cutlass idling as he stepped from the car, looking over the tree as he mulled over his options.

'You can go through,' a workman called to him. 'But it'll have to be on foot.'

Blake parked and trudged up the long incline. The Jaegers' house struck him as a smaller version of his own, possessing an air of ramshackle opulence. But it was more neglected than Moonfleet and, even at first glance, Blake could tell this place needed new window frames, a paint job and the housing equivalent of a full service. He paused at the gate and looked across to the bay window at the right-hand side of the property. A woman was watching him. She was old, her face expressionless. Blake raised a hand and mouthed 'hello' with a cheeriness he didn't feel. Her expression did not change.

He pushed open the gate, crunched along the gravel path to the front door and rang the bell. Stepped back. The woman was still staring, not at Blake, but at the gate where he had stood.

Blake glanced to his left. To the north he could make out the top of a long stone building he knew was now the Ealing Hospital; for over a century it had been the Hanwell Insane Asylum, a grey, grim building surrounded by a tall, prison-like wall. A madhouse right out of Victorian gothic literature.

Blake shuddered, lost for a moment, but the sound of a key being turned tugged him back. He turned to the door. It opened slowly and what it revealed left Blake speechless for a second. His eyes narrowed and he felt his throat constrict. And in that brief moment everything he had felt about the case evaporated as certainties melted with the speed of thought.

The young woman in front of him registered his expression and her voice held a hint of concern. 'Hello?'

Blake tried to speak but couldn't. He was looking at a face he had only ever seen in photographs.

'What's the matter?' the woman asked.

'Nothing,' he murmured.

Blake was looking at the face of Lucy Jaeger.

'There's been some mistake,' Blake stammered. 'I was told ... We were told you were missing and hadn't been informed that ...' His voice tailed off.

'I'm Odette Wilde. Lucy's sister. Twin sister.' Her tone was matter of fact to the point of being brusque. As Blake took this in he was struck by how unemotional she seemed about his mistake. As if hearing his thoughts, she said, 'I get it all the time.'

Blake nodded.

'How can I help?' Odette asked. 'Are you from the police? Do you have any news about Lucy?'

'I'm from the police, but no ...' Blake showed her some identification that Josa had issued him with. Although he didn't offer it, Odette took it from his hands and examined it. As she returned it she demanded –

'Then what is it?'

Blake looked over her shoulder. Speaking to the face of the first victim was too distracting. 'I'd like a little of your time, if that's possible. I'd come to see Lucy's mother. Well, your mother. To ask a few questions. Does she still live here?'

'Yes. Ask a few questions, *or something*?'

'May I come in?'

'No. Mum can't speak to anyone.'

'Why's that?'

'Alzheimer's. You won't get anything out of her.'

Blake stopped himself looking across at the face at the window.

'Can I speak to you, then?'

'About what?'

'Your sister. I'm trying to find her.'

'She's dead.'

'How do you know that?'

'I've been over this a million times with you lot. Now and again someone else turns up and tries to help because that's their job but it never gets anywhere and if you knew Lucy, you'd know. She wouldn't ...' Odette made a gesture with her hand in the air to suggest disappearance. 'She's dead.'

She began to close the door.

'Yeah, I think so, too,' said Blake.

Odette hesitated. 'Thank you.'

Blake realised she was used to lies and guessed her gratitude was for his straight response. He nodded, sensed a window of opportunity and pressed ahead. 'I'm looking at this as a murder inquiry. I don't know if we'll get whoever's responsible. It's been a long time but generally results are pretty good for cases like this. If we have cooperation.'

A pause.

Odette swung open the door.

'What do you want to know?'

Odette guided her mother from the window into a large wing chair. It was a faded red and speckled in food stains. Jeanette Jaeger stared dead ahead, and the angle of the chair meant she was watching television. Blake perched on the sofa and looked at the screen. Howard Keel and Doris Day were scowling at each other between bursts of song.

'*Calamity Jane*, Mrs Jaeger. One of my favourites!'

Jeanette showed no signs of hearing him. Odette was reaching behind her, adjusting cushions and settling her mother. She then moved to the television and plugged in a small jack attached to a long, cream-coloured wire. The other end held earphones. 'Mum likes her musicals,' she explained, speaking to Jeanette as much as Blake. 'Used to be a dancer. Old dancers never really lose it, do they, Mum?' She smiled, but Jeanette's face remained a blank. Odette gently fitted the headphones and, aside from a tiny, distant duet the room was silent.

'Music is really the only thing she responds to now.' Odette took a seat next to her mother. 'Well, not so much anymore. But it used to get through to her. Not so much now.'

'I've read all about your sister.' He didn't add that Odette had been a brief footnote. A one-line irrelevance. And the reports certainly didn't mention they'd been identical twins. Instead, he recalled, 'The notes said you lived abroad.'

Odette nodded. 'My dad died when I was three years old. Mum did a great job bringing us up but there's always one rebel in the family. I ran away from home when I was sixteen. Mum got me back. I did it again. And so it went until the VSO got me a place in Bangladesh working with kids from the villages. I was seventeen.

Got married in my first few months there. Hence Odette *Wilde*. Separated after a few weeks. Stayed in Asia for a while then travelled about. Long story short, I never spent much time here.'

'Until?'

'I got some bullshit diabetes. Diabetes. At twenty. So I came home because of the dear old NHS. Mum had Alzheimer's then but she was okay. Still knew who we were and stuff.' She took a breath. 'But even in the months I was receiving my initial treatment she went right downhill. Lucy was the one that looked after her. I …' She broke eye contact for the first time. 'I escaped. Still lived here. But I escaped.'

'And when Lucy disappeared?'

'That's the one good thing about the Alzheimer's. By that point, I mean when Lucy disappeared, Mum couldn't tell us apart. Never had any idea anything was wrong. Lucy never left, in her eyes.'

Blake studied Jeanette's immobile face.

'Does she remember anything at all? Do you think she could help in any way?'

'She's not got Hollywood Alzheimer's, Mr Blake. That's not how it works.'

'Hollywood Alzheimer's?"

'Yeah, you know in movies, people with Alzheimer's always get a whiff of their favourite perfume or see a photo of themselves kissing their husband on their wedding day and for five minutes it's fine and they're restored to perfect mental health. It doesn't work like that in real life. You feed them, help them go to the bathroom, the bedroom, keep them comfy and try to defend their dignity. Because they can't anymore.'

'I'm sorry.'

'Don't be.' Odette's voice was hard as granite. 'Have you got any kids?'

'I've got a daughter.'

'Be good to her,' she said, and looked at her mother.

'And that's it,' Odette concluded. 'That's her whole life story. All about my sister.'

Blake nodded. 'Thank you.' She had revealed precisely nothing he'd not already known or surmised. And even as she'd spoken about Lucy's hobbies which he knew so well, he'd zoned out, not hearing but watching her talk, studying the face of her dead sister come alive. 'And what about you?' he asked.

'Me?'

'Still the rebel?'

She shrugged. 'This is what I do, now.'

Blake didn't move.

'Lucy was always the one who looked after Mum. The sister who had nothing. The stay-at-home one.' Odette tilted her head. 'Now it's me. That one is me.' She leant forward. 'Sometimes, since she died … sometimes I feel like I'm becoming Lucy.'

Blake's shoes crunched across the gravel as he walked away from the house. He reached the gate and turned towards the door where Odette stood watching him go. He looked at her face. His hand rested on the gate and he already knew he couldn't leave.

*Sometimes I feel like I'm becoming Lucy.*

'Odette!' he called to her. 'Odette, can I can stay with you today?'

'What for?'

'I want to see your sister's life.'

'Jesus, you're pretty sick. If you think –'

'Please, Odette!'

'– that I'm going to give up –'

'What?' He hesitated. 'Please.'

She stood back a little and let the door swing open.

He sat on the sofa and watched her. She fed her mother, forcing each spoonful of mush into her mouth, patiently pressing and congratulating when the bowl was empty. Blake sprang from his seat a couple of times, taking Jeanette's cloth napkin and wiping away morsels of food that fell to her cardigan. When Odette helped her mother into the bathroom Blake offered his assistance. It was declined.

Jeanette Jaeger never said a word. She never registered Blake, and her only acknowledgment of her daughter was a physical one. When Odette placed a beaker to her lips and tilted it, the old woman moved her head back, took in some of the water and swallowed. All interaction operated on this basis of physical prompting. Blake could see Odette's job was a long and thankless one, but the young woman did not complain.

Hours passed. Blake sat quietly watching Odette tend to her mother, smoothing her hair down, removing her cardigan when the afternoon grew warmer, instigating another beaker of water, changing the DVD of *Calamity Jane* for *Carousel* as the credits rolled, and then making dinner. He watched her feeding the old woman, helping out again when food fell. Odette ignored his actions, but this close to her, Blake could see the pores of her skin.

Jeanette was in bed by eight. Odette poured herself a large glass of Sancerre. 'Wine!' she called through from the kitchen. 'Want some?'

'Love some!'

Odette returned to the front room and handed Blake his drink. He said 'Cheers', and went to clink her glass but she was already downing the wine. They both sat on the sofa. 'How long do you think you can keep this up?' he asked her.

'Dunno. It's not something you think about. You just get through the day and have another bottle of wine.'

'You must think about something.'

'Sometimes I hope a big movie star will get Alzheimer's. That's how things happen. Someone rich and famous gets it and suddenly it's important. They pump money into research. Public awareness is raised. They might discover a cure.'

'I doubt it.'

'Thanks.'

'Sorry.'

'I know, an impossible cure is … impossible.' She refilled her glass.

Blake wondered how many men had told her she was beautiful. When he'd seen the six possible women who Dempsey and Mason

387

declared could be Victim Zero, he had known immediately. The other five had been sexy and pretty and perhaps beautiful in a conventional sense. But only Lucy's face held a quality that made you look closer and wonder what it must be like to be so mesmerising. To have that gift. Greek legends suggest that Helen's was a face that launched a thousand ships, and Blake could believe that men – or at least one man – would start a war over the vision of beauty that was Lucy Jaeger. Her identical twin, Odette, shared that beauty but now she stayed at home and dreamt about an impossible cure. 'Do you go out much?'

'Oh, yeah. Me and Mum. Can't get us out of the shops. And on Fridays we normally hit the clubs.'

'Sorry.'

'Stop being sorry. Have another drink.'

As she topped up his Sancerre he said without thinking, 'Thanks, Lucy.'

Odette shot him a look but didn't correct the mistake.

# CHAPTER 103

At midnight he trudged over the gravel again. At the gate he asked, 'Can I come back tomorrow?'

The following morning Blake rose early. He showered in haste, looked into his shaving mirror and moved his razor close to his face. No, he was wasting time. He left his house, unshaven, and drove to the foot of the locks. He walked briskly to Odette's house and she opened the door before he'd had chance to ring the bell.

Simon Maxwell glanced to his left. Josa Jilani was nodding and squinting a little, like she often did when she was trying to concentrate. She could have been receiving instructions for a household appliance she had no intention of ever using, or listening to a mechanic explaining what was wrong with her car engine. Her eyes and body language indicated interest, but her former boyfriend could tell it was forced.

They were sitting in the front office of Wingfield & Son, Funeral Directors, and Wingfield Senior was explaining the practicalities of collecting Preya's body – when the police felt ready to release it – and transporting it to a local mosque where Josa and a group of family friends would wash the corpse, preparing it for burial. Simon had already explained that Preya's body would be wrapped in a shroud when the undertakers collected it, a common practice when a Muslim has died in violent circumstances or otherwise suffered some form of mutilation. Throughout all the explanations, Josa simply nodded and squinted.

Wingfield paused and smiled. He affected a mixture of concern, sympathy and mild joviality. He was a short, broad tugboat of a man with a friendly West Country accent and he obviously knew Josa from previous burials. 'And regarding the money side of things … that will be …' He didn't say the price, indicating a brochure on the desk, his finger falling on the exact amount. 'And we do ask for that in advance.'

'Sure,' Josa replied, handing him her debit card. 'I just have to phone my bank. Authorise such a big transaction.'

'No problem.'

She stood and walked from the room as she made the call.

Silence, and Simon felt uneasy as Wingfield smiled at him. 'She's a lovely girl,' the funeral director commented.

'Do all clients have to pay in advance?'

'There's a big Muslim community around here. I know a lot of the imams. They're my friends. Good people.' Another grin. 'But in a few cases, after the burial, the clients have disappeared and we've not been paid, so for Muslim services we have to ask for money up front.'

'What? And that's never happened with Christians or any other community?'

'Well, it has, but …' Wingfield spread his hands. 'You do understand, don't you?'

'Oh, yeah,' he replied, his disgust made clear in the sneer of his voice. 'I understand.'

Josa appeared back in the doorway. 'We're ready to go,' she said.

The day passed in slow motion, Blake watching Odette from the sofa, rising less frequently to help as Jeanette was fed. At eight o'clock a bottle of Sancerre was opened, and at nine another, then another. They never mentioned Lucy or her disappearance. Blake caught a taxi home at 2 a.m. In the dawn light later that morning he jogged from the blocked-off road, along the canal and to the

Jaeger's house where Odette was waiting for him at the door. He spent the day watching her, ignoring Jeanette now, transfixed by the dead, beautiful face that shot him infrequent looks, but never a smile.

That evening she passed him a glass of wine and, as he took it from her, their fingers touched for a moment. A little later he asked, 'Can I stay tonight?'

'You are so not my type.'

'I don't mean it like that.'

'D'you see this as some sort of sanctuary?'

'I don't know.'

'Are you still kidding yourself you're here for my sister?'

Blake paused, his eyes never leaving her face. 'But I am,' he replied.

Odette threw her glass against the wall.

The following morning Blake arrived earlier than usual but the broken glass had already been swept away.

That afternoon, as the dusk ushered in the evening and Odette bathed her mother, Blake stood and walked around the front room. He hated it when Odette was removed from his immediate presence and, for some sort of distraction, he lowered himself into Jeanette's wing chair. He looked ahead. Saw his reflection in the old-fashioned television screen. *Christ.* He looked drawn and dishevelled, and, in a characteristic movement, he ran the palms of his hands across his face, as if flannelling away the grime of the –

His phone rang.

'Hello?'

'Danny.' Jack Dempsey's voice. 'It's me.'

'What's wrong?'

A long pause. Then, 'Danny, this is the phone call you never wanted to get.'

# CHAPTER 104

## *Earlier that day*

A bowl of burning incense flickered on one of the work units. The scent emanating from it mingled with the smell of camphor – camphor that would be added to the water when the body was washed for the third and final time.

Islamic custom dictates that a corpse is washed an odd number of times by people of the same gender. Preya Jilani lay on a long, narrow table that stood to one side of the room, her body prepared for this ritual of *ghusl*. She was supine, and although her face, hands and feet were bare, the area from her lower neck to the middle of her shins was covered by a single piece of material. Its fabric was white but thick enough to remain opaque, even when drenched.

Josa quietly closed the door, paused and then looked around. The room reminded her a little of the mortuaries and surgeries she had visited over the years. Echoey, airy with white tiled walls. But the detail she remembered most from the moment she turned around was not her sister's face or the sheer physical presence of the corpse. It was the curtains.

To the right of the table, Josa could see a window that led through to another room. The orange curtains that covered the glass were drawn. Orange curtains. Not just orange: a bright, bursting orange hue that seemed at odds with the location.

Orange had been Preya's favourite colour, and that flag of vibrancy gave her sister an unexpected and irrational sense of calm. She breathed in, deeply.

A little later, Josa's gloved fingers curled around Preya's right palm. She lifted it and the helper tipped a red jug, allowing water to cascade over both sisters' hands.

She washed Preya's right hand from the tips of her fingers to her wrist, three times. She then moved to her sister's left side. Another sluice of water and Josa repeated the ritual.

At first, Josa had thought she would wash her sister for the sake of others who would ask if she had performed *ghusl*. But as she finished cleansing Preya's face she understood a little more about the process. How it helped her. She looked down at her sister and felt that by preparing her, she had made herself ready.

She raised her face, bathed in orange light. Looked to the helper who had held and poured the water from the jug. 'It's done,' said Josa.

# CHAPTER 105

The undertakers were dressed casually in jeans and jumpers, and although they treated the body with courtesy, there was no sense of distress. This was simply a job that had to be completed. With a workmanlike swiftness, they carried Preya's shrouded body across the cemetery, exchanged a few words of guidance to each other and reached the allocated space.

Moments later, the corpse was lowered and laid sideways in the grave.

Time passed. Josa wasn't sure how long, but she felt the ground beneath her feet as she made her way to the plot; felt sodden soil on her skin as she picked up a fist of earth. She hesitated by the graveside. 'Goodbye, Prey. I'm sorry.' She wanted to weep, to wail. She'd done her job. Organised the funeral as quickly as possible … Wasn't this the bit where she was entitled to fall apart? She threw the earth onto her sister's body. 'Love you.'

Half an hour later, the four of them were alone. Josa by the graveside and, about twenty paces back, Holly, Dempsey and Mason stood watching her from the top of a small hillock. The grey gloom of evening was setting in fast, as if the sunlight was eager to leave the cemetery.

'Where's her mother?' Holly whispered.

'She was there,' Mason said with a sigh. 'The old woman, face like granite.'

'Heart like granite,' Dempsey muttered. 'Did you see the way she ignored Josa? Is that supposed to be a mother's love for –'

'We've both seen it before, Jack. That hatred, that anger … that *burning* that can follow a loss. No one can control a rage like that.'

'Apparently she's flying back to India tonight to be with *the old family* for a few months. Good riddance, I say. We're Josa's family now.'

Mason took a breath. 'Don't be too harsh on the old girl.'

Dempsey shook his head, unconvinced.

Holly made her way down the incline and joined Josa. 'How you doing?' the teenager asked. 'How was ... you know, having to wash ...?'

'Yeah, it was okay. I'm glad I did it. I thought it would feel weird but it just felt right, you know? Kind of ... *real*. Washing her felt like I was doing something practical for her. For Preya.'

'Good.' Holly studied Josa's face. 'That's good.' The older woman hadn't turned away from the grave. 'It gets easier. I know it sounds weird me saying that because I'm just a kid, but I know what it's like to lose someone and how much it hurts and ... Anyway. I'm really sorry and if there's anything I can do ...'

Josa still didn't move. 'Thanks.'

Holly nodded. 'I'll see you later.' She turned to walk back to Dempsey and Mason.

'Holly! That's kind of you to say. About losing someone.' Josa managed a weak smile. Looked at Holly. 'Right now it just feels all-consuming, you know? Sometimes I want to cry and break down but most of the time I just feel empty. So what good would crying be? What good would anything be? It's like nothing matters anymore but everyone is still trying to bother me with stuff that is just *bullshit*. Either trivial stuff or things that I can't be bothered with because it just doesn't matter anymore.' She sat on the ground by the grave. 'I don't know. How long did it take you to get over your loss?'

'Dunno. When it happens you make all these little pledges to yourself and other people. Like vows. And you believe them – about how you're going to start living your life. Then a few months down the line you realise you've not done any of them, then a couple of years later you realise it did have a massive effect and continues to impact, but not how you thought.' Holly sat next to Josa. 'Sorry. That's probably not what you want to hear.'

'No, it's … Do you mind me asking? When did your mother die? I mean, pass away.'

'She didn't.' Holly sounded surprised. 'She's still alive.'

'I thought you were talking about your mum.'

'I was.'

'Your dad said you'd lost her.'

'Yeah.' She nodded. 'Sometimes I think it would have been easier if she'd died. No, I don't mean that. Don't tell anyone I said that.'

'Hey, this is just between us two. So, what happened?'

Holly sighed. 'My mum's American. Dad met her when he was really young. Not many years older than I am now. When he gets tipsy he gets teary-eyed and says it was a brief encounter. Anyway, they parted and Mum didn't tell him about me.'

'Whoa!'

'Yeah. Then they met years later and it could all have gone a bit Jeremy Kyle but actually it was, well, pretty beautiful. My mum and dad got on and hey, we were one big happy family for a few years until … *It wasn't what my mother wanted.* At their own anniversary party she looked around and decided it wasn't what she wanted. So she left us. There was nothing dramatic, no single thing to blame. I wish there had been. We just weren't for her. She said she had dreams to chase. *Jesus!* She should have thought of that before … Anyway, she tells Dad that her folks and sister are willing and more than able to bring me up.'

'And what did your dad say to that?'

'That he'd rather die than lose me.' Holly smiled. 'Then it was just the two of us. With Uncle Jack, of course. I dunno. I sometimes wonder if it was my fault she left. Don't tell Dad I said that, will you? I know it still bothers him. He sometimes tries to broach the question – casually to see if I'm okay. Cracking on like it's nothing so he doesn't make anything worse. Like I don't know what he's doing.' Another ghost of a grin. 'I love him so much but he's hopeless sometimes. I don't know what he'd do without me. And I don't know what I'd do without him.'

Josa had tried to give Holly space by looking at the grave again, but now she turned to face her and she saw that tears were rolling down Holly's cheeks.

Dempsey took a step forward but felt Mason's hand on his arm. 'Give them a moment, Jack.'

'Hey, it's okay,' said Josa, moving closer to Holly and embracing her.

'God, I'm sorry,' she sobbed. 'I came here to see if you were all right and, God, look at me. I'm so sorry. I haven't cried about it for ages. Honestly.'

'Hey, hey, hey. It's all right.' She broke off from the clinch. Put a palm across Holly's cheek. 'You and me. We'll always be all right. And even when we're not, they'll never beat us.'

'Because we're survivors.'

'No.' Josa sounded firm. 'Because we're fighters.'

And in the wintry gloom, they embraced again, clinging on to each other as the last of the sunlight ebbed away into dusk.

Three hours later Jack Dempsey strode into the Lillie Langtry and weighed up whether to go for ale or spirits. He'd intended to get straight back to work at the Empress State Building but like a dowsing rod involuntarily arching towards water, he'd felt himself pulled to the bar where he ordered a pint. He took a long pull on his beer and sank into a seat on an empty table.

'Jack!'

He looked up to find the weather-beaten face of Detective Sergeant Bob Michaels. 'Bobby! Pull up a chair!'

'I'll be back in a tick.' The DS grabbed a large whiskey and soda and rejoined Dempsey. 'It's bad news, Jack.'

'Then it'll wait until the second pint.' He took another gulp of beer. 'Christ. What is it, then?'

'I heard your boy, Danny, is following up the angle that Lucy Jaeger was a victim of this bloody serial killer.'

Jack nodded. 'So?'

'Lucy was a family friend. I've looked into her disappearance. Personally, you know? And when Josa Jilani made it known within the division that she thought that this Salinger character was the killer, well, I did a little digging.'

'You did a little digging?' Dempsey said. 'And what did you unearth?'

Dempsey didn't bother finishing his pint. He trudged wearily from the pub, intending to call Blake from the ESB. In the event he phoned from his mobile, making the call almost immediately as he walked across Lillie Road. 'Danny,' he said when the other man picked up. 'It's me.'

'What's wrong?' Blake demanded.

Dempsey looked towards the Lillie Langtry, then back to the ESB and exhaled. 'Danny, this is the phone call you never wanted to get.'

'The phone call I never wanted to get? I get those every day.' No response. '*What is it?*'

'It's Lucy Jaeger,' Dempsey replied. 'The girl you're investigating right now. Our former Victim Zero.'

'What d'you mean, *former?*'

'Danny, this is a thousand-to-one thing, but I guess it's better we found out now.'

'What are you talking about?'

'Lucy Jaeger was a family friend of Bob Michaels.'

Dempsey could tell that Blake was straining his memory. *Detective Sergeant Bob Michaels had been the right-hand man of Don Walters, the Hitchcock Murders' original senior investigating office.* 'I remember him.'

'I've just spoken to Bob now. When he heard your theory that Paul Salinger was the killer he looked into any link between the Professor and Lucy's disappearance.'

'I know where this is heading and I don't want to be on board.'

'Danny, listen to me! He's already looked for a link between Salinger and Lucy Jaeger. And there isn't one! Christ! I'm sorry to have to tell you this, but you were wrong, Danny.'

'Never!'

'Aw, come on, son!'

'Did Michaels actually confront Salinger and ask if he knew Lucy Jaeger?'

'Yes! Showed him a photograph of Lucy. No recognition. Nothing. Salinger did not know Lucy Jaeger. That's fact. Incontrovertible fact.' A long pause. 'Danny, are you still there?'

'He didn't look hard enough.'

Silence, and Dempsey realised that Blake had hung up.

Across London, in the warm, strange house in Hanwell, Daniel Blake stood alone in the front room.

Odette appeared in the doorway. 'You okay?'

'Fine.'

She nodded towards Blake's mobile. 'Who was that?'

'No one,' he replied, slipping his phone back into his pocket. 'Just a wrong number.'

Blake spent Friday watching Odette, thinking about Lucy. At 8 p.m., with her mother in bed, Odette went through to the kitchen and called to Blake. He found her holding a bottle of claret, and although he was no expert, he could tell it cost good money. 'Not a screw top,' she explained. 'So if you could do the honours.'

'We've got to stop this,' he said.

'Why do you still come here?'

'I shouldn't. Why do you still allow me to come? Want me to come?'

'Jesus-fucking-Christ! Because what else have I got?'

'An impossible cure.'

'An impossible cure. An impossible cure. Do you want to know what I really think about? Do you? I think about her dying. I wonder when she's going to die and I'm going to get her money and my life back and then the guilt makes me want to die and then there's nothing! Nothing! And people like you ... Would you still be sat through there if I didn't have this face? Just watching, watching, watching! And you're not even watching me! You're watching Lucy!' She was screaming now.

'I want someone to take notice of me again. *Me!*' She thumped her chest with her palm. 'Me, me ... *Lucy!*' The last word had been a slip of the tongue, but it froze Odette.

'Hey, don't worry. You're just upset.'

'You wanna see upset? You wanna see what upset looks like?'

Odette grabbed a steel carving knife from the kitchen worktop. She flashed it in Blake's direction. 'This is what upset looks like!' she raged, as, raising the knife high, she ran towards him.

# CHAPTER 107

In one blurred movement she brought the knife down, slipped the blade under the cuff of her jumper and sliced away the sleeve. She switched the knife to her left hand and cut away the other sleeve with equal slickness. 'It looks like this!' She held out her pale, slender arms. They were covered in a storm of deep, red slashes and pink scar tracts. 'That's what guilt and upset looks like!'

'Come here.' Blake embraced her for the first time. She held no sexual allure for him, so he was not afraid to press her close.

She raised the knife. It was poised over his spine.

'It's okay,' he murmured reassuringly.

And then, in a snap, sudden movement, her fingers straightened, allowing the knife to fall to the floor.

They stood quite still for several minutes. Odette sobbed and Blake guided her forehead into his shoulder. Finally, gently, he pushed her back. 'Let's open that wine, eh?' But he didn't break eye contact.

Is this what Lucy had felt? This helplessness and guilt? Had one person offered comfort? She'd have clutched it as Odette had done, and that one man who offered hope had exploited her vulnerability, enjoyed her beauty and murdered her.

'Oh, God!' spluttered Odette. 'You're thinking of her. You're still thinking of her.'

It was impossible to disassociate Odette's face from Lucy's, and everything that had happened during that long, obsessed week suddenly made sense to Blake. He stepped back, head spinning. 'That's how it was for the killer,' he murmured.

'What?'

Blake looked at the knife on the floor and then back at Odette.

For the first time he saw *her* and he knew that this scarred, lonely, beautiful woman was the one who had caused all the murders and hurt. Odette Wilde. Another step back. Head reeling because *he had it*! In that moment he had cracked the Hitchcock Murders. 'It's you ...' he whispered.

Whoever had looked into Lucy's face as he murdered her had seen Odette. In his imagination, it had been her sister he had killed. Blake took a third step back. The killer had only ever seen Odette Wilde when looking at Lucy Jaeger, just as he had been watching Lucy for these past few days. No link! Of course not! As the killer ended Lucy's life, in his head he'd been murdering Odette, not her sister. *The link was with Odette*. With trembling hands, Blake reached into his jacket pocket and pulled out a photograph taken at the launch of Salinger's book. He held it towards her. So certain. So sure now. He jabbed his finger at the face in the photo and said, 'Do you know him? You know him, don't you?'

She looked at the image and then at Blake. He knew she wasn't lying when she replied, 'No.'

Blake let the photograph fall to the floor.

That was it. Everything. No more. He had been wrong so many times, hopeful and distraught and redundant. Everything he thought of ... But the killer, Odette, Lucy ... a shift of thought.

*You are so not my type.*

God, he was tired. He should have asked ...

He snatched the photograph from the floor and pointed at another face. 'That person. There. Do you know that one?'

Odette remained silent.

'You do!'

'We had an affair ...' Odette's voice was low, barely audible. 'Oh my God ... when I broke it off, the ending was hellish, but ... Are you saying my ex-lover murdered Lucy?'

Blake looked at the photo and into the face of the killer.

# CHAPTER 108

He vaulted the gate, landing awkwardly, but the tumble merged into a shambling sprint along the canal towpath. By the time he reached his car he had his mobile in his hand and was already calling Josa. After a couple of rings her voicemail kicked in.

'Josa. It's Blake. I wanted you to know that I've got a link.' He ran his palm over his face. *So much to say* … Where did he start? 'I think we've got the bastard who murdered Preya. The link is the killer's ex-lover. Odette Wilde.' He caught his breath. 'Josa, we can get the person responsible for taking your sister's life. I wanted you to be the first to know. I'm going to confront the killer now. At the University. In Salinger's office. It's part of a plan, because there's one more thing I need to do, but …' He looked around, across Hanwell. The sky was a striking red behind the old asylum. 'I'm sure you don't want to hear the details on a message so I'll talk to you later. Bye, Josa.' He hung up and accessed his phone's directory, selecting the killer's name. A moment later he heard 'Hello?'

Blake's eyes didn't leave the asylum. 'I think we should meet,' he said. 'Tonight.'

Blake immediately regretted making the second call so soon. But the adrenaline was surging through his blood, urging him onwards, and after so much sitting and staring it was time for action. But he had to reach Salinger's office first. His plan depended on it.

He revved the engine of his Cutlass and screeched away, tearing down a series of lanes before burning onto the Ruislip Road. He roared up to sixty on this stretch, the Ealing greenery a blur as he raced towards central London. He tore onto the A40 and pushed the car to eighty before a jam on the approach to Shepherd's Bush brought all traffic to a standstill. He swore. Hauled the steering wheel to his left, mounted the pavement and cruised alongside the stationary queues of vehicles. Hung a sharp left and swerved around the back of White City, soon making good progress again, but ...

He cursed, knowing he'd lost valuable time. Minutes later, regretting his hasty call, he pulled up outside Capital College and prayed he wasn't too late.

Blake circled the outside of the deserted university building looking for an open window. It took him less than a minute to spot one and he clambered into the empty lecture hall. He recognised the room from his and Josa's first visit. It was dark and silent now, rows of benches waiting for the clamour of students. He glanced at the screen. Salinger had shown a clip of *Frenzy* when they'd been here before. Blake recalled the scene – the killer strangling his victim with such awful pleasure.

*Lovely, lovely, lovely* ...

Blake bounded up the stairs. The door was unlocked and he slipped quietly into the main building. The lights were all switched off, but illumination from the outside street lamps leaked through into the corridors giving the place an eerie yellow glow. Despite his attempts at stealth, his footsteps echoed as he jogged through the passages. After a couple of wrong turns he reached the corridor he was after and, at the end of it, he could see the door to Salinger's office.

*Pad, pad, pad* ...

He jogged to the office door. No light was visible beneath it, indicating the room was empty. He silently thanked God. Blake figured he'd beaten the killer to the rendezvous after all. He tried the door. Locked. But the mechanism was laughably simple, and Blake pulled his picklock from his inside pocket. After a moment's work he heard a click, the lock was defeated and he pushed open the door.

# CHAPTER 109

Josa rang the doorbell of the grand old flat on London's Portland Place then stepped back, expectant and nervous.

It was Monday night, and Preya had been dead for six days, but still Josa had not confronted the man her late sister had lived with until shortly before her death. Now she intended to change that, talk to him face to face and –

Her phone rang. She glanced at the screen. *Blake.*

She smiled. He'd been good to her. Constant texts and messages, but giving her the space she'd requested. She felt ready to talk to him now and went to press *answer* but at that moment the door swung open.

Josa slipped the phone into her pocket.

Blake stood in the middle of the Hitchcock Room. It looked unchanged from his first visit. Hitchcock memorabilia, stills from the films, the alabaster bust of the director, the battered sofa, ordered book shelves, Ottoman chest, chipped desk, posters on the wall … He recalled talking to the killer in the room, a conversation that felt like a lifetime ago. Blake glanced at a length of string hung with photos that made a smiling face across the wall behind Salinger's desk, directly in front of the door. It held four photographs. Blake looked at them in turn – close-ups of injuries, each a frame from a Hitchcock movie. He tore them from the line and removed six A4 photographs from a tube in his inside pocket. Quickly, eagerly, he began to pin them to the line.

In the corridor outside, someone approached the office. If the late-night visitor had been walking normally the sound of footsteps would have reverberated through the passageway. But the approach was cautious and quiet. In the office, Blake worked with his back to the door, too engrossed in his task to notice the careful footsteps as they neared the room. In the corridor, a hand extended and turned the door handle.

Josa looked around the drawing room where she'd spent so many evenings with Preya. She was struck by the number of framed photographs that her sister's ex, Michael, had kept on the shelves. She'd been shown through to the room by his housekeeper and, as she waited for him to appear, she lifted one of the photographs and checked the shelf it rested on. The dust indicated the photo had been there a while. Josa replaced it, happy that the photographs hadn't only been reinstated after the murder.

She checked her phone. One message. She went to access it but Michael bounded into the room. 'Josa! Hi! Lovely to see you! How are you?'

*He didn't know. Christ! Preya had often joked about how wrapped up in their work he and his staff became, but with all the press coverage she'd assumed that the news would have reached him …*

She paused. 'You've got so many pictures of Preya …'

He shrugged, caught off guard by the comment. 'I still love her very much.'

Josa nodded. 'Such a shame about the baby thing.' Talking on autopilot now, wondering how to broach the terrible news. 'That you guys couldn't compromise and –' She stopped. Michael was shaking his head. 'What is it?'

Michael looked puzzled. 'We didn't split up over that. Hasn't Preya told you?'

## CHAPTER 110

The killer opened the door, hesitated and looked into the office. A heartbeat, followed by a step forward. Blake held his breath and sensed the other person scanning the room. A long, long pause.

Blake stood in the one part of the office that afforded him a hiding place – directly behind the open door. He knew the killer was looking at the six photographs he had attached to the line, each one showing the face of a young woman. Blake heard footsteps and the figure closed the door, gently pushing it to, but fortunately not looking back. No, the killer was too interested in the photos, walking straight to one of the portraits and snatching it from the line. For several seconds the killer gazed down at the image.

'How interesting,' said Blake. 'Six photos to choose from and only one catches your eye. The shot of Odette Wilde. The girl you didn't recognise when Detective Sergeant Bob Michaels asked you about her. Now that's interesting, don't you think?'

Slowly, the killer looked up.

'Smile,' said Blake, 'The camera is loving you, old chum.' He had captured the killer's movements on his camera phone and stood pointing the handset across the room. He held the device in his left hand. His right hand gripped a gun. 'And look what I found in your desk! A lovely little Beretta Cheetah. And in shiny nickel, too. Just like in the movies. Not planning on using it tomorrow, were you?'

'When this Hitchcock Murders thing blew up, a friend of mine worried the killer might come after me and so he gave me that. I've never used it.'

'But you just kept it lying about.'

'What do you want?'

'What do I want?' Blake's voice betrayed his incredulity. 'What do I want? I want you, sunbeam. You killed the sister of someone very dear to me. You murdered a friend of mine. And you slaughtered innocent girls in a bid to … Christ, in a bid to … I don't know what.'

'Shall I tell you? Fill you in on the details?'

'Not interested. The video of you picking Odette's photo is all I needed. She's the link. You see, a part of Odette just wants to be left alone, and it's vaguely possible that if asked about you, she'd have denied that you and she were lovers. But you recognised her. There's the link. *Gotcha*. And I have it on film, so to speak. The Hitchcock Murders are over because the killer was foolish enough to be caught on camera.'

'This isn't over.' The words were not delivered as a rant or a promise, more as a matter-of-fact observation.

'Oh, this is over.'

'Because you say so? No, no, no. I am a murderer. I have not simply murdered – I am a murderer. I trust you appreciate the distinction, because a killer needs to accept his status – otherwise he'd go crazy. But you know all about that.'

'I think we're both a little crazy.'

'What's to stop me from simply taking that pretty little gun and shooting you between the eyes? And then leaving.'

'Ah now, there you go,' Blake said. 'You tried to emulate Hitchcock and never quite managed it, and here's another example of you not really getting the Master's art. Hitchcock knew when to end a movie. Don't pad it out. When the killer's been caught or killed, cut to the end card. That's it, I'm afraid.'

The killer nodded. 'Hitchcock shot an extra scene for *Vertigo*, you know. After Scottie saw Maddie fall to her death, we originally saw him return to his apartment but Hitch realised he simply didn't need the scene. He knew an ending when he saw it. And so do I. But if this ends here, we have a problem.'

Blake's eyes widened in mock concern. 'Oh, aye?'

'The audience wouldn't believe it. They'd feel short changed. Because they, like me, would know that the Daniel Blake character may be holding a gun, but he would never use it.'

'And you know this how?' asked Blake.

'I know this because I know you. I've researched you. Oh, you've used a gun before, haven't you?'

'Shut up!' Blake snapped.

'Ye-ahhh, you've used a gun before. On top of the cathedral. Overlooking the world, you took a man's life.'

'I said shut up!' The Beretta wavered in Blake's hand.

'You murdered! You murdered another man! Took his life in front of his child! You murdered him, and that image will stay with his son for the rest of his life. How d'you feel about that, Danny?'

'It wasn't like that!'

The killer took a step forward. 'No? Then what was it like? How did it feel to take another man's life?'

'Stay back!'

'How did it feel in your head?' Another step forward. 'And how does it still feel today? In your hands? It was a Glock 17 you used then, wasn't it? A touch heavier than that little Beretta. Can you still feel the weight of the weapon in your palm? The weapon you used to murder someone. Still feel the reverberation in your fingers as you pulled the trigger? Do you look at your hands sometimes? I bet you do.'

'This is your last warning.' The killer was only two steps away from Blake. 'Stay back'

'Smell the perfume of cordite that every gun blast exhales?' Another step forward. 'Do you still *live* the murder, Danny?'

'Every day,' said Blake and began to squeeze the trigger.

The study door burst open and, for a moment, both people in the room looked towards it. The killer saw an opportunity and sprang forward, colliding with Blake in an attempt to push the gun's muzzle to one side.

Throughout the near-deserted university, the single shot sounded like an explosion. It echoed through the corridors and empty lecture halls where long ago, the murders had evolved.

# CHAPTER 111

'Then why did you split up?

'That word you just used. *Compromise*. You couldn't teach Preya what it means, could you?' He offered a fragile smile. 'I called her bluff and said that from now it couldn't be just her way or the high–'

'Michael, there's something I've got to tell you,' Josa interrupted. 'About Preya.'

He blanched. 'Oh, God. She hasn't met someone else, has she? This sounds stupid but I'd planned to get in touch with her and see if she'd consider taking me back, even if it –'

'No,' Josa interjected, 'it isn't that.'

'Then what?'

Michael's housekeeper bobbed into the room. 'Sorry to interrupt. Mrs MacDee on the line for you. It's an emergency.'

He swore under his breath. 'You don't mind if I take the call, do you? I'll be back in a minute.'

'Sure.'

As he left the room, Josa accessed her voice message.

*'Josa. It's Blake …'*

Blake looked down at the blood that leaked through his shirt and suit jacket.

For a moment, he only felt a localised area of intense heat. The shock and pain followed a second or two later. The bullet had seared into his body at point-blank range. He looked up, meeting the triumphant gaze of the killer.

The message concluded with, '*Bye, Josa*', making her blood run cold. 'He's going to face the killer on his own,' she murmured.

Michael reappeared. 'This is going to have to wait,' she told him. Moments later she was in her car, gunning the engine, praying she could reach the university in time.

Blake swayed like a drunkard. In his position behind the door he could not see who had pushed it open, but badly wounded, he lacked the energy to move forward. He felt an overwhelming desire for the new arrival to be Josa, to be help of any kind, and the hope gave him enough strength to call out, 'In here!' The words emerged as a whimper.

The killer brought a hand down hard onto the Beretta and it clattered to the floor.

The newcomer stepped into the room and Blake's heart fell. It was not Josa. He swayed again, this time more violently. He saw a blurred movement. Something was happening. Two figures embracing. He groaned and the universe spun. Blake hit the floor and passed out. The last thing he saw before the blackness claimed him was the calm, almost serene face of Professor Paul Salinger.

Josa's car screeched to a skidding halt outside the main university building. She leapt out, unbuttoning her jacket as she flipped open the boot of her vehicle.

A crowd of about a dozen students from the nearby halls of residence clustered around the entrance to the foyer. One of the older lads was pointing inside. 'I've been on clay-pigeon shoots with my dad and that was definitely –'

Josa reached them, interrupting the student with a terse, 'What happened?'

'We heard a gunshot,' he replied. 'We came to see what was going on.'

A younger student chipped in, 'But all the doors are locked.'

'Call the police!' Josa demanded. 'Tell them to get armed backup over here – now! And tell them the request comes from Detective Chief Inspector Josa Jilani. Stress *now*, and stress *armed*!'

Josa reached across to the first lad and took the laptop case he was holding. Without saying another word she thrust it through the nearest window. 'Any damage, send me the bill.'

Josa Jilani stood at the end of the corridor that led to Salinger's office. She pulled a Ruger SR9c from her handbag and took a moment to ensure the gun was comfortable in her hand. The Ruger is a compact 9mm semi-automatic, popular in the US for its accuracy and ease of use. Jack Dempsey had given her the gun in case of an emergency and Josa figured this amounted to an emergency. She tossed her handbag to one side.

Josa walked slowly towards the room at the end of the passage. She could hear nothing but her own heartbeat and knew it was a bad sign. Silence, in her experience, was always a bad sign.

She reached the door, kept the Ruger firmly grasped in her right hand and turned the door handle with her left. Gently, she pushed the door open. Straight ahead of her she could see a Beretta aimed directly at her head.

'Come in, Josa. Join the wrap party.'

She paused. Her gun returned the compliment, pointing dead ahead. She peered through the darkness. Whoever had spoken stood in the far left-hand corner of the room. Although hidden by shadows, the figure's right arm was extended, meaning the pistol was clearly visible. The person's voice was breathless, making it difficult for Josa to identify. The figure in the shadows spoke again.

'I'm going to have to rush you. Come on in. You've got two old friends already waiting for you.'

Josa's arm didn't waver as she took two tentative steps forward.

'This is over. You know that, don't you? It's over. In about a minute this place will be flooded with police. Why don't you give me your weapon and we can talk?'

'I don't think so. The director decides when to call cut, and as I directed this whole movie, I'll be the one to fashion its finale. I started the Hitchcock Murders, executed them and elevated them. But they're not quite over yet. One more victim and then we can roll the end titles. Now, which one of you will take the final bullet?'

Josa took another step forward. To her right she could see two people tied to chairs. The first was Blake, obviously in a bad way. Blood leaked from a stomach wound and his face was a ghastly, green sheen of perspiration. A rectangle of gaffer tape was stuck across his mouth but he was looking at her, still conscious. She had expected Blake, but the man by his side shocked her.

In the other chair, his hands tied behind the back of the seat, sat Professor Salinger.

'Or perhaps we should go big on the last murder. Make it a group thing. Lots of blood. I always admired Hitch's use of Technicolor. Much underrated, so it would seem appropriate.'

The figure in the shadows moved forward, stepping into the light. Josa felt herself gasp as the woman's identity was revealed.

'What do you think, Josa?' asked Cordelia Smith.

# CHAPTER 112

Josa edged to Blake's side and, keeping her gun trained on Cordelia, said, 'Don't worry. I phoned Dempsey. The cavalry's on its way.' She twisted around to tear the gaffer tape from Blake's mouth but Cordelia stopped her.

'Touch him and he dies.'

Josa paused.

'You're going to have to do as you're told. You're a policewoman. You should be used to that.'

'Where do you think this is going, Cordelia? Do you think it's going to be like a Hitchcock movie come true and some cunning disguise is gonna get you past the cops? That's not how it works in real life.'

'Thanks for the newsflash. But I'm the one you haven't been able to stop. Shall I run that sentence by you one more time? You haven't been able to stop me.'

'Cordelia.' It was Salinger's voice. 'What the hell have you done? Why?' His voice trailed off.

Cordelia Smith – prim, prissy, uptight Cordelia Smith – said, 'I knew Odette Wilde. Did you know that? I knew her.'

'I knew you'd met to say hello at functions she'd attended with me. But she was just another face, I never thought you'd even remember her, let alone –'

'Oh, yes. We were at a launch party at a bookshop in London. She walked in and you sauntered towards her, opening your arms. You said, *Ms Wilde!* and embraced her. That was the first time she saw me. As she peered over your shoulder. And in that moment we both knew, we both somehow knew that we shared something. You. In our different ways, of course. So there was no jealousy, or even annoyance. But we were joined by that complicit understanding.'

'And that's as far as your relationship with her went?' Salinger said.

'Oh no. After you ended your affair with her, she came to me in tears. Called at my home. Could she come in? Could we talk? I was so surprised to see her I said yes and we chatted for hours. She was such a child, full of questions.' Cordelia gave a mother's smile. 'Had you spoken about her to me? Did I think you loved her? She didn't understand *anything*, and I became quite fond of her. She was so innocent. *Seemed* so innocent.' Cordelia mimicked a look of confusion. '*What have I done wrong?* she would ask me. *You know him. Tell me what I've done wrong!* I would hug her. Hold her. Sometimes for hours. But her visits became less frequent. She met another boy, more her own age, I think. She told me about him as if gloating. At you, Professor Salinger. And me. We met once more after she told me about this new boy she was seeing. She told me she was in love again and told me – *she told me* – to, '*Let the Professor go*'. She had done, and now I must. She said that sometimes you had to have the courage to jump.'

'And for that!' exclaimed Salinger. 'For that you killed her?'

'I killed her for you! This boy she was seeing worked on the university paper. She told him she'd been seeing a senior academic in the arts faculty and he wanted to run a story on it. Apparently she had photographs. They wanted to ruin you, Paul. I couldn't allow that. And when she saw the horror in my eyes, she laughed and laughed ...' Cordelia smiled. 'One night I drove around to Odette's house. She wasn't in but her sister, Lucy, was. She seemed a sensible young woman, not a silly young child, and so we drove and talked. We ended up on one of those river boats on the Thames – the sort that serve drinks but don't actually go anywhere. There was a party going on inside. But it was raining, so we were the only ones on the bow. I *explained* the situation.' There was a long pause. 'She simply shrugged.' Cordelia's face became a mask of confusion and hatred. 'Sat on the ledge at the head of the bow and just shrugged. As if none of it mattered. I pushed her. Not a hard, vindictive push, but enough to let God decide. She floundered on the edge for a moment, trying to regain her balance. And I shrugged. God shrugged, too.'

'You killed her,' said Josa.

'She fell,' replied Cordelia. 'There's a difference. You wouldn't believe how fast flowing the Thames is. I saw her body swept along the river. Ten metres in as many seconds. She was bobbing up and down, screaming, gulping down the water. But there was no one to hear her. No one to save her.'

'She just fell!' shouted Salinger. 'A heated argument. A tussle. An accident. There's not a jury in the land that would convict you, Cordelia. Just let us go and we can sort this out.'

'But the others, Paul. I saw the effect Lucy's death had on Odette and it was wonderful. She became changed. It was as if the colour had been drained from her life. The Technicolor Ms Wilde was now living in black and white. She evolved into a different person. Really, a different person completely. And the grief she felt and showed, well, that wasn't grief for her sister. It was grief for the loss of her old self. It was beautiful to watch. I had cleansed the world of a patch of dirt. I had made the world a cleaner place. It felt marvellous. I had to continue, but I had no concept of murder and so I simply relied on what I knew best. The Hitchcock Murders. I had been proofreading your book for months. Again, it was the Lord, guiding me. The Hitchcock Murders became my Bible. Showing me the way. Giving me the light. To see in the darkness a path to righteousness, a way to cleanse my soul and cleanse the world. Becka Hoyle and then the other harlots ...'

'And my sister?' asked Josa in a whisper.

'You tried to break Paul!' Cordelia snapped venomously. 'I could see what you were doing! Knew you were out to destroy him!' She took a breath. Calmed herself. 'But I knew. In my turn, I knew how to destroy women like you. I had already been shown the way. You take the sister, murder and stand back.'

'You are evil,' said Josa. 'This has nothing to do with any God. Your sadism, your cowardice, your –'

'Well, I'll soon find out. I am seeing the Lord tonight.' She placed the muzzle of her gun against Blake's forehead. 'And unless you drop your gun, Miss Jilani, I shall shoot your friend in the head and we'll all be judged side by side in the realm of the Almighty.'

'If I drop my gun,' replied Josa, 'you will kill him and then me. No deal, Cordelia.'

'I leave this stage on my own terms,' Cordelia said. 'Not looking down the barrel of a gun. Now drop it.'

'No.'

'You think you can pull that trigger? Smite me where I stand?' She shoved the barrel of the Beretta into Blake's face. 'If you shoot me, my death spasm will most certainly result in the death of Blake. I have no doubt you are eager to kill me, but is that bloodlust so great that it overpowers your desire for your friend to live?' She paused. 'It's a genuine question. In a moment I shall put this gun to my head and pull the trigger. That's a promise. It is a done thing unless you shoot me down. So, I shall count to three. If on three you have not dropped your gun I shall pull the trigger. Blake will die. I shall then raise the gun and shoot either myself or you. Haven't decided yet. Or perhaps you will have shot me. Either way, I face my judge tonight, and do I look scared to you?'

'You don't escape that easily.'

'I'm going to count to three. If you haven't dropped the gun by the time I reach three, I kill Blake.'

'I'm not dropping this gun. And I'm not letting you take your own life.'

I'm going to count to three.'

'Don't do it.'

'One.'

'Don't do it, Cordelia'

'Two,'

'Don't do this.'

'Three.'

# CHAPTER 113

Josa dropped her gun.

A couple of seconds passed and Cordelia said, 'I'm disappointed in you. I reached three. Your friend dies.'

Josa's eyes flickered to the Ruger she'd discarded. Could she grab and fire it in time to prevent Cordelia pulling the trigger?

'I'm joking!' Cordelia declared. 'When you write your report about me ...' She removed the Beretta from Blake's face and trained it on Josa. '... don't forget to stress I was merciful. I do not want to be portrayed as some monster. Most will understand, but you will be tempted to lie about my crusade, and that would be sinful. *Now turn around.*'

'What?'

'Turn around. You're about to get what you want. An ending to all this. But more than that ... American academics have rather a good word for it. Closure. Now turn around.'

Josa didn't move. The Beretta returned to Blake's forehead.

'Okay, okay!' Josa yelled. She turned her back on Cordelia, but as she moved, in her peripheral vision she saw her stoop and whisper something into Salinger's ear.

The Professor cried, 'No! No!' and Cordelia shouted at Josa –

'Close your eyes!'

She half-turned her head. Glimpsed the Beretta being raised and angled so it was pointing at her.

'Turn around!'

Josa faced dead ahead and screwed her eyes tightly shut in an involuntary acceptance that this was it. That moment of blackness lasted only a moment, but felt like an eternity.

Cordelia's final words were a cry of, 'I love you, Paul!'

Josa realised it was the end and, just in time, she opened her eyes.

Three gun shots and then silence.

## CHAPTER 114

### *Fourteen minutes earlier*

Blake looked down at the blood that leaked through his shirt and suit jacket.

For a moment, he could only feel a localised area of intense heat. The shock and pain followed a moment later. The bullet had seared into his body at point-blank range. He looked up, meeting the triumphant face of the killer. A face he knew so well. The face of Professor Paul Salinger, the man who murdered Becka Hoyle, Ebba Lovgren, Elaine Hargreaves, Sarah Robinson and Jill Kennedy. The killer whose deranged, internal relationship with the world's greatest film director had spawned the Hitchcock Murders. The mad, manipulative butcher who now grinned at Blake's torment.

'Now, I'm no doctor,' Salinger said, 'but that's gotta hurt.'

Blake swayed like drunkard. He tried to call out, 'Help!' but his voice failed him. The Professor brought his hand down onto the Beretta and it clattered to the floor.

And then someone else was in the room. The new arrival stepped into the study, but from his position behind the door, Blake couldn't see who it was until they'd moved forward and, in a rapid blur, he saw Cordelia Smith embrace Salinger.

Blake's universe spun and he tumbled to the floor. Cordelia peered down at him. As if underwater, he could faintly hear her asking, 'Is he dead?'

The last thing he saw before the blackness claimed him was the calm, almost serene face of Professor Salinger. And the last thing he heard was his reply. 'Not yet.'

Blake sank momentarily into oblivion but adrenaline and willpower dragged him into a murky consciousness. He didn't know if he could move and didn't fancy putting it to the test. Through barely opened eyes he could make out Cordelia and the Professor.

She was holding Salinger's face in her palms and asking, 'What have they done to you, my poor, hunted creature?'

'Thank God you came, Cordelia. I have to leave now and I wanted to say goodbye before –'

'To leave?' She still held his face and now she scrutinised it. 'Why? You've done nothing wrong. You can explain that.'

'Done nothing wrong?' He took her hands in his. 'Cordelia. I've murdered.'

'In my eyes and the eyes of the Lord you've done nothing wrong. Those girls. Those *jezebels*.' She spat out the word and, despite his semi-conscious state, Blake could see that Salinger was uncomfortable with her reaction.

'Cordelia. You can't help me. I've got months left before this bloody cancer finishes me off and I don't want to spend my remaining days being grilled and gawped at from behind prison bars.'

'Don't speak like that!'

'It's true! I couldn't bear it, I'd rather –'

She placed her palm across his mouth. 'Never say that. For my sake' She removed her hand. 'Never even think it.'

'I'm sorry.'

'Hush now. There must be something we can do. Who knows you killed those whores?'

'Blake phoned me minutes ago. Just before I called you. He said we should meet tonight. Here. Said he was just leaving the house of …'

'Yes?'

'Odette Wilde.'

Cordelia didn't even pause. 'But he arrived alone?'

'Yes.'

'Did you sense … I mean, did you get the feeling that he'd only just found out that you executed all those harlots?'

Salinger hesitated, and Blake realised that this angle hadn't occurred to him before. 'Yes,' the Professor murmured, a slight excitement tingeing his voice. 'I sensed that very strongly. But he's bound to have –'

Cordelia whirled around and looked directly at Blake. He closed his eyes and desperately prayed she'd not spotted he was conscious. He heard footsteps and then the sound of her breath. She was still recovering from her jog to the study. For a moment he held his own breath. And then he heard –

'It must be in here, somewhere … Here it is! Ha ha!' She pulled Blake's mobile phone from his blood-stained jacket pocket. 'Let me see. Today he has made two phone calls. One to Detective Chief Inspector Josa Jilani, directly before he contacted you. Don't you see? He's only told her. That's all. *We can still do this!*'

'But if he's told her …'

'Look!' She thrust the phone towards him, tapping the screen. 'This is his call log. It shows the call to her lasted just a few seconds! He'll have told her nothing. Besides. Maybe we can ask her in a moment.'

'What?'

Cordelia nodded to the window in the corner of the room. They both saw Josa's car screech past them.

'She's alone …' murmured Salinger, and something in his tone told Blake that he was starting to believe that he could still get away with the murders.

'Listen to me, Paul. I want you to help me tie Blake up. Then I'm going to tie you up. When that bitch gets here I'm going to confess, and, believe me, it will sound realistic. I've spent so many nights wishing it was me that wielded the knife that … Come on! We're wasting time!'

Blake tried to flex his muscles. To gauge the levels of his ebbing strength. But the torso wound and resultant loss of blood were sapping his body and he could barely feel a thing. Cordelia and Salinger hauled him onto a chair and hastily tied his hands together using lengths of gaffer tape, looping the tape through the slats of the chair to lash him to the seat and ensure his hands were secure. Then Salinger was tied, albeit loosely, to a chair.

'What's your plan?' he asked. 'Tell me!'

'I'll deliver my confession. Record it with this ...' She took a Dictaphone from the Professor's desk. 'But at the end I'll shoot Blake and Jilani and then myself.'

'Cordelia, you can't! That's crazy!'

'It will give you time. People will have heard that gunshot. The police will be here soon. They'll probably arrive shortly after Jilani. But if I'm right, when they enter this place there will be you, alive, and two corpses. Well, three. I shall have ... moved on.' A flicker of a smile. 'But my confession will remain intact. And we'll be together again shortly. But in your remaining days, write. Let them know. And enjoy God's earth before you reach His kingdom.'

'You would take your life, just to give me more time?'

Cordelia nodded energetically. 'I hadn't told you this, Paul. But I had planned ... I had intended that when the cancer took you, I would follow immediately. Now I can help you.'

'Cordelia, I ...' Salinger stopped. They had both heard the footsteps and knew Josa has almost reached them.

With a huge effort of will, Blake raised his head and announced, 'And he's back in the room!'

Salinger shot him a look of hatred. 'Blake!'

'Oh, yes! And just one thing.'

'What?' Cordelia snapped.

'You're both fucking mental if you think any of that will work.'

Cordelia's eyes widened and she stepped forward to silence him, striking his head with the butt of the Beretta.

'Gag him!' Salinger ordered, and she tore off a strip of gaffer tape, quickly moving it to his lips. 'Just one, thing, Salinger. You've studied the Master of Suspense for decades ...'

'Let him finish,' the Professor said, locking eyes with Blake.

'Well, after all these years – watching him, reading him, trying to emulate him – you've only half succeeded in becoming Hitchcock.'

Salinger's eyes narrowed. 'Half succeeded?'

'Yep. You're just a cock.' Blake winked at the Professor and Cordelia slapped the tape across his mouth.

'A profanity,' she murmured calmly. 'Your last words as a mortal man were a profanity. You'll scream a lot more oaths where you're going, Blake.'

But amidst all the blood and craziness, Blake felt that the most surprising moment of the whole exchange with Cordelia came at the close. She lightly kissed his forehead and, in a tone that suggested tenderness and genuine regret, she said, 'I'm so sorry.'

His eyes pleaded with her and she paused before looking away from them.

Josa's footsteps had reached the office door.

"After I fire three shots I'll be dead and so will they. That's when you must act. Goodbye, my love.'

Josa Jilani pushed open the door.

# CHAPTER 115

Josa half-turned her head. Glimpsed the Beretta being raised and angled so it was pointing at her.

'Turn around!' Cordelia commanded.

Josa faced dead ahead and screwed her eyes tightly shut in an involuntary acceptance that this was it. That moment of blackness lasted only a moment but felt like an eternity.

Cordelia's final words were a cry of, 'I love you, Paul!'

Josa realised it was the end and, just in time, she opened her eyes.

Three gun shots and then silence.

Blood everywhere. The study that for so many years had been a cosy refuge and vibrant hub of lively debate was silent. The movie posters that depicted scenes of heightened horror and beautiful people were sprayed with the awful truth of murder. From the fabric of the unframed print, Alfred Hitchcock looked down on the scene, his face and the raven on his shoulder dappled red with blood and bits of brain.

Hitchcock's enigmatic smile didn't look remotely out of place.

Jack Dempsey looked from the mint julep the bartender had just placed on the coaster to the vibrating phone in his hand. *Caller unknown*. Shook his head. Snatched a quick mouthful of the cocktail and pressed *answer*. 'This had better be good!' he boomed. 'Is that Mr Dempsey?'

'Very rarely. That you, Stevie?'

'I didn't think you'd remember me!' The young policeman

replied. 'Mr Dempsey, one of our men just took a call from the university. After all the prank calls from there recently it was given a low-priority status. But I just happened to see the verbatim report. It's Josa. She's gone to the university and, from the message she passed on, it sounds like she knew she was walking into trouble.'

Dempsey was already on his way out of the bar.

Of course, Josa had anticipated the first discharge and expected it would be the suicide shot of Cordelia Smith. With the second shot came the immediate realisation that this might be some kind of lethal spree and the Beretta could be used to kill everyone in the room. Josa spun around to face Cordelia and was in time to witness her final act. She had placed the barrel of the gun in her mouth and began to tighten her trigger finger. Her head tilted back as if trying to avoid the bullet – Cordelia's last shred of self-preservation making her brain try to dodge the bullet even as it ordered its dispatch. Her finger pulled further back and the gunshot sounded like cannon fire in the enclosed area.

Cordelia's head exploded.

Looking back on that moment, Josa wondered why she hadn't made one last-ditch effort to stop her, or why, when her blood and brains were splattered all over her and the room, she hadn't screamed or even registered a modicum of alarm. In truth, she told herself, she had subconsciously recognised the inevitability of the act. Without saying a word or giving the vaguest murmur of concern, she watched the corpse fall backwards. Cordelia's spine hit the wall, and she wobbled and crashed face forward to the floor.

Josa looked at Salinger and Blake, both lashed to their chairs. 'Are you two okay?' she asked.

'I'm fine,' replied Salinger. 'Well, I say fine.'

She was surprised by Blake's reaction. His eyes were wide with fear and he was shaking his head furiously.

'You'll be okay,' she muttered. 'Could get used to you with

gaffer tape across your lips. First time I've seen you with your mouth shut.'

Blake was frantically trying to communicate with her, but as she loosened the last strands of tape that bound Salinger's wrists, she said, 'Sorry, Blake. Gotta look after citizens first. You know that.' She grabbed a letter opener from the desk and began to cut through the remaining layers of Salinger's bonds. Blake's eyes were wide windows of terror. His cries of 'No!' too muffled to be comprehensible. Paul Salinger shot him a covert smile.

If there had been an inevitably about Cordelia's final deed, the act that followed was completely unexpected.

Josa finished shearing through the last thin film of tape that bound the Professor. 'There you go,' she said, standing back as she freed the killer.

# CHAPTER 116

## *Fourteen seconds earlier*

'American academics have rather a good word for it,' said Cordelia. 'Closure. Now turn around.'

Blake felt the barrel of the gun pressed against his forehead. He experienced a pang of ignominy that his death might be associated with a term as glib as closure. But in the reflection of Norman Bates' portrait above the desk, he could make out Josa turning around a second before Cordelia withdrew the gun. Blake saw the older woman lean across to Salinger. She held the Dictaphone out of audio range and whispered into the Professor's ear. Blake strained to hear her words ... Just close enough to catch them ...

'I'm sorry, my love,' Cordelia said with quiet sadness. 'I can't do it. I'll fire three times for the sake of the confession they'll hear –' Her eyes darted to the Dictaphone. 'When I'm dead, which will be after the third shot, stop the recording. Then kill these two. The police will hear three shots on the tape and assume ... I'm sorry, I don't have the courage.'

She slipped the Dictaphone into his hands, stepped back, and in a show of pitiful desperation, shouted, 'I love you, Paul!'

Josa finished shearing through the last thin film of tape that bound the Professor. 'There you go,' she said, standing back as she freed the killer.

He rubbed his wrists. 'Thank you, Josa. You've no idea what that means.'

'No problem,' she assured him.

Blake's wide eyes saw the Beretta Cordelia had dropped, inches away from the Professor. He watched Salinger lean forward as if stretching his constricted muscles, but gagged and tied to chair there was nothing he could do to stop him from reaching for the gun.

Josa was hovering over the table. 'She did a more thorough job with the tape on you, Blake. I'm gonna need some scissors ...' She scanned Salinger's desk as his fingers curled around the Beretta.

'Ah, you may say, no problem,' Salinger said to Josa's back, 'But you really are a life-saver.'

He raised the gun, pointed it at Blake and fired.

'How long till we reach the university?'

'Like I said,' replied the taxi driver as the black cab screeched around a corner. 'We should be there in ten! What with the traffic and –'

'Just put your foot down!'

Dempsey thumped the side window with his fist. Five years ago he had been too late for Daniel Blake and he'd been haunted by that failing for every day since. Now, he knew, he could exorcise the ghosts that had plagued him for half a decade, but only if he reached Blake in time ...

He wasn't to know that the exorcism of Jack Dempsey was for another day.

The blare of a car horn brought him back to the moment. He glanced out of the window and saw drivers furious with the liberties his cabbie was taking.

'That's the way!' Dempsey yelled and held up a fan of bank notes. 'Make it in five minutes and there's five hundred quid in it for you.'

'Five hundred?'

'You heard me.'

'In that case …' Dempsey was thrown back into his seat as the cabbie floored the accelerator. 'Hang on!'

As Salinger pulled the trigger, Blake found the strength from somewhere to kick out. His shoe connected with the muzzle of the Beretta and the bullet shot harmlessly wide, burying itself in the study wall.

'What the hell?' said Josa, spinning around.

'I picked up the gun,' Salinger yelped. 'He went mad. Kicked out at me and the bloody thing went off! Christ almighty!'

Blake saw that Josa still had the Ruger in her hand and that every second or so, Salinger's wary eyes flickered towards it.

Josa ripped the tape from Blake's mouth. 'What the hell are you doing?'

'He's the killer! Josa, he's the killer!'

'What? No, really. What?' Salinger sounded more bemused than aghast. 'You kicked the bloody gun. It went off. That doesn't make me a killer.'

Josa looked concerned. 'Are you all right, Blake? You've got a nasty gash across your head and you've taken a bad –'

'Tonight I came here and confronted him. He admitted he was the killer.'

'This is ridiculous! You heard Cordelia admit to the murders,' argued Salinger. 'You both heard that! Don't tell me that never happened.'

'That whole charade was intended to buy you time!' Blake snapped. 'Tell him to put down the gun, Josa.'

'Professor Salinger,' she began, 'if you could just –'

Salinger stepped back and raised his gun. 'I don't know what it is with you two. Hounding me from the start. You heard Cordelia confess. What else do you want? You want me. Won't stop until I'm dead so it'll look like you were right all along but –'

'He knows I know, Josa! This is a bluff. In a moment he'll ask you to put down the gun, and if you do, he will shoot us both. When the cops arrive he'll play them the tape of Cordelia's confession. They'll hear three shots and assume Cordelia shot us both and then herself. He will walk free.'

'You're insane!' said Salinger.

'I've now got "tied to a chair by a loony" on my CV. Of course I'm insane. But I know exactly –'

'Just put down the gun,' Josa interrupted, looking at Salinger. She sounded reasonable, but overly deliberate, as if talking to a simpleton. 'And we can all move on.'

'I don't trust you. I'm sorry, Detective Chief Inspector, but can you blame me? You pursue me and pursue me and when you find out someone else committed the dreadful crimes, you still want to pin them on me. I'm scared. Please put down your gun. I'll then give you mine if you give me your word you will treat me fairly and hand over Cordelia's tape to your colleagues.'

'You have my word,' replied Josa.

'Not enough,' said Salinger. 'I want your gun.'

'Don't do it!' Blake shouted.

'He's got a point, Blake. We're all jumpy.'

'Let's just both get rid of the guns!' Salinger implored.

'He's playing you, Josa.'

'I think he's telling the truth, and you're in no state to see that,' she said. 'I'm going to put down my gun,' she continued, and placed it on the desk.

'Josa! If you take your hand away from that gun he will kill us both. That's not guesswork or a hunch – it's a certainty. A stone-cold certainty. He will kill us both.'

Josa looked from Blake to Salinger.

'Why are you saying this?' the Professor demanded.

'Josa!'

'I'm moving my hand away, now.'

'No!'

'Thank you,' murmured Salinger, in a voice as svelte as velvet.

'I can prove it!' Blake screamed.

Josa's hand re-gripped the Ruger. 'What?'

'I can prove it.'

'This has gone on long enough!' Salinger raged. 'I'm going to —'

'You're too smooth for your own good,' Blake interjected before mimicking the Professor's intonation, adding, '*Thank you.*'

'Oh, what the hell do you mean? I don't know what's caused this vendetta against me but it's getting out of control.'

'He's right,' said Josa. 'Blake, if you can produce evidence right now, then great, but if not I drop the gun and we move on because —'

'I can.'

'What?'

'Produce evidence.'

Salinger chipped in with, 'What are you talking about, man?'

'I'm talking about proof that you are the murderer. And I can produce it. Right here, right now.'

'You've got proof that I'm the murderer and you only decide to mention it now?' Salinger laughed. 'As a matter of interest, why didn't you mention it earlier?'

Blake shrugged. 'Only just figured it out. The svelte *thank you* did it. That's you all over. So supremely in control. So supremely confident. And in copying the murders of Alfred Hitchcock, your ego would have insisted on emulating the single most audacious element of his onscreen killings.'

'What are you talking about?' Josa demanded.

'This is madness!' Salinger spluttered. 'Are you seriously going to let him continue?'

'Yes.'

'Remember when we first met Cordelia and Salinger? We knew that she'd suspected him. But nothing more. My guess –'

'Oh!' the Professor cut in. 'Your *guess*?'

'My guess is that shortly after our first meeting with him, when I said he was the killer, he realised that if anyone would find out, she would. So instead of murdering her, he recruited her. And to do that, he couldn't tell her the truth. So he made up some bullshit about cancer. And he probably said that he'd ended the relationship with Odette Wilde and that Lucy had begged him to take her distraught sister back ... Some baloney about them fighting. An accidental death. Whereas all Salinger wanted, in the beginning, was revenge. Wanted to see Odette suffer but couldn't risk touching her as their affair might have emerged and he'd have been in the frame. So, he killed Lucy Jaeger. There was no spur-of-the-moment madness. It was planned and savoured.'

Salinger glowered at Blake, and in that split-second, the look told him he was correct. But the Professor turned away quickly, shaking his head. 'You heard Cordelia say she pushed Lucy into the Thames. That's why her body was never discovered.'

'You told us where Lucy was, the first time we met you. You told us.'

'Of course I did. In your world, of course I did. And I wrote a signed confession in peacock's blood and –'

'The locations where the victims were discovered. They were as much a part of your Hitchcock game as the method of despatch. That's why the fact that we never found Lucy bothered me. Why would that be … *unless it was part of the game*. The fact that we never found her was in your eyes a crucial part of the Hitchcock Murders.'

'You said he told us,' Josa said.

'And so he did. The first question I ever asked him in this room: *What's your favourite Hitchcock movie?*' As he recalled the question, he faced Salinger who replied –

'*Rope.*'

'Exactly,' said Blake. 'One of Hitchcock's most brilliant and audacious thrillers in which the body of the victim is right there, hidden, but right there all the way through the investigation.' Blake directed his gaze to the Ottoman in front of him. 'In the wooden trunk.'

'You think …' Salinger began.

'Yes, I do,' Blake replied.

'That Lucy Jaeger is in there?' concluded an incredulous Josa.

'Yes, I do.'

'I've had enough,' Salinger said, 'of all this madness. A minute ago you saw sense, Josa, and you were going to put your gun down. And now –'

'And now I'd like you to move back, sir.'

'No! I've had enough of this.'

Josa raised her Ruger. 'I'd like you to move back, sir.'

Their guns pointed directly at each other.

'You trust his word over mine?' Salinger reached for the Ottoman's lid. He paused for the briefest of moments as he ran his hand over a faint red heart, about the size of a fifty-pence piece, that was inked into its ancient wood. 'Fine!' He flipped open the lid to reveal a mass of DVDs.

Blake shook his head wearily. 'That's just the top compartment. To open the main compartment, use the rope handles a little further down.'

Josa glanced at the Ottoman and saw hinges about half-way up the chest, indicating a lower chamber. It was obvious that this was accessed by opening the top half of the chest which in effect served as a lid for the lower compartment. The two rope handles – one at either side of the Ottoman – would flip open the top compartment.

Salinger could see that Josa had worked out that the chest had a lower section. He smiled with wry resignation. 'You want to see what's in the chest?'

'Yes.'

'Are you sure?'

'No. And I hope to God he's wrong. But I have to know.' She looked at Blake. Nodded. 'You take one side, sir,' she continued, her left hand grasping one of the lower rope handles. 'And I'll grab the other.'

One-handed, and without lowering the Beretta, he complied.

'Thank you,' Josa said. 'After three we lift.'

'Very well.'

'One, two …'

'Strangely enough, and you may not believe this,' Salinger said, 'But I always felt it would come to this.'

'Three.'

They hauled back the huge wooden lid and were confronted by the secrets of the antique Ottoman.

# CHAPTER 119

She ran her hand over the heart on the top of the Ottoman. Paused. And then, careful to prevent her nails catching on the wooden lip of the lid, she pushed it upwards using the heel of her palms.

He saw her look inside the chest, her face lighting up as she pulled the dead creature from its coffin. She cooed. 'Look at this!'

The dead fox. Mother called it a stole, but to his seven-year-old eyes it was a limp, lifeless fox. And although he found it gruesome, like bells to Pavlov's dogs, its physical presence made his heart pump faster with anticipation. It meant she was going out. For a few precious hours, at least, he would be free of her attentions. She wrapped the fox around her throat. 'What do you think, Paulie?' She put the tip of her index finger to her lips and shot a coquettish look into the air above him.

'You look beautiful,' he replied.

'Come here!' She embraced him and he smelt the beer on her breath and the flowery perfume she squirted on her throat. 'You're a good lad. Why can't you be like this all the time? Then I wouldn't have to …' She pulled back and he instinctively covered the bruise over his right eye.

His father walked in. 'How you doing, big fella?' His father really was beautiful. A short, balding man in his mid-forties, but to his only son, a hero. He'd already rebuked his mother for the blows to his face earlier that day, and for once she hadn't retaliated. In fact, right now she looked happy. Excited, even, with a look in her eyes that he'd never seen before.

His father knelt down. 'I'm taking your mother out for a few hours. Are you going to be all right on your own?'

*Going to be all right?* It was the best thing in the world! And ten minutes after they left he crept downstairs and switched on the television set. It took a minute or two to warm up and present a picture but that pleased Paul as it gave him time to curl up in his father's armchair. He took a deep breath and could smell his dad. Smiled. And was it there? Yes! Good old Dad! Wedged between the cushion and the seat itself, the Saturday Secret Bar of Chocolate.

*Don't tell your mother!*

'Thanks, Dad!'

By now, jaunty music was coming from the TV and its screen stretched into life. *Alfred's Hitchcock's The 39 Steps.*

At home, with his father's love, his mother's absence and an old film. He didn't know the word Utopia, otherwise he'd have applied it to evenings like this.

Years later, when the business with Josa and Blake was done and the countless analyses reeled on, most commentators called him a misogynist, but they weren't quite right. Paul Salinger loved women; he was just terrified of them. All of them. His job at the university allowed him to enjoy young virgins who were easily impressed by restaurants and experience, but when he'd met Odette she hadn't been fooled. She was young and lithe but bursting with knowledge and street smarts, and yet somehow, *somehow* she still adored him. He would swear to that. They'd met by chance in a supermarket and, after three weeks of heaven with her, he had gone down on one knee and proposed. She'd laughed. Was he serious? She'd just been crossing the much-older-man thing off her list. Even three weeks had been stretching it but hey, he had a big TV and small libido so the pay-off had been –

*Stop it! I love you!*

She was taking pleasure in this.

*Get over yourself! Go back to fucking your students. And don't call me again.*

Salinger visited her sister. Odette had spoken about her often enough and he inferred she remained one of the few people whose opinion counted with his former lover. But as Lucy had started to soothe him, to tell him that Odette could be insensitive and unkind, her voice faded out. He stared at the girl who had slighted him and something snapped. Her neck.

Later, of course, he could never admit that the crime was one of petty frustration. It was more. Had to be. It was the beginning of his homage to the Master. The one person who had always been there for him. The one who would understand. The Hitchcock Murders may not have begun with the death of Lucy Jaeger, but they were a sequel to it; a justification for his part in her meaningless demise and an attempt to prove that Odette, his mother and the rest of them had been wrong. He grasped the prospect of immortality, fame and respect, using it like a trident to prod back all those grinning harpies.

The movie finished and the BBC2 announcer declared that there would be another Hitchcock classic the following Saturday night.

A rattle of locks.

He looked up, suddenly terrified. They never came back this early! He peered over the wing of the armchair and saw his mother appear in the doorway. Her eyes were wide and her face pale.

'It's your father … He stepped in front of a lorry …' Paul Salinger knew there and then, knew with an unshakeable certainty that she had pushed him. The look in her eyes … 'He's dead!' she blurted out. 'I tried to save him!' She couldn't look at her son. 'Tried to help him, but …'

The dead fox around her throat was awash with dark crimson, its fur torn and matted with blood.

# CHAPTER 120

'Three!'

*Josa and Salinger hauled back the huge wooden lid and were confronted by the secrets of the antique Ottoman.*

The face that stared up at them was discoloured and eaten away by the onset of decomposition. The eyes had rotted away to a soft white pulp and her naked body was caked with old brown blood. Her mouth was locked in a scream but her hair had been brushed, as golden and kempt as a model in a shampoo commercial. The corpse was sealed in a transparent plastic bag but its features remained clearly visible.

The face of Lucy Jaeger, 21-year-old Lucy Jaeger, silently screamed up at her as if finally getting the chance to express her own horror at her end.

'Oh, God, I'm sorry, Lucy,' Josa murmured.

Salinger saw his chance and seized it, rushing at her, brushing aside her gun with one hand and punching her hard in the stomach with the other. He moved forward in a shoulder charge, ramming Josa into the wall and raining a series of hard blows into her torso. He was strong and kept his head low, meaning that Josa, unable to escape from the corner, was only able to pound his back with a number of ineffective thumps.

Salinger's fury was demonic and he beat her for a full fifteen seconds – a frenzied onslaught. She could feel ribs snapping and felt nauseous from the pummelling. Salinger stepped back. Lunged for her neck. He grasped her throat and, roaring with anger, began to squeeze, tighter and –

In one elegant movement Josa drove her forearms between his wrists, forcing them up and apart. He may have been stronger and crazier, but she was well trained and could now confront him head on.

He threw a punch at her face and, with an expert's ease, Josa blocked it using a rudimentary kung fu move, sweeping her left arm upwards in a ninety-degree arc, deflecting the blow and leaving her attacker exposed. Her right arm was already moving forward. As she had been taught, she made contact, not with her fist but the butt of her palm, smashing it into her opponent's jaw and thrusting upwards so the heavier fighter was almost lifted off his feet.

Salinger staggered back and the space between them gave Josa the opportunity for another well-practiced kung fu move. She pivoted her body, raising her right leg high so her foot was level with her left thigh. She brought it hammering down on the Professor's knee. He screamed in agony and staggered back but Josa was relentless.

Back in her Hendon training days she'd been one of the best boxers in her intake. She'd trained hard, and the punches now came with a practiced ease. Two hard jabs. The first broke Salinger's nose, the second hurt him some more and a third left him looking like someone had poured a jar of bolognese sauce onto his face. She threw a sharp left into his kidneys and by now the only thing keeping him upright was the narrow cabinet he was pinned to.

Josa stepped back and reached for one of the two guns that had fallen to the floor. Before Salinger could register that the onslaught had stopped, Josa was pointing her Ruger at his chest. The professor was breathing heavily now. He looked into her eyes and Josa saw that it wasn't because of physical exhaustion.

'Go on, Josa.' He smiled. 'Make me a legend.'

The gun wavered.

'You know you want to. I murdered your sister. Stabbed her in her shower just to recreate a movie. Pull the trigger.'

Josa was aware she could drop Salinger at that moment and come up with a story that no juror would disbelieve.

*Detective Chief Inspector* Jilani had fought back and disabled the suspect. But now *Josa* looked into the mind of the man who had stabbed Preya.

'Do it!'

Josa looked at Blake. He nodded. The muscles around her eyes fractionally tightened. *What?* Had she misinterpreted him? But no matter because –

'No!' Her mind was made up. Her resolve clear. 'I'm afraid not, Professor Salinger,' she declared. 'You're nicked.' Josa let her gun fall to one side. 'No happy ending for you.'

Salinger shook his head. 'Endings, endings, endings. Studios, distributors, producers ...' His hand, hidden behind his back, had nudged the alabaster bust of Hitchcock. ' ...they all try to alter the final scene.' His fingers curled around the bust. 'Which is madness because ultimately ...' And from nowhere his arm had launched into a haymaker right. The bust smashed into the side of Josa's head and she staggered back, blood pouring from the wound. 'Only the director should decide the ending.'

Salinger picked up the Beretta and pointed it at Josa. 'And guess what?' He fired twice and the sheer force of the shots threw Josa off her feet. She crashed to the floor. 'I've decided.'

Blake watched as Salinger fired another couple of bullets into Josa. She lay in a slick of her own blood, unmoving. He peered hard, looking to see the rise and fall of her chest, but he could see nothing and knew that taking that many shots at such close range would mean –

'And now!' Salinger smiled at Blake. He began to remove his necktie. 'It's been fun. Creating my own legend. Following in the Master's footsteps, and yes, I suppose even bettering his own achievements at times. But ...' He gripped his tie, wrapping its extremities around the fingers of both hands as he approached Blake. ' ...let's get to the end scene, shall we?'

'Leave now and you have a chance of escape,' said Blake. 'You delay and you're dead.'

'Thinking of me? How kind. But really, you needn't.'

He gently looped the tie around Blake's throat.

'I know it's over for me,' Salinger told him. 'How far could I get with a leg that feels like a broken twig and a face like this? And after all this, even the police will be able to figure out what's happened. Bless them. I had intended to go on a little. A few more murders. Well, many more murders had been the plan, but you know what? Whenever I give a lecture about *Family Plot*, which was Hitchcock's final movie, I always say how it's apt and funny and a knowing, farewell wink to the viewer. But I think it's rubbish. Every time I write about Hitchcock's later movies I so wish he'd ended with *Frenzy*. The brilliant, *brilliant Frenzy*.'

Blake tested his bonds again but he was held tight, completely unable to move his arms or shift from the chair. 'I've got a nasty feeling I know where this is going,' he murmured.

'All my brilliant murders. They will make me famous and people will respect me as an artist. Yes, go on, then. As a genius! They'll regret not exploring and harnessing my talent, but for centuries – *centuries* – they will read me, study me, debate me, wank over me, make me live on the silver screen.' He tightened the noose and slowly began to throttle Blake.

# CHAPTER 121

Blake's vision was swamped by Salinger's looming face. 'You're the perfect murder. You'll immortalise me ... Lovely!'

Even now, exhausted and on the verge of death, Blake still picked at the gaffer tape binding his wrists; a useless act of personal defiance.

*'Lovely ... lovely ...'*

Blake couldn't breathe, and at first his chest felt like it was going to explode, and then his head became hot as if submerged in boiling water as he sensed his veins about to burst.

*'Lovely!'*

Blake could only see Salinger's face now, and an irrational anger seized him. An anger that came with the thought that his final sight would be the look of joy on the face of his killer ... and even as he began to feel less and less and the pain in his chest numbed into nothingness, he resented his murderer's hold over him ...

*'Lovely ... lovely ... lovely ...'*

Blake felt, saw, felt ... Blackness, nothingness, a prologue to death, his sole link with the living now just a single repeated word –

*'Lovely!'*

As he started to slip away, Blake wanted to die with a memory of his own. He was determined that his final sensation on earth should not be the sound or sight of Salinger. He tried to focus on a memory ...

Blake is back in hospital. He can smell the disinfectant on the floor and hear the *beep-beep-beep* of the monitoring device. In the green darkness he can see his old friend, Don Walters, lying dying on the bed.

*That memory …*

He stands in the shadows watching her make a vow.

*That vision …*

Josa Jilani, so proud, so resolute, so kind and to Blake's eyes, extraordinarily beautiful.

The last memory he wanted of this life was *that* sight – the first time he ever knew that Josa Jilani would always, somehow, be special to him.

And even in those seconds which he felt sure would be his final consciousness, that look in her eyes still had the same effect on him … Bang!

That memory was good enough for Daniel Blake. Christ, in death, that explosion, that *bang* felt real. He had heard it boom and felt the reverberations through his body. Those echoes wiped away the blackness, and as his vision cleared he realised he *had* heard a gunshot. Salinger's face swam into view but this time the Professor looked astonished. The noose around Blake's throat slackened and he took in lungfuls of air. Salinger straightened his back and Blake saw a bright red poppy bloom across his chest.

He took a step back and looked down to where the shot had come from. Saw –

Josa Jilani, lying prostrate on the floor, still covering him with her Ruger. Her eyes drooping, her body so weak she could barely raise the gun.

Professor Salinger smiled at her. 'But I didn't, I didn't …'

Josa looked at him. She wanted to tell him that the last woman he had murdered had saved her and done for him, that Preya Jilani had constantly nagged her to wear a bullet-proof vest in any potentially dangerous situation. *More rules and regulations than the Home Office …* Her sister's common sense and love had saved her and defeated him.

But she remained silent, too tired to gloat, or even focus.

'I didn't say cut,' concluded Salinger, and Josa fired one last time before he slumped to the floor.

Josa blacked out.

## CHAPTER 122

She had no idea whether she'd been unconscious for hours or minutes. It had, in actuality, been several seconds. She could see Blake, pale and drenched in blood but trying to talk. She could hear nothing, but could lip-read his words, 'Josa! Stay with me! They will be here soon! Stay with me!'

'Oh, Blake,' she murmured and her gun fell to the floor.

For minutes, nothing, and then sprinting footsteps clattering down the corridor.

Todd Martens – Marty – appeared in the doorway. Josa's hopeful eyes fell away. She knew his devotion to Salinger was too strong. The young student took in the silent, bloody scene. 'No, no, no …'

He stood in the doorway, whimpering, unwilling to move forward, as if remaining outside the room would render the truth it held a fiction. But his murmurs became a scream, and, shocked by his own outburst, he inched forward and then ran to Salinger's side. He knelt down and gently shifted the Professor's head onto his lap. 'You can't be dead! Come on! Essays to mark! Books to write … No!' He brushed back the older man's hair with tender fingers, then howled at Josa and Blake, 'You murdering bastards!'

A strange, momentary silence … And then the room was pulsing with blue light thrown from the police cars that had arrived en masse in the quadrangle immediately outside the study.

Blake tried to smile at Josa.

Dempsey burst into the room, all oaths and angry recriminations, then gently urging Josa back to full consciousness. Uniformed officers joined the party moments later, instantly followed by medics who buzzed around Blake, Josa and Salinger.

One found a feeble pulse in the Professor's carotid. 'He's alive!'

Dempsey groaned. 'Pity!'

The paramedics stemmed the flow of blood from Salinger's wounds, officers ushered Marty away and a couple of constables sealed off the room.

Josa hobbled over to Blake. 'You okay?' she asked.

He stood and swayed unsteadily. A medic moved forward to help him but he said, 'I can manage, thanks.' And then in reply to Josa, 'Not so bad. Come here.' Blake hugged her.

But in that embrace, Josa experienced what was for her the most chilling moment of the evening. Across Blake's shoulder she could see Salinger being lowered onto a stretcher. For several seconds he lay immobile beneath the bloodied, iconic print of Alfred Hitchcock. The director seemed to be watching them both. Then Salinger stirred. Looked at her. *Smiled.*

Josa had seen the smile before, always on the faces of criminals who had been apprehended but knew something that the police didn't. Often it was a knowledge that they'd walk, or there was a loophole officers weren't yet aware of. Sometimes it was a grin that meant she had not been in time and that dreadful consequences would –

– that ghastly, heart-freezing smile was now playing on Paul Salinger's lips.

'You're too late ...' he whispered. 'The best is yet to come ... And there's nothing you can do to stop it.'

The theft didn't even make the papers. But for the Hitchcock Murders it was a pivotal act and, ironically, Karen Sherwood was the only reporter who even bothered to look into the crime. One week after the bloodshed in Salinger's study, the solicitor's firm of Francis and Company had been broken into. No one connected the burglary with the serial killings, not even Karen Sherwood, who knew the case so well. 'What was stolen?' she asked old Mr Francis. 'That's the strange thing,' he replied. 'They got into the safe but left all the valuables. Just took a bit of post we'd not got around to processing ... The police think the burglar must have been disturbed and fled without getting what he wanted.' He smiled nervously. 'You're not going to write a big article on it, are you? We don't want the fuss or the –'

'Don't worry,' she interrupted. 'I won't be writing this up at all. No offence, but …' She peered into the open safe. ' …it's just not important enough.'

The Old Bailey trial of Professor Paul Salinger began exactly six months after the suicide of Cordelia Smith and proved a much briefer affair than most observers had anticipated. Less than twenty days after its highly publicised beginning, the judge summed up and the jury retired to consider a verdict. Josa, Blake, Dempsey and Mason retired to a nearby pub. It was mid-morning, too early for beer, and so the four friends chatted over coffees. Their anxiety was becoming almost palpable when Josa's mobile rang. After a brief phone conversation she said, 'They've reached a verdict. We've got twenty minutes.'

Half an hour later, the foreman of the jury stood. The judge asked him if they had reached verdicts for all the charges that had been levelled at Paul Salinger. He replied in the affirmative. The first charge was read out and the judge asked, 'Do you find the accused guilty or not guilty?'

The foreman shot a glance at Salinger and announced the verdict.

Pandemonium broke out.

## CHAPTER 123

In the days following the arrest of Salinger, away from London, away from the constant snap of cameras and journalists' questions, Blake had made good progress in his return to health. Josa had taken time off duty to recuperate, joining Dempsey, John Mason, Holly and Blake in Cornwall. For a couple of months the five of them stayed in the American's cottage by the shingle beach, never talking about the murders or the Professor, but enjoying a different existence and *modus vivendi*. A local doctor visited twice a day and, although he endlessly clucked and fussed over his two patients, he proved a good man and invaluable to their recovery.

'Holly has really enjoyed having you around,' Blake told Josa one evening. They were alone in the cottage's front room, both of them sitting by its roaring fire. 'Thanks for ... you know.'

'No. What?'

'Well, I can see how much it's meant to her, so thanks for making the effort. All the girlie chats. Trips to the shop together. The stuff I'm not very good –'

'No effort. She's great. I like her. You know, once upon a time I thought that I was going to have ...' She stopped. Stared into the fire. Looked up. 'She's got a lot of you in her. But I still like her.'

'Quite right, too. She's brilliant. Gets it from her old man.' Blake grinned. 'Nah, really – friends moan about their teenage kids, but Holly's never really been any trouble. I mean, we have differences of opinion now and again, but we talk them through. Sort them out. You know?'

'She sees it as team work.'

'What?'

'She sees you two as a team. Since you both lost her mother.

She feels the world did her and you a massive injustice, so now she thinks it's Holly and her dad versus the world. And she's determined to win.' Josa gave a reassuring smile. 'I said she had a lot of you in her.'

'I don't think it's quite like that. She never really speaks about her mother.'

'Oh, she does.'

There was a long silence. 'You once told me you needed space and I hope I've respected that. But even when this thing is over, I hope maybe you … I don't know. I've tried so hard, because I love her, but you know, maybe it's not been enough and it would –'

'Don't worry,' Josa told him.

'Thank you.' He smiled. 'So what are you going to do?'

'I don't know. Help with the case. I'm guessing there must be something I can do. Then I honestly don't know. Right now I feel like I want to leave. Walk away from all of it.'

'That would be a shame.'

Josa shrugged, looked into the flames again. 'I spent so many years trying to escape being an outsider. But we all are. You, me, Dempsey … That's us. Not a status. More a condition. You know? Does that sound … Oh, I don't know. Maybe it's not so bad. Maybe it's how you deal with that exclusion. How you perceive what you're excluded from and what it actually means to you. And you know, Blake …' She smiled at him. 'Sometimes there's nothing warmer than the togetherness of outsiders.'

'You are what you are. Which is brilliant and remarkable, by the way.' Blake squeezed her shoulder. 'You can't just walk away, Josa. You can't in any real sense *leave*.'

'What about you?' she asked. 'Are you going to go back to doing what you used to do? You could do a hell of a lot of good.'

'Me? No. Christ, it was a miracle I came through this thing. My guilt, my fear of the rain … No. I couldn't. The work I'm going back to is much more dangerous but at least it's a personal mission. *Other people's murders* …' Blake paused. Shook his head. 'Besides, I don't feel cleansed yet. After what happened on the Cathedral Tower I can never be mended until it's over and somehow …' He took the poker and stoked the fire. 'It can never be over.' A loud crack and the fire spat out a cinder. It landed harmlessly on the hearth. 'When you shot Salinger ... point blank, almost, why didn't you shoot to kill?'

'I don't know.'

'I think you do.'

She held his gaze. 'Because it would have meant Jahannam. Hell.'

'He deserved it.'

'I wasn't talking about Salinger.'

The light from the dancing flames flickered across her face as she glanced down at her hands.

Josa was the first to leave. She'd stayed with Holly and 'the boys' for eight weeks, and during that time she'd only left Cornwall once, when Blake had driven her to a Newcastle match. The Magpies had been playing away and Blake had gone along with her, explaining he'd never had the slightest interest in football but was willing to give it a shot. Josa took great delight in his inability to grasp the offside rule. 'You're just a boy!' she laughed. 'Boys can never understand football!'

On a couple of occasions she'd had friends down to Dempsey's village to stay the night, and she'd been amused and flattered by Blake's reaction to them. He'd made an obvious effort, picking them up from the station, cooking elaborate meals and making sure that anything they wanted was never too much trouble. It reminded Josa of how Preya's boyfriends and hopeful suitors had once treated her as they attempted to win favour with her sister. When she'd recognised this parallel, she'd smiled. Just another moment where she missed Preya for reasons that would hold true for the rest of her life. The smile faded.

Still, she had important matters to distract her and keep her focused. The Crown Prosecution Service was building its case against Salinger. It was conclusive, but they had known conclusive cases destroyed by loopholes before, and Josa was determined to help. The trial was set.

Josa had hoped that at some point before the trial, Salinger would announce his guilt, like an entertainer taking a bow. Blake warned her against such optimism, reasoning the Professor wanted the theatre of an Old Bailey trial. Sure enough, he entered a plea of 'Not guilty' and exercised his right to waive counsel and represent himself throughout the proceedings. The CPS team was overjoyed. 'There's an old legal saying,' one of the barristers said with a smile. 'A man who represents himself has a fool for a client.'

'He's no fool,' Blake retorted sharply.

Josa nodded her agreement, still bothered by the smile he had shown her and the words he had whispered as he was stretchered out of his study.

But for the CPS, the trial began well. Salinger floundered on the legalese and soon discovered that real-life court proceedings bore little relation to *The Paradine Case*. By day three, to Josa's annoyance, people were congratulating her. She believed in an ultra-cautious approach, but was still surprised to get a call from Blake shortly after the day's proceedings concluded. 'Bad news,' he told her. 'I think we've got a problem.'

Blake, Josa, Mason and Dempsey met in Gordon's Bar, a louche little subterranean establishment tucked away about twenty paces from Embankment station. They were huddled around a small table in a dimly lit corner. Dempsey had been the last to arrive and asked, 'So, what's wrong?'

'In a couple of days they'll get on to Kim Gilmour's murder,' Blake replied. 'And there's something not quite right about it. You know, I'm just not sure …'

'We know Salinger did it,' Dempsey retorted, a fraction too quickly. 'He's bragged about it to anyone who'll listen to him.' He paused. Josa raised the bottle of Merlot they were sharing and Dempsey nodded, mouthing his thanks. She began to pour him a tumbler of wine but the bottle slipped from her grasp. The American caught it.

'Sorry!'

'Forget it! We're all jumpy,' Mason said. He pulled a tissue from his pocket and mopped up the small spill of red wine that seeped across the table. 'So, go on,' he added. 'What's on your mind, Daniel?'

'Salinger enjoyed the immediacy of it. He tried to get Tony Taylor to do his dirty work with you, Josa, but that's only because it was a rush job and he had no choice. There was something tactile about the way Salinger killed. He enjoyed physically overwhelming his victims. Controlling them. Feeling them ...'

'But primarily,' Josa countered, 'he was reproducing the movie murders.'

Mason nodded. 'The murders Hitchcock directed.'

'That was his motivation, sure,' Blake agreed. 'And the means by which he executed the murders. But something just doesn't fit with Gilmour's killing. On that night. By the church ... I glimpsed the person responsible. I don't know who it was but ...' He hesitated. Dead silence around the table. 'It wasn't Salinger.'

Dempsey leant forward. 'Let me get this straight. Are you thinking he had an accomplice? Someone who killed Kim?'

'Not even that,' Blake replied. 'Salinger wants us to believe he was responsible for all the Hitchcock Murders. He wants the hype and hoopla of the trial, but my point is – I think he wants all the, well, let's call it 'praise', and I think he's wanted it from the word go, which precludes the possibility of an accomplice.'

'So,' Josa murmured, 'you think that Gilmour's killing was opportunistic? Someone using Salinger's crimes as camouflage?'

'Yes. Yes, I do. And now I'm wondering if we should warn the CPS of our doubts.'

They discussed the matter at length, finally resolving to keep their suspicions private. 'Anything that upsets the apple cart at this stage could be devastating,' Mason reasoned.

'Worst-case scenario,' Dempsey said, 'the judge orders a retrial. That would play right into Salinger's hands. The tabloids' reporting has been a scandal – they convicted him six months ago and since the trial started they've got worse, because it's obviously such an open-and-shut case. Look, if it goes again – if there is a retrial – the defence could argue any subsequent trial would be prejudiced by biased reporting.'

'There's no way he'd get off!' Josa insisted.

'True enough,' Blake commented, 'but the judge could panic and cut a deal. We do not want that.'

'So, we're agreed then?' Dempsey said. 'We keep our suspicions to ourselves.' All four nodded. 'More wine!' boomed the American, and replenished their tumblers.

'But you know what ...' Josa murmured, 'We're all avoiding the obvious question here.'

Blake leant back into the shadows. 'I know.'

Josa took a sip of her wine. 'If Salinger didn't kill Kim Gilmour,' she said, 'who did?'

# CHAPTER 124

'Do you find the accused guilty or not guilty?'

Josa looked around the gallery. She could see a few familiar faces from the investigation. Stevie, Yvonne Salter, Julie Spragg and, of course, Todd Martens, his focus forever fixed on Salinger. She also recognised Chloe Robinson, daughter of Sarah Robinson, the third victim to be discovered. The relentless journalist Karen Sherwood sat on the back row and – Josa did a double-take – almost unrecognisable in jeans and a hooded top, Simon Maxwell.

Only Blake seemed to be distracted, looking down at the phone he'd smuggled into the courtroom. *Why hadn't Holly got back to him?*

Josa realised she was holding her breath.

The foreman shot a glance at Salinger and announced the verdict.

Pandemonium broke out.

Blake raised his glass. Salinger smiled.

'Cheers,' the Professor said as they clinked glasses. He took a sip. 'You not drinking?'

Blake shook his head, said nothing.

'Don't be a sore loser!' A pause. 'Once, you asked if it bothered me that when you Googled my surname, you got reams and reams about J.D. Salinger and I was buried away in the fifth or sixth page. Guess what? I Googled my name earlier and –'

Blake held up his phone, its screen showing the Google results for 'Salinger'. The Professor dominated them.

His surprise at Blake's anticipation threw him for a second, but he regained his composure fast. 'And that is just the beginning. I was found guilty today. That verdict launched the brand of Professor Paul Salinger, and I am so looking forward to the years of fame that lie ahead. Two things excite me most. My conversations with you and the steady release of my diaries, letters, articles, videos …'

They sat in a small, bare room below the Great Hall of the Old Bailey, facing each other across a desk that was empty aside from the glasses of water that Blake had privately insisted upon. Three uniformed guards stood behind Salinger.

'Because without them,' he continued, 'this fame would be short-lived, and after a brief period I'd be of interest only to the cognoscenti of true crime. I mean, if all I had to tell my tale was prose, I'd be lost. Who reads books any more, right? But, my dear Daniel, my legacy will be so much more than a simple book full of prose. I collected so much ephemera … conducted interviews with myself, videoed some of the actual murders, took photographs, even wrote an introduction to a book and signed it as Alfie …' He was laughing now. 'All safely stored away on a single USB stick in the possession of a friend of mine. Over the coming years he will drip feed it to an expectant global audience via the internet. They'll try to block it and have it removed, of course. Good luck with that! The videos alone will cause a sensation that will resonate throughout history! I shall become bigger than you could possibly imagine. A new breed of killer to inspire others. As I said to Josa, the best is yet to come and there's nothing you can do to –'

Blake held up a blue USB stick between his index finger and thumb. The item he had stolen from Salinger's solicitors, Francis and Company.

The Professor blanched. 'No, that can't be, can't be …'

Blake nodded.

'That's not yours! That's not …' He turned to the trio of guards. 'That's stolen property, that's *stolen property!* Give me that!' He lunged across the table but a couple of the guards dragged him back, pinning him to the upright of his chair. Blake shook his head, indicating they should stay, but take no further action. 'Give me that!' Salinger roared. 'That is my legacy!'

Blake's hand hovered over his glass. More a pause than a hesitation. He let several seconds pass. Parted his index finger and thumb. The USB stick fell into the water.

'*No … no … no …!*' Salinger's shout transformed into a terrifying shriek. '*Noooooooooo!*'

Blake removed the stick from his glass of water, snapped it in two and placed the halves in his pocket. Hours before he'd cut almost all the through way the USB stick in order to make the gesture and now he took in the effects of it.

'You've destroyed me,' Salinger murmured.

Blake nodded and stood up.

'When will you be back to see me? Interview me? Learn about me?'

His reply was a smile and a slight shake of the head. Blake didn't need to articulate the word to make it clear: *Never!*

He walked to the door, nodded to the attendant on the other side, and it clanked open. Salinger was on his feet, needing all three guards to restrain him this time. He was yelling Blake's name, over and over again.

The door slammed shut.

Blake hadn't spoken a single word to the Professor and as he walked away –

'*Blake!*'

– he didn't bother to look back.

Blake used the spare key Josa had lent him and let himself into her flat. They were late! Typical. He sat down, switched on the television and glumly surfed through a few dull channels.

The original plan had been for him to meet Holly at Waterloo and travel to Josa's together, but he'd received a text from his daughter's phone saying Josa had called and was in south London.

Blake idly glanced over his shoulder. Josa's bedroom door was open. It looked surprisingly bare.

The text message had gone on to say that Holly and Josa would make their way across town together, all meeting up at the flat. Blake walked into the bedroom. Pulled open a wardrobe. Empty. His phone was immediately in his hand, making the call.

'Josa! Where are you?'

'I'm gone.'

'What?'

'Where are you?'

'I'm at your flat. As we arranged.'

'What are you talking about? I came to a decision. As I intimated in Cornwall. To *leave*. Leave all this behind. To start again somewhere else. I've got a ticket to ... well, never mind. I was planning to break it to you and Holly Belle together when we met, but she texted to say you couldn't make it and so I left. I was going to call you.'

Blake froze. 'Holly texted you that?'

'Oh, thanks! I was half-hoping you'd show just a little regret that I'd decided to disappear!'

'Josa ... I didn't say that to Holly Belle. Whoever texted you ... Whoever texted me from Holly's phone ... It wasn't Holly ...' His mouth was dry and he could barely speak, but he heard his own cracked voice conclude, 'Something's happened to her.'

Josa tried to calm him down. '*Phone her!*'

Blake called her number immediately, left an urgent message, and then texted his daughter. '*Hi sweetheart. Where are you? Give me a call just to let me know you're safe.*'

Almost immediately his phoned beeped and a surge of relief swept over him. It was from Holly's phone. He clicked open the message. Read the thirteen words and found himself unable to breathe.

'*Your daughter will now pay the price,*' the message read, '*just as Gilmour paid the price.*'

The thirteenth floor of the ESB was deserted. Chairs were stacked in one corner and white sheets covered the desks. The teams that had worked here were being shifted to another part of the building, with the entire floor undergoing redecoration before its new occupants moved in.

Josa looked across the still, silent space, remembering team talks, the incident board, the people she had worked alongside and –

'It's over there, isn't it?'

One of the decorators interrupted her thoughts. He was a short, stocky man, pointing to her office in the corner.

'Yes, that's the one.'

They strode across the floor, light sensors picking them up, illuminating where they had walked but not where they were heading. Josa unlocked the door to her office. 'Give me ten minutes to box up the rest of my stuff.'

They were alone, which pleased Josa. She had baulked at the prospect of meeting any of her old comrades. She intended to collect her things and leave, and the man by her side had volunteered to help move her belongings. A discreet withdrawal, with no fuss or false sentiment. She stepped into her room and took it in as if she'd never seen an office before.

'No problem.' The decorator's boot tapped against the side of the large cardboard box that stood next to the desk. 'I might as well get cracking with this.'

Josa looked at the container and recalled bringing it into the ESB the evening her promotion had been confirmed. It contained mugs, diaries, framed photographs and other personal ephemera she thought she'd need but had never once missed. 'Yeah, sure. You can move that now.'

'Up to the fourteenth floor, with the rest of your team's stuff?'

Josa shook her head. 'No. Could you take it down to reception, please?'

'Reception?'

'Yeah. I'm not going with my team.' For a crazy moment, Josa thought this kind-faced man was trying to persuade her to stay, just as her boss, Liz Canterville had done. The former Home Secretary said she understood her desire to get away from the service, but would list her time away as compassionate leave. *Anytime you want to come back to us, Detective Chief Inspector Jilani, the door is open …* But Josa replied as she now responded to the decorator. 'I've left the police.'

He nodded.

As he lifted the large box with ease and walked from the office, Josa took out her mobile and made a call. 'It's me,' she said. 'Did you get through to Holly? What's the situation? Need my help? Or was it a false alarm?'

She hadn't noticed the square of pale, pressed-down carpet that marked the spot where the box had stood for so many months, or the envelope that lay on the edge of the flattened area, addressed quite simply, *To Josa*.

Daniel Blake read and reread the message, praying that he'd misinterpreted its meaning. But the words were cruelly unambiguous. He sat paralysed for several seconds, shaking as he stared at the declaration. Somehow he managed to move his fingers. Called Holly's number. No answer. A beep. Another text message. '*I am monitoring you. Tell no one about your daughter. Tell anyone and she dies. How are you feeling now, Danny Boy?*'

Blake stared at the message. 'Oh no, oh no, oh no …'

He almost dropped the phone when it began vibrating. The caller ID indicated Josa was calling him. 'Hello?' He could hear how feeble his voice sounded.

'It's me,' Josa said. 'Did you get through to Holly? What's the situation? Need my help? Or was it a false alarm?'

Blake held the phone to his ear, gazing dead ahead but not seeing anything.

'Hello! Paging Daniel Blake! You okay?'

'I've just heard from Holly Belle …'

'This is a terrible line. I can hardly hear you. Did you say you'd got through to her? Is everything okay, then?'

A tear rolled down his cheek. 'I don't need your help,' Blake said. He hung up and closed his eyes.

# CHAPTER 126

The moment Salinger had been found guilty, something changed in Josa. For months, helping to build the case against the man who'd murdered her sister had given her purpose and focus. She had recognised this, even during her time in Cornwall, and gradually came to feel that once Salinger had been dealt with she must leave the service. If she could not save the life of a loved one, how could she get up and go to work every morning, seriously believing she could protect the public and the team around her? And with this belief came another dread.

He could phone no one. Tell no one. *He never felt so alone* ... Blake sank his face into his open palms, forcing himself to think. *Think!* He had to do something! Start piecing this together otherwise ... No! He couldn't even consider that! Christ! *Who the hell could have —*

The television was shouting at him, its incessant chatter an assault on his senses. He picked up the remote control and pressed buttons at random, attempting to turn the set off. The cassette in Josa's DVD/VCR whirred into life, and without looking at what video had begun to play, Blake hit *pause*, silencing the television.

He stood up. Paced the room.

*Christ!* The very concept of anyone snatching his daughter, harming her in any way ...

His legs turned to water and he grasped the back of the sofa for support. Breathed deeply. 'Get a grip!' he snapped to himself.

Josa's VCR had a one-minute still mechanism, meaning that if the machine remained paused for more than sixty seconds, the tape would automatically start playing again. And so as Blake tried to grapple with his current dilemma, his past began to play out before him. The tape that Josa had watched after they had first met. The only VHS she'd ever played on the machine had remained forgotten for over six months. But now the footage it held was about to tell Daniel Blake everything he needed to know.

# CHAPTER 127

Guildford Cathedral, five years earlier. Not that Blake recognised the building on the television, scarcely registering the video at all for several moments.

'Go, go, go!' someone from long ago shouted.

Blake glanced up. Looked at the screen. Blurs and shadows, but … he knew that gothic stonework …

*Where was Holly? How had he allowed this to happen? Would he ever see her again?*

He began to turn from the television but heard a dead man's voice.

'… he's up there now with Diaz and the boy like he's bloody Don Quixote. He should have left this to the police.' Kim Gilmour. Something began to dawn on Blake. Something so awful that he would have given his life – there and then – to reverse the process he realised had been set in motion.

'Oh, God, no,' Blake murmured. He forced himself to sit down and relive the murderous evening that had crippled him for half a decade. He saw officers arguing, Mara Diaz arrive, Gilmour ordering the armed police to storm the tower and finally, the loyal, ever-dependable Jack Dempsey stating that he'd venture to the top of the tower, declaring he'd rather go up *alone*. In fact, he was insisting on it.

Blake didn't need to watch to the end of the tape. He knew. He recalled the events surrounding Gilmour's killing and closed his eyes. Why had it taken him so long to recognise what had been obvious all along? He rewound the tape a few seconds and played the crucial moments again. The moments that revealed the identity of Holly's kidnapper. Blake shuddered. *Or her killer.* The possibility hit him again like a mallet. He sat in a state of shock, finally pressing *pause*. He had seen enough …

The other dread was one of debilitation. She could not do her job, she reasoned; the job that had meant more to her than anything. And this perceived failure infected her confidence like a virus. Her insecurity about one issue replicating itself over and over again until Josa Jilani half-forgot who she was.

As the trial wore on and she was needed less and less, she noticed something that shocked her.

Her hands were beginning to disobey her.

The scorching sensation was nothing new, but now she felt her fingers weakening.

For years, her fears had affected her physically, the burning sensation tormenting her hands as if hell itself was catching up with her. *Almost there, Josa* … Holding her hand and giving it a gentle, painful squeeze. But this was something new and unexpected.

When she was with Blake, she knew, the burning had stopped. It was because he gave her a belief in herself – through his words, through his trust, through his jokes, through that look of pure adoration he gave her, even when he thought he was wearing his sternest poker face. And he needed her. To curb his anger and insanity and, with the symmetry of a perfect relationship, to fuel his belief in himself.

As Josa found herself trying to understand the feelings she held for him, she missed her sister more than ever. Preya, always such a buccaneering spirit in relationships, would have advised full steam ahead, but Josa recalled her previous sense that she was better at ending relationships than sustaining them. If she kept her friendship with Blake on a platonic footing, she would never lose him.

And the final guilt: so soon after Preya, was it even right to feel *love*? The first time the word occurred to her in relation to Blake, she had been surprised, but her overwhelming response was self-reproach, quickly followed by fear.

She had loved her father and her sister. Lost them both. So if it came to crunch – if ever Blake needed her – she doubted she could save him. And as her hands began to fail, so that doubt and a dozen others began to grow more potent.

Small, embarrassing moments like spilling the wine in Gordon's were regrettable but no big deal. Yet Josa couldn't help but wonder where it would end, or indeed, whether it ever would. As her confidence ebbed away she could feel herself losing her grip in more ways than one.

...because suddenly he knew. He recalled the events surrounding Gilmour's killing. Raked his fingers through his hair. Why had it taken him so long to recognise what had been obvious from the start? Josa had even asked the vital question at Gordon's bar in London. *If Salinger didn't kill Gilmour, who did?* The answer was inescapable, of course. The one person with enough twisted reason to want the man dead. And now that same person was taking revenge on him.

He stood in a state of shock, finally slipping his phone into his pocket, aware there would be no further communication. But the numbness was ebbing away. *And replacing it he could feel –*

Some bastard had taken Holly Belle! Had dared to harm his little girl!

*Fury.*

He ran his hand over his face. Recalled Josa's eyes, flame red in the light of the fire. '*She sees you two as a team.*'

Blake grabbed his jacket.

'*She thinks it's Holly and her dad versus the world.*'

Daniel Blake's rekindled anger began to burn through his terror. He marched towards the door. He knew where Holly was and who had snatched her. Despite their former friendship, Blake would show no mercy. This was betrayal on a massive scale, but he didn't give a damn. There was something infinitely more important. His daughter had been put in jeopardy and the bastard who had taken her would need to kill him or be killed. Simple as. One or both of them would be dead before the day was through.

Blake glanced out of the window and across London. Armies of huge, dark clouds hung over the city, as if gathering for battle. Rain would shortly fall. Blake registered this added jeopardy, but didn't hesitate as he threw on his suit jacket and raced from the flat. Right now, a monsoon, tsunami and tornado rolled into one wouldn't have slowed him down for a heartbeat. His daughter had been dead right when she thought it was them versus the world.

Holly Belle Blake was in trouble, and her dad was coming to get her.

## CHAPTER 128

Finally she had turned a little to her left and seen the envelope. Reached down, and as she neared it, recognised the handwriting on its front.

'Oh, my God!'

She picked up the envelope and opened it.

He tore up the three flights of stairs and only paused on the final step. Took deep breaths and glared at the closed wooden door ahead of him, as if trying to stare through it and discern the outline of his destiny. Exhausted from the climb and the events of the last hour, he rested his forehead on the door, momentarily reluctant to push it open. Finally, he tried the handle. It turned easily, as it had done five years earlier.

Daniel Blake pushed open the door and stepped onto the tower of Guildford Cathedral where he'd saved Jamie Diaz's life on that long-ago night.

He'd visited the place many times over the past half-decade, endlessly walking across its copper floor, examining the architecture, sometimes sitting on the edge of the wall watching the sun fall. He never knew what he'd been searching for and certainly never discovered anything, except more questions, more regret. But now he found his daughter's kidnapper waiting on the far side of the tower top, exactly where Thom Diaz had once waited …

'You know,' Blake said, 'just before I pushed open that door, I still hoped I was wrong.'

The figure turned around and flashed that broad, familiar smile.

The sky brooded in the background. A deep crimson smudged by dark clouds. There was a storm coming.

Back in Josa's flat, the truth had tumbled onto him. But there was a moment of video that confirmed his belief. He'd recalled his encounter with the unidentified person outside the church where Gilmour had been murdered. The fleet figure who had clearly been overseeing the killing. Blake had been weakened by the rainfall, and the Chief Superintendent's murderer had almost shot him at point-blank range ... Now that moment came back to him ...

*His opponent had the gun. As if in slow motion, the figure moved backwards, leaping back in a controlled graceful movement ... so slowly, as if allowing Blake to enjoy his final moments ...*

The grace and elegance of the person's movements had struck him, even then. Almost balletic in the way she'd stepped back to give herself space to shoot him.

And there, on the video ...

*One of the younger officers steps in her way. She moves back, away from him, although even this tiny movement is like a step from* Swan Lake, *the magical princess skipping away from dark forces ...*

Christ! No wonder Josa had almost recognised the figure outside the church where Gilmour had been fatally wounded. She'd seen the tape. Seen the person responsible for the death of her old boss.

What was it Odette had said? *Old dancers never really lose it.* Well, this one had lost it.

On the top of the Cathedral Tower, back where it had all started, Blake looked at the woman who had murdered Kim Gilmour and kidnapped Holly. 'Hello, sweetheart. I'd like my daughter back. You get one chance to walk away,' he told Mara Diaz. 'And this is it.'

'Daniel Blake. Here we are again,' Mara said. She held a gun in her right hand. 'Your family and mine.'

'Where's Holly?'

Mara stepped to one side. Slumped against the waist-high wall of the tower, Blake saw his daughter, blood pouring from a gash above her left temple. She was handcuffed. Wrists in front of her. Holly seemed to be coming to, and on seeing her father, her face lit up. 'Dad!'

'Hello, darling. Daddy's come to take you home.'

'It doesn't work like that, I'm afraid,' Mara revealed. 'Different numbers this time. Two of yours. One of mine. We both know why that is. And why she has to die.'

Holly looked at her father with terrified eyes. 'Dad, what's going on?'

'I'll tell you what's going on, dear.' Mara stooped low so her mouth was over the girl's ear. 'We're going to teach Daddy a lesson. Would you like that?'

'No.'

'Oh, come on, Holly Belle,' she rasped. 'All the times he's denied you something ... and think of all those parental orders he's barked out over the years. Don't you want to teach him a lesson?'

'No.'

'Strange child,' Mara murmured. She straightened her back and smiled at Blake. 'Maybe the fall will knock some sense into her.'

Blake took a step forward and Mara raised the gun, pointing it at his head. He froze. 'This is nothing to do with her,' Blake snapped. 'Let her go.'

'Your father's been here before ...' Mara's eyes didn't move from Blake. Nor did the muzzle of her gun. 'Tell her what happened the first time, *Danny Boy*. Explain why she's here. Why you *knew* this is where I'd bring her to, to get some justice.'

'I tried to save someone,' he replied. 'I did save someone. Here. On this spot. Five years ago. *Your son.* I tried to stop Thom but ... Mara, we can talk about this, but let Holly go.'

'Who are you?' Mara screamed. 'Who are you to give orders? To maintain this pretence of reason? You murdered my husband!'

'I tried to save –'

'And you murdered my son!'

Blake paused, horrified. The wind was picking up now, howling and hissing over the old stonework. He stared at Mara. He had realised far too late that the only person who could want Gilmour dead was the widow of the man who'd been killed during an operation he had commanded. But this new element was a mystery to Blake. 'What the hell do you mean?'

'He took his own life!' she shrieked. 'Do you have any idea what you did that night? He was an intelligent little boy. And beautiful! And what you showed him ... We never spoke about what happened. How you and Gilmour murdered his father. Then one day he said to me ... he said he wanted to be just like his dad and I thought we were over it. And then, on a school trip ...' She was crying now. '...he jumped from a castle wall.'

'Oh, Jesus, Mara, I'm so –'

'I don't want your pity! I want justice.' She stooped low again, clutching Holly close to her. 'I'm going to kill you now, Holly Belle Blake.' She poured the words into the girl's ear. 'And as you fall, just remember it's your father's fault.'

'Mara, I'm begging you,' Blake pleaded.

'Why couldn't you have stayed beaten?' Mara screeched. 'I visited you for years. Whenever I thought you might be happy – at Christmas or birthday times, I came round and made you relive what you'd done. And seeing you in the state you were in gave me a little comfort. Then when you phoned me in New Zealand and said you were back on a case, I guessed you were starting to recover. You were starting to live again! What life did I have?'

Blake shook his head. 'So you flew straight back to the UK. Murdered Gilmour. Why didn't you just kill me then?'

'One of Thom's old friends in the force told me that your prime suspect was this Paul Salinger character. So, anonymously, I told Salinger a few of your secrets. Just to see if he'd twist the knife. Beat you. Then after you took him in, it struck me that you'd think he killed Gilmour and that maybe his defence could prove he didn't so he'd walk free. I wanted you alive a little longer just in case that happened. I'd have loved to see you broken by his triumph. Yeah, I'd have relished that. But when the judge summed up it was clear Salinger would be found guilty. I didn't have to wait any longer. But I'm not here to kill you. I'm here to punish you, like you punished me.'

Mara leant down, grabbed Holly by her collar and hauled her from the floor. The teenager appeared groggy and Blake guessed the blow to her head had –

'No!' he shouted.

Mara was lifting Holly even further, swinging her towards the edge of the tower wall. Time seemed to slow down, as it had five years earlier. Blake saw the most important thing in his world dragged onto the tower wall, and screamed.

'Please! Mara, please!'

Mara grinned, moving her left hand to Holly's chest.

Blake knew if he ran towards her, Mara would shoot him. But he would take the hit, gladly. He was desperately trying to calculate how many bullets he could catch and still force himself forward, bulldozing both himself and Mara from the tower and saving Holly. It had to be worth –

The first few drops of rain struck his face and he recoiled involuntarily. Mara caught this. Beamed at him. One last gloat. 'You cripple!' she sneered. 'Too broken to even save your own daughter.' She shook her head. Looked at the girl who lay helpless along the tower wall, nothing between her and the 160-foot drop. 'Look what you're putting your poor father through!' she said, beginning to push Holly over the edge. 'You are so grounded, young lady.'

Mara was pushing. Holly was screaming. The girl's left leg dangled over the edge of the wall, her shoulder now over it and, as her body's weight teetered on the verge of pulling her into oblivion, Daniel Blake did something extraordinary.

# CHAPTER 130

He turned away. A smart about-turn so his back was to Mara. She could scarcely believe it. 'Just watch!' she shrieked.

*Just watch.* The words confirmed Blake's intuition that for Mara, it was vital he witnessed the death of his daughter. He knew it was the only bargaining chip he held, so he'd have to play it deftly and quickly.

He replied without pleading or panic: 'No.'

'Dad!' Holly screamed.

The sound of her terror ran through him like an electric shock.

'Just watch!' Mara's shriek sounded barely human.

'I've seen enough death,' Blake replied, and heard a low rumble of thunder in the near distance. He looked into the night, aching to turn around, but knowing that if he did –

'I want you to watch!'

Blake scanned the tower wall ahead of him, chose a very precise spot and began to walk.

'I'm going to murder your little girl, Blake!'

'Dad! Please!'

But he didn't even spare them a glance over his shoulder. Instead, in a surprisingly sprightly move, he skipped onto the tower wall and, without looking around, announced, 'You think that seeing my daughter die adds up to justice. And I know there's only one part of that equation I can change to alter the outcome. Subtracting myself.'

Mara's anger exploded in demonic fury. 'You bastard! Watch this! I said, *watch this*!'

'Mara!' He gestured to the dark panorama in front of him. The cauldron of stars and lights dotted across Guildford. 'I can't tell you how, but really, *really* … I always knew it would end here.'

Mara began to understand. 'What?'

And at last Blake turned around. As he'd hoped, Mara had withdrawn her hand from Holly's chest. He still didn't have a hope in hell of reaching her, but it did buy him a precious moment. Daniel Blake smiled at his daughter. He could feel his eyes welling with tears. 'I was always so proud of you, your mum and me both. Thank you so much for saving me. Have a good life.' He raised the palm of his right hand. 'I love you, Holly Belle.'

Even as he spoke her name he was stepping back. His left foot hovered over nothing but 160 feet of empty air. And then, with a force of will that made him want to vomit, he snapped his right foot back, and so for a brief, bizarre moment, Mara could see him dropping. Now it was her turn to run, although she knew, *knew* with an absolute certainty that she could not reach him in time. 'No!' she shouted.

*I always knew it would end here.*

Daniel Blake had plunged from the wall. No *might do*. No *could do*. He had fallen – no, deliberately *stepped* – from the top of the Cathedral Tower in order to save his daughter. An almost unbelievable sacrifice, and for Holly, an almost unbearable escape.

Mara collapsed, crumpling into a half-screeching, half-sobbing heap. Holly tumbled to the tower floor and, without pausing, ran to the door. She bolted through it, gone before Mara looked up. The woman's vengeance, her all-important revenge had been torn from her grasp.

Daniel Blake had plummeted from the tower of Guildford Cathedral to protect his daughter. As the storm grew louder, Mara's incoherent howls also increased in volume, but there was no one on the tower to hear her.

# CHAPTER 131

Holly Blake stumbled down the last of the steps, pushed open the heavy door that led to the chancery and pelted to the choristers' door, her footsteps echoing across the marble floor. Less than two minutes ago she'd seen her father step from the tower and the sight had compelled her to run, to escape the scene and the awful action that occurred there. But now, pausing in the doorway of the cathedral, she had stopped running and the image of her father falling almost blinded her. She squeezed her eyes shut and screamed, 'No, Daddy!'

She wept so heavily she could barely breathe. A roar of thunder made her stop for a second, automatically opening her eyes at the sound of the storm. And what she saw, right there in front of her, made her gasp with surprise.

On the top of the tower, if the imposing figure of the Golden Angel had looked down for a moment, she would have seen a dark comma on the copper floor. If she could have heard, she would have listened to the wailing subside, only to be replaced by a monotone repeat of a single syllable: *Blake*. But even that mantra became slower, the pauses in the repetition becoming longer until the dark comma fell silent.

And then Mara Diaz sat bolt upright. She looked at the area enclosed by the low red wall, as if seeing it for the first time. She tried to imagine her husband and son, to envisage how it must have been for them that night, but the visualisation became too painful. She dragged her sleeve across her eyes, wiping away tears in a quick, brusque fashion that suggested, *time to move on from this place.*

The wind had picked up and the thunder was rolling nearer. Lightning lashed around the tower, and the sky was turning as dark as midnight, heavy with storm clouds. The light sprinkling of rain had become a downpour and, as more water struck her face, Mara whispered, 'This is how it must have been.'

And then something else struck her. A realisation. A suggestion, or rather, an unformed idea. A thought which changed the course of her life.

Holly ran from the cathedral and smashed into him, throwing her arms over his head and around his shoulders, embracing him as if she would never relinquish her hold.

'It's all right,' he told her, and when she pulled her head back she saw that familiar smile. 'It's all right, princess,' Jack Dempsey repeated.

His smile suggested he didn't know, and that awareness brought back the tears. 'Dad … jumped … tower … dead!' she stammered.

But Dempsey placed both his palms on her shoulders, ducked his head and pushed her back a little. He took a small master key from his pocket and unlocked her cuffs. He had no time to tell her that John Mason had phoned him minutes earlier, quickly and concisely explaining his fears concerning Blake and giving him the location of Holly's mobile. Instead, he simply placed a finger across his lips and waited until her wailing petered out a little. The big American looked deep into her eyes. Lightning cracked above them both.

'It's not over yet,' he said.

# CHAPTER 132

Mara realised that this is how it must have been, not simply for her husband, but for Blake. In fact, her situation found a direct parallel with his, five years earlier. A plan gone horribly wrong. Death. The tower. She had looked at this rooftop differently a moment ago. And hadn't Blake said that he'd done something similar? Been repelled but puzzled by the cathedral and yet drawn to this place. He had mentioned ... she tried to recall ... He'd returned to the site of the tragedy. Learnt about it.

An amorphous idea was forming in her thoughts. She tried to grasp it. He had read about the cathedral, yes, and learnt its secrets. For a moment she struggled to remember what had happened here several minutes earlier. Of course, the fall dominated her recollection, but before that, when he'd turned his back on her, he hadn't simply walked to the wall. He had paused as if in consideration. He had been selecting, choosing a very precise place on the wall. Why?

*He knew this place ...*

The unformed idea was solidifying, the epiphany it promised almost visible now. Mara looked at the exact spot Blake had jumped from and narrowed her eyes.

Dempsey walked slowly, forced to tug the reluctant teenager in his wake. 'Come on!' After a dozen paces he stopped and turned to face her.

'Look ...' he whispered.

She couldn't see anything, or at least nothing unusual. Just the cathedral, looking more ominous than ever in the stormy darkness.

'No! *Look!*' Dempsey insisted as he jabbed a finger heavenwards.

Mara stared at the spot Blake had stepped from. She tilted her head as if a different angle would lend insight but the idea remained frustratingly incomplete. She got to her feet, still focused on the patch of wall Blake had chosen. *He knew this place*. A huge bellow of thunder and a loud, close crack of lightning jolted Mara from her reverie. She shook her head, turned away from the wall and began to walk to the door that led to the staircase.

She turned the handle. Then paused.

Holly strained her eyes. It was dark, and whatever Dempsey was pointing towards was a long way away.

'On the tower!' he prompted.

After a couple of seconds she saw what Dempsey was indictating and her face exploded in joy. 'Is it?' she asked.

Mara slowly let go of the door handle, letting it slide through her fingers. He knew this place so well and he'd been choosing something after he turned his back on her. Those two facts had to be connected. He had been carefully selecting the spot because ... She whirled around and once again stared at the wall he had stepped from.

'It's him,' replied Dempsey.

Now she knew where to look, Holly could see him clearly. About an arm's length below the parapet that ran around the top of the tower, a couple of feet from one of its corners, the teenager could make out some sort of corbel. She couldn't discern its features but it was in fact one of three similar protrusions projecting from the tower, each jutting out exactly twelve inches and decorated with a female face. This trio of figures symbolising the enduring virtues: Faith, Hope, and Charity …

Clinging to Hope, so far above her, Holly Blake could see her father.

Mara took a tentative step forward. And then another.

Daniel Blake could feel each minute curve of the stone in his palms. His fingers were interlaced, looped over the corbel. This way, he stood a chance of hanging on for a few minutes before risking an attempt to somehow haul himself over the parapet.

But the muscles of his hands were weakening and, worse still, he could feel the rain falling harder, finding his fingers, loosening his grip …

As he'd stepped from the wall he'd felt the heart-freezing sensation of plummeting, then almost had his arms pulled from their sockets as he'd grabbed the stonework. That fall had been bad enough, yet did he really believe that he could spring from the corbel to the tower wall? But that was his plan. That was all he had left, and both figuratively and literally, there was only one thing he could do: hang on to Hope.

Mara was running now.

Holly saw her father looking over his shoulder, down towards where she stood. Was he looking at her? Her view of him was too indistinct to tell with any certainty, but clearly Dempsey thought he was peering at them because he shouted, 'It's all right, Danny Boy! She's safe! Holly Belle is safe and well!'

Blake had spotted them moments earlier but, aware that Mara was near, he'd remained silent. He felt certain that Dempsey knew this too and so the fact that he'd just bellowed the news about Holly could only mean one thing ...

Blake turned his head skywards, already aware of what he would find.

As his face angled upwards he felt rain hit his flesh and he gasped in pain. The whole sky exploded in a mad, massive frenzy of thunder and lightning. And at its epicentre he could see Mara Diaz, gun in hand, looking down on him, smiling.

'Hello, Daniel,' she said.

# CHAPTER 133

'Oh, this is perfect!' Mara smirked. 'Absolutely perfect. You know, you're a trier, I'll give you that.'

'You've lost!' Blake shouted back, 'Go ahead, shoot me, do whatever you want, but you've lost, Mara. My daughter is safe and you can't harm her.'

'Can't harm her? Blake, she's going to see her father fall to his death. That's a lot of bad dreams.'

'Fuck you!'

'And whenever she gets close to someone she'll have to tell them this story, again and again throughout her life. And she'll have to tell them why the situation arose and she'll have to acknowledge it was your fault.'

'You're insane! I should have just let Thom kill himself and Jamie!'

'He would never have jumped if you hadn't been there!'

'He wanted to die and take Jamie with him! And it was your fault. So when this is over, think about that – it was your fault! You should have been there for him! But you never were because you wanted me! You murdered your husband! You!'

'No!' She pointed the gun directly at Blake and he stared up at her, through the rain, daring her to pull the trigger.

'Do it!' he yelled. 'The only thing you've got left is the gun in your hand. Well, use it!' He was shouting very loudly now, his words given force – given grandeur – by the howling storm that raged about them. 'Come on! Do it!'

Dempsey turned to Holly. 'I need you to go inside the cathedral for me, darlin'.'

'Can't you do something? We've got to do something!'

'Holly, you've got to –'

'We've got to get up there,' she screamed. 'To stop her! Save him!'

'Even if we could get up there in time, I'd never make it across the tower rooftop to –'

'We've got to do something!'

'Holly Belle!' Dempsey eyes flashed with anger. 'Listen to me! This will be over in a moment and the way it ends depends on me. And to get it right I need space. Please. I'm begging you to back off, because I can't lose my boy again.'

Holly saw his eyes were full of tears and she nodded, beginning to understand. Jack Dempsey looked up, through the night sky, through the storm and through half a decade of guilt for not getting it right when it had counted. Now, in the most desperate of circumstances, he had a chance to save Daniel, save himself and exorcise the ghosts that had tormented him for five years.

'I believe in you,' said Holly. 'Do it, Uncle Jack.'

'Is this it?' shouted Mara. 'Your last act of defiance for your little girl? That's fine. She'll always half-wonder if it was suicide. Whether her father was a coward as well as a murderer.'

'Christ,' yelled Blake. 'You blamed him, didn't you?'

'What?'

'After Thom died, you blamed Jamie.'

'I loved Jamie!'

'Listen to what you call me! A murderer! A coward! The man that saved your kid's life!'

'Shut up!'

'And you gave Jamie a hard time, about all of it! Didn't you? Told him he should have stopped his dad from jumping. If he'd loved his daddy more, he wouldn't have jumped. Ring any bells,

Mara?'

'That's it!' she screamed. 'No more. I'm in control here. And I choose to end it now!'

'That's why Jamie had to end his own life. To get away from you!'

'You bastard!'

Through the driving rain, Blake could see her steady her aim so the muzzle pointed directly at him, before her finger pulled back on the trigger. He roared, 'I love you Holly Belle!' and squeezed his eyes tightly shut.

In the screaming, savage storm, the gunshot was just another noise.

# CHAPTER 134

Blake heard a gunshot and, registering the discharge, realised he was still alive. He looked up, and in the rain and darkness could just about make out Mara's silhouette. Her gun was still pointing in his direction but her aim was wandering, as if taunting him as to where she would fire the next bullet.

'Is this it? How you get your revenge? Sadism? Make you feel good, Mara?'

The rain was hard and incessant now, and Blake's grip was slipping.

'Well, take your best shot because in three seconds I'm letting go. You're not dictating my final moments in this world.'

The gun continued to sway left, then pointed at his head before arcing to his right.

'One!' Blake shouted, beginning the countdown to his own death. 'Two!' He could barely cling to the corbel any longer. He was about to fall, and faced with the choice of taking his own life or a bullet from a maniac, he chose control.

'Three!'

As he shouted the last word two things happened simultaneously. He began to loosen his grip, feeling his palms sliding over the smooth, damp stone. And a flash of lightning tore open the sky, momentarily illuminating the top of the tower. In that electric moment, Blake saw not just the silhouette of Mara but the woman herself. Or rather, what was left of her. Her face held a look of complete astonishment, and in her forehead, in the dead centre of her forehead, he could see a gaping hole.

Dempsey lowered the gun. He knew Holly had not listened to a final plea he had made, to turn her back. Not to watch. She had seen him shoot and now she turned towards him.

Blake felt Mara's blood hit his face and he saw the gun finally fall from her hand. It struck him just above his right eye, cutting into his flesh. Perhaps it was his imagination, but the woman with a hole in her head appeared to be alive, willing a few more seconds of life in order to say something to him. Her mouth opened and closed three times – he was sure of it – but she was unable to speak and, as loud thunder seemed to shake the tower itself, she pitched forward, tumbling over the cathedral wall. Mara's body collided with Blake, crashing heavily into his shoulder as she plunged towards oblivion, knocking his right hand from the corbel.

Mara Diaz was dead before her frame smashed into the roof of the lower cathedral.

Blake spared her a glance. The fingers of his left hand tightened on the ancient stone, but the rain, just as it had done half a decade earlier, made any firm grasp impossible. His muscles had been sapped of their strength. He had nothing left. His left hand slid from the corbel, the fall dragging Daniel Blake from Hope into nothingness.

And even as he fell, he reflected that Mara was dead and those he loved were safe. Maybe that was enough. No one left to save him, though, with Holly and Dempsey so far –

No, that didn't matter. They were safe. And it was finished. His death didn't matter. As he fell into nothingness, Daniel Blake was finally at peace.

# CHAPTER 135

## *Fifty-seven minutes earlier*

'Dear darling Jos,

Dad loved me, but you were always the apple of his eye and he always said that you – Josa – could do anything you put your mind to. I know I was always jealous of the relationship you had with Dad and maybe I even resented him for it, but I hope it's never shown. But you know, when you got the promotion I realised Dad was right. Our Josa can do anything! You know I've always loved you more than anything or anyone, but in a weird way, I think this has brought me and Dad closer. Because he may be dead, but I feel I understand him better. We're together, he and I, at last, in our belief that you are the most marvellous and beautiful girl in the world.

We both know you can do this thing, and we both love you to the moon and back again.

Love, always, Preya XXX'

Josa's eyes had filled up long before she'd got to the end of the written note she found in the good luck card from her sister. She felt the confidence stir inside her. She took out her mobile.

*Blake had sounded so strange on the phone a few seconds earlier. She had known something was wrong, but ignored it.*

But it was time to start repaying the faith of others. She scrolled through her phone's contact list and found the number she was looking for. Pressed it.

Josa imagined her sister on that night, swinging by the ESB en route to the restaurant and leaving the card at reception for someone to bring up before –

'Hello?'

'You need to call in a favour!' Josa said. 'Like now!'

On the other end of the line, John Mason told her, 'I'm all out of favours!'

'Then find a few! Call your old friends! I need a location fix on two phones. Danny's and Holly's. Can you do that for me? And get Dempsey on board?'

'Is this about Daniel? Is he in trouble?'

'He needs my help,' Josa began, '*our* help. And right away. Listen …'

## *Fifty-seven minutes later*

Yet Blake only fell a couple of inches. Looking back on that moment he could always recall the sense that he was plunging to his own death, and it was as though an angel had caught him. A split second after he slipped from the corbel, he felt a tight grip on his left wrist.

Blake looked up and saw her, stretching over the wall. She had come back for him. She looked down on him and gave her life-saving smile.

'Josa!' Blake yelled up to her.

'I've got you,' said Josa Jilani.

She would always remember that moment. The rain and wind on her face and Blake, the man she had saved, held in her hands. The doubts and demons beaten. Her grip was strong and unshakeable.

Dempsey's gun had only held one bullet. Now he tossed the weapon to one side and closed his eyes. While pulling the trigger he'd been calmness personified but the pressure of taking the most important shot in his life finally hit home and he collapsed to his knees. Holly fell too and hugged him. She could feel him weeping. After so many years of pain, Jack Dempsey's ghosts had been exorcised in the storm.

'Look!' said Holly. 'He's safe!'

Dempsey opened his eyes and saw Josa hauling Blake over the parapet.

Exhausted, Blake fell from the wall onto the floor of the cathedral rooftop. His phone was already in his hand and he noted the battery was almost dead but might have enough juice to allow a quick call to –

Dempsey answered immediately with, 'We're okay, we're both okay ...'

'And I'm fine!' Blake shouted above the wind, thunder and lightning. 'Thank –'

The line went dead, the battery finally giving up. But Blake had heard all he needed to know. Josa helped him to his feet and he gently rested a palm across the side of her face.

'Thank you,' he said. 'God, thank you, thank you, thank you ...' He embraced her, and for several moments they stood in the storm, holding onto each other, Josa burying her head in Blake's shoulder.

'I thought you were leaving,' he told her.

'I couldn't.'

As Josa felt the cold, torrential rain drench them both, she suddenly remembered Blake's phobia. She looked into his eyes. 'The rain,' she murmured, 'we've got to go.'

'It's fine ...' Blake said. 'It's all over.'

And, still holding Josa in his arms, he tilted his head back so the rain splashed onto his face, gently washing away the blood from his skin.

## END CREDITS

Thanks first and foremost to Nicci for so much understanding, encouragement, patience and guidance. I have absolutely no doubt that without it, I'd have been found dead outside The Phoenix years ago. Thanks also to Rocco, for showing how Daniel Blake would approach the big situations and giving me Jamie's line about the cathedral; to Dempsey for clarifying Jack Dempsey and to Holly Belle, simply for being Holly Belle.

I'm grateful to Ibrar Ahmed of the Association of Muslim Police Officers for so much assistance and insight and to Merle Nygate – a brilliant writer who was kind enough to advise and encourage my efforts. Also to Rik Kershaw-Moore who has a mind like the Black Museum and never ignores my mad, midnight texts and never fails to deliver. Doctor Helen Burgess for her insider knowledge, and Bryony Dixon, whose enthusiasm for silent movies, back when I worked at the British Film Institute, opened my eyes to Hitchcock's early works ... Thank you, all.

Many writers have a disparate group of friends who offer advice and support and generously pretend they'd rather be talking about some half-baked, half-finished manuscript than getting another round in. My 'team' is second to none and I send big thanks to my sister Sara, Liz Cooper, Rob Fairclough, Lawrence Jones, Ayesha Khan, Heidi Rasmussen, Derek Ritchie and Steve Rogers. Special thanks to Lucy 'Lucifer' Roberts for going so far above and beyond that she was virtually on the moon.

And I couldn't leave out the Cutting Edge crew – Paul, Martin and Hatty – who decided to unleash *The Hitchcock Murders* on the world, even if it meant working with me. And yes, I know I can be a bloody nightmare and something of a liability, so thanks for all your help and kindness... Seán, my horrifically thorough editor – I'm lumping you in with that rabble, mon ami. Cheers.

Jonathan Zane, Jonathan Zane, Jonathan Zane... So many whiskey-fuelled nights and early mornings with you telling me about The Protocol in such spell-binding detail. No, not a bit of it was used. But yes, The Protocol's time is a-coming...

And finally, to my mum, who has always been there for me throughout good times, bad times and what-the-hell times. Thank you. *The Hitchcock Murders* is for you and Dad.

**Josa Jilani and Daniel Blake will return in**
*They Keep Killing Marilyn*

## After Leaving the Theatre:
## Filmography and Final Thoughts

I don't pretend to know Alfred Hitchcock as well as Professor Paul Salinger does, but one of the perks of writing this book is that people often want to talk to me about Hitch and his films. I'm sometimes asked to recommend a Hitchcock thriller but it's almost impossible to choose a favourite because there's something very special about everything he directed – randomly select any movie in the following filmography and I guarantee you'll have chosen a work full of interesting moments and touched by genius.

If you visit my website – gavincollinson.com – you'll find some thoughts on Hitch's under-rated films, viewing suggestions for newcomers to Hitchcock, info about Josa, Daniel et al, and much more. You can also contact me via the site. I'd love to hear your thoughts on *The Hitchcock Murders* and if you email me a question, I always reply.

The Hitchcock filmography below covers all his work as a director. Aside from *The Mountain Eagle* (Hitchcock's 'lost' movie) all his feature films are fairly easy to get hold of, providing you have a few quid and a search engine – even titles like *Lifeboat*, which were once tough to track down, are now just several clicks of a mouse away.

# Alfred Hitchcock Filmography

**Silent films:**
The Pleasure Garden, 1925
The Mountain Eagle, 1926
The Lodger: A Story of the London Fog, 1926
Downhill, 1927
Easy Virtue, 1927
The Ring, 1927
The Manxman, 1928
The Farmer's Wife, 1928
Champagne, 1928
Blackmail (silent version), 1929

**Talkies:**
**Blackmail (talkie), 1929**
Hitchcock's first talkie, shot at the same time as the silent version. As such, it's difficult to avoid mentioning the scene that every critic seizes on – the sequence where Alice, distraught after killing her attacker, is repeatedly jolted out of her dark thoughts by the word *knife* – that single syllable stabbing though an otherwise half-heard exchange. Although often overlooked due to his prowess with visuals, it's a reminder of how ingenious Hitch could be with the soundscape of his movies.

**Juno and the Paycock, 1930**
Possibly the most depressing plotline of any Hitchcock film sees an impoverished, dysfunctional family enduring a series of miserable set-backs (serious injury, 'shameful' pregnancy, disastrous love affairs, destitution, murder and so on) and therefore when one of the main characters announces, 'It's true! There is no God!' you can be sure she's earned the line. Hitchcock makes the film (based on a play) feel like an intimate exchange and it's interesting to compare his stagey handling of *Juno and the Paycock* with later works, most obviously *Rope*.

**Murder! 1930**
Herbert Marshall plays Sir John Menier, a celebrated actor-manager who turns detective to save an innocent young woman who has been found guilty of a crime she didn't commit. Hitch has great fun with the soundscape of the movie, most notably with a sequence that's recognised as the first 'internal monologue' scene ever featured in cinema history.

**Mary, 1930**
The German-language version of *Murder!* with Hitchcock shooting both movies at the same time using the same sets but a different cast. (Mary was once almost impossible to get hold of but has recently been released as a DVD extra on a number of higher profile Hitchcock films).

**The Skin Game, 1931**
A story of two feuding families which ends miserably with one of the family members committing suicide, leaving her father to claim he is a broken man. Reviewers were underwhelmed. 'Mr. Hitchcock's imagination is never particularly keen during this production,' The New York Times declared. 'Now and then this director has a fairly good idea but it is never brilliant…'

**Number Seventeen, 1932**
A murder mystery that Hitchcock didn't want to make but eventually shot as a comedy thriller, played largely for laughs. He declared it was a 'disaster' and although the plot is as creaky as the old house where the majority of the action takes place, it has a certain down-at-heel charm. The opening sequence is probably the best, heavy on atmosphere and totally devoid of dialogue. In it, we enter 'Number Seventeen' and after several spooky minutes, discover a corpse. The shrill whistle of a nearby train represents the scream of one of the men finding the body – a clever wrinkle Hitchcock would use more memorably in *The 39 Steps*.

**Rich and Strange, 1932**
*Also known as East of Shanghai*
*Rich and Strange* is a comedy - the tale of an 'ordinary' suburban couple who win a large amount of money that changes their lives, mostly for the worse. The film emerges as a strange one, unlike anything Hitch ever shot before or after and indeed, the opening sequences are more Charlie Chaplin than the Master of Suspense. In 1932 it proved a commercial and critical failure but it can be viewed as an interesting curio with a mournful, haunting quality that at least makes it a memorable movie.

**Waltzes from Vienna, 1933**
*Also known as Strauss' Great Waltz*
A musical romance that charts the writing of *The Blue Danube* and the piece's first public performance. If that sounds an unusual choice for Hitch it's because, as he told François Truffaut, *Waltzes from Vienna* marked the lowest ebb of his career and he only agreed to make it because he had no other film projects and was desperate to stay working. But better times and much better movies were on the horizon…

**The Man Who Knew Too Much, 1934**
When the daughter of Bob and Jill Lawrence is kidnapped the couple are, of course, distraught before they choose to fight back and take matters into their own hands… This was Hitchcock's first picture for Gaumont British and given more of a free hand, he crafts a fast-moving, witty, inventive and vital work that's a real signaller of the greats to come.

**The 39 Steps, 1935**
Richard Hannay teams up with a reluctant, beautiful blonde and embarks on a cross-country chase to discover: *What is the secret of the 39 Steps?* Hitch had undoubtedly created some very fine films during his debut decade as a director, but this is his first great; not simply one of *his* best works but arguably the best British movie of the 1930s. The Hitchcock standards – the innocent man on the run, feisty blonde, the ingenious MacGuffin, thrilling chases and romantic

subplot – are all present and delivered with barnstorming élan. The film has such charisma it could set up its own charm school.

## Secret Agent, 1936

*Secret Agent* – an action-packed spy yarn - isn't as narratively tight as *The 39 Steps* and although Madeleine Carroll and Peter Lorre are both back, Robert Donat (so perfect as Hannay) is sorely missed. John Gielgud is okay as the lead but he lacks Donat's twinkle and it's said that he blamed Hitchcock for making the film's villain more charming than the hero. Despite this, it remains a very watchable movie and Peter Lorre is great as 'the Hairless Mexican'.

## Sabotage, 1937

This dark account of foreign agents, terrorism and bombs going off on London Transport is an effective, chilling thriller and in his depiction of Verloc, Oskar Homolka crafts one of the great Hitchcock villains. Hot on the heels of *Secret Agent* - which feels like it's trying to be a combination of Hitch's preceding two works - *Sabotage* has a sense of something new. It lacks the humour of *The 39 Steps* and the Boy's Own style of *Secret Agent* but it's an edgy encounter and the most unsettling of all the movies Hitch made during this period of his career.

## Young and Innocent, 1937

A man accused of a murder he didn't commit must find the real killer... Possibly the most under-rated of Hitchcock's British talkies, *Young and Innocent* is a fabulous thriller that repeats *The 39 Steps*' trick of combining dark, sinister motifs with light humour and a bickering romance. The opening scenes that lead to Guy strangling his former wife are as disquieting as anything Hitch had previously delivered and the interplay between Derrick De Marney (Robert) and Nova Pilbeam (Erica) is a delight.

## The Lady Vanishes, 1938

When the elderly Miss Froy vanishes whilst on a train, it's left to plucky Iris Henderson and another fellow passenger, to find out how... and why. In other words, it's another express delivery of humour and thrills with a bit of whodunit on board for good measure. Michael Redgrave gives a perfectly weighted performance as Gilbert, the romantic lead, and although Margaret Lockwood shines as Iris Henderson, it's entertaining to see Googie Withers trying to steal every scene she's in. To a modern audience, Gilbert's eccentricities can appear more annoying than endearing but that doesn't prevent *The Lady Vanishing* from emerging as one of Hitchcock's very best British films.

## Jamaica Inn, 1939

Smuggling, pirates, romance and derring-do in darkest, nineteenth century Cornwall... This version of Daphne du Maurier's 1936 novel represents another under-rated gem. Critics have attacked the movie's departure from the source material and derided Charles Laughton's OTT portrayal of Sir Humphrey. But his preening, egotistical, self-delusional villain is for some viewers, fabulous fun and the film as a whole delivers big on atmosphere and excitement.

## Rebecca, 1940

The 'new' Mrs de Winter is tormented by the memory and strange lingering presence of her husband's dead first wife... Hitch's first American movie was his most expensive film to date but ended up winning two Academy Awards (including Outstanding Production) and raked in millions at the box office. He allegedly claimed it was not 'a Hitchcock picture' because of the levels of interference producer David O. Selznick subjected him to throughout the production, but *Rebecca* is an absorbing movie, beautifully shot.

## Foreign Correspondent, 1940

An American journalist travels to Europe and becomes enmeshed in an assassination plot... *Foreign Correspondent* harks back to Hitchcock's Gaumont British works in terms of pace and action, although the war plotline gives the film a more serious edge. It's another under-rated thriller with many visual triumphs. The murder in the rain, for instance, is the kind of sequence that could inspire any writer...

## Mr. and Mrs. Smith, 1941

Two New York sophisticates - the eponymous Smiths – discover their marriage is not legitimate. They've been happily 'married' for years but will this shock news make them reconsider? Hitchcock tries his hand at a screwball comedy and anyone who could remember *The 39 Steps* wouldn't have been surprised by his success in the genre. Pleasingly, leading lady (and close friend of Hitch) Carole Lombard directed Hitchcock in his brief 'walk on' scene, forcing him to redo his very simple cameo many times, much to the amusement of the 'real' director and his crew!

## Suspicion, 1941

A shy young woman is charmed by and marries a charismatic chancer, then begins to suspect he's trying to murder her... Cary Grant, Joan Fontaine and Nigel Bruce are all on splendid form and some of the famous visuals – Johnnie walking up the stairs carrying a tray of milk is the obvious one – are daring and imaginative. But it's hard to forgive the film's cop out ending, a finale that Hitch himself disliked intensely.

## Saboteur, 1942

An innocent man must go on the run when he's falsely accused of starting the factory fire that killed his best friend. He's forced to find the real culprit who, in the movie's climax, plunges to his death from the Statue of Liberty. Another under-rated chase movie full of arresting Hitchcockian touches - it deserves to be seen more.

## Shadow of a Doubt, 1943

When 'Uncle Charlie' visits his extended family they're elated as he's something of a hero to them. But his niece begins to suspect he's a killer... Hitchcock reportedly called this his 'favourite Hitchcock movie', possibly because of its authenticity of American detail. It's a taut, smart look at the omnipresence of evil and when asked by the press to sum it up, the director replied: 'Love and good order is no defence against evil'.

## Lifeboat, 1944
A riveting, surprising film, *Lifeboat* is set almost entirely within the confines of a small boat. It's been described as a kind of 12 Angry Men with added sass, sea and females with Tallulah Bankhead delivering the picture's stand-out performance. Hitchcock was nominated for a Best Director Academy Award for the movie, losing out to Leo McCarey who scooped it for *Going My Way*.

## Bon Voyage and Aventure Malgache (both 1944)
Hitch decided he needed to help the war effort 'back home' and therefore returned to England where he made these two propaganda films in French for the British Ministry of Information. Both serve as tributes to the French Resistance and were made to be screened in newly liberated areas of France, but evidence exists to suggest the authorities found both works too cerebral and not heroic enough, meaning neither was extensively seen until years after the war had ended. It's worth noting that around this time, Hitch also shot footage used in the short, *Watchtower Over Tomorrow* (1945), a documentary produced in the US that attempted to show how another World War could be avoided. He was uncredited for that piece and for a short propaganda film he directed called *The Fighting Generation* made in October, 1944. Lasting less than a minute, it starred Jennifer Jones and was intended to galvanise audience members into buying War Bonds by showing the good work being done by nurses' aides treating soldiers injured in war.

## Spellbound, 1945
Gregory Peck plays an amnesiac who may – or may not - be a killer and Ingrid Bergman is the psychiatrist (and love interest) who helps him when he's forced to go on the run. The film's tagline was the memorable, 'Will he kiss me... or kill me?' and its evocative score won an Oscar for composer Miklós Rózsa.

## Notorious, 1946
*Notorious* is at once a spy story and a twisted romance in which Ingrid Bergman plays a woman asked to marry a Nazi in order infiltrate his villainous circles. Cary Grant, playing the agent the woman truly loves, is used perfectly by Hitch who extracts every ounce of his star's charisma, guile and vulnerability.

## The Paradine Case, 1948
Courtroom drama in which a married barrister falls for his client who stands accused of murder. Hitch loathed the story and hated the casting of Gregory Peck and Louis Jourdan. Selznick's interference became intolerable and to top it all, he didn't like the technical equipment he was given to make the picture. And yet *The Paradine Case* comes across as a confident, competent take on the courtroom sub-genre and

Charles Laughton's winning performance makes up for what Hitch considered to be casting missteps.

## Rope, 1948
Two young men murder an old pal and conceal his corpse in a trunk, which is then used as a table at a party they throw for friends who have no idea about the killing... The first of Hitchcock's Technicolor films is well-known for taking place in real time and comprising only ten shots, each one (aside from the final two), lasting approximately 8 minutes. The photography is gorgeous and James Stewart simply awesome as the nonchalant academic who gradually begins to realise that he is in some way responsible for the murder of a former student.

## Under Capricorn, 1949
An Irishman travels to Australia where he's reunited with a woman he was close to, many years earlier. But she seems to harbour a dangerous secret... This historical melodrama set in Sydney and starring Ingrid Bergman, bombed at the box office, possibly because audiences now wanted Hitchcock to serve them thrillers. Despite many British and American reviewers panning *Under Capricorn*, French critics hold it aloft as one of Hitch's great works.

## Stage Fright, 1950
An innocent man on the run, false identities and a heroine falling in love with the officer investigating the case she's wrapped up in... *Stage Fright* seems to serve up many typical Hitchcock plot devices but the ending delivers a great twist and we're given a truly disturbing villain. The movie was shot in England and boasts one of the starriest casts Hitch ever assembled with Jane Wyman, Marlene Dietrich, Michael Wilding, Richard Todd, Alastair Sim, Sybil Thorndike, Kay Walsh, Joyce Grenfell and Patricia Hitchcock (in her movie debut) all adding to the film's charm.

## Strangers on a Train, 1950
Two people 'swap' murders after meeting by chance on a train. Each must kill someone nominated by the other – trouble is, one of the strangers didn't realise the other was serious and is now trapped in a situation where he finds himself in league with a psychopath... Raymond Chandler was one of the screenplay's co-writers and the finished movie was a smash hit with the press and public alike – a much needed triumph for Hitch after the relatively disappointing receptions afforded *Under Capricorn* and *Stage Fright*.

## I Confess, 1951
When a priest is accused of murder, he's unable to reveal what he knows because the real killer has already admitted his guilt to him, but during confession. It's a dark, humourless film that Hitch felt he should have injected with more irony.

## Dial M for Murder, 1954
A former tennis star plans the 'perfect murder' but when his beautiful wife kills the man he sent to strangle her,

things become more complex... Another superb thriller from Hitchcock who was content to keep the action, for the large part, confined to one apartment. Ray Milland is adroitly cast as the murderous Tony Wendice and Grace Kelly excels as his adulterous wife, Margot.

### Rear Window, 1954

Whilst recovering from a leg injury, a house-bound photographer passes the time by watching the residents of apartments opposite his own home. He becomes convinced one of them is a murderer, but no-one will believe him. The movie received four Academy Award nominations, including one for Best Director and many believe *Rear Window* to be one of Hitchcock's top 5 pictures. The critic Roger Ebert eloquently summed up its success, noting, 'The experience [*of seeing the film*] is not so much like watching a movie, as like... well, like spying on your neighbors.'

### To Catch a Thief, 1954

A retired jewel thief is suspected of returning to his old ways after a series of copycat robberies across the French Riviera. In order to clear his name, he sets out to catch a thief... One of Hitch's most fun and sumptuous frivolities sees Cary Grant at his most charming and Grace Kelly the epitome of poise in what proved to be her final film for Hitchcock.

### The Trouble with Harry, 1956

When villagers find the corpse of Harry (recently deceased) outside their little community in Vermont, there's a difference of opinion as to what to do with him, not helped by the fact that several individuals each believe they killed him! An out-and-out comedy, making this a rarity for Hitch during his US years, *The Trouble with Harry* was that it was not well-received. The director called it 'the most English' of his American films and it's an important picture as it marked the first collaboration between Hitchcock and the iconic composer, Bernard Herrmann.

### The Man Who Knew Too Much, 1956

A reworking of his 1934 movie of the same name, this version stars James Stewart and Doris Day who sings '*Whatever Will Be, Will Be (Que Sera, Sera)*' during the lively proceedings. When François Truffaut drew comparisons between the original and the remake, Hitchcock famously stated that '... the first version is the work of a talented amateur and the second was made by a professional.'

### The Wrong Man, 1957

The true story of Christopher Emmanuel 'Manny' Balestrero, a New York musician who, in a case of mistaken identity, was charged with armed robbery. Due to its subject matter, *The Wrong Man* shows fewer Hitchcock flourishes and comes across as a solid, serious docu-drama. It's notable for being Hitchcock's penultimate film shot in black & white and the first of his movies to feature an actress called Vera Miles – later made famous by a certain shower scene...

### Vertigo, 1958

What happens when you become obsessed by a woman who is killed? And what insanity awaits if you found someone who reminded you so strongly of her, that you felt compelled to model them into your lost obsession? Hitchcock achieves near perfection with this towering masterpiece. The incredible visuals, Herrmann's music, sublime acting and ingenious storyline combine to create a thing of cinematic beauty. Contrary to popular belief, *Vertigo* was not panned on its initial release, but received a broad spectrum of critical opinion. In recent years its brilliance has been more widely recognised and in 2012, in Sight & Sound's once-a-decade critics' poll, it replaced *Citizen Kane* as 'the best film of all time'.

### North by Northwest, 1959

Advertising exec Roger Thornhill is mistaken for a man wanted by crime chief Phillip Vandamm. Cue a chase across America in which Thornhill is pushed to his limits, helped and hindered by a stunning but glacial blonde who isn't all she appears to be... After the serious stew of *Vertigo*, Hitchcock brings ice-cream to the table in this deft, daft and quite wonderfully enjoyable movie. The iconic crop duster scene may be the sequence most people remember but the quiet roadside exchange that immediately precedes it, the auction and a frantic finale offer further moments to relish. A total joy.

### Psycho, 1960

A young woman steals money to start a new life with her lover but finds death at the Bates Motel. The establishment's owner, Norman, discovers her corpse and is in two minds about how to handle the grisly murder... Shot in black & white by the crew Hitch used for his TV show, the feel of Psycho can distract from its extraordinary structure and characterisation. One of Hitchcock's crowning achievements and possibly the King of All Horror Films, it's easy to overlook quite how daring this venture was back in 1960.

### The Birds, 1963

In the quiet backwater of Bodega Bay, the birds begin to attack humans, as if mobilised and driven by the presence of sophisticated 'city girl', Melanie Daniels. *The Birds* is another work of genius. The attacks carry an extraordinary sense of terror that's made more potent by their inexplicability and Tippi Hedren, making her feature film debut as Melanie, is a revelation.

### Marnie, 1964

Marnie is a thief with a powerful secret buried in her childhood. And Mark Rutland - the wealthy businessman she's forced to marry - is the man determined to unearth that secret. Another engrossing study of obsession, false identity and childhood trauma, *Marnie* marked the end of an era. It was the last Hitchcock film photographed by Robert Burks, edited by George Tomasini and scored by Bernard Herrmann, all three men stalwarts of Hitch's pictures. It was also the second and final film to star Tippi Hedren who once again excels in the lead.

### Torn Curtain, 1966

Professor Michael Armstrong is a US scientist who publicly defects to East Germany, but the move is a sham and the American is operating as a double agent... Critics have ripped into *Torn Curtain* but it contains many gripping scenes. Armstrong's attempt to escape back to the States, for instance, forms an excitingly tense and skilfully prolonged finale that indicates that the 'Master of Suspense' was still capable of holding an audience spellbound.

### Topaz, 1969

A French intelligence agent becomes mixed up in the events leading up to the Cuban Missile Crisis. It's another Cold War espionage thriller which meant familiar ground, thematically speaking, but Hitchcock was wholly unhappy with the film's production. He'd been rushed into the shoot with a hastily rewritten script that wasn't even finished when the cameras began rolling and this could explain why *Topaz* – a perfectly watchable film – does not hit the heights of his previous works. But any notion that Hitchcock was 'past it' would be dispelled in his very next movie...

### Frenzy, 1972

Police are hunting a serial killer who strangles women using a necktie. They have a suspect, but it's the wrong man and after he's arrested, it looks like the charismatic but mad murderer may have escaped justice... Unsettling, brutal and brilliant, *Frenzy* is Hitchcock's last film made in the UK and echoes his first British thriller, *The Lodger*. Once again Hitch is ahead of his time, shocking and delighting audiences with a range of audacious devices and sleights of hand. Based on the book, *Goodbye Piccadilly, Farewell Leicester Square*, it became Hitch's fitting farewell to England.

### Family Plot, 1976

A couple of con artists become embroiled with kidnappers in Hitchcock's final movie, a modest light comedy that proved a commercial and critical success. After a culminatory plot twist, the last scene of the film shows a character called Blanche walking away from the action, looking into the camera – at the audience – and giving a knowing, complicit wink. In retrospect, it's hard not to interpret this as Hitch's own, typically unexpected parting message.

---

In addition to these feature films, Hitchcock directed a ten-minute comedy short, *An Elastic Affair* (1930) starring Cyril Butcher and Aileen Despard. Sadly, as with *The Mountain Eagle*, the work is currently a 'lost film'. *Elstree Calling* (1930) is a British movie comprising several musical vignettes, each pretty much unrelated but connected by a perfunctory story concerning a man attempting to tune his TV set into the musical numbers. These linking segments were directed by Hitchcock. He also directed a short sequence in the *The House Across the Bay* (1940) as a favour to its producer, Walter Wanger, plus several small items that fall into categories including 'unfinished', 'unreleased', and 'non-commercial', such as home movies, screen tests and sound tests.

Incidentally, whilst serving as an assistant director in the early 1920s some cinema historians suggest he directed a number of scenes, but even on modern TV and film sets, it may *look* as if ADs and occasionally producers and other crew members are directing key moments of the action; I've therefore confined this filmography to known fact. Although it's fun to speculate – and yes, *The White Shadow* (1924), I'm looking at you – this isn't the place. And we haven't the time.

Aside from his feature films, Hitchcock directed for television, and most notably, many episodes of *Alfred Hitchcock Presents*, the US anthology series that originally ran from 1955–62. More specifically, Hitch was at the helm for the entries entitled *Revenge* (1955), *Breakdown* (1955), *Back for Christmas* (1956), *The Case of Mr. Pelham* (1955), *Wet Saturday* (1956), *Mr. Blanchard's Secret* (1956), *One More Mile to Go* (1957), *The Perfect Crime* (1957), *Lamb to the Slaughter* (1958), *Dip in the Pool* (1958), *Poison* (1958), *Banquo's Chair* (1959), *Arthur* (1959), *The Crystal Trench* (1959), *Mrs. Bixby and the Colonel's Coat* (1960), *The Horseplayer* (1961) and *Bang! You're Dead!* (1961).

Hitch directed an episode of *Suspicion* (1957) called *Four O'Clock* (1957) and an episode from the first season of *Startime* entitled *Incident at a Corner* (1960). He only directed a single episode of *The Alfred Hitchcock Hour* – an entry called *I Saw the Whole Thing* (1962) which proved to be the last drama he ever directed for TV.

Without the man who gave us these works, this book would not exist. So, thank you, Mr Hitchcock, thank you, Alma, and thank *you* for reading *The Hitchcock Murders*. I hope Paul Salinger didn't give you second thoughts about the Master of Suspense and that you continue to enjoy the old boy's films.

Having said that, it's probably nothing, but just one final word of warning. As a friend. The last time I visited the professor he told me that when he's released he intends to stalk the streets, peeping into front rooms and silently breaking into houses where he can see the occupants are watching a Hitchcock movie. He plans to monitor them, unobserved, and if he catches anyone failing to laugh on cue or bite their nails at the right moment, he will kill them, there and then. But please, don't let that put you off Alfred Hitchcock. Enjoy his films. I'm sure Professor Salinger was joking... Wasn't he?

Good night,

Gavin Collinson